47th Street Black

a novel

BAYO OJIKUTU

THREE RIVERS PRESS
NEW YORK

Published by Three Rivers Press, New York, New York.
Member of the Crown Publishing Group, a division of Random House, Inc.
www.randomhouse.com

Printed in the United States

Design by Lenny Henderson

Library of Congress Cataloging-in-Publication Data
Ojikutu, Bayo.
47th Street Black / Bayo Ojikutu.— 1st ed.
p. cm.
1. Chicago (Ill.)—Fiction. 2. Friendship—Fiction. 3. Gangsters—Fiction. 4. Violence—Fiction. I. Title.
PS3615.J55 A15 2003
813'.6—dc21

2002012314

ISBN 0-609-80847-8

First Edition

47th Street Black

For Ma, Dad, Grandma, Bisi, Sherri, and Carolyn.
The good I do in this life is inspired by,
and in honor of,
you all.

Acknowledgments

I LEARNED SOMETHING from one of the characters in this piece—in one of the early chapters, a protagonist chides a street wanderer for falling into the trap of investing faith in miracles. "Niggas," this character says, "always tryin to give the respect for doin the good and right thing to some other kinda shit. Some other shit floatin in the air." In the spirit of avoiding such a philosophical cop-out, then, I will keep this as "real" as it should be, make my guy Mookie proud:

I've encountered some outstanding teachers over the years—writing instructors and otherwise—without whose guidance my aesthetic pursuits would be void, and obviously, this novel undone. Father Thomas Crawford (odd time, and place, to thank a priest, I know), the pastor of St. Kieran's Catholic Church, and his congregation taught me all that a ten-year-old Black boy from the South Side of Chicago ever need know—the potentially good and the profusely vile—about race relations and the power of the patriarchy in sacrosanct America. Mort Castle was the visiting instructor for the very first writing workshop that I ever participated in, during high school. Without his early encouragement and essential advice I may never have placed a pen to paper after age sixteen. These things do mean so much to the young.

Richard Stern of the University of Chicago—everyone on campus warned me about Professor Stern when I inquired about his workshop as a graduate student beginning the journey—but he was nothing except sage, generous, respectful, and compassionate with my work. I caught Professor Stern on NPR a few months ago; it was so great, in that nostalgic way, to hear his gravelly baritone. Peter Vandenberg of DePaul University, the freest, most challenging, invigorating, revisionist academic (that's an almost oxymoronic stream of adjectives affixed to *academic*). In eight credit hours, over two quarters, he changed the way that I perceive the world of the mind.

John Coltrane, Miles Davis, Malcolm X, Toni Morrison, Philip Roth, John Edgar Wideman, Ralph Wiley, Martin Scorsese, Haki Madhubuti, Amiri Baraka, Charlie Parker: these I thank for doing, saying, creating so many insightful, moving, and true things. Within the aesthetic and social world, their works are my inspiration.

My agent, Caroline Carney of Book Deals, Inc., my editor, Chris Jackson, and everyone else whose tireless efforts impacted this piece amongst the editing, sales, and marketing departments at the Crown Publishing Group. They have taken so much care with my work, endeavored to render my aspirations realized, and they have been largely successful. I will be sure to let Mookie know: in Midtown, miracles do happen.

And Ms. Toisan Craigg. Back in 2000, Ms. Craigg took a risk on my work. I remain humbled, and I will never forget.

The dispossessed men who continue to enter the transitional living program on Green Street between Halsted and Monroe through the O'Hare Outreach program in Chicago. So much sorrow there, so much pain, so much joy, so much red, white, blue, brown, and black truth. Working with, and for, these gentlemen gave weight and credence to my own belief system.

Lastly—and this is where my acknowledgments must take on the tone of the liner notes of a hip-hop album, for that is where I am from, I give it up to my crew. My South Side, G-Wood, South Burb,

Chambana, black-and-old gold, deuce-trey, too tuff, Monday Night, hooping, keep-it-real, true crew. Over the years, they've taught me all that I know of the psychic tugging war that is Black male interrelations. Now, like my family, and my muse, they are stuck with me for life. Thanks, all.

47th Street Black

Prologue

BEEN RUNNIN FROM WHITE FOLK long as I can member. That's what brung me to Chicago, up North, them swamp crackas chasin me back home. And runnin was the only thing to do. If I'd stayed down there they woulda got me one way or the other. Crackas hate for you to be lookin at they women—and that's all they knew I done, jus glanced at a pink gal from our side of the street. If they'd known I'd been bangin one out back uh Mista LeValley's place, ain't no chance they woulda let me make it outta Louisiana. Woulda found a way to string me up by the throat right there in the swamp. They don't like for you to be lookin at they women, naw, and bangin one is nuff to send you straight to hell. Jus as bad as killin a cracka it is, maybe worse. Least if you kill a cracka, he ain't gotta hear his woman laughin and screamin and groanin with no colored buck on top of her. That's sure good cause to chase your ass straight to hell.

Papa always said to watch myself with them pink gals. Said they had to send one of his bruthas up North after the war cause he'd been caught blinkin wrong at a white woman on the bus. And he said he knew a coon who they'd strung up not too long before that, jus for talkin to one at the soda shop. Jus for talkin to one. They found that coon out in the Bayou with a rope round his neck and nothin but a blade cut where his thing use to be. That was what Papa said.

But Papa, he knew how it was. When he said be careful, he jus meant not to be messin with them pink gals out in public, and sure don't let Mamma find out nothin bout it, public or not. I know Papa had him a few pink women when he was comin up, them white-trash, slutty ones, since the rich ones won't get with you unless you they butler (see, if you work in they house, it mean you ain't jus no regula coon). The white trash, though, they don't care. They like to do it with us, cause they done heard all kindsa stories bout colored bucks. I know they's jus as good as the rich ones, too—there's somethin altogether different bout bein inside a pink twat, rich or poor. Hearin um scream and moan and groan behind they cracka man's back make it all the better. Mamma don't understand, not at all, but Papa knew. He jus meant to keep it outta the white man's eye, to get yo twat in the shacks and outhouses and back fields cause a cracka man don't see no difference tween the rich ones and the trash neither. A colored bangin his woman, that's all he see. So they gonna chase you if they find out. Papa woulda said it was my fault for lookin at that pink gal in public first off. Shoulda been satisfied bangin trash in Mista LeValley's outhouse. "You lucky to be gettin way with that," Papa woulda said, holdin tobacco in the left side uh his gum, jus so I'd know he'd heard some uh that pink screamin and moanin for hisself. That's how come I ain't tell Papa nothin fore I ran up North; I knew what he was gonna say. Plus I knew if Mamma found out she woulda strung my yella ass up by her damnie.

But this North ain't been no better, least not Chicago. Been up here half my years, since '49, and been runnin from white folk the whole time. Landlords, police, jobs, Talians. Course, they come up with better reasons to splain why they's chasin after you—say you ain't been payin your rent, or you stole some clothes outta Woolworth's, or you ain't been to work in weeks, or you took they money. But they still jus wanna string you from the tree. When I was young,

Mamma use to say how goin up North'd be the answer to our woes. When I wrote to her, first thing I let her know was how up North ain't no different from home, seein as I'm still runnin from swamp crackas. She came on to Chicago, though, no matter what I said. Now she know for herself that ain't nothin changed long as we round these white folk.

I suspect when it come down to it, they still mad causa me bangin one uh they women. Yeah, I shoulda known better after what happened back home. But my mind was thinkin how Chicago ain't Louisiana and how things is different up here, good livin to be found in this place. White folk suppose to be like them Roosevelts and Kennedys up North—lovin freedom, lovin niggas, lovin free niggas—that was what my mind was thinkin. Plus, I missed my white-trash twat from Louisiana, that special-feelin twat, and all the power it use to make me feel. This particular white woman I kept runnin into on 47th Street, she was somethin beautiful, too, not white trash at all. Blond girl, dressed like she was in the movies—glitters and furs and heels—crossin and uncrossin them creamy legs every time I walked past her. Lady wasn't no white trash, she was one of them pinups I use to give myself to in dirty dreams dreamed in Papa's shack. And hell, why was she always comin to the clubs on 47th if she didn't want some? So what was I gonna do, turn her down when she come talkin to me? That's what I was getting all slicked up for when I went to the jazz clubs, so she'd get so hot that crossin and uncrossin them creamy legs wasn't nuff no more and she'd slide my way. I knew she ain't come all the way to 47th just to hear no jazz music. Lady was after her some colored buck.

How was I gonna know Vinnie Povich was her man? Wasn't studdin him no ways, not really, not while I banged that blond woman. Wasn't thinkin bout nothin but how she moaned and screamed and said she loved me, made my thing so hard it hurt as she swallowed me up. That's all I cared bout. Fuck her man—goddamn cracka.

Yeah, I'd heard all bout Vinnie: two-bit half-Polish, half-Talian gangsta from off Western Avenue. Shit, he didn't mean nothin to me, specially not while I was doin it to his lady. I mighta worked for them cats, but I ain't have to respect um none, or care who they woman was. She was crossin and uncrossin them creamy legs for me, goddamnit. Don't matter what they said, or what she said, I sure as hell didn't rape that lady. Begged me to come up in that tight twat, she did, said she loved my yella ass and everythin.

I don't trus no Talians no ways, don't trus nobody stupid as them. It's causa them I know all white folk ain't got brains. This's the biggest thing I learned since comin to Chicago. Talians is dumber than us, both them and the spics. Why else would somebody who born white, in control of everythin, sittin in the fronta the bus, growin up to be mayors and governors and presidents, ownin buildins and pink women with creamy legs and tight twats, why would somebody who born with all that try so hard to be a colored? It don't make no sense a'tall to me, but bein round them Talian gangstas, I found out they'd all give they mammas to be a coon. Look at um—always talkin shit and holdin they big balls and killin each other and eatin food with some kinda red sauce on it. What's that but a nigga? It don't make the Lord's good sense to me. They can trade places with me for a day, let me marry Marilyn Monroe and chase they white asses round the streets and see if they still wanna be colored so bad. I swear, them and the spics is the most ignorant crackas God ever born.

That's how come I went on and stole they money, them Talians. Don't respect um a bit. Vinnie let me get way with bangin his blond woman, so I figure he bout the stupidest cracka who ever lived, him and Tommy Ricci. So, seein as I don't respect the bastards, why should I go round collectin lottery money for um and deliverin it to they doorsteps? Why can't I keep it for myself? Couldn't figure no good answer, so I went head and stashed it. Fifty G's, brung off the

47th Street rackets last Sunday. Took it to Mamma's place on Ellis Avenue, gave it to her cause she came up from home without no real money. Fuck them Talians and they doorsteps. They ain't gettin nothin, cause I done took it all. They fault for bein so goddamn stupid.

"Naw, Johnny boy. It's your fault for lookin at that pink gal out in public."

That's what Papa woulda told me. Talians may be stupid, and they maybe even fooled like they was lettin me get way with bangin one of they women, but they don't play when it come to takin they loot. Somethin else I learned since comin up North—money's everythin to Talians and all other crackas, no matta how stupid they is. It's my fault for forgettin this lesson, my fault for stealin that cash. Shoulda known better than messin with what belong to the cracka man, specially after Mamma wrote to tell me bout how they done Papa after I ran. The cracka man ain't nobody to be trifled with, not his women and specially not his loot. Shoulda known better. Sorry, Papa.

So I'm runnin down 47th Street at three o'clock in the mornin not causa lookin at no pink gal's creamy legs or bangin no Talian gangsta's twat, but causa stealin they money. I hear they Chevy roarin bout a block back of me. So I run into a alley, cause they most sure'll get me if I keep runnin on the street. See, I'm stupid for stealin white money, but I ain't stupid nuff to let um catch me for it. This here alleyway is too tight for that fat Chevy. I'm safe.

It's cold, though, colder than it was on the street. Ain't never gonna get use to that bout Chicago, how cold it is. Middle of April in Louisiana, it's round seventy degrees warm. But back there I woulda never made money nuff to afford the slick threads I'm wearin and these Stacey Adams steppers and the gold chains round my neck. And I sho couldn't uh picked up no white woman in no jazz club or stole no Talian's profits down South. That's how else I know crackas is stupid. Why they go and put freedom in this cold, ugly North stead of in the pretty warm back home?

There go good livin at my back, lookin for its payback. Somehow these Talians got they ride up between the brick walls and they's still chasin after me. I hear the garbage cans tumblin outta the way and the steel scrapin gainst these buildins. But I ain't lookin back, naw, cause lookin back'll slow me down. Learned that runnin from the swamp crackas. All I know is my Stacey Adams steppers is hittin on the gravel and my white suit jacket's flappin in the wind and there's the end of the alley, right up ahead. That's where I'm safe at, on Ellis, where Mamma's place is. I'll run on up in there and make sure the money's still under her bed while she holds the crackas off with Papa's huntin rifle, jus like back in the swamp.

But God done swept me up and thrown me to the gravel. Don't know why He always on these crackas' side, but He is—I know causa how He hit me square in the back before droppin me. I look down and my nose drips blood to the gravel, makes a pool where I'm layin. I can't hear the Talian's Chevy no more, so I look up. The back door's open and one of um is standin over me.

"Get up, boy."

I look again and recognize Mista Joe Defelice, one real stupid Talian. I don't move. What, he think I'm gonna help him string me up? So this skinny wop grabs my arm and tries to pick me off the ground. I ain't really strugglin, but I weigh myself down so he can't lift. I'm makin this hard cause I'm tired of God always bein on they side.

"Vito, come and help me. This's a heavy bastard."

"Just shoot his black ass and leave him there then."

"That ain't what we're told to do. You know this, Vito. We gotta take him out like any other cocksucker."

"What for? You mean we gotta put this *melangiano* in the car and carry him all the way over there? This ain't no regular *pazzo* we're talking about here, Joey, this's a filthy spade. What're you talking, take him to the warehouse?"

"That's what we're told to do. Come help me and stop crying, *fannucc.*"

They pick me up and throw me in the Chevy's backseat. I can't see the face of the third Talian, the driver. But I know Vito and Mista Joe Defelice good. Vito's the fat man they call the Hack. Since he here, I know what bout to happen. Tommy Ricci don't use him to do nuthin but hang folks on meat hooks by the asshole, torturin um till they pay up whatever they want. That's what they gonna do to me out there at the warehouse, let me hang till I hand over loot they figure still belongs to them.

Mista Joe Defelice, he Tommy Ricci's man over the lottery. Defelice's the cat I was supposed to bring the fifty G's to last Sunday night. But he don't look mad right now, more like he sick, like his skinny head's achin. I don't care cause since I'm bout to get hung on a hook like a slab of ribs, these Talians and all other crackas can kiss my yella ass.

Mista Defelice holds my head down to the vinyl. "What was you thinking about, Johnny?"

"Fuck you." I ain't scared uh nothin no more, goddamnit. Not now.

"What'd you say to me? We gave you a good living, me and Mister Ricci. We put money in your pocket, clothes on your back, gave you a nice car, a place to hang a hat, all this. What'd you have before we took you off the street, huh? And what is you doing in return to show gratitude? You steal what's ours and you say fuck me. What is you thinking? Do you know I'd shoot you right here if I didn't wanna get your filthy blood on this nice man's car?"

"Fuck you, you muthafuckin wop bastard."

"This's your boy, Joey?" Vito's fist slams into my face. The hurt rips my cheek—swear I'd whip him not for Defelice holdin me down, cause I ain't scared of um no more, goddamnit. "This idiot don't got respect for nothing. What was you helping him for, Joe? He's one uh them that's watching the television too much. Thinks he don't gotta show respect. Thinks he's not a nigger."

"Use your brain for a minute, Johnny. Where'd you put our money at?"

"Fuck you and your fat-ass wop mamma. You ain't gettin nothin from me, muthafucka."

So this stupid, fat Talian, Vito, gets to beatin on me, cause I'm held down and he feelin brave. My nose ain't drippin no more, it's pourin outta my lips. But they point me to the floor, so they Chevy vinyl don't get dirty. Jus like some coons, these Talians is.

Vito stops beatin me and laughs like he crazy. "Hey, Vinnie, ain't this the *pazzo* that was making it with your broad?"

The Chevy stops. The third Talian turns round from the front seat and gets to groanin. "Say his name again."

"Johnny," Defelice tells him, "Batiste."

"This's the cocksucker I been looking for," he says, "yeah." Ain't no shock in Vinnie Povich's voice; don't sound sad or mad, not joyful or satisfied neither. This weasel who heard bout how his blond woman howled while she was lyin up under a yellow buck from the swamp, he sounds calm and smart to me, like he knew his answer before the Hack asked the question. "Same fucking bastard. Whaddya say, Joe?"

Vinnie turns to the steerin wheel before Defelice can answer him and drives again. They ain't beatin me no more, jus got this shinin on they faces, this waitin kinda shine. I feel a turn and look up, see we in another alley. The door opens and Vinnie gets outta the car. Mista Defelice wipes blood off his hands, on my white pants leg, and Vito jus sits, rolls of fat jigglin with a crazy boy's giggle. "Dumb nigger."

I hear the trunk slam, then my door opens and somethin's draggin me into the alley, somethin that don't need help from Vito. I look to the sky again, but I don't see the moon cause the weasel's standin over me with black steel in hand. The swamp crackas finally caught up to me—or I caught back up to them, runnin so fast. Either way, I hope he strings me up. At least Mamma'd have somethin proper left to bury, that way.

Damn Talian mutt jus points his pistol at my crotch and fires. I start to screamin and cryin, but ain't no ambulance, no police, no Roosevelts or no Kennedys, no God bout to come save me, and in the back of my head, I know this. I chew my lips quiet. Time to go to hell for bangin that tight pink twat that belong to the cracka man. Papa told me, told me to keep it outta the white eye—musta thought I'd caught freedom cause I'd made it to 47th Street. Dumb nigga.

Vinnie kicks me in the stomach, then lets me lay with my nose and my nuts bleedin on the gravel while Vito and Mista Defelice watch from the Chevy. The man with the pistol stops and gets to groanin, and I hear Defelice callin to him, "Wait, Vinnie," he say. "Mister Ricci said . . . warehouse . . . lotta loot . . ."

The Hack's still laughin, though, and Vinnie, he grunts like he's gotta do this. "I hate killing *melangianos*. Makes me feel dirty, like I'm one of yous. Dirty like mushrooms in dirt." He raises the .38 from the hole tween my legs to the place where my screams and tears came from. The laughin done reminded the weasel of his reason for bein here. "You ever gonna look at a white woman again?"

"No suh," I cry out like I'm down South, back home. And I am—all the runnin these years jus to end up back home, bleedin from where my thing use to be and scared cause I got this damn life in me. I wish I could take back all the "muthafuckas" and "wops" I called these crackas, seein as that ain't my place to say. No point in makin um chase after you, not if the faster you run from them, the more you bound to catch up to they asses. But it's so much pain, I forget to say sorry for my foul mouth. And it ain't till he sees me screamin again, like a baby jus outta the hole, sees tears and snot flowin with my blood, that he squeezes the trigger and puts me outta these nigga woes.

1

If I be a master,
where is my fear?

—MALACHI 1:6

1

WE USE TO WATCH THE BIG CARS roll west on 47th Street, Lord's sun shinin off black paint jobs, brighter than it shined against skin. We'd follow um for blocks—Southpark down to where the strip met Indiana Avenue at least. But they didn't never stop, not for us, not even for the red lights. Just rolled on through, afraid we'd jump on the fenders and take the joyride west, I suppose. Didn't want no ride, though, least I didn't. Alls I wanted was for the rich men hidin behind them car windows to show they faces, to nod. Gimme my respect—that was all I wanted.

The ol souls walkin the strip, they was the ones who told us why the big cars never stopped. Said them limousines had somewhere to be, business to tend, folk to bury. So I'd ask the darkest, drunkest of all—ask if we knew them cars wasn't never gonna stop, how come we kept followin west on the strip?

Ol 47th Street Black'd laugh, like I was a stupid young'un whose soul hadn't been lost long enough. When his chuckles was done, his voice'd creak from under his straw hat, like Grandma Rose's devil'd possessed him, talkin bout, "If this's all the Lord's gave us to do with life, what's wrong in followin big cars, boy? We know ain't none of um gonna stop, we just hope to catch up one day."

Then I'd laugh, cause that ol soul was the stupid one. Me, I didn't hope for no ride, just for that rich man to gimme my respect.

* * *

Mookie and me met way back, around '57. I remember comin out to the street—we lived in what they called West Kenwood back then, on 45th Street—and seein a little colored boy hittin balls up against folks' houses. I think he'd cracked one of Grandma's windows and I'd gone to check on things, to stop "all that heathen poundin," like how the ol lady called it. Minute I set eyes on Mookie out on the block, though, I couldn't do nothin but watch them baseballs getting crushed. Cat swung with a lead pipe, all by himself in the middle of our street. Coulda stopped him if I'd wanted—Mookie wasn't nothin but a bit bigger than me back then—but that sweet swing and the float it brung had me locked. Wasn't how the balls beat up the frame sidings or knocked over lawn decorations or shook up the fences. Mookie just made them fly so high—fifty, one hundred feet in the air and on down 45th Street. He was only a boy, eight or nine years ol himself, just a boy givin no thought to how far his balls popped or what they tore up, not studdin a thing but his swing.

"What you doin?" Took five minutes to get that outta my mouth.

"What?"

"Said what you doin? My grandma told me to look on the street and find out what the racket is."

"Ain't no racket. Playin ball."

"By yourself?"

"Naw."

"Who you playin with, then? Don't see nobody else out here. Mus be playin by yourself, and you just don't wanna say it."

"Playin with the Lord."

"Huh?"

"Ain't nobody else out here to catch or pitch to me, so I'm playin with the Lord."

Woulda got his tail whupped black to green if Grandma'd heard that kinda trash comin off his lips—so I knew right from the jump, the boy didn't have no good home trainin. He tossed his second-to-last ball above his head and slammed it to 45th Place.

"Jesus bringin them balls back for you to keep playin?"

"Don't know. He ain't yet." Mookie got to throwin his last ball in the air and lettin it bounce gainst the street. "You wanna pitch to me?"

Mookie rolled the last ball out where he wanted me to stand, and I followed into the street. After he'd whacked it away, I ran the neighborhood, collectin balls he'd already knocked about. We was best boys from then on.

Mookie first became the man in high school. Between 39th and 47th Streets at least, he was the man. Playin football—gave up swingin at balls for throwin um long and far—was what done it for him, tossin touchdown passes for Wendell Phillips High School, winnin games and standin as they hero and all. A dark-skinned, wavy-headed star, that was Mookie those last two years of school. That was when the young gals really started throwin themselves at him, when he was tossin them touchdown passes. Hell, if anybody shoulda believed in a pot of gold promised a colored boy, then it was him, specially after seein his snapshot on the *Defender* sports page them times. I didn't play no football, framed too tiny. Wasn't nothin I coulda done out on the field that size. No hidin in Mookie's shadow out there—nigga was too busy gettin worshiped. So I sat in the stands, cheerin for him just like another one of them silly gals.

But that was over, Mookie bein a football star and all, by the end of junior year. Colleges didn't want him as no quarterback, wasn't ready for a colored to be winnin games. Wanted him to be takin handoffs, tacklin, gettin tackled to the ground where he belonged. Proud young cat like Mookie didn't wanna hear that shit, so when he came to understand didn't nobody outside the Forties blocks want him for no touchdown-throwin hero, he stopped goin to school altogether. Took to runnin the streets, stealin baseballs outta the Salvation Army store, shootin craps, and smokin squares. No more Phillips High touchdown throwin for my man Mookie, just livin life as one of Grandma Rose's godless street hoods instead.

That was what I saw him doin from the classroom window—shootin dice across the lot, down there free in the March sun—the day I decided to drop outta school and roll with Mookie for good. Ol Mister Manley stood behind his desk up front, usin his wood stick to point at words that meant not a goddamn thing, scribbled one under the other on the blackboard. My blink slowed to the heavy fade that came on whenever Manley got to dronin his gray sermons and jabbin at the wall with his stick. I looked down on Pershing Road not cause I peeked Mookie's shadow out the corner of my eye or heard craps crackin off a wall then—just runnin from the man, like every other day. That was how come the muthafucka'd put me in the front of the classroom first off, so he could keep that ol stare fixed on me, make sure I wouldn't get away with sleepin through lessons. His fault for sittin me close to the peephole so freedom'd keep my eyelids open no matter his hum.

Down there, Mookie crouched to his knees at the middle of a circle of dropouts from the Low End, dark dice (couldn't tell for sure up high, but maybe they was red) leavin outta his hand smooth, rollin and bouncin against the concrete without losin they pop, then dancin that jumpin bean dance off to Phillips High's brick. Dice hopped high on that ground, too, like concrete was too hot for restin (but it was cold that day—saw ice clouds breathed from Mookie's mouth) and craps shot fast down the line, though he'd barely shook before lettin go; and when they landed against the school, brick chips bounced off the walls big as the craps that made um.

Those Low End cats stood tall over Mookie's squat, but they was still covered in the shadow brung by my man as they gawked his roll. Shock on they faces, cause lookin down to concrete they'd found a shootin star high above. I swore they cheered like the girls in the football stands, too. Couldn't do nothin to stop themselves, even as they dropped more dimes into Mookie's winnin pile.

Seein them free on Pershing Road, I had to go to the toilet. Mister Manley took questions from the class behind me, usin the stick to point at brown hands raised here and there about the room, happy palms makin no more sense than the words scribbled in fronta me. Good, happy goddamn palms. I didn't have a clue of the lesson's subject till I felt that pee throbbin in my crotch, pressin against my balls and thighs all of a sudden. "Heroes," the history teacher'd hummed. And the words on his blackboard came to eye as my right leg tapped a jig under the desktop: *Patrick Henry,* the wall read, *George Washington, Ben Franklin, Daniel Boone, Abraham Lincoln, General John Pershing,* under *American history's great figures.*

"Who recalls the seven shared traits of these great figures from our history?" Manley said. "From yesterday's reading. Somebody remember one? Ah, Deborah—"

The palm his wood stick fixed on dropped, and the big-toothed girl with the mini-beehive sat up straight as a pole before answering, "Strength."

"Good, Deborah—strength. Another from someone else . . ."

I raised my right hand. The words didn't make no sense to me—heard talkin, couldn't make no logic outta it—but squirts stung inside my skin, beggin to trickle into my drawers. Didn't move from my seat, though, no matter my knees shakin and palm wavin high. *Always raise your hand, wait to be excused from somebody else's table, boy,* Grandma'd always said. I heard her under Manley's hum, too, learnin that to me over and over till her lesson wasn't no different than the classroom's hero tales.

And the ol man saw me wavin, more frantic than happy like the rest—shit, I was right in fronta the bastard. I caught them gray eyes rollin on me for less than a second before his stick pointed to the back of the room. "Someone else . . . Wilfred?"

"Patriotism," the Puerto Rican boy said.

"Good," said Manley before pointing past me again. "Someone else with another—"

My left leg tapped, faster than the right, fought off a drip.

"Honesty."

The beehive girl giggled.

"Morality."

Mookie stood from the circle, and the Low End fools patted him on the back and shoulders, gave him due dap for hustling they change before the next roller grabbed hot dice from the wall.

"Selflessness."

Just one squirt into my drawers, and I felt better—for a second, better. Legs went still, and as Mookie stepped outta the circle, I breathed. Could follow Grandma's words and stay put in that place just then, and learn. Manley's hum was soft, my body still and peaceful.

Then the rest of the hot juice bit my crotch for a turn to trickle themselves. Legs crunched together till I felt the wet cotton of that drip left in my drawers already. And that only turned the juice inside hotter, madder, screamin to be let free as the first, free all on the floor of Manley's learnin room. Screamin for righteousness. I dropped my fist into my balls to keep the flow inside, and bit lips to forget that sting. Right leg couldn't feel the left for the crunch and the beggin sting and the knuckles diggin at my sack. Whole while, the other hand waved, and Manley pointed every which way but up front.

"Courage."

I remembered Reverend Goode durin one of his Sunday sermons at Grandma's Ebenezer, talking about how the Cath'lics counted seven deadly sins a nigga could commit in life, crimes against God sure to get the soul damned to hell fire afterwards. Sounded same as them hero traits jiggin in ol Manley's classroom. Remembered wantin to piss on myself in that Ebenezer Baptist pew, too.

Three cats left the circle down on Pershing, no more change, and Mookie's shadow squatted against brick again. He rolled rocks without shakin, smooth and quick as a blink. I waved my palm into one ear, then the other, as I heard a drip under my chair.

"Muthafucka, do you see me sittin here?" The classroom went quiet except for my echo and that second free drip under it. Stingin stopped for good—the flow inside'd won, my fight done, and heat let go all over and around me. My right hand splashed in the pants leg. "Goddamnit, been wavin at you ten minutes . . . you see me or what, goddamnit . . . fuck wrong with you?"

"Excuse me, Jacy"—that was how Manley'd say my name, "Jacy," like one goofy, white word, instead of how my grandmamma named me proper, J.C.—"watch your filthy mouth, boy. Is there some problem?"

"Yeah, there's a problem, muthafucka. Been wavin my hand at you all this time. Goddamn problem . . . like this." I waved again, ear to ear, and the beehive girl giggled, followed by the rest—heard laughin from the cats in Mookie's circle down below, even. "Wavin right in your face, stupid ass. What, am I invisible? Sonofabitch."

"You've got yourself a detention, Mister Rose." Manley dropped the pointer at the blackboard and sat behind his desk, scribblin on a yellow pad. "I saw your hand, boy. Your classmates answered the questions. Too late—you've earned yourself a detention now."

A group mumble took over Manley's hum. Fillin up the walls, that fool chitter-chatter and the drip from my seat, trappin me inside still. I heard, and I watched him write me off, like he couldn't see wet drippin outta me.

"Muthafucka." I jumped from my chair and kicked the desk outta my way, back to the mumblin beehive girls and brown boys.

The puddle splashed and pee stank sharp and hard in his classroom. I smelled it, at least. "Had to go to the bathroom, damnit. You ain't see me?"

Manley looked up from my detention and pity took the place of his eyeballs' roll as he saw my trousers hangin low from the crotch. Muthafucka wanted to apologize—I knew it—but he bit his top lip and grabbed the pointer. "Jacy, boy, if you had to go, you should've gone. Nobody was stopping you from getting up to go to the restroom. That's what you should have done—you are smart enough to know better. Should have gone. Sit back down now, Jacy."

"Stupid muthafucka . . ." I ran the six strides to Manley, still heard my drawers squishin together, and the beehive girl gigglin long with the rest of um. Ran to the ol man though he screamed for me to stop; "Sit your black ass down," I swore I heard him say, so my legs swallowed that path fast as coulda been.

Heard Mookie down on Pershing, too. "Hot seven," he said, and dice cracked against the wall.

"I'm wet." Didn't have a clue what I was runnin to him for till my arm crushed into Manley's throat and screeched the ol man's chair into the blackboard wall. Classroom was quiet then—no mumblin, no drips, no gigglin at a sorry, soggy bastard, no oohs or ahhs from them scary niggas—just quiet and shocked same as the Low End dropouts watchin Mookie shoot on Pershing Road. I jammed Manley's head into the blackboard till clouds of chalk rose up from his scalp, and *Lincoln* smeared into his gray. His eyes couldn't roll no more, just spread wide and empty. He tried swingin that pointer at me, tried to put me back in my right place—but I snatched the stick outta his weak right hand and crashed wood sideways into the muthafucka's nose. Splinters popped all round, against my cheeks even, and blood ran from a rip opened at the bone that joined Manley's empty stare together, and then from his nostrils, bright red blood down pasty skin.

His hand rose to his face, wiped before the flow reached his lips. He looked at the pink palm. "Bastard," he yelled, and the classroom was full of all kinds of dark oohs then.

I ran again, squished though the door and down two flights of steps, droppin the pointer piece somewhere before makin it out to March sun. Nobody chased after me or paid me no mind as I went, and I heard no alarms soundin when I pushed on the emergency exit door. Ran out there to Mookie's crap-shootin circle, passin wind and Low End hustlin dryin my trousers.

Be six years more years before I came across any more school learnin. Never could go back to Phillips High—didn't want to or nothin—but never had a choice about steppin foot back inside that joint. Manley was waitin patient there, I heard, lookin to teach my ass a true lesson about his history.

* * *

I still loved watchin Mookie swat at balls. Somethin to behold, that swing. Shoulda kept playin baseball instead of football; he woulda stayed a hero like that.

"You gonna pitch to me or what? Slow bastard."

"Wait."

"What? Wait for what?"

"We ain't got no more balls."

"No more balls? What you mean, no more balls? What you got there in your hand?"

"I mean after this one, we ain't got no more. You scattered um cross the streets."

"That ain't none uh my fault, J.C. You know that ain't my fault. You just been throwin them soft pitches and I ain't have no choice but to hit um like that there. What else you spect me to do?"

"Just don't hit this one so hard, is all. This our last ball. What we gonna do without no ball?"

"You just run your little ass round the block, take some more outta the secondhand shop. That's all you can do. Else we be done with this and go get us some squares. Head to Englewood, sit on the curb and watch the Cath'lic chicks comin outta the girls' school, comin in and goin out. Or you take your ass back on over to Phillips. What else's there to do? You don't wanna take yo ass back to Phillips. You know it."

"Ain't goin back. Suppose to be in history bout now."

"Pitch the ball then, slow bastard."

"All right. You ain't gonna hit this one hard, right? Not hard like before."

"Pitch the ball, J.C. I ain't gonna hit it hard. For real, just pitch it."

So I did, threw the thing fast so maybe Mookie couldn't hit it at all and we'd keep swingin at that one ball long as the sun stayed above. Didn't wanna go smoke no squares or sit on no curb, was tired of lookin at Cath'lic gals. Didn't wanna do nothin but watch Mookie's swing in that alley just off 49th Street.

He smashed that last pitch. Damn ball jumped up to heaven and stayed for a good long while, too, didn't come down till God'd gave it wings it couldn't fly with, wings that wasn't made to give flight to balls hit by Kenwood boys. When it dropped down from heaven, rejected, the thing crashed behind a ol garbage pile at the alley's street end.

Mookie ran his circle, touchin tin garbage lids like they was bases and laughin as I thought about what we was gonna do with ourselves. "You said you wasn't gonna hit it like that, Mookie. You said for real. Now what?"

"Go to the pool hall," Mookie said as he crossed the last lid and grabbed hold of one of the open cans, pantin to catch his breath.

"Naw, Mookie. I wanna play ball. Ain't even get to bat really. You said you wouldn't hit it like that."

"Go find the ball then, you wanna play so bad." He got his air and stood straight to put those black, waitin eyes on me. "Find it and we'll keep on so you can get you a good at-bat."

I ran the alley, not laughin like Mookie, but smilin cause maybe I could watch him hit the ball to heaven one more time or crack a window on the back side of one of them 49th Street stores.

The smell came on me as I ran. Wasn't no regular alley odor, cause a alley odor hung in your nose and stayed till you figured out how to breathe without takin in the stink. Wasn't my nose that caught the April noon's foul air no ways, more like my whole body'd soaked in it and got drug below gravel. Nose couldn't do nothin but sink with the rest of me.

"You smell that, Mookie?"

"What?"

"Smell like stale shit."

"We in a alley. What else you spect to be smellin?"

"It's a different kinda stink I'm talkin bout. Smell like somethin rotted all the way out."

"Like yo grandmamma after she take her panties off? Yeah, I smell it."

"Respect to Mamma Rose, fool. I smell somethin for real. Like somethin gone bad over here."

"Don't know. May be a dead rat. Find the ball, J.C."

Climbed over the cans and didn't come across nothin. I swore I knew where the thing'd fell, saw it drop right down into that pile. But I couldn't barely breathe for the foul of trash and that other, rotten funk chokin me. Only smelled worse as I pushed away the wet bags and cardboard boxes. And holdin my nose didn't help none—funk found its way in through my eyes and my ears and my mouth, took wind. Couldn't figure how the ball'd dug itself up under that pile neither. But it had; swore I'd seen it fall there. Nowhere else for it to be.

Somethin gleamed under them pieces of trash. I pushed the last garbage away just as that air was bout to do me in, and our ball did lay there, right in the lap of a whiskey-drunk bum. Nigga'd fell asleep under trash, his skin shinin bright while still givin off rot funk. At least I figured the cat for a sleepin bum, seein as how he'd stretched himself out in that alley with his eyes shut tight to wrinkle the forehead. He wore some fine clothes, though: suit, tie, gold chains around his neck and rings on his fingers bringin the shine, along with them polished Stacey Adams steppers. Except for the skin gone ashy with too much sauce, he was a clean-lookin man. Light behind that sick shade like he wasn't a full colored. And his mouth was opened up, teeth pearly white besides a front one that sparkled gold. I didn't figure what his trouble was till I pushed his shoulder and saw the wet blood on his suit jacket as his head tilted loose, neckbone unconnected from the body. Enough blood swam at the crotch of his pants to make a puddle like curb rain after a storm. I found our ball floatin there.

"Mookie!"

He walked up slow. He knew I'd found a crushed rat or somethin else foul, so he walked to me like he didn't wanna know why I screamed. But he couldn't stop himself from askin still, "What's wrong, J.C.?"

"Look." I stood over the body, stakin my claim, and Mookie squatted near the bum without touchin him. I wondered what he was gawkin at, so I bent down and caught them gold neck chains shinin in Mookie's eyes, brighter there than they'd shined under trash.

"You know who this is, J.C.?" He looked at me. "You know who this is? This Johnny the Baptist."

"Johnny . . . who, Mookie?"

"Goddamn Johnny the Baptist. Don't you be listenin to the cats in the pool hall?"

"Pool hall? What for?"

"If you woulda, you'd uh heard um talkin bout this Cajun. Say he come from down South to work for the Outfit years back. Collectin street taxes from the stores on Forty-seventh and runnin the numbers loot over to um. Became a rich man round this way, drivin a Caddy and gettin all the high yellow women to chase after him. Then he went and started losin his good sense, did some gangster's broad and stole some of they racket money. Outfit put a contract on him and his dumb ass ain't even leave the city. Word been goin round ain't nobody seen this here Cajun for days. Say even his mamma gave up, hot-tailed back to the swamp talkin bout how she gonna get her a house like the crackas, with a salon on the street level. Figured the gangsters'd caught up to her boy. And here he is—Johnny the Baptist. You spose to listen to the ol men in the pool halls, learn bout life, J.C. Hear how stupid Cajuns end up dead in alleys."

"Why you disrespectin his name when he ain't doin shit but layin here?"

Mookie snatched the chains off the Cajun's dead neck without answerin, no different than had he been robbin the sports page off a bum passed out on the El train. Them was some fancy gold necklaces, too, one thick and ribbed close to the neck to choke, if he'd had any air left inside; the other hangin low down, so far Mookie had to dig under Johnny's shirt and fiddle before snatchin it loose. Stole them gems right off the Cajun's smeared neck, and stuffed them into his socks.

"What you doin? Man, ain't nothin you can do with them chains. Once a pawn shop round here see that blood, they gonna say yo black ass robbed somebody. Then they gonna call the police. Then what you gonna do?"

"You notice it don't stink round here no more? You smell it now?"

He was right. I couldn't say how, didn't seem like a funk my nose coulda got use to smellin. So it musta took over, left us with nothin else to swallow, no clean wind to compare it to, like fish—fish couldn't drown cause they never got another choice in life except breathin water.

"You gonna take them rings or what, J.C.?"

I lifted Johnny's cold hands quick and smooth, much like my man as I coulda, and tried to pull the gold off the swelled-up fingers. Wasn't comin, though, not the fat diamond on his right pinky finger, or the J-shaped gem on his left index, not even the thick bracelets on his wrists. Them hands was makin sure Johnny the Baptist had somethin fancy to be buried in. "Can't get um," I said, and licked my lips. "What you gonna do with them neck chains?"

"Remember the beginnin of this past football season, we was playin Mount Canaan? Member that? You came, huh?"

"You was playin quarterback?"

"Course. Just this past season. You member the game I'm talkin bout?"

"Think so—I do."

"Remember this black limousine pullin into the lot and droppin off some fancy folk to watch the game? Lookin like the president comin to see his boy? Member that? I asked Coach who they had on they team important enough to have a limo bringin his people to the field. Know what he told me? Say they got a boy over there, a white boy, whose father's a big-time gangster. I ain't believe him, even when the whole rest of the team got to bumpin gums on that same shit. So I asked this kid—what's this kid's name from down the block who folk send him to Canaan?"

"Herman?"

"Yeah, Herman, little faggot boy Herman, that's who I asked. He ain't wanna say nothin first off, acted weird. Then he get to tellin this tale bout how the only football player over there who folk come to games in limos is a cat name of Tony Ricci. Herman claim this guy's ol man don't do nothin but own a secondhand shop on Ashland Avenue, far as he know."

"Yeah?"

"That's what Herman's faggot ass claim. Now remember . . ."

"Nope, I don't member shit. Nope, Mookie."

"Listen. Remember my uncle Leon, the one who own the store over on Garfield? You know he don't just sell groceries in there. He got liquor too—Jim Beam, Jack Daniel's, Johnny Red, 20/20—all kindsa whiskeys and wines. But you need a license to sell juice in the city. And the Outfit got that liquor license shit tied up so you gotta go through um to get one round here, and after you get it, you gotta pay um to keep it. So ol Johnny would come by the grocery store to collect the fee for Uncle Leon's license. They got all kindsa rackets, them gangsters. That's how come they be ridin round in limousines."

"Okay, Mookie, I still don't see what none of that got to do with this dead bum in fronta us here."

"Johnny ain't no bum. Listenin is everythin in life, J.C. If you learn to listen, you'll be a smart man, won't end up like this Cajun." Mookie stood over me, gold chimin in his socks. "Don't nobody, not even white folk, get rich just off ownin no pawn shops on Ashland Avenue. Not rich enough to be ridin in limos less they dead first off."

* * *

We'd just walked inside a block of him and the ol man'd already started runnin his mouth. "Where you goin, little nigga?" "What you gon bring me back?" "Got a dime . . . need to get me somethin out the sto." And you couldn't say no to him, or have the good sense to ignore his cries. "Goddamn stupid monkeys is all you is," he yelled, "all you ever been. Little goddamn monkeys—all you'll ever be."

High as a fly on dog shit was what Grandma Rose woulda said bout Black.

From the time he rose outta the concrete at 47th and Ellis at the sun's first blink, strolled down to Kenwood Avenue, then back again before the sun'd shut eye on that place, 47th Street Black stayed drunk like so. So bubbly you couldn't even really call him drunk no more—Black just was. Never strolled too far east into Hyde Park or too far west past Michigan Avenue, cause then he'd be messin round with the lake or with the white folk over by the highway.

Truth be told, I wanted the ol man to go far from the strip, go on and take himself off somewhere where I couldn't hear him mumblin and stumblin bout that shit he mumbled and stumbled bout whenever we came near. Shoulda learned my lesson that very day, payin stupid mind to Mookie King. Only thing made sense after findin Johnny was goin home and figurin on what to do with them chains. Figurin somethin that made better plain logic than the riddles Mookie'd told in that alley.

But there I was on 47th Street, followin my man to the pool hall. He didn't even shoot pool back then—"Just wanna go listen, ask um bout these chains maybe. You know they know somethin," Mookie said. He was always minglin with poor bastards back then, always jivin with them fools hangin on the strip.

I heard Black almost soon as I smelled his sweet Mad Dog wine. He stood between Vernon and Southpark Avenues, leanin back on brick, straw hat tiltin off his dried-up conk, raggedy purple shirt opened just above his stomach, showin a hundred curled-up hairs and yellow scratches from sleepin on the street, dungarees brown to hide stains of whiskey, piss, and shit cause even a bum had pride. And skin black, empty, empty black—the nothin up under dirt, sky on top of night, black as that.

"Looky here," he said, runnin his mouth to the pavement under him. "Two little nappy heads runnin round in a place they don't know nothin bout. Pickaninnies betta go on and get they tails off my street before they get themself hurt. What you doin over here?"

I knew not to say nothin, cause Grandma Rose raised me up with good sense. “Don’t be getting close to them bums, boy,” she’d say, or “Don’t give um no money when they get to askin.” “Don’t sit next to um on the bus.” “And you better sho not ever let me catch you talkin to one of um in public, boy.” She was a good Baptist woman, Grandma Rose.

But Mookie’s people wasn’t churchgoers, so he didn’t know no better. And his head was hard as steel back then, mouth foul like gutter water, till he came across one of them ol fools on the strip and turned into a sweet, concerned angel boy for um. “What’s up, Black?”

“You ain’t hear me askin you a question? What you doin over here? Come you ain’t in school? Need to take yo ass back over to Forty-fifth. Don’t know nothin bout this place. None uh y’all know.”

“Don’t go to school no more,” Mookie told him. “Ain’t for a while.”

I was just bout at Southpark before the ol man’d said another word. “Stupid. Both of you just stupid. At’s all I got to say.” But *all* was a long ways off for Black, long as that wine was strong in him. “What’s that noise there? I hear it. Y’all ain’t getting nothin by this fool.”

“What?” Mookie looked, worried as if there was somethin Black could do to stop him.

“That noise down by the ground, by yo feet, boy. You know what I’m talkin bout. Sound like bells ringin. Loud as that, but pretty. Thirty pieces better than silver—sound like gold. So much, it’s comin outta your foot down there. I ain’t deaf, boy, I hear. And I see the shinin. Chimin, shinin, somethin. How come you ain’t sayin nothin over there?”

Black looked at me; him and Mookie stared at me. Felt like Reverend Goode at Ebenezer Baptist bout to tell his folk the Word—they was waitin on me to deliver gospel. “It ain’t nothin,” I said.

“I’m a fool, but I ain’t stupid,” Black said. I caught the fear in

Mookie's eyes—he was bout to run from the ol man's questions, make us both look shady. I moved in his front so the only way he could get by was to escape out into strip traffic or tear through Black.

"It ain't nothin, man," I said again. "What two little pickaninnies gonna be holdin on to gold round this place for? Don't sound like that make sense to me."

Black rubbed his hand against pink lips, streakin dirt across his mouth. "You tryin to con me, boy, or you tryin to talk logic to a fool? Either way, you stupid." Then he gave up, that quick, the strength of his drunkenness gone. Even ghetto wine would only let him go so far. The corners of his mouth raised, not smilin, but shruggin. "Where y'all headin?"

Mookie turned to the ol man and the run was gone from him, and he got to lookin at Black like he gave a damn, much as sweet angel boys really gave a damn. "Just down to the pool hall."

"Y'all little niggas don't know nothin bout shootin no pool. Oughta let me go on down there, show y'all what the game's bout. At's my game, you know."

"Naw, Black," I said, and pulled Mookie toward Southpark. "We goin home, chief."

Black let his back slide down the bricks. His eyes dropped, away from us, to the strip. "All right. Y'all go on bout yo way then. Get off uh my street. Don't nobody know nothin bout nothin over here. This my street. Go on back to yo mammies. Stupid little niggas—best take care uh yoself. Best be careful. I hear it ringin, I ain't stupid. Ain't no light at this end, but I see that shinin."

We crossed over to Southpark, but I didn't say nothin to Mookie, didn't let myself breathe. Wasn't till we'd made it to the pool hall door, more than a few blocks safe from the corner, that I opened my mouth and swallowed air clean of a bum's sweet wine.

* * *

We was in Grandma Rose's wood cellar, the night after findin the Baptist. I shined his chains—first time Mookie'd let me touch um even. He hawked them jewels like it was his treasure alone; didn't even matter no more that it'd been me who'd found Johnny first. And when Mookie handed them over, he said to just scrub um with vinegar and water, nothin else. "Till the gold part shines," he kept repeatin. "Don't clean all the blood away, just make um sparkle. Then give um here."

Hadn't told me the plan, but he had one. He'd done the figurin on his own—too much joy was in them eyes for there to have been no plan. "What the hell we doin?"

"Gonna take these necklaces to Ashland Avenue," he said from the cellar staircase.

"Ashland Avenue for what?" I looked at the gold. "What's on Ashland, the pawn shop you was talkin bout?"

"Yeah, the pawn shop. Just gotta find out where it's at exactly."

"What they gonna do with this gold? You think them white folk gonna give us money for it? That's how come you got me scrubbin? Ain't nobody bout to give us loot for no bloody chains, don't care how much I make um shine."

"Don't want loot. We can spend loot tomorrow and it'll be gone for good, least we won't never see it again."

"So what they gonna give us if we go to Ashland? That ain't no safe place."

"Just shine them chains, J.C."

I dropped Johnny's gold in the bucket. "Naw, man, what we bout to do?"

"Don't set um in it!" Mookie flew across Grandma's cellar. He reached into the vinegar water with his touchdown-throwin arm and snatched up the chains. "What difference it make what we gonna do? What was you spendin your time on before we found Johnny? Chasin baseballs round Forty-fifth? You said it yourself, what else we got to do with ourselves?"

"Go buy squares from the corner store and sit on the curb down in Englewood. Watch the Cath'lic gals comin in and goin outta the school, me and you. That's what you told me."

"Fuck that," Mookie said. "We bout to do somethin ain't gonna be over when the sun go down. Gonna take us to the end, like ridin in a black limousine. If we can be what they is, we ain't gotta play ball in no alleys, or watch no Cath'lic girls from no street curb. Won't even have to lie to our folks bout school no more. We ain't got nothin more to wish for, if we what they is."

"What is they, Mookie?" I took the gold from him and shined, just like he'd told me. "And how they gonna make us that? They got the Lord's power to change how we was born?"

"Yeah, they got the Lord's power. Gangsters, J.C. . . . evil men, gettin away with bad. Livin off it." Mookie rested on the steps again. "Ain't no more Johnny, so they gonna need somebody to collect from this place. I just wanna ride in a limousine like em, jack. Chains ain't nothin but somethin to show we found out the game. Just clean till they shine. And J.C.?"

"What?"

"Don't scrub all the blood away."

I looked at my hands, winced as the chains scratched skin. Then I cleaned without askin no more dumb questions, kept on scrubbin till Johnny the Baptist's chains reflected gold against dirty water.

2

MISTER TOMMY RICCI didn't look like no gangster, least not how them gangsters on the movies looked. The way he had on his short-sleeve opened to the chest with a bone-white T-shirt underneath and polyester pants pulled high above his waist, he coulda been ol Manley from history class. And his voice sounded like that of any cranky ol white man from the other side of Ashland. But he did have slick hair, slick and black as the back side of Grandma Rose's hand after you'd made her mad, while the wrinkled rest of him showed more than fifty years of livin. Tommy Ricci's whole body drooped to earth even, except for the face with its thin skin pulled high at both temples.

Only thing real evil-lookin bout his pawn shop's back office was the two characters in the room's corners. They both wore suit jackets and knit shirts, and they'd been whisperin with Mister Ricci as we walked into the room. Them two cats—eyes hidin in the dark and smiles like the devil—they coulda been gangsters. It was the six of us back there: Mookie and me, them cats in the office's wicked edges, Tommy Ricci and his son. Funny-lookin boy, Tony Ricci, with lips thick like a colored, and hair tall and black as the ol man's. Us and Mister Ricci was the only ones sittin down. The rest made a circle inside the walls.

The ol man checked Johnny's necklaces under his desk lamp. "These is fake. Nothing but gold plate."

Mookie frowned. "What you mean, sir?"

"Fake, I said, like the crap they sell at the Jewtown markets. Real gold don't show light like so. You get these things from Jewtown?"

"No, sir . . . I inherited them."

"From who?"

"My uncle."

"These belonged to a uncle? He gave em to you?"

Mookie stared at the floor, so I answered. "Yeah."

Mister Ricci's fingers fiddled in the gold. "Your uncle died of what?"

"Just ol," Mookie mumbled.

"Old?" Tommy Ricci lifted the pieces from his desk and held them underneath his light. "Was he having some kinda nosebleed when he died of this here oldness?"

"Huh?"

"Smeared blood on this one—you see?" Tommy Ricci pointed to the brown streak on the thick necklace, and Mookie grinned halfway. By then, I'd figured Mookie's game: Ricci had to see the stains of Johnny the Baptist's death if we was gonna be believed. Long as they saw that blood on our treasure, they'd know we had the true goods. "You stole this jewelry, didn't you boys?"

"No, sir," Mookie said.

He tossed the chains to the desk's edge. "Don't get me wrong here. I don't care one way or the other. You gotta make a living. If you steal, you steal. Now me, I'm just trying to get by as a simple man in a store. I've given you time I coulda been using to feed my family. Only sitting here because Tony says he's seen you play the football, likes what you do. That's important to me, because it means my son respects you. But you can't come into my place embarrassing yourselves with this bullshit, wasting my time. Not if you're good boys, you can't." He leaned back in the chair, gave us a chance to save ourselves.

"We didn't steal no chains, sir. We took um from a dead man," Mookie said.

The ol man smiled. "Taking from a dead fella is stealing. Didn't you boys know that? You heard of grave robbing?"

"Body wasn't in no grave. It was in a alley off Forty-ninth Street. We took these chains from Johnny the Baptist," Mookie said. Mister Ricci didn't move forward in his chair or look at the men in the corner, just frowned at us in orange light. That smile'd gone from his face faster than a rat after trash scraps. "We need jobs."

"Jobs? This's how one comes to me and asks for work? Tells me stories, insults me, and speaks to me of people I ain't never heard of? You're liars and thieves, the both of you. For what should I hire you?"

"I seen you ridin around in limousines, sir," Mookie told him.

"What's that mean? What's that got to do with you and a job? So what I drive in a limousine? What do you do? You got a high school diploma?"

"No, sir."

Tommy Ricci turned at me. "You in school?"

"No."

"So what do you expect to do for me with no schooling and no diploma? You wanna sweep up my floors? This's a secondhand shop. Ain't nothing for dirt lying around here."

"We wanna do what you do, sir, that's all we want," Mookie begged.

"And what do I do? You wanna ride in my limousine? That's what you want? I'm a man trying to run a store. A little man, that's my living. There ain't nothing you can do about running a store these days without a goddamn high school diploma even."

"How do we get on your side?" Mookie's voice was more sad than pitiful in my ears. "That's all I wanna know."

"You can't. Tony, I'm done with these your friends. Get em outta here and tell em not to come back unless they got money to buy or something worth my time to sell."

We stood from the circle and Mookie grabbed after Johnny's bloody necklaces, wrappin um in his white handkerchief. Only after he'd stuffed the chains into his socks did we back outta the office without lookin away from Mister Tommy Ricci.

We was walkin down the east side of Ashland when them characters from the office came for us. I heard um back there, plastic shoe heels clickin against the street. I kept lookin south, though, cause we was done with them folk and they pawn games far as I knew it. But, sure enough, Mookie peeked over his shoulder.

We hadn't even made it to the corner of 63rd and Ashland when they called out, "Hey, you twos! Stop!"

Mookie did like they said. Me, I kept walkin—just slowed up a bit and turned to watch the heels click near.

"We gotta ask yous some questions." You woulda thought the big, stupid-lookin one with the mustache crawlin on his lip was in charge for the way the words came from outta his mouth that day—bouncin off the church across the street for all Ashland Avenue to pay him full mind. "You twos was yapping about a alley on Forty-ninth, something about a dead fella up in there. When'd you see this?"

"Yesterday," Mookie said.

"You think it's still there or you think police over that ways found it out?"

"Don't know." I'd stopped three steps ahead of the conversation. "After we took the chains, I covered him up with trash, piled it on top like I found him."

"When's pickup day over that ways?" he asked the smaller man.

"Not till Tuesday."

"Tuesday. It should still be there, you figure?"

The small man nodded. "You twos know where this here alley is exactly? This place where you found Johnny?"

"Course," Mookie said.

"Okay, good. You wanna meet us in front of the secondhand shop tomorrow night maybe, so you can show us. I don't know that neighborhood too good, can't find my way around it for nothing. But we can't have stiffs lying around the street, not even over there. We gotta clean up this mess that ain't even our mess. This bullshit of a mess—ten o'clock, say? Can you twos get outta your house at that time?"

"What's in it for us?" I said, cause I was done with the game and wanted um to know it. Mookie's eyes showed hope, though; same fool hope that shined in them whites right before he put alley lead on one of my pitches.

"For yous? You'd be doing us a favor, me and Salvie here. This'd get back to Mister Ricci," the big one said as the other folded his arms. "You said you wanna do the same thing Mister Ricci does for a living?"

"Own a pawn shop, that's what he does," Mookie said, talkin fast to hold the smile inside. "That's what he told us."

"I known Mister Ricci since I was about you twos' age. He's like a father to me, cause he's the smartest man I ever came across. Smart men, they're smart cause they talk with what they do, not with what comes outta their mouths." The other frowned as the big one's words echoed south. "You said you wanna be like him, seen him driving in nice cars, right?"

"Yeah," Mookie said.

"Ten o'clock," the big cat repeated. "You meet us in front of the store and we'll make it worth your time."

I nodded cause I couldn't figure nothin better to do with myself just then, nothin but swingin at baseballs in a 49th Street alley and sittin on curbs, smokin squares and watchin Cath'lic gals.

"Walk with me, fella." The small man took Mookie at the shoulder and pulled him to 63rd Street, past me. But when he talked, his words was for both our ears. "You done a stupid thing today. Wasn't so much you stole necklaces off this stiff. Wasn't that you brung yourself all the way over here with them things just to lie to Mister Ricci. Them things was both stupid, yeah. But the most stupidest thing you done today was to come to somebody's neighborhood and tell em you wanna be what they is. What is that to tell somebody, huh? You think me or Angelo or Mister Ricci or anybody would ever come to Forty-seventh Street to tell you we wanna be what you is? If we did, you'd oughta kick the dog shit outta us for being a bunch of idiots. We'd deserve it. Be fucking stupid to tell you something like that, no?"

"Figure so."

"Of course you figure so. So you learn from this fucking thing you done and be happy we didn't beat you shitless just for being a couple *pazzos*."

The big one smiled. "You need bus change to get you back over there?"

"No thank you, sir," Mookie cooed.

"All right. Remember, ten o'clock we'll see yous." They turned and clicked back to the pawn shop.

We stood at the bus stop on 63rd still, me and Mookie, when I saw them two in they big gangster car. They drove to the other side of Ashland Avenue, over where the sun set, with Mister Tommy Ricci sittin in its backseat. I looked at Mookie, saw his whites gleam with touchdown passes and balls bout to get crushed, then back to the street, as the ol man's head turned quick so I wouldn't catch him watchin our corner.

The car faded with Ashland Avenue and I knew for sure—much as they wouldn't want to do it—one day I'd make them plastic heel bastards gimme my due respect. That thought filled me as Mookie let go the smile he'd held outta fear.

2

3

"I LOVE YOU, Mookie. . . ."

Bullshit. Only a few got any love. Mamma shows it to me most, my little sister, Geri, from time to time, J.C. when he gets caught up actin like a sissy. Can't even say if Papa loves me for sure. Never says so, never says much of nothin. Definitely no words like "I love you" never came to his mouth far as I can think. Hell, in the end, only one I know who gives a damn about lovin a nigga for sure is me.

"I love you, Mookie. . . ."

This broad on top of me, though, she's a good-lookin liar, so I let her bullshit slide. Twenty-two and just outta college, lookin like them ol movies of Lena Horne, the ones where she coulda passed. How many eighteen-year-ol South Side colored boys can say they fuckin a rich, high yellow broad who look like Lena or somethin white and pretty off a magazine ad? An older broad who lets um shack in they ritzy Hyde Park apartment, where you can just about see the lake?

Ain't no secret to what I want with this Mora broad, then. She's fine and older, got loot and her own place, and she fucks like a rabbit. No mystery to that. But what's this college-educated chick want with me? I ask, cause I can talk to her more than I could with them Low End gals I use to fuck with it. Mora's got brains. I ask cause I wanna know why she with a eighteen-year-old hoodlum when she could have any of these negro doctors or lawyers who be runnin around Hyde Park these days. She don't need my no-good paper, seein as her folks left her all they loot when they passed. I ask cause I don't understand it. I ask and she gets to tellin these "I love you" lies, lyin and moanin this pretty, painful moan.

Then she explains how negro professionals ain't got what she wants. Plenty try to get with her cause she's fine—offer marriage and a future and such. She reminds me about how she got her own money again, so she don't need nobody else's stash. Says after livin four years with nothin but white folk in college, she just tryin to come home.

"If I wanted that fantasy shit," she say, "the real fantasy shit, I woulda married one of them white boys on campus."

"Oh yeah? Married one?"

"They was lovin me on the sly, you know?"

"Mmh," I say.

What she wants outta her man is the truth. She ain't lookin for no negro tryin to be president. Just wants a nigga who knows he's a nigga, one who don't try to be nothin more than that. Seems like I'm perfect for her then, cause I'm real. A big colored boy who dropped outta high school and lives off bein a thug and only God knows what else. She ain't tellin no sexy lies when she says this neither, just answerin my question with what she feel. So I don't ruin it, don't tell her how, except for the big and colored part, wantin to be like some ol white men makes me what I am.

"Aah . . . my God!"

She screams and lies to me again. I cum, we sleep—that's our love, and there ain't none better. Jivin, sexin, and sleepin; good lovin.

"Someone's calling you."

Mora ain't in the bed no more. But I hear her voice, I swear it's her candy voice. Bells too—they gone now, but I heard um. Somewhere in sleep, I heard um ringin. Why ain't she in bed? Clock says nine-thirty and the sun's mornin hot, soothin with its burn. So I lay back where I was, cause I ain't got nowhere special to be.

"Someone's calling after you. . . ."

She walks around the bedroom in one of these silk robes, ain't wearin nothin under it but yellow skin. The way she's lookin reminds me how I want my first boy to lay in this high-bright womb.

Again, like I'm deaf and dumb, "Someone's calling after you."

"What?"

"One of your friends, on the phone."

I ain't gave her number to nobody but Mamma and Geri. When I come to Mora's apartment, I'm lookin to get away from the life. This's where I, only me, comes to sit and look out and just about see the lake. Her crib is my peace.

I snatch the phone, though I ain't mad at her, and set it on the satin sheets. "Who this?"

"What's up, nigga?" J.C. cuts into my ears. "My fault for botherin you at your woman's place. Got a message."

"Message?" I look at Mora. She rubs my chest soft and sings what sounds like a gospel tune from church. "How you get this number?"

"From yo mamma. Called over there and told her I had dime to drop on you."

Mora's at that part of the tune, the chorus part, where she's croonin "alleluia" over and over. Either it's the chorus or she don't know the real words. Whatever, I'm hard as what I got can get and I don't wanna be bothered with the little man. "What you talkin bout, J.C.? I'm half sleep."

"Wake up, cause Fuoco's lookin for you."

I listen now—enough to hear pool balls crashin at his back—so Mora's song and my hard dick ain't but whispers on the other side of glory. "Salvie? Lookin for me?" I jump outta the bed and grab my slacks, not even thinkin about my drawers. "He mad?"

"Naw, least he ain't sound it. Just said he needed you for somethin. Said to meet him at noon on Forty-seventh, at the overpass."

"What for, J.C.? Ain't everythin took care of over here?"

"Far as I know, yeah. Like it's supposed to be. The pushers on Forty-third been bullshittin, but I'm handlin um soon as possible. It's Saturday, right? I'm doin that first thing tomorrow."

"First thing. Yeah." Silk slides up my legs. "You don't think he callin for that, do you?"

"Calm down. Meet the cat and see for yourself what he gotta say."

I hang up and look in the gold-rimmed mirror. I've got myself dressed without thinkin nothin about the effort. That's how these ol men mess up my head. J.C. usually ain't the one who gotta gimme juice, but when the gangsters light fear's flame under me, confidence is burnt up. Ever since we came across um in Mister Ricci's pawn shop, my thoughts've had Salvie Fuoco and them on the brightest, highest throne. J.C.'s always said fuck um, and I go with that talk long as the little man's around, just so he'll keep lookin up to a nigga. But the minute he's gone, or when Salvie or Angelo or Joe Defelice or, God forbid, Tommy Ricci himself come around, I ain't shit. Even though, like J.C. been arguin for the last year, we make our livin hustlin the streets no different than these ol men.

Ain't nothin I can do about what's in this head of mine. So I get to lookin for my jacket under the bed, behind the door, in the bathroom. Ain't no tellin what Mora's wild ass done with it.

She finishes her tune. "Where you going?"

"Got business," I say, and find the jacket hangin inside her walk-in closet. "You need somethin in the street?"

"No thank you."

"You sure?" I reach for my wallet and take out a C-note. "You don't need nothin?"

"I'm okay."

I drop the hundred on top of her satin sheets, kiss her, and I'm gone back to my world. Don't care what she say. Since money's comin in from my deeds, least I can do is make like I'm givin her a little bit even when she don't ask. That way, if she's lyin about lovin me, I still own this peace she brings.

* * *

47th Street done changed. Changed from how I recall it as a shorty, from the center of colored life to these rows of shut-down shops and empty buildins. Seems somebody went and dropped a bomb here—a big, black atom bomb layin waste all the way down to State Street. But there's life here, if that's what it is, life that walks the strip searchin for the 47th Street that was. How can the ol place have gone so fast, less than a year, I swear, and why'd it leave these gutted buildins, vacant lots, and searchin wanderers? How come it ain't just take it all, outta mercy?

Most know me on the strip now. It's a good feelin, bein known. I'm Mookie the 47th Street hustler man to them, runnin the happenins in these parts. Fame comes with the crime. Eyes light up as I roll by slow in my shiny convertible T-Bird. The hands rise to wave, barely in time for me to notice. Can't do nothin but blow the horn and drive on no ways. Salvie's waitin.

I stop at a red light at Michigan, and the voice calls. "Lemme get a ride, Mookie," it says. "You got all kindsa room in that fine car, enough for me. Gimme a ride to where I gotta be."

I look up and 47th Street Black's on the corner, yellin like he do every day, always in need. "Where you gotta be, Black?"

"On Forty-third," the skinny drunk slurs under his straw hat.

"Forty-third ain't but just over that way, man," I say, pointin north outta the car. "What you need a ride for? Come you can't walk?"

"Mookie, you got all kindsa room in that car," Black says. "Ain't puttin you outta yo ways to drive an ol man a few blocks, not in such a pretty car. Just take me for a ride. Lemme sit in the front seat."

"What you gotta be on Forty-third Street for, Black?"

"You know, Mookie. Mary Ruth's over there, waitin on me."

I laugh and the light turns green. "Gotta go, Black. Got places to be. Catch me tomorrow."

"You ain't bout nothin, Mookie," he yells over the T-Bird's purr. "Wait till you get my age and you need a ride up the street. See if you can get a young coon to stop for you. That's how the Lord be workin things. What go round . . ."

I don't expect to live long as Black no ways, so what he sayin don't mean nothin. No use to long life if all I got is a corner to stand on, straw up on top of my head, and some junkie broad hobblin around 43rd Street lookin for me. Might as well live good and happy now, live and take joy in my ride's shiny purr. Then, I can go on and be gone from this place.

There go the lot where the ol Snake Pit Blues Lounge used to be. I remember the night me and J.C. went to take care of the owner, Jackson, how that slick bastard whimpered and cried like a pussy as his blood stained up the office carpet. Figured he'd have the good sense to pay Salvie then. But a thick-skulled fool like Jackson was too stupid to accept who was runnin the show. Word come down from Tommy Ricci himself that, payup or no payup, Jackson had to be put outta his nigga misery. So Salvie sent me and J.C. to burn the Pit. And here it sits, gutted like the rest of the strip. Jackson disappeared off the face of the earth afterward, least from the livin face. Word is Salvie and his nephews, Angelo and Paulo, buried him out in Indiana.

Salvie's Chrysler is parked by the 47th Street overpass. I look close and see somebody in the front seat with him, so I stop the T-Bird on Wentworth and walk fast across the street, cause I know Salvie's been waitin more than a minute.

I'm sweatin from the summer sun—ain't scared, just hot from this sunshine and the suit I changed into. That's what I tell myself, what I gotta believe. Don't wanna let my fear show in fronta him, even if I can't help from lookin up to these ol men. Gotta give um they credit—they above us in this game. When these Italians was sufferin they woes, see, they knew good enough to start themselves a mob and take over the world. Tommy Ricci can shut down our South Side quick as Daley, quicker maybe, causa his mob. Maybe I am sweatin outta fear then, fear cause I can't figure how they knew to lift themselves up to the rest of the white folks' level, up there while we wander these tore-down streets.

I get into the Chrysler's backseat. "How you doin, Salvie?"

"Hey, kid." He sounds cheery, so I relax in the cushy upholstery. He's wearin one of these gray haberdasher hats over his shiny eyes, funny tan skin—olive, they call it—and tight mouth. He ain't sweatin a'tall. Gotta get me a hat like Salvie's.

Don't recognize the man sittin next to him. Pale ol fella with no lips and silver eyes from what I can see on this side. He don't bother me none cause, from this wrinkle in his stare, he's more scared sittin on the 47th Street overpass with a nigga and a dago in a brand-new hat than I am sittin behind him.

"You know Bernie here, kid?"

The ol fella turns a little, tries to look me square in the face, but it don't work for him. "We ain't never met."

"This's Bernie from South Shore," Salvie tells me. I shake the ol man's hand, feel the wet in the palm. "And Bernie, this's Mook, our guy in this area. Bernie's got a job he wants you to do, Mook. There's a *pazzo* over here—"

"Can I tell the story?" Bernie cuts in with a wore-out voice—sounds like it use to whine before his throat'd rotted out. "Lemme tell the story, Salvatore, so he understands from where I'm coming."

Salvie leans on the door. "Go ahead with it then. Don't matter to me. Maybe it's best coming outta your mouth, since it's you who can't handle your own business."

Salvie don't respect this Bernie. I hear it, this disrespect, in his words. Means he ain't got no fear of the cat. That's how it works for them. Fear comes outta respect, not the other way around like it do for us. "All right, kid, Mook or whatever it is—you listening?" Bernie stares out the windshield as he talks, so I take him for shady. "I keep a book over on Seventy-ninth, in my neighborhood. That's still my neighborhood over there, you know? But I encourage everybody to place their bets with me. Jews, Gentiles, Catholics, Episcopalians, Italians, Polish, whatever. And the coloreds too, your people. I know the policy and the numbers thing you got ain't what it used to be, so I welcome your money. Always had open arms to any kind, cause I believe in the rights of a man to place a bet. And I'm a understanding type, the peaceful kind. I listen when my clients gotta buy a dress for their little girl's high school dance, braces for their son's teeth, a anniversary gift for the wife. I got a family, I know these things exist. So I let people slide when they ain't got the dough to pay up. That's the kinda guy Bernie Shepherd is, don't let nobody tell you different. But people coming along to take advantage of me and treating me like their whore, I got problems with that. Makes me sad, hurts me to know I opened my arms to somebody who won't nobody else even crack a door for, only to get spit on."

"Bernie's got a welcher problem." Salvie interrupts like patience has ran off and took joy with it. "There's a cocksucker name of Tobias from your neighborhood, Mook. This guy spent how much?"

"Forty bills," Bernie says. I whistle. "Bet the Sox heavy all spring long. Fucking loser."

"Four grand with Bernie here," Salvie goes on. "And the guy comes to him, begging for a loan, cause you know Bernie's into that thing, too. But he ain't about to give nothing to a bastard who can't even cover his points. He ain't stupid. So he tells the guy to pay up his fucking loot, gives him two weeks. Time passes, no money, nothing. Now Bernie says he seen this fella driving around in a brand-new Buick over there in South Shore."

I chuckle. "You sure it was your guy in this new car? You got a good look at him?"

"Of course I'm fucking sure," Bernie says. "What's this fucking kid laughing at, Salvie? I've got no time for no kinda wise-aleck. What's he mean, am I fucking sure? I don't never forget a face. Long as you do business with me, I'm gonna always know what you look like."

"See, Mook, Bernie was telling me about this problem. Told me where his problem lives. So, I got to mentioning how I had a reliable guy over near there. Told him how good you been doing business for me, how you're running things on this side of town. I said, 'If there's anybody over in that area who can get the money what's owed you, it's my guy Mook.' "

"I ain't trying to kill nobody." Bernie's words barely make it through the whine now. "Not even this putz who's not paying me what he owes. I ain't no murderer. I'm a bookie. Just put a hurting on this fucking Tobias and get me my money. And if he still don't wanna pay up, talk to him like how you people talk to each other. Take the car from him if he says he don't got my four G's. Take and bring it to my chop shop out south. Corner of One-twenty-seventh and Princeton it's on. You'll see it, even if it's nighttime. This putz gave us a bad address, but we found he lives on Fifty-ninth Street, two-oh-seven East. Salvie says you can handle this job, no problem. Whaddya say, kid?"

I ain't studdin Bernie. Figure it's cause he don't strike fear in me, figure this's why I ain't sweatin over him the way I sweat over the rest of um. How's somebody I don't give a fuck about, who don't scare me none, how's this type gonna tell me to collect what he's owed? Ain't nothin to stop me from keepin whatever we get from this Tobias. J.C.'ll beat the shit outta Bernie the bookie if he tries to cause a problem over us keepin his loot. J.C. enforces for me before he enforces for them, see, cause we gonna be doin somethin bigger than hustlin these streets for Salvie Fuoco one day.

But Bernie's sittin in the front seat, next to the man. So what am I gonna do? "Yeah, I can handle the job."

I feel Salvie gettin cheery again. "Thanks, Mook. You done the right thing, doing us this favor. I appreciate it. Take care uh that this week, after you've collected everything else."

"Course, Salvie," I say before leavin the backseat.

I'm in the T-Bird holdin its steerin wheel and starin at 47th Street, what I can see of it. Ain't moved a lick, too tired; maybe from bein woke at nine-thirty, or maybe I'm worn down causa the sun. I don't know. Could be I just ain't comfortable with a muthafucka I don't know, a muthafucka I don't respect, havin me shake up a cat from my own home. Ain't even bein offered no cash to do this. Putz or no putz, Bernie's welcher is from here. Now, if one of them Jew businessmen from South Shore or Beverly had come to 43rd Street and found him a hooker—the colored hookers them Jews love, they part of our territory—did the girl, then not paid her, what woulda happened? Could I've gone to Salvie and asked him to get a meetin with Bernie? Could I've made Bernie catch the Jew who'd welched on a Black whore? Do Bernie gotta right my mistakes if I can't do it myself? He should, cause I know he's more scared of my black way than me of his gray—but he ain't gotta do shit in the end. He's more the gangster, and that's all what matters.

Somebody's knockin on the passenger side. I look, expectin 47th Street Black, but it's Salvie. "Lemme in, Mook."

I open the door and he still ain't sweatin, even though he's walked from way across the street in this sun's blaze. I know he's hot, but this guy ain't sweatin a'tall.

He sits. "How you doing?"

"Fine," I say. "I'm fine, Salvie."

"Ain't acting fine. Been acting like something's on your mind since I seen you. What's the trouble?" He knows I don't respect Bernie, and that I ain't no kinda street enforcer. Salvie even knows that when we handled Jackson in the Snake Pit, I wasn't the one who swung the bat. They know it all. "Listen," he says. "I hate to have you take care uh this thing here, considering it's that fucker's business he ain't collected what's owed him. That ain't none of your fault, ain't your problem even. You don't work for him. But think of it like this, Mook—think of this Tobias as a obstacle to you getting what you need to take care uh yourself."

"What you mean, Salvie?"

"See, if this welcher don't pay Bernie, then Bernie can't pay us, right? And if Bernie don't pay us, how we gonna pay you? Tobias, whoever this bastard is, he's standing in the way of your money. If you think of it like that, it's second nature to bust him in his skull, you see?"

"Yeah, Salvie," I say, barely loud nuff for my own ears.

"I understand, believe me. Twenty years I been in this business, Mook. It was hard putting hurtings on *paisanos* first off, especially after spending that year fighting Il Duce in the War. Them orders to hurt Italians over there wasn't coming down from my own people neither. But if those who you call yours, who talk and pray like you do, if they's the people holding you down, why should you give two fucks about hurting em? They ain't your brothers if they don't know to get outta your fucking way when you're trying to make some money. Twenty years from now, you're gonna know that the only people you got is those who'll die before they get in the way of your livelihood. These fuckers on the street who look like you do—fuck em. They ain't nobody to you."

I nod and get to lookin at the summer sun. It's burnin even through the T-Bird's windshield, so I turn to Salvie. Of course he's right, cause these ol men always know this goddamned truth. "Course, Salvie," I say.

"Now take me to my car before that fucking Jew steals something from it," he says. I drive across Wentworth and drop him at the Chrysler.

Salvie steps back into that sun. "Take care, Mook."

"Me and J.C.'ll get that handled this week," I say, cause I know that's when he wants it done. I wheel the T-Bird around and drive down 47th Street again, back to where I came from.

* * *

Silk suit, Marshall Field's tie, Florsheim steppers—like a negro professional goin to church, I look. Don't care what Mora says. When we go out, I ain't gotta be no nigga, specially now that I'm respected in the neighborhood. I'm enough of a coon when we in her ritzy apartment, playin out her fantasies, and when I'm takin care of Salvie's business. But if I'm gonna live this hustler's life, at least I should be allowed to look at the lake and be somethin more than that when out in public. Ain't no other eighteen-year-ol cats who dress like this here. Can't none of the rest of um afford to look like what I find in Mora's rich mirror. I got the loot, makin five hundred dollars cash per week now, so I can play the part. Just for the show of it.

"How I look?"

There go Mora behind me. All gussied up in that little dress, brown curls dancin around her light forehead, and them tight, special curves floatin on top of the bedroom carpet. Yeah, like Lena, or like the finest white woman who ever walked the face of the planet, that's what she looks like. Couldn't have got with a woman this beautiful no other way, even if I'd kept playin ball. Only a hustler who's smart enough to dress up like a negro professional gets with women this fine. The business must be worth it, then, cause Mora's part of my wages.

"You look good, baby," I say without turnin from the mirror glass. "What about me? How I look?"

She don't know I'm watchin her face in the reflection, so she frowns, red-painted lips twisted like she don't approve. But she ain't gonna say nothin about it now. Too late. "Handsome. You look very handsome, Mookie." She walks to the door. "You ready to go?"

Figure she still set on wantin a all-around nigga, one who don't know nothin better than just that. Nigganess. I don't care, cause long as I'm droppin C-notes on these satin sheets and drivin her around in my shiny T-Bird and makin her scream when we together, I can dress how I wanna. I look in the mirror again and straighten my tie. I can pass for one of um, a negro who got a good job. Look like one at least. In fact, what's the purpose in goin off to school and gettin a professional degree like they be doin? I ain't been in no school for two years and I'm starin at a pretty, wavy-headed man in the mirror, a man wearin a $350 suit and standin in a ritzy apartment with thick white carpets, satin sheets, and walk-in closets close enough to the lake. And this cat in the reflection, he got a fine high yellow woman waitin for him so they can go eat at Miss Nelly's restaurant. And when we come back home, we gonna fuck till the night's blue end. Don't go to no school or to no church, and I feel like a professional negro gangster.

"Come on, Mookie!"

I feel like a gangster, and I look like the man. Can't nobody tell me different as I leave out to dine with the real professionals and this college-educated woman on 49th Street, over in that part of the world Salvie gave me to run. Just off the strip, over where they treat me right cause they know who I am, or wanna know who I am, over where all of um want somethin from a gangster wearin his best blackface.

* * *

Honeys, just like us cats, got a role to play on the strip. While we strut our pistols and gold, our Stacey Adams and gabardines, honeys supposed to be on the corner, balancin on heels too high for legs so thick, painted pretty—lipstick red enough, blush bright enough, perm straight enough—for your eyes to play like what they see is somethin other than a Black mamma. If you ain't from 47th Street or Kenwood, even if you is from 47th Street or Kenwood, you call these honeys "whore," "tramp," "broad," "heifer." In that same breath, you call us "nigga," "coon," "spook," "spade," "colored fool," "loser." Now, ain't no wrong in nobody usin these words, cause this is how we live. And we livin like this cause this is how Salvie, Tommy Ricci, Daley, the president of America want us to do it.

Only way a honey's gonna get hers in this world is if she learns to walk like she's dancin in them heels and falls on her bare brown back with them thick legs in the air when white fingers snap and dollar bills drop, same as only way we gonna get paid is by hustlin the streets, talkin the jive, clutchin our manliness, and pullin a pistol on another coon when need be. Problem is, after playin so much of this game for um, we get to believin the shit lives in our souls. This's how come I need Mora. I figure, long as I'm livin like this here, the lady at my side'll know better than confusin herself as some kinda Black whore.

But this is the real world they brung us to, this is what we gotta do to make it through, who is we to argue? Just some jive I learned from that cat, 47th Street Black himself.

This mamma J.C.'s with ain't no more than fifteen years ol, though, can't be. I know by how she don't say nothin while we eat. When I started goin with Mora she'd get to talkin her college-speak over our heads, leavin us so we couldn't say nothin back to her. But we done long figured out she ain't really sayin nothin brainy, just usin big words to tell us what we already know. So, since we cracked her bullshit game, we know how to talk back to her till she shuts up.

But the honey sittin next to J.C., she started out not sayin a goddamn thing, like she's starstruck. I ain't sure what's affectin her like this, whether it's Mora's big talk, J.C.'s dick, or my wavy hair and silk suit. I ain't figured her out far as that go—I will, but I ain't yet. She's made up all sophisticated, so you can't tell first off that she's a young mamma. But she don't do nothin but sit here, lookin dumb and stuffin her face same as me and J.C. All the while, Mora's got this look on her face like she's puzzled, puzzled but jazzed, by our ghetto ways.

J.C.'s always gettin with young girls. Suppose it's cause he's short, and cause younger chicks usually got smaller brains and bodies than ones our age. Easier to run um that way, he says. Plus, J.C.'s no-account mother was young when she had him, so it's in his blood. Can't think of no time when I seen him with one childish as this girl, though, but I ain't surprised. Says he can't stand broads complainin about bendin over and kneelin just so his little ass won't get lost. I got more love and trust for J.C. than everybody except Mamma and Geri, but he got a helluva problem about standin so tiny. That's how come he gets all loud and mad and ready to attack over bullshit; that's how come he such a good enforcer for me now. Nigga's angry with God for robbin him of size, and he's takin it out on those who cross us. Gotta be mad to do evil like J.C. do it. God musta wronged me along the way, too, seein how I'm livin this life. I just ain't figured out exactly how it is He played me on the short end.

Mora takes this young girl off to the ladies' room, guess to stop her from actin so hungry and stupid at the table. Mora's tellin her that, even if a colored man bein a coon is sexy, a colored female's always gotta be on her whitest behavior to keep her nigga's attention. Don't nobody wanna be with no stupid Black woman, least not out in public. That's what Mora's doin, givin her this good advice.

So I'm lookin at J.C.'s bushy-haired brim, his cracked brown lips and untrustin eyes, but I'm thinkin of the girl. "How ol is what's-her-name, this broad you with?"

"Christina," he say, like he's insulted I can't recall her name. He looks at the ladies' room. "You ever seen a ass on a shorty like that before?"

"Ass?" I frown and remember the blessed hill I peeked as she walked off.

"Fourteen," he say, "that's how ol. With a ass like that there. Ain't but a shorty."

"Fourteen?" I play him off, cause from the soft blink in J.C.'s eyes, he's diggin the girl. "Why you messin with sugar that young? She barely in high school, ain't but jailbait."

He laughs. "You ain't seen it, Mookie. Who besides her mamma and daddy gonna believe she's a kid? Not no police. They wouldn't even arrest me, couldn't do it, be too busy starin at that ass. Them fourteen-year-ols, the ones barely in high school, they what a nigga need."

"Oh yeah? Niggas call that jailbait, last I heard."

"Don't act like you ain't never been between no young legs before. The finest lovin is a young girl's lovin. You know that. You been in some fourteen-year-ol womb before. Don't lie."

"I have," I say, "but I was fourteen, or somewhere round that same age when I was in it. So ain't no way I coulda told you no difference between young lovin and nothin else. That's all I knew back then, that young, stupid, poor love."

"It's in the tightness," J.C. says, smilin like the devil, "the beauty of young girls. They ain't had no lotta sex up in um, so they stuff ain't quite broke in. It's tight like vise grips on you, like it love you so much it don't wanna let go. First time I had her, bout a month back, she was raw, brother. Pussy was fresh, you know, left a mess up under us. Now your woman's fine and all, but I know she wasn't fresh when you first got up in her."

I smile, act like I ain't got no envy. "Naw, she wasn't, can't lie to you bout that. But she still screams when we together—calls out for Jesus even. Likes it painful like that. Your young girl don't never be screamin, do she?"

J.C.'s eyes is wide and I'm happy cause I'm one-uppin his joyful pride. "She's only fourteen. What you want? How ol is Mora—twenty-one, twenty-two? Something'd be wrong with her if she wasn't wild like that . . . screams?"

"Swear to God. Be screamin and moanin and callin for Jesus by right name."

J.C. licks his lips. "She calls for Him? All right, she's somethin else, I give it you. But Christina? Girl's tight and fresh cause she's young. Ain't no choice but to keep ourselves quiet cause we be in her folks' crib or down in Grandma Rose's cellar. But you gotta figure her bein set like so be makin her wanna scream, don't you?"

I nod. His pride's used up, gone from his words and his eyes. I look to the ladies' room myself to make sure Mora ain't comin out yet. "We got a job, J.C."

"Job? That's how come Salvie was lookin for you?"

"Yeah, he gave us this thing to do. Gotta bust up a muthafucka name of Tobias. Lives on Fifty-ninth Street, two-oh-seven, you know, in the three-flats. Owes four G's to a Jew bookie in South Shore."

"Four G's?" J.C. whistles. "A Jew bookie? What's wrong with this cat?"

"Don't know," I say, and look at the lights hung high over Miss Nelly's dinin room, sparklin in J.C.'s eyes. "I don't know. That ain't even the worst part. This Tobias, they say he ridin round town in a brand-new Buick. At least that's the word."

"They want us to kill his ass or what?"

"Naw, naw," I say. Mora and the young girl is near. "They say bust him up, and take the car if he don't pay."

"When?"

"Tomorrow," I say as our ladies sit. "Tomorrow. Sunday night."

—

Can't figure what's got into J.C. now. I guess he's tryin to show off for me and the young girl cause I one-upped him. Orderin all kinda wines and desserts and snappin his fingers at the waiters, tellin um to move faster, speakin loud for everybody around to hear. Mora looks embarrassed. Can't tell if the young girl's impressed or not. Just sits here with a pearly smile on her face. Been lookin like this since her and Mora came back from the ladies' room. Guess that's how she's followin Mora's advice, grinnin this pearly smile instead of actin like a coon.

He pops his fingers at the waiter now. "Come here, Willis."

The bald-headed man runs to our corner. He's scared silly of J.C., still wipin sweat from his scalp as his shadow hits the tablecloth. "Yes sir? Can I help you gentlemen?"

"Yeah," J.C. say. "Go get Miss Nelly and tell her to come on out here. She's here, ain't she?"

"Yes sir. In back."

"Ain't busy or nothin?"

"No sir, Mister Rose. She's always free to greet her regulars."

"She's free? Well, go on get her then, boy."

The waiter runs off to the kitchen, sweat shinin on his head again. Christina looks impressed now—that pearly smile is gone and she's cooin in J.C.'s ear. Mora don't look embarrassed no more neither. I hope it's cause she about to meet Miss Nelly and not causa J.C.'s showin off. Don't wanna have to one-up his little ass again.

Miss Nelly's a beautiful woman. Got this gray hair that don't never move on top of her head, just sits up there like a crown. And she ain't flashy at all, no sign of shinin jewelry or nothin. Instead she's always wearin gowns down to the floor to let you know she's rich without slappin you in the face with her dough. She wears a different one in the pictures on these walls (photos with Jackie Robinson, Ernie Banks, Louie Armstrong, Duke Ellington, Count Basie, Joe Louis, Cassius Clay, and every other big-time negro across the land). Got one of these rich gowns on tonight, the ol woman do. Her skin's the perfect brown, brown enough that she ain't the blackest black, but so brown and proud that she ain't carryin much white folk close in the family blood.

"Morris, how are you, dear?" She slides past J.C.'s chair and opens her arms up for me. One day before too long, I'll have Mamma set up like Miss Nelly. Rich, so don't nobody mistake her for no whore neither, with a crown on her head and flowin gowns on her body. "How's the food, dear?" She looks around the table, makin certain our plates is empty. "You filled up?"

"Just fine, ma'am," I say. I peek at the young girl and she ain't studdin J.C. no more. Her eyes is fixed on me and Miss Nelly. "Thank you."

"Hello, Miss Nelly," J.C. yells across the table.

Miss Nelly don't like J.C. causa the rough way he treats Willis when we collectin Salvie's money. Bad enough she gotta pay them Italians off so they won't take all her licenses and shut down the restaurant, worse to have a little shit-talkin, bushy-hair eighteen-year-ol bargin into her joint and slappin her geechy waiter around. J.C. just ain't never understood bein loud and talkin trash ain't always the best way to do the job. Sometimes you gotta go that route, long as you back your talk up. But my way, cool and quiet, is best when dealin with fine folk like Miss Nelly.

"Hey, Willis," J.C. yells to the dinin room's far end now. "Come get a picture of us with Miss Nelly, boy. Hurry up!"

It don't take the wet-headed man two minutes to get the camera set up to snap a photo of the ol woman and us. J.C. feels better, I think, better cause it seems like he's somebody even if Miss Nelly don't like his ass. Least the little girl coos in his ear again.

"Gonna go on the wall long with the rest," J.C. say. "Ain't it, Miss Nelly?"

She looks at me outta the corners of her eyes. She hates this bastard, that's what these hazel eyes say. "Soon as I find more room." Miss Nelly walks off and it's just me and J.C. and our women again. Once Christina's done breathin in his little ear, we leave for a ride down 49th Street.

By time we get to Ellis, and J.C. and Mora is payin mind only to folk comin and goin in the streets outside the T-Bird, Christina's whisperin soft in my ear, telling me she ain't no dumb little girl. She know what's what—she know who's who around here, too. "Yes, I do," the little girl say.

* * *

"Who is it?"

We stay quiet for a good while, standin on the third floor of 207 East 59th Street, breathin hot air against a black door that maybe ain't black at all, just can't really see it good in this dim place to tell otherwise.

"Janitor," J.C. say, rubbin the pipe at his side. "Here to fix the stove."

The door cracks opens enough for the frame's chain to jam the lock. "Don't need no janitor. Ain't called the landlord for nothin."

J.C. kicks the door loose, snappin a piece of wood free and throwin the lock across the room. He keeps that stubby right leg out from his body and the welcher trips at the ankle. But Tobias catches his balance quick enough to run from the little man, who drops the pipe to leap over a raggedy couch, landin in the crib's far corner and trappin this fool. I grab lead as it lands outta J.C.'s grip and close the broke door, waitin.

Tobias is cryin and hollerin, his screams bouncin off the apartment walls loud to wake the long dead. "What the fuck! You ain't no kinda janitor. Got my rod in back."

J.C. grabs the man at his shirt collar. "Shut up, muthafucka. You got four G's back there, nigga?"

Tobias' eyes go blank, like the emptied-out look we found on Johnny in that alley. "Who are you?"

J.C. slaps him—Tobias got damn near twice his size, but the little man slaps snot outta him still—palm tearin into the welcher's skin, and bangs his head against this polka-dot floor until the tile's design ain't no different than what leaks from the welcher's skull. "I said, you got the money you owe or what, bastard?"

Tears from Tobias' whimperin leak pink, but he pushes himself from J.C.'s grip and runs to the broke door.

"Get him, Mookie!"

I'm froze between the welcher and his exit. Answerin more to J.C.'s voice than to the body rumblin my way, I cock the pipe against my shoulder and grip my hands tight at its base. "Get him before—" I turn lead on Tobias same as I use to do playin stickball in alleys. Catch him at the swing's hard point, his jaw meetin the point and bringin my hands to shake. He drops to the tiles, splashes in his blood.

"Damn, Mookie. Ain't have to hit him so hard. Not in the head. Look, he ain't movin."

J.C. looms over Tobias so his lips is close enough to his nose to taste breath. Can't tell if the welcher's eyes is closed causa all the pink on his forehead. The little man taps the fool's head and foam spills from the mouth along with stained teeth chips, and my legs freeze again. "You killed him, Mookie. Can't get money from no dead cat."

Tobias ain't dead—just playin possum, and I know it. "Shoot his ass, then," I say, after my hands is through shakin. "Make sure."

"That ain't right, Mookie. He's dead. Why can't you give a man his peace?"

"Nigga was stupid to owe a Jew bookie four G's and not pay, then drive round town in a new Buick. Don't deserve no peace," I say. "Shoot his ass so we can tell Salvie we took care of this."

J.C. brings the .45 from under his suit jacket and readies the back bolt, its empty click soundin against the walls over the echo of Tobias' last scream.

This welcher rises from the floor now, rusty fists pullin at air, or at somethin I can't see that's come to help him. Tobias' eyes open wide through blood streaks and he gets to screamin again as he stumbles to his exit.

I swing the pipe, swing down this time like I'm hammerin his spine, and he drops next to the door chain. J.C. puts the .45 away and kicks as I beat. Each blow is below the neck cause we ain't been sent here to kill—Bernie's a bookie, not a murderer, see.

"Do we look like your muthafuckin landlord?" J.C.'s yellin between kicks. "You can be late payin us without gettin shit but a note put under your door? That's what you think? What the fuck is wrong with you? Shit, Mookie, watch that thing."

I remember how, while I was young, Papa use to say I had a habit of swattin up like I was playin tennis. By the time I got to high school, I was takin level cuts at pitches, keepin the bat even between my shoulders and my waist. Now all I feel is the downward slam of this lead against Tobias' back.

J.C. puffs spit from his nose, and his leg ain't poundin the welcher no more. "You got the money or what, stupid?"

"No cash," Tobias mumbles.

"Got no loot?" I stop swingin and he leans on his side, moanin. "Word on the street's you been ridin round in a brand-new car. How you ain't got paper, but you got a new load?"

"Spent on the Skylark."

I laugh and practice swingin against air. "You knew you owed four G's to this guy. How you gonna spend loot you coulda paid him off with? You just a stupid muthafucka, ain't you?"

"Fuck him. What I'm supposed to do, ask for his Jew say-so before I do what I gotta? It's 1967, joe. I ain't studdin whitey no more. Fuck him."

"You just givin um all your loot in bets and new cars. What kinda nigga logic?" J.C. kicks Tobias in the side again. "What we gonna do bout this?"

"Said I ain't got no loot." Tobias coughs and holds himself. "Bought a Buick, a Lark. Signed on the line."

"Gimme the keys," I say.

"Keys? Keys to what? My Skylark? You sick?"

J.C. kicks Tobias in the throat to keep him from screamin. I swing at his side but miss. Don't matter, cause the welcher's chokin on curses as he reaches into his pants pockets and hands me silver keys.

"All right, let's go," I say, and toss the set to J.C.

I stand over Tobias as J.C. opens the door and steps into the hallway. Thinkin about bashin this fool over the head one more time cause he's tried to stand in the way of my livelihood, like Salvie said, about the blood that'll flow and the wings I could grant him. But we already accomplished what they sent us to do here.

"Come on, man." I walk over Tobias and follow the little man down the stairs, holdin the pipe to my side.

J.C. turns to me. "Always wished I could swing it like that, Mookie."

4

IT'S LOSIN AND KNOWIN you can afford the loss. That's the best feelin a colored boy gets outta bein rich, cause he know he's comin out on the short end when it's said and done, be he rich or poor. I look at the other dark faces in the circle, the pain tearin into mouths, the winces cuttin eyes, and the frustration grippin fists as dice bounce against the back wall of Calvin's barbershop. I remember when I was a boy, Mamma'd bring me here to get my holiday trim, remember noticin the same ol cats on each trip sittin around before sneakin to the shadows—only half the souls came into Calvin's lookin for haircuts, see. Rest of um showed up for the parlor sinnin. I'd ask Mamma what they was doin back there, since didn't no heads look like they was shaved after comin to light. Mamma'd tell me to shut my mouth as she handed ten dollars to the ol soul at her side. He'd sneak to the shadows himself and, sometimes, he'd come back, head full of hair, and make her smile. Other times he'd come back and Mamma'd turn frustrated, or maybe he wouldn't come back at all. Couldn't never get my holiday trim on them frustrated days.

Wasn't till junior high I learned Calvin was runnin a crap game. Word was crap money paid Calvin's rent and kept him in solid business, seein as there was so much barber competition on 47th Street. Little nappy head like me couldn't go shoot no dice myself. Calvin's crap room was for ol men who thought they was hustlers, the high rollers and pimp-daddy types. You could even run across cops back there, let the street tell it, rollin dice and not thinkin about no wrong to it.

Use to hear stories about five G's droppin outta pockets on Calvin's games. Heard about the room gettin robbed by jokers mad causa losin they stakes, too. Some cat got blasted durin one after-hours stickup—they say Calvin let the shooter walk outta the shop, but didn't nobody never see ol boy alive again. Ain't been no stories told about robbin Calvin since.

"Twin tres . . . come on, sugar. Fall right for Big Daddy, come on . . ."

These back walls can't take me away, pockets is too deep. But they can't send the Holy Ghost through me neither, not like they do for the tricky-rollin ol men whose numbers always fall. Ain't gotta use no trick rolls to protect what I got—holdin on to far too much for that. So when the cheaters get to hoppin around and smilin and talkin trash to the losers at they side, I laugh. I know the little paper bringin um joy ain't nothin. I seen what real money looks like, how it lives. Salvie and Tommy Ricci and Joe Defelice don't jump around and act wild when they make real money. They sit and count it with the same knowin look they woulda had if they'd lost, which don't never happen no ways. This ain't the big payday, and they'd know it, cause sinnin go on every day. So much more cash to make later, proper count just gotta be kept. Them ol men always gonna win, but they can afford the loss. That's another cause behind why I wanna be like um. If they gamble, they ain't doin it to keep or lose they souls. They the judges who make the final call on what numbers fall on Calvin's wall.

"It's on you, Mookie."

"Nine, jack, sweet September," I say. I quake the dice in my right hand, but I don't say no prayer, don't do no hopin or no funny finger tricks. Just shake for a second and toss um against the wall. I stand up from my rollin squat and watch the crapshoot.

Ain't shit but a eight fall. Rest of the back-room souls moan, me bein so respected on 47th Street now, but I don't speak. Just look away from the G I dropped in the green cash mountain and walk outta Calvin's back room. Don't matter I lost two weeks' pay. J.C.'ll come back to collect Salvie's cut of the souls Monday, and I'll get mine right back.

* * *

Uncle Leon's store is on Garfield Boulevard. Little place, down the way from the Jackson Park El tracks and facin a empty lot where police cars always sit. The buildin's got apartments on top of it—small, dark joints seem like nobody live up there, at least lookin at the empty windows on the outside. Eyes facin the street without showin joy for the livin or tears for the rest, these windows peerin down. This's where Uncle Leon's lived long as I known, watchin the rest of us from up high.

My father's older brother was the family success before I got into the hustle. Came up from Kentucky with whatever money my grandfather'd left and used it to buy that store from an ol Polack runnin from the darkenin boulevard. While my pops chased baseball dreams down in the Negro Leagues, Uncle Leon became a businessman. Started sellin Mad Dog and Jack Daniel's and Jim Beam and all the other ghetto potions along with the groceries and became a rich man, rich for a colored.

All that ain't doin him no good right about now—he stands next to the cash register where somebody's shot holes through the metal tryin to get at his loot. Police, same police who sit across the street as the world falls around them, just stumbled outta the store drunk off Jack Daniel's themselves, promisin to catch up with those who done him this wrong. Uncle Leon just smiled at um. This's the sixth time he been robbed since June, and they ain't done nothin about it yet. He says he got this trouble cause Chicago turns plantation hot in the summer and makes cats forget they North, makes um act like no-couth Mississippi pickaninnies. Plus, all the heron and reefer runnin through blood around here only turns the heat worse. Ain't nothin no police can do but get drunk off Jack Daniel's whiskey, Leon say. So he's called on me.

"How ol is you, Junior?"

"Eighteen."

"Eighteen," he repeats, and huffs like he don't much care for this number. His eyes jump around the store searchin for customers who ain't nowhere near today, searchin, before fallin on the holes in this register and flinchin like they see a .22 about to pop off again. His fingers touch one of the holes, and I whiff the air in his store. Smells like smoke, drunk pigs, and bad fruit hangin high. "How old do you think I am?"

I look the pudgy, baldin man over. Him and my pops is spittin image other than Leon's rich fat. I'm told I got the same pretty southern looks they use to. I don't wanna believe it, cause if I do, it means I'm gonna age bad and end up a phony ol grocer, or as a nigga who can't hold a good conversation with nobody but the television set. "Let's see," like I'm thinkin it over. "Pops is twenty years over me, so he's thirty-eight. And you got him by a few years, so that makes you round . . ."

"Forty-three," Leon says. "That's how ol. What you think I been doing with these years?"

"Don't know. Been in this store for most of um, far as I remember."

"That's not what I've been doing, Junior. Running a grocery store's no ambition. It's something a man uses to get where he wants to be in life. Your father played baseball because he wanted to be big-time. A colored DiMaggio, that's what he wanted, had thoughts of ending up an American hero. Me? I've just been looking to be accepted. Kept my mouth shut back home, fought in Korea, got my checks from the army, came up North, and bought this store. Now, I don't want to be a hero, don't figure there's such a thing as a colored hero. Just want to walk down the street and not have folks looking at me out of the corners of they eyes, cause I belong to the very same world they belong to. I pay Uncle Sam, pay the streets, and still keep this mouth shut. Wouldn't you expect the police to protect such a good citizen, a war veteran? I'm just trying to make a living, not asking for anything but some security. You, what are you trying to do with yourself, Junior?"

I look outside at the police cars. "Don't know, Uncle Leon."

"Seems like folks your age are doing much of nothing. Just tearing down what we spent these years and took these journeys to build, that's all. You especially. You give your life to evil, serve it, and you don't use the bloody money you make to do anything but parade the streets in fancy clothes and nice cars. Where's that getting you? Everybody in these parts tells you they love you, the police dance around you when you come in here like they're scared of you themselves. You feel like a big man. But what are you journeying for?"

"Said I don't know, man." My words is loud and I'm walkin to the door. Ain't leavin, just lettin him know I don't wanna hear no more preacher talk. "To be accepted, man. Just like you. You say everybody act like they love me and police respect me instead of you. So I got what we both been lookin for."

"You're going to hell for it, boy," he says. "Who can live like you and not end up there?"

I stand by the exit, lookin at the police. They stare back; I feel um. "What you call me for, jack? What you want?"

He grits fake pearl teeth as he rubs the cash register gunshot hole. "Come to understand things after getting robbed these times without anybody looking out for me. Been taking this world's nonsense for more than what it is. Look at that Uncle Sam on the posters real good. He looks like somebody, and it ain't Jesus. That's how come he can lie and tell me to fight for him, that he's gonna protect me in return. Uncle Sam's a mighty fine liar, that devil. So we've just about been serving the same master, me and you, you figure?"

"Maybe," I say, and look around the grocery store. At the rot meat and molded breads and sugar-sweet juices. "Maybe so."

"But if I've been giving my life to Sam all these years," Leon says, "at least I can say I've done it to make things better for my family and me. I figure it's been for good reason, then. That's what you should be able to say twenty-five years down this road, Junior. I don't want you to be a man who sinned because of pretty girls and shiny cars and clean suits. If you've got to sin, you should be able to say that you've done it for the sake of loving your own."

"Uh-huh." I stand away from the door.

"They respect you," Leon rambles on, "but they come into your family's store, steal from you, shoot at your blood. The police respect you, but they sit over there watching while your people get robbed? What kinda respect is this you got?"

"Nobody know we kin."

"Doesn't sound like much to me. You think the folks who did this could go to Salvie Fuoco's neighborhood and rob somebody there? You think they'd get away with it cause they didn't know they were robbing his people? You think so?" Leon chuckles hard, so fat rolls under his grocer's apron. "All I want is for you to go get those who did me this wrong, Junior. I hate to ask this of a boy who's half of my age, but you've got the power to make it so this never happens again. At least you should use wrong like they use it, to take care of your own."

I nod at my uncle and leave the storefront without sayin nothin else.

"How else you expect to come about forgiveness in the end?" I don't know the answer to his question, don't even know what Leon's talkin about, so I let his words echo against brick.

* * *

47th Street Black was a runner and a crook, a nigga's nigga, like me. Now he's the darkest bum livin on this corner where the strip meets Michigan Avenue, nothin more. He told me the story of how his people came from Arkansas once—we all got such a tale, cause that's where we from, down Deep—back before I was in the business, when I had time to sit on curbs and listen to a yellow-eyed man's jive.

Him, his mamma, his grandmamma, and his two brothers got sent for by a relative who'd run from home years before. This uncle was suppose to have somethin set up for um, somethin nice and North, so Black's people piled in the back seats of the first Greyhound they came across and wound up on this strip back in '46, before it crumbled.

That somethin nice and North ended up a tenement above the relative's pinball parlor on 47th and Ellis. The uncle was a concrete hustler—"the blackest, snakiest, lyin-est, connin-est con you ever crossed paths with," in Black's words—runnin hookers outta the parlor's shadows and numbers outta the back rooms while his pinballs set off 47th Street's flashin lights. In exchange for givin um a place to live, he put them folk to work. The grandmamma swept floors and dusted the pinball machines, the mamma sewed clothes and cooked for the whores, the youngest brother sold soda pops to the arcade players and johns, and Black and the brother under him ran numbers. Delivered the receipts straight to Clean Willie White till the Outfit sent Salvie, Tommy Ricci, and Joe Defelice in to take over the lottery and replace Clean Willie with Johnny Batiste.

All the folk around here came to know 47th Street Black's people, not only from the service they provided, but cause them folk was the very blackest muthafuckas livin on the strip back then. This place drew wanderin folk from Arkansas, Alabama, Kentucky, Louisiana, worlds where the sun roasts slave souls fierce as coal. To mark somebody as havin the darkest skin on 47th was makin some kinda powerful statement then. But, let Black tell it, his people's skin had a vengeance to the shade, so dark and spiteful it let you know that, no matter the wrongs done them by they down Deep masters, by the cracks in this street, even by God Himself, these folk would rise up and shine in the end.

That's what vengeance did, shined against the skin, and the sun too, the sun shined on them niggas, made um sparkle. As I'd sit and listen to him, look at him, 47th Street Black'd get to claimin he had his family's same kinda shinin, spiteful skin. That's how he came about the name, cause that's what he was known for, his skin black as night on the strip. No matter how ugly he looked in my eyes, this bum'd stand on his corner and brag about his color, like he was proud of it. That's how I first figured he was a crazy bastard.

Now, Black—I don't know his God-given name, for all the listenin to this ol man I did, don't know what he gonna call himself after 47th Street's gone, shade unseen—he was close with Johnny the Baptist back in the day. Black was older, damn near thirty already, and shoulda been the man bein looked up to, but Johnny was the one makin paper, the collector the strip's profits was delivered to. "My main man," Black'd call the Baptist with a yellow tear. Johnny'd give Black and his brothers wads of cash (no more than singles and fives, but that was big-time for the cats of their day) to take they ladies to movie shows, or put somethin extra on the dinner table for Mamma and Grandmamma, or buy threads so they could look clean like the real players. The Cajun took a special interest in Black and introduced him to the finest women from the strip's ol jazz clubs. One of them is the lady Black still goes to see over on 43rd. And Johnny found extra work for Black on the streets, teachin him a little about the hustle, about workin for the man. They got close enough for Black to be one of the only souls left to know the reason Johnny called himself "the Baptist" wasn't causa his proper name, but cause he wouldn't never do no Sunday collectin till after he'd drove his yellow Caddy over to Reverend Goode's nine o'clock service at Ebenezer Baptist.

But everythin ended between them two after the Outfit sent Johnny to the uncle's parlor to collect back taxes. The ol man'd slowed down, see, and his rackets'd got to sufferin after the Outfit showed up on the strip. So the snake decided the easiest overhead to cut'd be his street taxes, seein as the Italians was lookin for a percentage of earnins. If you wasn't makin what you used to, you sure couldn't give um the same cut you'd been givin um. Makes sense, but the sense of math don't got chitlins to do with profit in Tommy Ricci's mind; he sent Johnny over to teach the uncle how to show respect. What Mister Ricci didn't figure on was that this fella who brung his people from down Deep wasn't nobody's punk. The ol man put a .22 inside Johnny's left nostril, told him to never bring his yella ass back to 47th and Ellis again. Not a week later, the parlor wasn't but a black cloud floatin in the South Side night. Problem solved.

Yet whoever it was lit the fire didn't know, or didn't give a goddamn, about the four street girls, the stacks of lottery receipts, the twenty-five G's in cash, Black's uncle, his grandmamma, mamma, and two brothers, all sleepin upstairs in the tenement when the flames took out the buildin's only good steps. They screamed, then burned to ashes that, let Black tell it, still shine in the mess of Ellis Avenue.

Folk on the strip figured Johnny was the one to start the blaze, and that's who Black himself blamed. All that kept him from his rightful vengeance was that he was wise enough to fear the Cajun causa who he had behind him. But the day Johnny Batiste disappeared, Black was found at the corner of Michigan, singin alleluia to the spring sun in praise of the Lord's merciful justice. He ain't left this curb since. Nowhere else for him to be now.

I never asked Black about the hustlin game, never brung up the subject or reached for his counsel or nothin, even though he was in the business back before Mamma even gave me birth. Knowin Black, I figure he woulda told me that he stands on a half-dead street corner, his uncle's soul burns in Ellis Avenue flames, and only God and the Italians (and me and J.C.—Black don't know it, but we was there, too) can say what came of Johnny Batiste, so there ain't no counsel to offer when it comes to tryin to make it in these streets.

"What go round," is all Black woulda said.

We're at his corner, 47th and Michigan. The streetlight's green, but we ain't movin. I got the Thunderbird restin, top down, against the curb. Still, folks honkin as they pass, either cause we in the way or cause they want us to notice um.

J.C. sits in the car, droppin his hands from the windshield. "Where's Black at?"

"Can't say. Don't know where that fool could be," I tell him. "You said he supposed to meet us at two?"

"That's what I told his ass."

Two-twenty-five, my watch say. We been sittin at the corner for a good thirty minutes. I turn up the sounds cause Otis's on.

R-e-s-p-e-c-t / Find out what it means to me

"There he go," J.C. says. I look from the radio dial and see Black's straw hat fallin outta a blue smoke cloud. There go his yellow eyes and burnt skin, and them rotten teeth. He tries joggin to the T-Bird but trips bubbly over the sidewalk. I reach outta the car to catch him before he scuffs my paint job, but J.C. props himself on my headrest and springs like he about to whack the ol man, pushin him away. "Where you been? You makin me look bad. Told you what time to be here, drunk bastard."

"Sorry," Black wheezes.

I grab his arm, cause it looks like he's about to fall on the car again. "What you find out, man?"

"Huh?" He frowns, eyes dartin between the two of us. Then he feels somethin in his ripped pockets and smiles that brown smile. "Word round this way's that the fool who robbed your uncle's store is the same fool who pumps gas on Thirty-fifth and Southpark. I know who it is the street's talkin bout, seen him over on Forty-third sometimes. Tall boy round your age, name of Henry. Don't sound like no colored name, do it? Sounds like a king's name to me: Henry. But that's what they call this here boy, the one they say robbed your store."

I let Black go and he stumbles back into the street. "Thanks, man. J.C. paid you, didn't he?"

"Yeah, I got paid."

"How much?"

He reaches into the rips, watchin J.C. in dim eyes, and pulls out two bills. "Ten, that's how much he gimme."

"Twenty," J.C. snaps.

I laugh and turn on the T-Bird's engine. "You gonna be all right, Black?"

"Yeah, I'm okay," he says, wheezin again. "I'm okay. Just drive me over to Forty-third Street in this fine car, Mookie."

I watch J.C. shakin his head. "Ain't that where you just come from? When you walked over here, wasn't you on your way from Forty-third?"

"Yeah, my baby's over there for me. Now, after I put in this work, Mookie, used my time to do you a favor, seems like you could take me where I gotta go. I ain't have to do this. Specially since whenever I see you, I'm greetin you with friendly smiles and waves, tellin your monkey ass to have a good day while you shootin car fumes up in my lungs. Now you bout to do it again. What kinda gratitude is this? Ten dollars all the life of a kind man is worth? Gimme a ride to where I gotta be, Mookie."

Ain't lookin at J.C. or Black, just at the sun, soakin in its burn. "Get in," I say, and rub my eyelids.

It takes the ol man five minutes to climb into the convertible—me and J.C. don't help him at all. When he's in, he gets to singin what sounds like Mora's gospel love song, "alleluia" over and over. Guess them is the real words. I take the right turn into 43rd Street's blue clouds.

* * *

Ain't much for a pool player. Only come to the 47th Street hall to listen to the ol men's talk and Muddy's blues. But pool been Salvie's game as long as I known him. Usin his cue stick to chase these colored balls (he always chooses the colored) around his favorite corner table, just to get to the black ball and put it away—this is a hustler's game.

He's made J.C. into a player. Little man's picked the game up so good that Salvie's dusty face sweats as they race to bury that eight ball. J.C. ain't never beat the man—with half a bill on the table, stakes outta his own pockets, ol Salvie ain't about to be no easy loser—but J.C. gives him a good run as far as I can tell. One day I'll be able to play like the two of them. Today, I sit on this bar stool, lookin over the game and learnin from what I see.

"What's up, Mook?" Salvie's eyes rise from his shot, starin through his frown. "You wanna get on here next? I'm about to finish your partner off in a minute. After I get through taking out this fella, you'll pick up a stick or what?"

"Mmh." Salvie's shot bounces against the table's edges and dances past the black ball. "You know I ain't no pool player, Salvie.

Gotta get some practice in before I come on the table with you. Ain't ready yet."

"Much as you twos are around here, always hanging out in this joint, I figure you was a fucking pro by now." Salvie watches J.C.'s shot bounce against the opposite wall from his own and line up just about even with the eight ball. "How come you ain't taught this guy how to play, J.C.? What's wrong with you?"

"Can't teach nothin to nobody." J.C. shakes his head. "Tryin to get this down good myself."

Salvie stares at the table. He taps his stick against my bar stool. "He set me up for a perfect shot. You see that, don't you?"

"Yeah, I see it."

"Never do that," Salvie says. He measures the shot and licks his lips cause he knows the little man's beat again. "So when you gonna learn, Mook? Ain't nothing more to it, like I say. Picking up a stick and going after balls, when you gonna learn?"

"I don't know. No idea. Whenever the time comes," and I look off to the players' smoke, into a corner as far from Salvie's table as I can find. "You hear my uncle's store got robbed again?"

"Your uncle's store?" Salvie still ain't shot yet. He stands over the eight ball and admires the game's end. He don't even bend until wrinkles show on J.C.'s face. "The one on Garfield?"

"That one—the grocery store. Cat stepped in there, pulled a rod, and blasted cracks in the loot box. Walked off with everythin. Took the brother for crazy green, like the last times. Got all his shit."

"Hold up, hold up, Mook. Talk to me normal. I ain't from Forty-seventh Street like you fellas. 'Cat'? What the hell's that mean?"

"A guy, Salvie."

"A colored guy, that's what a 'cat' is in this situation?"

"Goddamn, Salvie—a colored guy entered into my uncle's grocery store, took out a gun, and shot two holes in the cash register. All the store's profits got—"

"Money was stolen," J.C. corrects.

"You understand when I say it like that?"

"Yeah, I got it. Long as you speak regular talk, I got it." Salvie licks his lips, drawin out the end to this game as J.C. moans. "So what?"

"It's the sixth time he been robbed this summer. Six times, man. The police ain't doin nothin bout chasin this cat. My uncle's shop can't take no more of this shit. You the man—boss—over here, Salvie. What can you do?"

"Me? What I got to do with this? I didn't tell nobody to stick up you people's store. That ain't our way, Mook, you know this. Walking into some place and putting a gun to somebody's head, shooting holes in registers cause you so desperate for a few dollars. What's that sound like to you? A junkie trying to pay for his fix is what comes to my mind. I ain't got say over that, Mook, not at all. What you want me to do?"

"I thought you was the chief around here. Thought you had say over everythin." I watch Salvie's cue stick tap against the pale ball, just enough so it brushes the eight into the far pocket. "His name is Henry. Be pumpin gas over on Thirty-fifth and Southpark. My uncle pays y'all for protection, don't he?"

"Watch it, Mook." Salvie stands, chucklin at J.C.'s loss. He snatches a week's wages from under the little man's ashtray and laughs, lower and smokier now, while he counts the five fresh C-notes in J.C.'s face just for the sake of stickin the loss deep. "Your uncle pays us, sure. And we pay you. What do we pay you for? Takin care of matters over here, if I ain't mistook. Your uncle's store is on Garfield. And didn't you just tell me the stickup guy was a colored? Ain't all this your territory, what you get paid to do? Ain't it? You say you found the fella's name, where he works, all of this. For what do you come to me? Long as I get a cut of Leon's money, however you two handle your troubles, what do I care? That's what I always say—you people gotta learn self-reliance. You take care of this cocksucker yourself, Mook."

J.C.'s got the balls racked in the triangle again. Heavy breathin takes the place of his moan. "We gonna go again or what, Salvie?"

Salvie looks at me and rolls his eyes. "You need to learn how to play, Mook," he says, and crouches to break the next game, C-notes pokin outta his trouser pockets. "Ain't a goddamn thing to it."

* * *

Henry do look somethin like a king. About six foot four and walkin so straight that his head's always to the moon or sun, whichever's in the sky. For the three days I been watchin him, I ain't seen him bend for nothin, not even to fill these cars with petro. He's figured this way of liftin the pump, flippin the gas switch and feedin tanks in one motion, all without stoopin to do it. That's how royal he is. Wears his gas-pumpin uniform pressed and tucked so he's always clean, no matter this work he do. Thought 47th Street Black'd picked out the wrong cat till I watched him takin loot outta the service station register. Then, on the second night, I follow him—in Papa's beat-up Pinto, definitely not in the T-Bird, too smart for that—to a grocery store on 31st. I sit across the street while he robs the joint and knocks the man behind the register upside his ear with a .22. The tall spook walks back to the station when he's done, his pockets stuffed with grocer cash. Seems 47th Street Black was on the business good. This Henry's the bastard king I'm lookin for.

Another thing about him is that he's forever walkin to where he's gotta go. I wait at the station durin the early hours and each mornin he's come in on foot. And, at night, when his duties is done, he walks back to his kingdom, wherever that is. A full day standin up, fourteen work hours plus day and night walks. Can't imagine havin no life that involves bein on foot all day, not while I wear these fancy steppers, or walkin back to my crib, not when I can drive my shiny T-Bird. But Henry don't seem to mind, just struts around smilin like he's happy to be in this place. Guess standin and walkin so straight on these feet is all it takes to make him a king.

But it's the third night now, and I seen enough. As he leaves outta the station, takin more of the register loot, I drive after him. Keepin about half a block back, I roll west on 35th Street. Ain't till we pass Prairie Avenue that I pull close to the midnight-empty sidewalk. "Need a ride, partner?"

The king spook looks down at me and frowns like I'm funny. "Naw, live right up here on State, few blocks head. Don't need no ride. Preciate it, though, brother."

I feel the metal of Salvie's .38 stabbin my side. "Sure?"

"Yeah, I'm sure. Said it's just a few blocks up this way—up in the Gardens."

"Man, you know a grocery store on Garfield Boulevard? Over that way." I point left across my shoulder.

Henry don't even flinch, just looks down again. "Got a couple over there," he say. "Garfield's a long street. That's how come they call it a boulevard."

"I'm talkin bout one in particular, between Wabash and State. Got windows look like black holes on top of it. You know the one?"

"Yeah. I know that store. You say you lookin for it?"

"That's what I say."

"Don't know why you wanna go over there. Plenty of markets around this way. Bigger stores, got everythin you'd want. But if you need the one you talkin about in particular, all you gotta do is make a left up here on State and take that on down just about three miles, then make another left at Garfield. Better yet, go head and get on the Ryan, take it east till you get to the boulevard, and you'll run smack into the place. Don't know why you wanna go there particularly; got better stores around this way. Besides, that one's closed by now. It's past eleven, brother. But hell, if that's the place you want, it's that way, between State and Wabash, like you say. Lee's, it's called."

"Leon's," I say. Henry ain't stopped walkin a'tall, so I keep Papa's

Pinto rollin. "Ain't so much the store I'm after. Got somebody to meet in fronta there. Cat by name of Mookie. You know who I'm talkin bout?"

Henry laughs. "Only nigga I know with that kinda name is a fake gangster runnin around here in a shiny red convertible. Thinks he's top shit, but don't do jack but work for honky like any other cat. He a friend to you?"

"Somethin like that." I slide the .38 away from my stomach. "If he was, would you speak the same bout him?"

"No disrespect, but you asked for my opinion. Now, if you was scared to know or didn't want the truth, you shoulda kept from askin."

"What if I told you my friend Mookie is kin to the man who runs that grocery store? Leon, the man you call Lee. What if I told you he was Mookie's uncle?"

I stare at Henry, look right through him till I see the sidewalk behind, waitin for somethin. But this face won't blow Henry's cover—his blink don't even skip a beat. "So? What that got to do with me? He still a half-assed, fake-pimp muthafucka. That's all I know the cat to be."

I yank the parkin brake and stop our roll. "Come here, my man."

Henry frowns after he looks the Pinto over. He don't think I'm nobody, so he walks to the passenger side.

"What if I told you this bout Mookie?" I'm talkin to his stomach, can't even see the face now. This cat ain't stoopin over for me. "Told you this fake-pimp got say over when we go from this place, me and you, can send us up or send us down? Would you still hold your tongue against him like you doin?"

Henry's laugh echoes through the Pinto's rusted roof. "If he could do all that, he wouldn't be no fake, would he? I'd say he was the Lord God Himself, if he could do all them things. But we wouldn't be talkin about Mookie no more, cause ain't no fake-pimp nigga got that kinda power."

I snatch Salvie's gat from my slacks and show Henry a king's true power, this power to judge. His body jumps from Papa's Pinto—ain't but a hole flowin red where his stomach was. I hear the gun echoin against the projects around us, at least till the screamin drowns it out. Henry, who was so happy to have feet and too proud to bend over to talk to a fake gangster in a Pinto, drops to 35th Street. This's my first time seein him when he ain't standin up, this's my first time, so I smile as he wiggles on top of the sidewalk.

I lean out the window to see who's comin to tend to his pain. But the street stays empty. The passenger door opens slow, and I slide outta the car, standin up after all these hours. I watch Henry twist, wait for him to die. But this's a strong fool—he won't go nowhere just yet. I think of Uncle Leon: "Least you can use evil like they do," he said, "to take care of your own." So I follow his gospel and judge the spook's soul worthy. One, two, three, the sounds bounce against the poor buildins and the screams is gone. I look down and 35th is covered by the swamp of what was proud bastard king Henry.

I'm back inside Papa's Pinto and drivin off, Salvie's hot gat dropped under the driver's seat. He'd hate that I left a body lyin around, even on our streets—but killin bastard kings is the messy part of this life now.

5

ABOUT SIX FOLK BETWEEN ME and Uncle Leon's counter, and so many more fiddlin around with his no-good groceries, makin up they minds on how to best poison themselves. Business is back to normal in Leon's store, no matter that the register still got holes the size of baby fingertips in its front, sharp edges torn from Henry's .22 blast. I peek across the street and the cops is still there, watchin people come and go through Leon's door, little dark children smilin cause they mamma's gonna feed they hunger soon.

J.C.'s parked outside in the T-Bird's passenger seat, his hand poundin against my dashboard, like he frustrated. He looks at me through the red and white words on the store window—*Leon's Liquor and Produce . . . Servin Our Side Long As Need Be,* it reads rightways. The little man screams loud to hear through the glass and letters. "Come on, Mookie!"

I peek over the six heads at the ol grocer ringin up customers behind his counter. "Uncle Leon!" I raise my empty hands, so he see I ain't here to buy nothin from him. "What's up?"

"Ah, Mookie," and his voice sound like he gives a damn about me. The folk in front part into two lines, make a path between me and the register. The ol man smiles clean and white. "How you been, boy? Everybody, this's my boy, my nephew, Junior. You all know Junior?"

They all stare now. I sniff the store's air and it stinks like bad meat still. "Just come by to make sure everything's all right, man."

"Oh yeah?" His eyes go wide, shine like his teeth plates. "See there—that's a good boy. Everything's been real good, Junior. Your man came by, told me how you took care of that."

"My man?" Got no clue what he's talkin about with his "my man" shit, so I stare at the woman in fronta me with the thick specs hidin her eyes. "Good, good. Glad it worked out."

"Thanks, Junior." Leon's got a pint of Johnny Walker Red in his hand now, and he's holdin it out over the register, my way. I walk the path these folk make, watchin the eyes as they follow—children, ol men, honeys, all from my streets, follow me.

"What's this?" I ask the grocer as I touch the bottle of red liquor.

"Thanks," he says again.

He don't offer nothin more, so I turn to leave his place. I ain't lookin at um, but it feels like the faces is still fixed my way, children still smilin. When I'm gone, I hear Leon's voice through the door. "He's a real good boy," he repeats. "Takin care of business around here now."

I sit behind the T-Bird's steerin wheel, lookin at red bubbles flow inside the bottle. "Fuck is that?" J.C. asks.

"Got it for Black," I say. "Thankin him for helpin find ol boy."

"Mmh. What you get me?" the little man asks. I drive on without lookin through the ol grocer's window, or to the cops in the lot, or at the brick of Garfield. I drive back to the strip, and I figure on givin the Johnny Walker to the ol bum, even though the only one who could be "my man" bringin the news to Uncle Leon is Salvie. Black woulda asked for a ride to come this far south.

Me and J.C. sit in fronta ol Phillips High in the T-Bird. The car's shiny as always, but the shine's got a special strength today, strong to make you blink. That's what the young kids do as they walk past, blink at the Bird. Can't be from the sun's reflection, it ain't out today. "Think you should put the top up?" I look at J.C., wonder what he's doin with a pack of Salems; little man ain't smoked since before we started hustlin, and back then only outta boredom.

"Naw," I say, and look at the gray sky. "Ain't gonna rain. Don't matter how cloudy it is. If rain was comin I'd know bout it, so I woulda put the top up this mornin."

"Oh. God care enough bout your car gettin wet, He warn you bout rain beforehand?"

"Best believe."

"You sure He ain't mad with you?"

I reach for a square and snatch one from his pack, though I can tell from the twist in his mouth he don't want me to have it. "Angry for what? God kills every day, leaves bodies lyin all over the city. Remember how we found that stiff in the alley?"

"God ain't kill Johnny—Salvie and them did it, left him lyin there with the garbage."

"All right, you say they did it. But God ain't mad bout the crime. Not mad enough to stop um from bein rich and drivin round in big cars, runnin things on this side of the city. I done the same thing they did, left a nigga lyin on the street, not a goddamn thing more. So what? If the Lord allows them to ride round rich-style, makin fifty thousand dollars every week off doin somethin, then sits up and lets my car get rained on for committin the same wrong, that'd be mighty, how you say . . ."

"Hypocritical, that's the word you lookin for."

"Hypocritical of him. He'd be a muthafuckin hypocritical God to do somethin like that, no? I'd have to go far enough to say the Lord's prejudiced if he lets my upholstery drown for leavin a colored man lyin in the street when you got white folk out here livin high and dry as they make riches off the same wrong."

J.C. nods for a second cause he knows I'm right, then frowns from tiny raindrops fallin on his forehead. "This's the white man's world, Mookie. He gonna let them get away with what He'll punish us for. We been in this business long enough, man. You know how it works."

I put the square between my lips. "That much's true, I'll give you that. But what I'm sayin, J.C., is that the wrong we talkin bout here—killin a colored and leavin him on Thirty-fifth Street—ain't no big thing, not in my eyes. I mean, it's big for gangsters to get rich from doin it, but not big enough to make God angry. A colored man's forever a step away from dead anyways, so his years is spent not far from that dirt. You born out your mamma's womb like you comin outta the earth, you crawl round beggin as a boy, you bend down to pick cotton or lift crates as a man, then you die and they bury you back under the same ground. So ain't no big thing in killin Henry and leavin him there. That's what you get life for. I just saved God the trouble of whackin the guy Himself."

"So He's gonna make you rich in the end, like He do for these white folk?"

"Look at me now," I say, spreadin my arms. "Hell, look at you. How many cats you know dress like us and drive round in a fancy car? Ain't we just bout rich? Only He knows how much we gonna have before it's over. But we gotta end up with millions, no doubt. We in the hustle, J.C. Big-time."

He nods and no more rain falls on him. "Praise Jesus," he says.

"Praise His name." The square hangin from my mouth still ain't got no flame to it. "Gimme a light, J.C."

"Ain't got no matches."

"How come you got Salems without matches?" The bell rings and the Phillips students stroll from the school. "What they for if you can't light up?"

"They for Christina. She got a light all her own."

"You bought cigarettes for this tramp?" I toss the square outside the car. "You got me droppin you off at school so you can walk together with some fourteen-year-ol heifer and smoke squares you spent yo own money on? What's wrong with you? You can't do no better, J.C.? Look at all the fine honeys we come across on the strip, ready to throw themselves down for us."

"*You,* joe, not *us,* throw down for *you.* After I walk her home, where her parents ain't gonna be for another three hours, and after we smoke these, I'm gonna get into the best little cat-nanny this side of Forty-seventh Street. Ain't none a them 'fine honeys' got it like Christina. Then we gonna smoke some more. What you gonna be doin the rest of the day, Mookie?"

"I'll be at Mora's crib," I say, and J.C.'s smile disappears. I see the girl walkin to us, not lookin so sophisticated with her hair held up in one of these barrette buns, and J.C. leaves my car. "Remember to meet me at ten. We got work to do," I whisper.

I start to drive on when I catch her starin at me. First off, I think she's blinkin hard causa the T-Bird glow, but that ain't no two-eyed blink. It's a right-eye wink, along with a quiet kiss. I swear. J.C. gives her the cigarettes and she looks off, so I drive. I ain't goin to Mora's—just a lie I told to stop J.C.'s gloatin. Ain't goin nowhere but home.

* * *

We live in the Forties, still right on 45th. Ain't moved up enough in the hustle to get my people off this block. Been here since I was nine, so it's just about all I know. My people pleased with themselves for makin it here, see, like they accomplished everythin and don't need no more journeyin. This ain't nothin more than where we been trapped since comin up from Kentucky, far as I figure. I seen what Tommy Ricci drives around in, the hats Salvie wears, even how Mora's parents lived before they died. I know no gangsters, no true players, is meant to be in a place like this. Real players got homes on Pill Hill or in the suburbs, or over east where you can just about see the lake.

My ol man sits on the livin room love seat and watches the White Sox game on his television. He groans when somethin good happens, mad cause he figure he coulda done the same as them boys if he'd got his shot.

"What's up, Papa," I say as I walk into the room.

"Mmh," he says, like I'm somethin else the years done kept him from doin.

I walk on to the kitchen, and Mamma's slumped at the table, weighed down heavy from carryin a load long dropped by the ol man, this cross she ain't come to figure it's best to let fall. She ain't cookin or choppin no vegetables—do enough of that all day in the children's hospital cafeteria—just searchin through her newspaper. Got it spread over the table, hands, not eyes, tearin through columns.

"Afternoon, Mookie," she says. "You tell your father hello?"

"Course," I say, and watch the newspaper comin apart. "It ain't in there, Mamma."

"What? How you figure what I'm lookin for?"

"I don't." I touch her shoulder. "Just know it ain't there."

She makes a sound, almost like Papa, and looks at me. "You got money for groceries, boy?"

I take out my wallet and drop a fifty on the useless newspaper. I don't mind. Even if I wasn't no hustler, I'd be droppin loot on somethin for Mamma. Hell, I'm eighteen and still cribbin in her home for the most part. The least I can do is make sure food gets bought, or else what's the point of livin like this?

I walk upstairs, stepper soles creakin against wood as I rise. Geri's in my bedroom, playin Sam Cooke records. Of course she's layin on my good linen.

"What you doin, girl?"

"What it look like?"

I sit on the bed's edge and look at myself in the mirror. Tie ain't quite straight, so I fix it—ain't goin nowhere I know of now, but I fix it. "Why you always be in here? You got your own room, right across the way."

She sighs. "I ain't got no pretty bedsheets like these," she says, and rolls around hard to wrinkle the silk. "And I ain't got no record player. If you buy me my own record player, I won't come in your room no more."

"You better get you some kinda job, girl."

"Job? What kinda job you got?" Geri looks at herself, smilin like she know somethin she ain't got no business knowin. "That's what I wanna do."

"You ain't cut out for this kinda work."

"What you do that's so hard?" She tosses my pillow across the bed, dust spreadin its cover. "Where you be goin all dressed up every day?"

I laugh. "To my job, little girl."

"Doin what?"

"Workin the strip."

6

LISTEN TO THIS SAX. I ain't one who likes to hear jazz so much. Me and J.C. be listenin to the R&B comin outta Alabama and Detroit as we do our thing—Booker T and Aretha and Sam Cooke, may he rest. Down Deep music. Jazz is Mora's thing. She say you gotta have a ear with culture to appreciate this kinda sound; in other words, you gotta be one of them schooled fools to get down to it. But this music man we listenin to, when he gets to blowin his notes it ain't about culture or education, ain't even about music. I like to hear him play cause the noise he's makin is so Black and sad.

Mora and Geri sit with me at this fancy booth, and they mesmerized with the sax blower. Eyes wide, fingers runnin through hair, tongues whippin across lips. He's a pretty boy, I'll give him that, pretty causa his clear chocolate skin, sleepy eyes and shiny curls. Of course they gonna be mesmerized with such a pretty boy playin his sax so good and sad, else he wouldn't be up onstage. But I don't like for my woman and my sister to be lovin this cat so much, lovin him and leavin me sittin here lonely. Causa that, I can't appreciate this song just now.

"Go tell the music man to play somethin for my sister. It's her birthday. Tell him to play somethin nice."

The waiter looks at me, sees who I am, sees I'm sittin at the fancy booth. I slip him a ten and he runs off smilin, happy to take my money and scared not to do like I said.

"I got a request from a brother in the audience. . . ."

I look up from my rum to the stage. The music man's cleanin off the spot where his lips touch the sax. His eyes got sleep in them, though he's rested for a good while between sets. I notice Mora and Geri swoonin still over this sax blower and I feel more alone. I gag on my rum.

"Y'all know I don't dig requests. I gotta satisfy the ears of everybody who came out to listen to me, see. But this one comes from a special man with us tonight, a respected young brother on our side of town—Mookie King. He wants a song played in honor of his sister's birthday. Where you at, Brother King?"

I don't say nothin, cause I'm caught up with the folks starin at our fancy booth, with the eyes on my presence, the smiles, the claps here and there, claps for me. I'm onstage now and the club crowd's lovin me. Mora and Geri done turned away from the sax blower even and started gushin over me, the one who fed them. Like it's suppose to be. Ain't gotta say where I'm sittin at, cause they all see me here in the fancy booth. They see me.

"All right, Mookie. Remember I'm playing this only because you asked for it. Remember that. This is for you and your sister. What's her name?"

"Geri," I yell through the shadows.

"Geri," the sax man repeats. "Happy birthday, Geri."

He gets to blowin a tune and I bite my lip, not cause the crowd ain't payin me mind no more. Not causa that, but cause he's playin his sax Black and sad again. The noise makes me feel painful, not happy, for Geri's birthday. Is it my request that's brung the music, or Geri, or is this man just forever sufferin?

I see 47th Street's wanderers as I hear his tune, but they ain't lost on the strip no more, not even in the city. The souls is out in a forest, green and dark and muddy, a marsh maybe. And they got dirty faces, like they fell along the way, so dirty I can barely see them against the night and these trees. At least till the light comes, light like fire in the sky. The souls get to runnin, not to the light—which I expect, since the marsh is so dark—they run away from it, scared. More lights appear with the first, chasin the wanderers deeper into the marsh. Can't tell whether these lights just chasin for the sport of it, or if they tryin to catch these fools; least I can't tell till the first sets the slowest muddy coon on fire. I look up to see his soul in the sky, twistin in flames. I only know I'm runnin with the wanderers when I smell and hear more slow coons burnin around me, so I run faster. The sax blower's song stops as heat touches the end of me.

I open my eyes and he ain't onstage no more. I look around the fancy booth, at the lacy napkins and shinin silver forks, at the two fine women in Carson Pirie Scott dresses I afforded, and down at myself. I feel the cold steel against my side, protectin me from shadows and lights. What'd this music man's song have to do with the joy of my little sis's birth?

I'm sittin at the bar, drinkin a rich, spicy rum now instead of the cheap brands my lips is use to. All kinda folk around me. Educated professionals talkin soft and smart, drunk losers yellin in the joint's smoky air, hustlers and hookers preyin on loose wallets. All of um better be droppin loot in my collection pot by this Sunday, else me and J.C.'ll come for um. I finish my drink.

"Bartend, bring me somethin else," I say. "Another rum and Coke."

The man behind the bar walks slow to me, wipin his hands. "Brother over there say he wanna buy your next round. Say he wanna meet you."

"Who this?" The bartend points to the end of the liquor counter.

It's the music man, without his sax. He smiles and nods, so I wave him over.

"What's up, jack? Thanks for the tune, my sister appreciated it. It's her birthday today—I mean, tomorrow. When it passes midnight, you know, she'll be eighteen."

The sax blower gives up grip and I see the wanderers burnin in the night again. His touch is cold and shakier than mine—I'm lost in his marsh till he lets go my palm. "No problem, brother," he says, and looks at the bartend. "Can you get us those drinks? Bring me a Seven-and-Seven along with whatever this man wants."

"Rum and Coke," I repeat, and the sax blower drops a five-spot on the bar. "What you buyin me drinks for, chief? You ain't gotta do that. Thought you knew who I was."

"Of course, Brother King, I know who you are," he says. He's about the same height as me, with low eyelids hidin eyes with so much mist in um they almost ain't here. His skin's sweaty, shinin in the joint's lamps although his touch is cold. He's older than I am for sure, got more years than Mora on him look like to me. "That's how come I wanted to meet you. Hear you're a good cat to be familiar with in this part of town."

"Oh yeah?" I lean on the liquor counter as the bartender delivers our drinks and snatches the wrinkled bill. "Where you get this from?"

"Keep the change," the sax blower says. "Ain't no hard word to come about. The birds is always conversing about you as they fly through these parts. Mookie King this, Mookie King that. Dig the suit. Those ain't no secondhand Salvation Army threads. They sing importance."

"Okay . . . what's your jive, music man?"

"Sorry. You're a busy brother, Mookie. Don't mean to waste your time," he says. "Leroy Cross." He holds out his hand again and I look at the drink I asked for. If I sip it, I give him the one-up. Strip rule #1: a nigga owns you if you owe him, owns you no different than the C-notes I drop on Mora's bedsheets is supposed to lock her in my debt. So I shake his hand and see the song's burn instead of tastin this rum.

"What you need?"

"Ain't what I need so much," Leroy says. "It's just a favor I'm asking. Like when you sent that waiter to request a birthday tune. I'm looking for a song."

"Mmh."

"Like I say, I hear you're a important man from the birds," Leroy says, speakin as soft and careful as the professionals. "And I hear how you came about this importance, young brother like you. That you got connections with the man in high places, with some bad-ass honkies. These honkies, they control my trade, you know, decide when I get paid for blowing sax and when I starve because I've got nothing but the air in my instrument. Sound about right to you, Brother King?"

I smile and shrug cause I ain't bubbly enough to start runnin my trap. Salvie'd taught me to keep quiet when somebody brung up the hustle.

"It'd be helpful, brother to brother, if you put me in contact with these bad honkies you're with. On the city scene, you gotta be connected to get the good gigs, make real loot. That's the favor I come to you for. I don't dig requests either, like I say, but I played for your sister, and I bought you rum. You do this for me, brother?"

I'm still smilin and shruggin, but I can't look him in the eye no more. I watch Mora and Geri at the fancy booth. "Why you go and play that sad song for Geri? Ain't sound like no birthday ditty. That's what I asked you for, a tune for my sister."

"Wasn't a sad song, ain't meant to be," Leroy says. "It's Coltrane, called 'Alabama.' You say it's sad—it's more melancholy than sad in my ears—and that's only in the beginning, those first bars. After its silent break and into the bridge, the song's joy, nothing but. Maybe more relief than joy, cause melancholy's done with. It's where my people are from, Alabama. Wasn't a sad song, just what your request brought to my head."

"Made me think of coons burnin in the marsh."

"You didn't like it?"

"Naw, naw. Don't mean I didn't like it, ain't sayin that at all. I thanked you for playin, didn't I?"

Gets quiet, at least in the space where me and the sax blower sit. Leroy Cross's got hustler in his soul—slick talk, shadiness—enough to be a street player. He'd be good workin 47th, maybe good as us. Just can't see him bustin nobody's head open. He don't weigh but a buck and a half, and his body's so shaky.

"Who're the fillies in the big booth?" Leroy nods at Mora and Geri. "They're about the finest things in here tonight."

I cough. "That's my woman and my little sister, the one you played the song for."

"Figures," the sax man says. "Which one of um is Geri, the brown or light one?"

"The one that looks like Lena Horne, she's my woman, Mora." I sip on the rum finally. "The other is Geri."

"Geri," he says, like he's about to play her another birthday song. "Mind if I introduce myself?"

I cough again, splittin the smoke that falls between us. "First you ask for my help, for a favor. Then you wanna talk to my little sister? What's on your bird, chief?"

Even his eyes leak sweat now. "I play sax, brother, tenor. Gotta go with what inspires me. Others, somebody like you, might think what I do makes no sense, but if I don't follow inspiration, it won't come no more. When I got that note to play a song for your sister, I thought of 'Alabama.' And as I see her, I'd like to talk to her. Gotta follow what inspires me, cause it doesn't come along every day. So I ask if I can talk to the girl, out of respect."

"Respect?"

"Respect for you," Leroy answers. "You're a big man in this part of the city and your sister's about the finest thing in the joint. You're still gonna look out for me after I talk to her."

"How ol is you, music man? Ain't you movin on a bit to be messin with somebody her age. Told you she just turned eighteen. What is you, bout thirty?"

"Twenty-four." The sax blower finishes his Seven-and-Seven. "One night, I'm playing a gig on Stony Island and these chicks start to hounding me after I'm done, and there's a cat standing outside the joint as I leave, one of these Black Muslims in the bow ties trying to convert drunk and high and bluesed-up niggas as they come out the spot, turn them from Satan's tricknology. Stupid muthafucka, right? But I ask the brother for advice on the fillies chasing me, and he tells me God's set it up so every man's perfect woman is half his age plus seven years. If the filly's short on that range, he says not to let her catch up, because she lacks the proper amount of living for me—and if she's long, let her go, cause she's too worn to do me any kind of good. That's just how the Muslim said it. So if you figure it like that, your sister's about perfect. And she's the finest thing in the joint tonight. So what do you say, Brother King?"

I don't say a word, just sip.

"If I talk to her, you'll still help me." Leroy stands from the stool, touchin my shoulder with that burnin hand, and I still don't speak. "You're a good brother. Thank you."

He walks off to my fancy booth. I take the last drops from the rum glass and follow after him, drunkness causin me to trip so I'm far behind his strides, too late to stop him.

"What was the name of the song you played for me?" Geri's lookin up at the pretty music man with eyes as wet as the lips she's licked all night.

" 'Alabama,' " he coos, like one of the birds flyin through these parts.

I ain't even sat before I notice Mora lookin at him like she's still mesmerized with his jazz. I grab her arm and pull her to the bar, leavin Geri with this music man. Ain't till I reach the liquor counter, Mora next to me so I can escape the loneliness brung by his horn, that I decide to connect Leroy Cross with the hustle.

* * *

It's Monday, so me and J.C. is in the lot between 34th and 35th, countin cash in the backseat of Salvie's Chrysler. I can think back not too far, to a time when he didn't trust us to help tally loot. Just handed out our little cut after we'd collected these blocks and sent us walkin on home. Figured Black hands couldn't be depended on to count profits, not even the profits of his sin, the right way. Either we'd add it up wrong, or somehow we'd slip loose bills into our clothes while he wasn't lookin. Even made us wear short-sleeve T-shirts and pants with no pockets when we started helpin him.

But the two of us is on the up-and-up to Salvie now, cause we get paid nice and dress neat enough to not take more than our cut from the pot. Ain't no reason to disturb the flow if we livin good off how his world turns—so me and J.C. is worth trustin even if we ain't on Salvie's same level, at least not far as I'm concerned. We been faithfully collectin the cut from the coons and deliverin it to this same North Kenwood lot every Monday for the last two years. We take our five hundred cash from Salvie and spend it on fancy clothes and shiny cars and good, colored pussy. But we ain't no kinda threat to him. We just actin exactly how we supposed to act—two boys from the Forties drownin in nigganess while tryin to live like crooked ol devils.

"How's that count look, Mook?"

"Huh?"

Salvie turns to us from the Chrysler's front. "I said, how much you two got counted?"

I frown at J.C. cause I lost the figure in my thoughts. "How much we counted, J.C.?"

"Same as always," the little man says. "Fifty-six, four, and thirty-five. It's the regular dough, bout the same y'all bring in every Monday. Ain't nobody welched."

"You sure?" Salvie reaches for the shoppin bag. "Lemme see."

He shuffles through the bills quick and smiles his cheery, satisfied grin. He counts out a G, splits it, and hands the left fist to J.C., the right to me.

"Ain't it time for a raise, Salvie?" J.C. slips the pay into his suit jacket's chest pocket. "Costs to live around here, man. Gettin steep."

Salvie's hat falls off from his laughin. "Stop dressing like rich fucks then. Who said you had to look like some kinda fucking spade movie stars every day? I don't know how your bodies take all the lard you dump on your heads and the silk on your skin. Then you both smell like fucking flower beds. Near makes me wanna bend you over, maybe let you suck on my balls. Must be a helluva expense to walk around looking like sissies all the time. You don't see me in four-hundred-dollar suits, do you? That's how come I ain't never gonna need for a raise, how come I always got dough, cause I live humble."

"You the one who made us buy these clothes," J.C. says. "Told us we had to look presentable if we was gonna work for y'all."

"If you spend all your money to look presentable, is that my fault? But hell, you find a way for more money to get made, then the boss gets a raise, I get a raise, and down the line, you two get raises. And you can buy all the pretty suits and perfumes and shiny fucking jewelry you wanna buy. That's all what you gotta do. If we make more, you make more. If we ain't bringing more in, you can't make nothing past a certain point. And you two reached the certain point a long while ago."

J.C. pats his chest where the five hundred rests, and laughs. He's got the door open before I grab him.

"Got somethin to ask, Salvie."

"About money?" He's starin at me, breathin cold clouds cause J.C. lets the night inside the Chrysler.

"Ain't got nothin to do with money." I rub my hands together. "Least not my money . . . you got friends in the nightclubs around town, yeah?"

"Friends? Ain't no friends outside the front door to the house. I know some operators in that racket."

"These operators's shady, ain't they?"

He looks outside quick, watches cops roll by slow on 35th, waitin on they cut. "I'm shady, you're shady, they're shady, so what? What do you need, Mook?"

"I got somebody who wants to meet some people on that scene. Needs a word to be put in for um, to be looked out for."

The cops park at the corner of Calumet, and Salvie fixes his eyes back on us. "This some broad singer you tryin to screw, Mook?"

"Ain't a singer, Salvie, ain't no broad at all. It's a sax blower, colored guy name of Leroy Cross."

"Leroy Cross?" Salvie lights a cigarette. "I know this fella? The name rings bells somewhere. He got records out or what?"

"Ain't put out no records." J.C. gets interested all of a sudden. "You know Leroy cause he's a strung-out muthafucka. Moved to this side of town months back. Word is he been round the city his whole life, though, high since he was a kid. The kind to start blowin sweet on his sax so you fall in love with his ass. The junk pushers on Forty-third been carryin him ever since he been over here, so I figure he's welched on some other dealers cross town. Word is he's into Forty-third Street for hundreds, maybe more. Suppose he come to Mookie playin his sad song, beggin him for help. And my man fell for him. You know Leroy cause he been workin y'all for years, Salvie."

For a blink, there ain't no sound in the car. The ol man don't speak cause his throat holds gasps of smoke, and we too busy waitin for him to breathe to make a peep ourselves. Even this air inside the car don't move—waitin on Salvie, too, I figure. When he turns to us, he's got crimson in his eyes, and it's that crimson and his cracked yell that break the quiet open. "Do I look like a nigger?" He grabs J.C.'s lapels and bounces him against the vinyl twice. "I ain't no junk pusher. That's nigger business, spic and nigger business. Watch what comes outta your mouth to me, boy."

Salvie lets go J.C.'s jacket and the little man's eyes scream how bad he wants to bash the ol man's head bloody on concrete. He reaches to his side, to the gat underneath his suit, and I grab his arm. The stare is watery. I shake my head, cause I'm the cool one, and I don't say nothin more about Leroy Cross. Just hold on to J.C. so he don't shoot Salvie and get us hung. "Breathe," I tell him.

"As long as you twos handle my money, don't you ever let me see you doing no dope. All right?"

"What?" I still don't let go J.C.'s shootin arm. "Ain't nobody doin dope, Salvie. You know us."

"Better not be. I don't wanna see you doing it, don't wanna hear you talking about it. If you got some kinda thought to do that shit, or to push that shit, you go find another job. We don't put our hands on junk." Salvie's thin lips is wet with spit and leakin smoke. "That's what's wrong with you people. You and the spics. Too much junk on the brain. How do you expect to think straight when you're fucking around with that shit? Bunch of stupid colored cocksuckers. You understand me?"

"Yeah, Salvie," I say. "We understand."

He turns to J.C., looks like he's about to start pokin the little man's forehead, but thinks better of it. "You hear me? Stay away from that shit long as I'm givin you a goddamn cent outta my pocket. Stay away from it."

"I hear you, man." His fear hides under eyes that leak hate. "That all?"

Salvie drags on his cigarette again. "I can't work with no dope addicts. You all get the hell out, I gotta go."

We step from the Chrysler, and he leaves us in dust. J.C. kicks the lot's gravel, sprayin more rocks across the ground. "Why you ain't let me pop that muthafucka, Mookie?"

"For what, so we'd end up buried out in the Styx or in some alley?" I watch the dust fall about. "I got enough to worry bout. My sister's with this bastard you say is strung out."

"You let that muthafucka put his hands on me. He called me 'boy.' If somebody'd done that to yo ass, I woulda shot him my damn self. And if Salvie was a nigga, we woulda took turns stompin the shit outta him together."

I start across the street to the T-Bird. "Remember when we use to walk all the way home from here in tennis shoes and torn T-shirts? Remember, J.C.? Look at us. How you gonna sit up and let that ol man make you mad enough to fuck us up?"

"You talkin outta your neck, Mookie." He kicks rocks at me. "Just like them—sound just like um. It's only cause Tommy Ricci's little girl OD'd off some bad shit they make that 'no touchin dope' noise. What they care bout a nigga and a spic? What they care bout you or me? But you sound just like um, Mookie, talkin half-ass bullshit. We is what we is. It's too late for nobody to do nothin to change it. Fuck Salvie."

I feel raindrops. "Ol man's still the cause behind why we ain't goin home on bare feet and why we dressed like this. It's causa Salvie we in this thing."

"I said fuck him. Don't sell me short," J.C. says. He runs to the covered T-Bird as rainwater falls hard. "I swear before God, one day that muthafucka's gonna be on his knees beggin me for life, or else I ain't no man. What is we if we ain't men, Mookie?"

* * *

Geri ain't a bad-lookin girl. Got dark brown skin, strawberry lips, hair like a Martha Reeves wig, and these black eyes that curse you or love you, nothin in between. Mamma says she looks like me, pretty and southern. Not that I pay mind to her like that, her bein my little sister. But one way or the other, she don't look better than Mora, so she wasn't the finest broad in the joint that night we met Leroy Cross—no matter how high and misty-eyed the sax blower was when he saw her. Shoulda known somethin shady was up with him right then, from the jump.

Ain't nobody woke at home, so it's quiet except for my breathin and the rain hittin against the windows. No gray blarin on the television, no newspaper rustlin in the kitchen. Sounds like ain't nobody alive in the Forties except me, so much so that I think to check on my folks. God's got no cause to take um yet, and I know this, but this quiet makes me wanna make sure. I would run upstairs, but I see the girl through the windowpane, dancin her way across 45th Street. She jukes the storm water fallin around her, tries at least, then gives up and drowns as she comes close.

It's been me and my sister so long that I got her stuck in every faded thought in my head, stuck somewhere even if she wasn't there at all, or there but too young to open her mouth and have a word on whatever went down. It's hard to believe she don't know nothin of Kentucky, figure she should recall Morris senior chasin his baseball dreams durin them poor years. But Geri came up at the very tail end, just young enough to see it, then forget. That's how come she don't understand ol Mo same as I do, as a wordless man who limps around cause the only gift he was born with got took by another nigga, a hobbled man whose wound keeps him from livin life right. A man who ain't no real man at all, just a fool rottin on a love seat, waitin on the first of next month for his government gimp check.

Just if Geri remembered them years, she'd understand the life I live, be glad I'm a hustler, that I won't end up limpin. And she'd smack a bastard before she let um call me "Morris" or "Junior." Only if she held on to watchin her papa get took down in Kentucky.

I hear the front door openin, the raw rain fallin hard, and I sit up on his love seat. Geri steps from the shadow and stares at me like she don't know what right I got bein here. "Mookie?"

"I been waitin for you."

Her black eyes shine, even in the dark. "Why it's so quiet? Ain't nothin wrong with Mamma or Daddy, is it?"

"Naw, ain't nothin wrong with um." I stand and pace the four steps to Mamma's rockin chair slow as I can, without turnin away from this girl drippin wet. "Where you been?"

"Out."

"Out where?" I rock hard till I hear floorboards creak. "With who?"

"What you askin for? Where was you at last night? You steal something? Shoot somebody? What was you doin?"

I rock Mamma's chair faster. "I was at Mora's."

"You spend the night?"

"That's my business."

"How ol was you first time you shacked with her?"

"Eighteen," I say as she squishes herself onto Papa's seat. "And?"

"So why you askin me where I'm comin from? I ain't spent the night with nobody. I'm at home, ain't even twelve-thirty yet. You ain't got need to worry on me."

"What you talkin bout, Geri, is different. Mora's . . . mine. You know that," I say. "You been with Leroy?"

"So what if I have?"

"Why you so difficult, girl? I stayed up to talk to you for your own good and you givin me grief."

"What you gotta talk bout? What's on your mind, Mookie?"

"You and him, where'd you go?"

"Went to hear him play at Palm's. Then he bought me dinner over on Forty-seventh. What else?"

"Don't want nothin else." I stop the chair from movin and the creak fades. "That all you done? Ain't go no other place with him?"

"Boy, the Lord's messin with your brain for all the wrong you done. That's what your problem is. I came home after I listened to him play some more."

"Just tryin to look out for you, Geri. I heard some word bout him. You need to leave Leroy Cross' ass alone. That cat ain't no good."

She laughs. "You heard word? They say he ain't no good, huh? What you think the word on you is round here? I hear you ain't worth a damn yourself. Should I tell your woman to leave you alone causa it?"

"You ain't listenin to me. I know gospel truth on this fool."

"Who it come from?"

"Don't worry bout that. Just say I heard it from the street."

"Forty-seventh Street?"

"Heard gospel from Forty-seventh Street—Leroy's a liar, and a junkie. And what I hear um sayin is true."

Geri's quiet, starin at the March rain as it hits against the windows. She nods here and there as her head fights my words, then she closes her eyes long enough that I expect her to start snorin her heavy snore. Then she smiles. "You ever listen to Leroy play?"

"Course," I say. "Was there first time you heard him."

"He's from Alabama," the girl says, in some trance now. "You know?"

"Yeah, I know. Told me where he come from when we was at the club."

"That was the name of the song he played for me, 'Alabama.' You haven't heard him, Mookie," she says, still noddin. She moves her ass, but the raindrops have dried enough so her squish barely sounds. "If you'd been listenin, you wouldn't expect me to care nothin bout what he do. Tellin them lies and doin dope—what else you want him to do? You ain't heard him play. I believe in a brother who dies before I believe in one who kills, Mookie. He ain't hurtin nobody but himself by what he do. You listenin? It's the truth Leroy plays. You ain't heard him."

"I'm lookin out for you, Geri, tellin you what I know's wrong with the cat. You my sister. I don't wanna see you goin down with no junkie muthafuckas."

Geri smiles again. "I got work tomorrow." She don't walk upstairs, though, just squeezes her eyes shut tighter and sleeps on our father's love seat.

* * *

Leroy Cross lives on 43rd Street, between Southpark and Ellis. Fiend's Heaven, they call it. But his joint don't look bad, not from the outside. Ain't till I'm walkin up the stairs that the roaches and spiders get to runnin over my shoes and the air grips on my throat, chokin breath. Plaster drips from walls, dust cakes the banister, and somethin hungry ate holes in what carpet there is. The 43rd Street flat looked decent outside, but risin the stairs, I know this place's long lost. I knock on apartment number nine's door.

"Who is it?"

"Mookie King."

"Come."

I open the door all the way, look around before walkin in. His crib is neat. No needles lyin around, no clothes thrown around the floor, no parts of the filth behind. Seems the suffocatin rot can't come past his blue welcome mat.

"What's up, Brother King? You want somethin to drink?" Leroy's sippin from a teacup himself. He don't look so shaky and sweaty in his clean white shirt and jean pants. His sax is sittin against the frosted window and he's walkin to it as he talks.

"Naw, man. I'm in a rush. Just need to rap to you."

"Yeah?" Leroy sits on the windowsill and straps the instrument so it hangs across his shoulder. "Chill, brother."

"I'm cool," I say, and take off my coat. "I'm cool."

"So what's the word with your honkies? You get a chance to talk to them?"

"Yeah, I did that."

"I'm connected?"

I sit on the foldin chair he uses as dinin room furniture. "Naw, you ain't connected."

"Oh," he says, sippin on that tea. "What happened?"

I laugh before answerin. "How come you ain't tell me bout this dope? You got me runnin round here askin my bosses to do favors for somebody they know as a junkie. And you knew they knew. It's embarrassin, man."

"No . . . they know?"

"What?"

"They." Leroy gulps the tea quick to bring coughs. His fingers press the sax notes—he plays to interrupt his choke. "Your people know I'm using?"

"They run things over here, you understand that. They find it all out."

"Figure they do. So they said no because of that?"

"Yup. Say they don't do business with dope fiends."

"Dig that. Ain't they the hypocrites? It's because of them I'm in this bind. They dealt me my first hit. So I turn to them for help getting out of it. Only seems right. But they can't do it because I'm stuck in the bind they put me in. How's that for hypocrisy?"

"What?"

"Nothing." Leroy stands and lets the sax bounce against his body. His lips touch the piece, but he still don't make no music. "Dig this, man. I know I'm just about out of favors with you. . . ."

"Just bout? You all the way out, my brother."

"I know, Mookie. I haven't done anything but buy you a glass of rum and played a song. That doesn't go far these days, in this world, I know. But I need to be straight up with you. Is that all right? Got time for me?" I nod. "The truth of what brings me to you is I've got problems with these heavy pushers. The Banks boys down here on Forty-third want me. I owe them a grip, you see. I figure if these brothers'd found out I was connected with your people, they'd have to lay back. If your people own me, if they're making money off my thing, I can't be touched. That's how it works, right? I wanted the gigs to come from being connected, too, don't get me wrong—wages would've helped me pay those motherfuckers. But I was more on the covering-my-own-ass groove."

"Better go on and say what you got to say. Somebody, my mamma I think, once told me to never ask a colored man what he wants directly, cause he'll try for heaven and expect you to come up with at least a piece of the moon since you opened your big mouth. And if he don't get what he wants, he'll steal it from you. That's the mistake I made with you first off, man, not listenin to such advice. So I'm bout to get up and walk outta here as you finish this tale, and if you say somethin I don't like, ask for too much, it'll ride in one ear and ride on out the other. Then I'm gone." I grab my coat and start to the door.

"What I ask for, Brother King, is your protection. We know you're a respected brother around here, got last word over what goes down on the streets. I figure if these bastards know you're behind me, they'll have to clear it with you before making a move."

I stop walkin. "Listen at you. Got a lotta nerve askin me for a thing like that after how you embarrassed me. You want my protection from cats I got no control over. Why? Cause you stupid enough to put a needle in your arm, then stupid enough to think you ain't gotta pay for it? You got a lotta nerve askin me for that, man, lotta nerve."

"You gonna help me, Mookie? You said if I asked for something you didn't like, it'd go into and outta your ears. Don't sound like my favor ever left your head."

I put on my coat. "I'll see what I can do. But in return, you gotta leave my sister alone. If you leave her, the pushers won't touch you. That's the deal."

"Geri?" Leroy rests his forehead against the window. "What'd I tell you about inspiration, man?"

"Inspiration? You askin me for life."

"What's the worth of life without playing? All I have is music—I'm a tenor saxophone. All respect due, Mookie, your sister's important to me. Couldn't make the sounds I've been making not for her."

"Life or inspiration, that's our deal." I open the door. "You can't have it your way."

"I'm a Black man, Brother King"—Leroy stands straight—"nothing's ever going my way. No point in being afraid to ask, no chance I'm going to get what I'm looking for in the end. I'm just trying to play much music as I can while I'm here. Not looking for my way no more."

"That's our deal," I say, and leave apartment nine. I hear him blowin notes finally as I walk down these stairs. I hear him and, at the bottom step, I see one of the souls from the marsh, burnin still. Just can't tell if these ashes belong to the music man, or if flames burned my own soul free without me even knowin.

7

"JUNK. HEROIN. HORSE. It's taking over around here, Mook. We gotta get a bigger cut of it, something." The 47th Street pool hall's empty except for me and Salvie. There's a shadow movin around in back, but it's only the ol sweep-up man. The air's dark, and it stinks from Salvie's cigarette. A lamp blinks over the pool table, but it don't let me see nothin unless I'm bendin over for a shot. So when he's shootin, Salvie can't see me for the dark, and vice versa. That's what I'm lookin at as he speaks. Nothin.

"You gotta talk to those cocksuckers on Forty-third Street," he says. "Thousands they're making every day. Every fucking day, thousands. What the hell is going on, Mook? This *babania* thing is booming—so many fiends over here. And the two of them, the Banks, they got some kinda goddamn monopoly over the thing. This's our place here, and they ain't paying us enough to hold no monopoly over the kinda loot they bring in: fifteen, twenty percent, that's not much of a cut out of a business that's making money like theirs. You gotta go talk to these fat rat bastards."

I step away from the table. "What you want me to say, Salvie?"

He misses the shot. "Tell em they need to be coming offa thirty-five percent if they wanna keep on being rich spades. I don't give a fuck who lives here, what filth floats around in the wind, these is our streets, Mook. If they can't pay us the simple gratitude of thirty-five percent for dirtying up what's ours with this bullshit, then the Banks need to find themselves a new trade."

"These's some crazy muthafuckas you talkin bout." I aim at the eight ball again. "What they gonna listen for? They ain't worried bout no police muscle, nothin like that. They payin um off, same as us."

"These are our cops," Salvie yells. "Over here, these cops is ours. Running our streets. They do what I tell em to do. Fuck the rat bastards. Who are they? Two fucking street pushers? Am I right? You afraid of these cocksuckers or what, Mook?"

"Naw, Salvie, course not. When you ever known me to show fear for a muthafucka?"

"You're scared of us."

"Ain't heard of me fearin nobody I ain't supposed to."

"True, true. Better not fear nobody else," Salvie says before shootin past the eight ball. I bite my smile. "Look, if these fat-ass Banks don't got the sense to listen to what I tell em, and they ain't afraid of our cops on the street, then they don't need to be running this goddamn junk business over here, do they? What good is it for us to have two out-of-control sons of bitches making this kinda dough? You tell em thirty-five percent and hope, for their sake, they got the good sense not to complain about it."

I bend into the blinkin light and lick my lips. I don't aim or think about nothin, just nod and put the eight ball away. "That's it, Salvie." Outta fear or respect or whatever the fuck, I don't bother countin the $750 cash won from the table's corner. Just fold the bills and slide them into my shirt pocket.

He breathes his smoke. "That's it? It's this goddamn lamp what did it to me. Distracted my game," he says. "But fuck it. You got me finally. These cocksuckers on Forty-third Street, you take care of em, Mook. Don't you ever let nobody walk these streets without paying enough of a cut."

* * *

J.C. finally bought his own shiny ride early this week—Cadillac Coupe DeVille, long, gold, and smooth as a boat floatin on a lake of silk. "Forty-five bills. Cash green I gave them, Mookie," he keeps telling me. I figure everythin's all right since he can drive around fancy-style now, too. And Geri told me Leroy broke up with her yesterday. She had shiny tears in those big black eyes of hers, but things is goin like I want them to go.

We ride 47th in J.C.'s new car, everybody—righteous folk, wanderers, thieves, pretty young girls—starin at the little man and his ride. He's lovin it, been smilin since he came to pick me up this mornin.

"Stop." The brand-new brakes slow us so soft I barely notice, and we roll to the curb at Michigan Avenue. "What's up, Black? Come here, man."

"Who's that?"

"It's Mookie," I say as the ol man squints at us from his corner. "Mookie and J.C. Rose."

He strides to the Cadillac like he ain't had a drink yet this mornin. "Oh, Mookie. Didn't know who you was in this here car. Who pretty Cadillac is this?"

"J.C.'s. You see he's the one drivin."

"Oh. Yeah, I see. This a pretty car. Need to gimme your convertible and get you one of these, Mookie."

"Yeah, that's what I need to do." I blink at the dashboard's gleam. "Thanks for helpin me find Leroy Cross' place last week. Appreciated it."

"Ain't no thing, none at all. You gonna gimme the T-Bird or what? I need to get up off these feet."

"Yeah, man, you can have the Bird," I say. J.C. laughs. "I need one more favor, though. Got some word to be put out on Forty-third Street."

"What you need known over there?"

"About this same cat, Leroy Cross. The one you just helped me with."

"Same jazz man?"

"I need you to tell your friends over there to let him be. Don't want no dope sold to him, don't want no moves made against him. Nothin. Put that word out for me, Black, tell um Mookie said so."

"I take messages from Forty-seventh to Forty-third. Half a mile, that's it. I don't give no orders. What they gonna listen to me for?"

"Don't be bullshittin me, Black, you the top nigga over there, always will be." Black smiles proud yellow, though his ears know jive for jive. "Besides, J.C.'s got the same word on the street. Just so happens, he's connected with the pushers goin west. You tighter with the fiends and they pushers goin east. If word's comin from both ways, runnin up and down Forty-third Street, it's gonna be held to."

"You sure, Mookie?" Black looks around the sidewalk. "Think I just saw this Leroy on Forty-third early yesterday mornin, buyin his junk. When you a fiend, you a fiend. And when you a fiend, you gonna find somebody to sell to you. That's how Forty-third Street is."

"You saw him over there?"

"Think so, yesterday mornin. Comin outta the shadows with one of them peddlers. He looked happy. That's what I saw."

"He a fiend," J.C. says. "What you want?" The two of um look at me crazy, waitin for a answer.

"Don't worry bout it. Just get that word out for me, Black."

"All right, Mookie. When I'm gonna get your convertible?"

"Soon. What you need for now? Somethin in gratitude for your help."

"Nothin," Black says, and runs his hand across the Caddy's hood paint. "Where y'all goin to?"

"Got business," I say.

"Oh, business. Gimme a ride."

I turn to J.C., who ain't stopped lookin at me. "You think I'm gonna put that dirty muthafucka on my new leather? Forty-five bills cash green I gave them for this car. You musta flipped, joe. Hell no."

I reach into my wallet and find a ten-spot, press it into Black's hand before the ol man leaves. J.C. wheels his Coupe back to the street. "I can't figure why you care so much for these loser niggas," he say. "I don't understand it."

We drive west. But I'm lookin on my shoulder, watchin Black walk north, back to 43rd Street.

* * *

I feel the hurt outside our crib, so much hurt I can't open the door. At least for this moment, touchin this pain on the front porch is as much as I can take. The hurt and the everyday stink would whip me down. My stomach turns sour thinkin about it.

It's worry that makes me step inside. I wanna know where these thoughts come from. Geri's the only one supposed to be home now—fear comes to me second then, right after this worried curiosity.

Leroy is laid out on Papa's couch. His eyes's closed, snot and spit colored pus-yellow runnin from his face. I can't speak, don't understand. The room smells funky the same as if he was my ol man. I think to jump on the sax blower and whip him, beat at his dried hair waves till he bleeds. But Mamma's here, sittin on the black rockin chair, and Geri's on the floor holdin a rag to his forehead gash, ragged like somebody dug at his skin with a butter knife. Somethin took care of this cat good already.

"Hey, Mookie," the music man says, words barely makin it outta his mouth from the effort he spends sittin up. Mamma and Geri look at each other, worried. "I thought you were going to take care of that. . . ."

I don't say nothin, just walk on through to the kitchen. Pause only to glare at my sister, hope I'm lookin cold and hateful as I walk on. Must, cause she turns away quick. She should be scared—I wanna choke her for lyin about this goddamn junkie.

Papa's sittin at the kitchen table, smokin a square, his body slumped on the chair's backrest. Ain't no newspaper in fronta him—he don't trust black-and-white lies no more. I open the refrigerator, not wantin a thing, just waitin for the man to grunt at me. End up speakin first. "How come you ain't on the couch?"

"Boy beat me to it. Been here since early," he says. I think of Papa without his limp, when I was a boy.

I smile. "What's he doin on your couch?"

"Don't know. Guess he hurtin," Papa says. He sucks on the cigarette.

"He gotta go." I wait for him to agree.

"Mmh." Smoke breathes from Papa's nose.

I'm about to sit down across from him, but the funk makes me shake. I run back to the livin room. Leroy groans again and I grab Geri's arm, the one holdin the rag to his cut. Pull her to the porch and close the door behind. "How you gonna bring him up in my house?"

"Your house? This's Mamma and Daddy's house. You and me just livin here. I got right to have company same as you."

"Hell no you don't," I say. Geri's coal eyes jump. "You said he broke up with you, so he ain't got no cause to be here."

"That was last week. I ain't upset with him no more."

I frown. "You lyin. Y'all ain't never parted. He had you make that shit up."

"So? What right you got tellin him to leave me alone first off? That ain't none of your place to do, Mookie. I told you I wasn't studdin what you heard."

"He gotta go," I say. "Tell him to go."

"Naw."

"He's the one who made a deal. Said he'd leave you be if I did him a favor. That's how come I believed the bastard broke up with you."

"No he didn't. He ain't never said yes to nothin like that. That's only what you heard in your head."

"Ain't said no neither."

"You do the favor?"

I don't answer.

"Whose fault is that, Mookie? You gotta get a Black man's word in soil, then take it for the dirt it's worth. You know that."

"He gotta go, Geri. He's disrespectin me in my home. He know I don't want his ass with you. Tell him to get out."

"Shh!"

"What?" I look at the door. "This's my house, girl."

"Leroy ain't goin nowhere. Ain't got nowhere to be."

I give up. Ain't nothin I can say to this child, got no strength against these eyes. "What happened?"

"Ran into some of your friends," Geri says, and grabs the doorknob. "Figured you ain't did what you said you was gonna do. That's how come he came here. Why'd you say you don't want me with him? What'd you tell me before, that you didn't wanna see me go down with him? Didn't that come outta your mouth?"

"That's what I said."

She huffs. "Make them leave him alone then, Mookie. They're the only way we goin down."

Geri walks back to the music man. I can't walk inside again—smell too much of this hurt. I sit on the porch, cover my ears, and think about the hobbled funk before me and this Alabama fire still chasin after my backside.

* * *

Black?

No way this's the ol man strollin 53rd Street, back straight as a post, head free from his straw crown, eyes bugged wide, clear white and wide. Not the cat from my strip, way over here sluttin up the heart of Mora's proper Hyde Park, right across the street from this place I run to forget my world. Looks like Black—same skin dark to shine off the sun like he use to say, same long-legged hiccup walk of a fool lost forever between pimp and limp. And the eyes, stretched wide to pop almost outta the face, wide as them ol quarter-show cartoons of Mississippi pickaninnies carryin cotton and diggin ditches. Dancin around in his head, never settlin on nothin too long, unless it's comin at him, and then only long enough to curse the thing and get outta its way.

But it can't be him—I'm damn near a mile south and east of his curb, so far from 47th and Michigan ain't no way of knowin such a place even lives—can't be. This cat, whoever he is, pimp-limps forward, clean and awake, see, clear walks likes he's headed somewhere for real. Ain't no stumble to him, just a cool-ass, black hitch—this's a walk with a point to it. But it can't be my Black. Where's he goin to?

"Black?" I yell.

The ol man don't turn around at the sound of me neither; just stays on his way to wherever, and I breathe cause I knew that wasn't him. A long-lost, sober cousin, or the ghost of his brother rose up from the Ellis Avenue flames and grown ol maybe, wanderin streets cause that's what Arkansas souls do up North, wander, but he ain't my Black. I breathe and feel my lips spreadin. The smile's faded already by the time the ol man's head turns over his left shoulder, and his eyes dance again even from across this street, dancin now like they missed a beat, and when the shimmy of this ol record came back to them its noise wasn't nothin but a whisper.

His glide's interrupted. He stops just short of Dorchester Avenue, lookin back at the intersection he just passed at Blackstone, and in this place it's me standin on a curb. Here, Black's the one with business to tend while I watch the world fly past.

"What's up, Mookie?" Even his voice is wide and clear, clear as one wasted on so much burnin water over so many drunk years is gonna sound. "What you doin over here?"

"Me?" I laugh, evil and low enough that the ol man won't hear it. I hope. "Takin care uh my business. You need a ride?"

"Naw," Black says, but he don't move from his place. I cross the street to the T-Bird, jump in it, and Black still ain't made another step west since tellin me he ain't need no ride. So I ask again.

Now he glides to the T-Bird and climbs into the passenger seat without sayin nothin. I sniff his air, searchin for the stink of drink just so I know this is Black for sure, but I don't smell a thing but spring flower buds. His eyes stroll, though, as they soak in this Hyde Park we pass in my top-down T-Bird. "So where you headed to, chief?"

"Hospital."

"Which one?" I ask, without thinkin. "What's wrong with you?"

"Me, nothin," he says. "Goin to check on my lady at the University."

I blink, see Black's beanpole, high-bright addict of a ol lady scrunched up at the end of some 43rd Street alley, shootin heron between garbage cans. "She all right?" My guts turn at the question's stupid sound.

"Been feelin sick a while. Can't hold much of nothin down. Goin on damn near a month now. Told her to take her ass to the doctor weeks ago, Mookie, been tellin her." Black's words is full of worry, but his skin shines and the eyes stroll on ahead of us.

"She still hittin that shit?" I say, and my insides settle into rightful place.

"Stopped round the same time this started," he says, "a few days afterwards."

I laugh. "Then she goin through them fits fiends be gettin when they kick the monkey. That's all. What a doctor gonna do but give her more dope?"

"Naw. You ain't hear me—sickness came first, before she put it down." And I swear his eyes smile happy themselves. "Mary Ruth's pregnant. My ol lady's bout to gimme a baby, Mookie."

"You for sure?"

"Best believe."

So my insides turn again, till they all dizzy, as the ol man beams on Mora's glorious Hyde Park in this big, sober joy. "So what's she at the hospital for?"

"Just gettin checked for this here upset mornin stomach," Black says, and he looks at me as I turn on Ellis Avenue, head south to the hospital. "She ain't sick from gettin rid of it or nothin."

I feel his stare still. "How ol are y'all, chief?"

For a good minute, Black don't say nothin, so I repeat the question louder, cause I wanna know if he's gone all the way crazy on me. Not street-corner crazy, but that real kind of white-folk crazy where a muthafucka talks like he's makin good sense, with words comin out like they should mean somethin, but the logic behind the talk ain't nothin but babble. The kinda craziness they lock a nigga up for even showin the signs.

"I turned forty-four a month ago." I look at the black cracks hidin under the shine, and I frown. Always took Black for older than the stories shoulda left him, figured myself for doin half-assed math, or Black for tellin half-true tales. Just by the look of him, worn and cracked, the ol man was on the high end of fifty far as I could see it: all that whiskey and wine and a doped-out honey killin him over the years. If he'd had Mora's gold-rimmed mirror to look in, maybe he woulda seen what livin'd done to him long time ago and come to his shinin, bugged-out senses. But then what, after he'd stopped his street-corner craziness, then what? "And Ruth's thirty-two, thirty-three."

"Ain't you a bit long by the tooth to be havin babies, chief?"

"What how ol I am got to do with nothin, Mookie? Shit, I did my part, dropped my seed where it's suppose to be. Good seed, too. If I ain't too ol to be droppin good seed, then I ain't too ol to be no daddy." Black looks at me again; I see him in the corner of my eye, see his beam gone. "What you tryin to say, it ain't mine or somethin? That what you tryin to say? You know somethin, Mookie?"

I laugh, not so low and evil now, cause there ain't no need for me to rub foolishness in this ol man's face. "What do I gotta do with you and your lady, Black? You say she havin a baby, I'm just askin questions, makin sure everything's okay with you, chief. Ain't nothin else to know but what you tell me."

"Sure you don't know nothin?"

I give him no answer right off and the ol man looks in fronta us again. The T-Bird rolls to the university's hospital, and a tear falls from Black's left eye—they ain't as wide as they was no more, his eyes, got a squint to um now. Like they tired of seein all the happy cotton to be picked, or squeezin to keep another tear from droppin. "You drunk?" I ask, but I don't mean it, cause it's another stupid question. The smell of flower buds tells me he's clean.

"Ain't sipped nothin since the day Ruth told me she was givin me my baby, Mookie. Shit, we quit together. She put that needle down, I dropped the bottle. Gotta be right to grow the seed. What kinda kid comes up outta a dope-shootin mamma and a lush of a ol man? Gotta grow the kid. Wouldn't believe all the things you see good now that you livin clean. These things was here, and I knew they was here the whole time. Just couldn't see um. Like that right there." Black points high, to a bird with a blue belly jumpin out of a tree and flyin over the ride. "It's a miracle, Mookie."

"What miracle? It's a goddamn bird." I stop the car in fronta the hospital, watch the blue-belly bird float off behind the gray buildin, watch though I know it ain't no kinda miracle.

"Not the bird," the ol man says without movin. He's forgot this's the place he asked me to bring him. "Clean livin is a miracle, Mookie. Two niggas who ain't been to church, or no meetings, or no head doctors, ain't gone nowhere, but we got our lives put together. Dropped that garbage and we clean. This's what givin life do for you: clean you up, clear you up, let you see. It's a miracle."

I stop myself from laughin now, just barely. "Ain't no miracle, chief," I say, and reach across the ol man to push the T-Bird door so it cracks open. "You doin what you suppose to do—what you gotta do for your lady and this here shorty you got comin, just like she doin what she doin for you and the shorty. And for yourselves. What miracle? Niggas always tryin to give the respect for doin the good and right thing to some other kinda shit. Some other shit floatin in the air. Ain't no miracles, ain't no muthafuckin birds, ain't no magic up there. Take the credit for doin right, Black, it's yours."

Black still don't step outta my car or open the door no further. "You gettin stupid with age, boy," he say. "Just the fact there's niggas down here on the earth and a God up above, that's a miracle for you. Puts livin in its proper place."

I got things to do now, places to be. "All right, Black," I say, "I wish y'all the best, chief. You and your lady and the baby. I'll check you out on the strip. You'll make it back okay?"

"Always." He gives me his hand and, except for a smudge of ash between the thumb and last finger, the palm skin is as fresh as the smell of him. I grip him tight so he believes that I got faith in Mary Ruth's miracle. "And don't wish for us, Mookie. Pray."

Black steps outta the T-Bird and hitches to the gray buildin. Goin after his ol lady, who's givin him good reason and a life to grow. I drive on without watchin him walk inside, don't know if he makes it at all. I don't wanna see clean Black disappear behind the Ellis Avenue hospital, float off like that bird with the blue underneath.

* * *

The Banks brothers is the top pushers east of Southpark Avenue, make just about as much money week to week as we do, maybe a bit more by now. Only thing is, don't nobody but the junkies respect um, causa this business they in. Dealin dope don't bother me none. Like Mister Ricci once told us, "You gotta make a livin. If you steal, you steal." And if you push heron, you push heron. What should I care? Of course, most don't see it like this. They look at the Banks brothers and see street whores, look at me and J.C. and see restaurant waiters. You tip a waiter, respect what he does. A whore is a sinner with a soul damned to hell. Both just makin a livin in the service of hunger, that's the common sense most folk can't understand.

Folk around here is afraid of the Bankses, not afraid like they is of me—afraid cause I can shoot a cat, leave um in the street, and get away with it. They afraid of Willie and Julius cause these two'll kill you for no good cause, stab you if you walkin too close, shoot you if you talkin too loud. The pool hall cats say the brothers once tied a coon to the back of a Chevelle and drug him down 43rd Street cause he'd signified on Mamma Banks. The same cats say Willie and Julius is junkies themselves. I don't believe it, ain't never known fiends with weight on um like these two. On the other hand, when you makin much green as they is, you can shoot up and still buy yourself three squares a day, I suppose.

Julius been lookin at me outta the corners of his vampire eyes since I stepped into the 43rd Street alley, lookin and chewin on rock candy. "What you want, Mookie? Why you need to meet us?"

"Talk, that's all, just wanna talk."

Willie wipes his burnt hands against the Laundromat buildin brick as he moves away from us. "Bout what? What's important we gotta talk bout?"

I lean on a trash bin and watch this cat chase a rat with food scraps in its mouth along the wire gate. "You hear the word on the street?"

They look at each other, then Willie, the oldest, speaks. "Which word?"

"Word that ain't nobody supposed to mess with Leroy Cross. Don't mess with him, don't sell to him."

"Whose word is that?"

"Mine. Came from me."

"Oh," Willie says, and sits his fat ass on a cracked plastic crate, under his brother and me. "We ain't been told nothin like that."

I laugh. "Been out here for bout two weeks now. Out so long it's made it back to my own ears."

"Oh, I know what you talkin bout," Julius says. "You mean the nonsense that ol 47th Street drunk's been mumblin lately. That Leroy Cross shit."

"Yeah," I say. "That's what I said—the word on Leroy. Y'all ain't paid it no mind?"

"Told you we don't know nothin bout that."

"Wait a second, Willie," Julius says. "I did hear that shit. 'Don't sell to Leroy Cross, don't touch Leroy Cross, blah, blah.' Listened to the bum babblin for a full day or two. Then come to find ol Leroy's goin west of the avenue to take care of himself. So I figure whoever it was sent that word—you, accordin to your guy—went and worked out some under-the-table deal with the competition over that way. Stealin our good customers, seein as they pay Ricci thirty-five percent over west. You wouldn't do nothin like that to a brother tryin to make his money, would you, Mookie? Tell me I'm wrong."

"Ain't no shady business like that goin down, y'all."

"Good, good," Willie says. He snatches a rock candy from the box in Julius' hand and sucks so hard, his drool drips to my right shoe. I take the Stacey stepper off, wipe it clean to shine with my good pocket hanky. "You know how much money Leroy Cross owes us? Must not, cause if you did, I know you wouldn't be sittin up here tellin us not to touch his ass. This's our business, Mookie, none of yours. Fuck you."

"Fuck me?" I bend over, slip the shoe back on, and stomp gravel till leather squeezes my foot snug. "Lookit here, I ain't tryin to mess y'all around, nothin like that. We got a stake in Leroy, that's all."

"We?" Julius' tongue is sugar red. "Who's we?"

"You know who I'm with. We got a personal stake in the muthafucka."

"Stop it, Mookie," Julius says. "Our ears is to the street too. Word goes both ways. I hear Leroy and your sister is into some personal shit. She leaves his crib early hours, late hours, whenever. Remember, we live on this street, too. This ain't got jack to do with who you work for."

"Oh, Jesus," Willie grumbles through rot teeth. "I know you ain't studdin us and our loot over no bitch—excuse me, over that pretty little sister of yours. Don't tell me this's so, Mookie."

"Look"—I don't know why I'm runnin the smooth act on these two, I know it ain't gonna work—"how long we known each other? Years, right? Y'all know I don't wanna jack up your money. Hell, I want you to make as much scratch as possible. More you make, more I make. I'm only askin, for whatever cause, that you leave this one cat alone. So many junk fiends round here, how much can one less hurt? Just let Leroy be."

"Mookie," Willie says, "we respect you as a Black man. Black is beautiful, ain't that what they be sayin nowadays? I'll tell you what I can do—Leroy owes fifty a week since Christmas. That's December and this's the end of March. Comes to six hundred dollars, not countin interest points. You pay us that back, plus fifty a week from now on, the fifty Leroy woulda spent with us, and yeah, me and my brother'll let him be. And we'll waive the points. Best I can do for you, my man. You can afford it, I know, Mookie, cause you're a fair Black brother. And this's a good deal."

I take one of Julius' candies. "You two is some funny cats. You ain't supposed to be makin offers to me. You supposed to take what I bother to give. That's how things is, how they always been. At least over here, that's how they been."

"That's how they been, Mookie." Julius' red tongue spits. "But this here's a new day, joe. Numbers and policy and craps and that crusty nigga bullshit is fine and good, but it don't bring in what we do. Who's gonna shut this trade down? It's 1968. We recognize the Italians and the cops, and we pay um a little to keep our thing movin. But we make so much, it don't never matter. Things keep goin up. Hell, that's what we pay um for, to protect us from parasite niggas like you."

"Don't let pride get in the way of good sense," Willie says. "If you wanna make sure Leroy stays well, you know what's fair. If you think about it, Mookie."

The Banks brothers ain't crazy as I believed, but they got me shakin here. "Y'all don't know who I'm with," I say. "You ain't heard what I'm sayin." I walk outta this alley corner and away from this strip fast as can be. On my way back to 47th Street, to tend to Salvie's numbers and crap games and crusty nigga bullshit.

* * *

These Caddies roll like no other ride I ever been in. Ride so sweet and slow, no matter how hard you put that pedal to the floor, so sweet and slow it's like you floatin over the rest of the world. Roll low, too, but the float's so real that it don't matter—you just lookin down on the rest of the livin. Flyin over the dirty and the rotten and the poor and the wrong, better than all of it—you in a muthafuckin Caddy, chief. This's how come colored folk love um so. Lets us pretend freedom as we laugh—saved, drunk, and happy cause we up so high—at what's under us. Only car for a dead nigga to take his last one in is a Cadillac limo, see, cause that best of all Caddies lets him float one last time, above the dyin. That last ride makes the end worth it, I figure.

Gotta give J.C. his due propers for pickin up one of these butter-smooth babies, even at the penny he paid. And it's a pretty penny for any other car, forty-five large, but for this sweet, gold floater, every cent is a cent spent right. Even my T-Bird don't handle 47th Street like this rag-top Coupe. Floatin so the souls gotta look up as we pass, at angels. I should do like Black say, buy one of these fine babies for myself and give that Ford to the ol man. Let him ride in low style while I'm up in the clouds.

"Look at him," the little man says.

"Who?"

"Black." J.C. speaks the ol man's name and I blink, see I'm back down on 47th Street. Black sits at the Michigan Avenue corner, his back halfway restin on the brick buildin front, halfway leaned forward so his body's propped on bent knees, his head covered by straw and titled down so the face's hid from us. His arms wrap around his legs, pullin them close to the rest of him to make a ball of himself, and he shakes in the March drizzle like he's throwin up. So busy holdin himself together that he can't do nothin about this water fallin on him. Just squeezes himself till sickness comes from his gut and splashes to the corner of 47th and Michigan.

Black looks up, and his face's wet with drizzle and vomit and tears. He smiles, and the rot shows all the way over here. I roll down the window, let the rain drip on J.C.'s leather seats.

"What the fuck you doin?" J.C. snaps.

But I don't pay the little man no mind, fix my sights on Black instead. Clean and sober Black, with these shit-colored teeth. "You all right, chief?" I speak loud, figure he'll barely hear me for the noise of water smackin against the strip.

Black spits yellow into a puddle at his right and swallows somethin more. He wipes his face, just in time for it to get wet again. "Mookie?" he yells as J.C. stops the Caddy at the intersection sign, lets the jealous beaters and rust buckets roll past. "You pray for us?"

"Yeah, Black," I lie.

"Mmh." I hear his grumble clear. He looks to the sky, lets drips splash in his eyeballs. "Ain't no miracles. Ain't nothin makin no miracles happen up there. Just wet clouds."

"Put my muthafuckin window up," J.C. yells. I look at the arm of my jacket and the door's inside upholstery, feel myself sittin in water. I raise the window and look away from the ol man. "What's wrong with you? Jackass."

We leave the curb, but I peek at the ol man before he's gone from the Caddy window; and it ain't till now that I catch the bag at his left, just opposite the puddle where he spit himself. Brown paper rolled down to show the rim of a bottle shinin silver. Could be Jim Beam, could be Johnny Walker, whatever, whichever, it's waitin there, suckin up drizzle just for Black to swallow. Let the heavens tear him up inside before he spits into that puddle at his right, where the sky and whiskey and tears and sickness will dry, only to fall again a few days from now.

"What kinda fool?" J.C. says.

"Don't know," I answer before we float off this strip.

8

IT'S ONLY THE FOURTH DAY in April, and it's hot like all get out. Ain't no natural heat I feel neither, not like in the summer, but it burns. I smell the black smoke circlin as I turn west on 43rd, and there it go, in the sunset ahead of me. There the smoke hangs low, not fallin from heaven, but risin up from the street. Look like it's comin from the West Side. Its burn seeps into the car, creepin through the vents and settlin in the T-Bird upholstery.

I'm headed to Leroy's, back to that filthy flat above peddler's row to collect from the music man. My whuppin pipe rattles under the driver seat, lead bouncin against steel. Geri came home cryin last night cause Leroy'd called her outta her name. She claimed it happened after a gig and he was high, but I don't give a goddamn. I told him I'd keep the Banks brothers away, long as he let Geri be. Then I let him welch on our deal and still went and sang Leroy's song to the rats. Geri woulda said it was my fault, cause I shoulda took the music man's promises for what they was—the dirt words of a colored man. But I'm doin these things for her in the end, so how's he gonna cuss my sister? I been disrespected again, the way I see it.

I park not in front, but a block down the way and around the corner from Leroy's flat, so he can't look out his window and know I'm comin. The pipe is under my wool coat as I walk 43rd Street. I wanna think about beatin him, about the lesson I'm gonna teach, but I can't get this black smoke outta my head. I see it still, risin into the sky, and soot drops onto the street. So many folk runnin around on 43rd. Can't tell if they runnin to or runnin away, they just run. Smoke's so thick, it's covered the sun enough that it looks like night's fell early.

Ain't till I'm on the second floor, past the dust and spiders and fallin paint, ain't till I've passed all this that a new wickedness grabs me. It don't choke, just pulls me by the arm. I call it new cause it's took over the stink from my last visit, not because it's my first time smellin such filth. More so than my feet, it's this foul air carryin me to number nine's welcome mat. I touch the doorknob with my right hand, the whuppin pipe in my left. But before I open his apartment all the way, I see the music man. He's slumped in the foldin chair, his head leaned back like his neck is broke, snot runnin from his nose, and pupils spinnin in sleep-dead sockets. The needle swings from his arm, the belt still fixed around the muscle. His nose, mouth, and throat ain't movin to show the effort of breath. Like I say, I dealt with this wicked air before, in an alley off 49th, on an empty 35th Street, I dealt with it.

I let go the knob and tuck the pipe under my coat. And I turn back through the filth, down the stairs, kickin black ashes from the bottom step. West down 43rd Street I head, where the cloud takes over the sky and everythin else around me. The wanderers' call screams over the music man's song now—

"King is dead! King is dead! They killed him dead. . . ."

* * *

She use to be fine, fine like my Mora fine. I see it even now, under skin that ain't had a good scrubbin since long as I known her. She's yellow like sun on Friday in June, Black's woman, Mary Ruth, high and bright as the star. Her face, under all the 43rd Street dirt, circles around like the sun, too, circlin around the world. Or the other way around, yeah, the world circles around this high-bright 43rd Street honey.

And she's tall as a statue, like somebody built her up from the ground in honor of somethin—God did it, maybe, God built Mary Ruth to honor Himself. Figure she use to be taller even, back when she was still fine, before she came to this street. She hangs over 47th Street Black underneath this corner store awnin, protectin Black like she couldn't protect that seed he planted in her foul womb. As soot falls from the risin West Side smoke, I can tell Mary Ruth was taller, too—back when she wasn't nowhere near this place.

"Hey, boy," Black calls. I slow my run, stop to look at him. The ol man's done up in his best. Haberdasher's hat sittin straight on his greased-up hair, fat tie knot pulled so tight his collar wrinkles at the throat, shirt and pants pressed and clean like they came straight out the Goodwill store over by the lake, and them sparklin, polished Stacey Adams on his feet—black-and-white steppers with leather so fine I see sky reflected in wing-tip skin. "What's goin on out there?"

"Don't know," I say, and look at the cloud that settles around us. "Somethin on the West Side."

"West Side?" Mary Ruth laughs. "This Forty-third Street, Junior."

"Yeah." Mary Ruth knew my ol man and his brother when they first come up from Kentucky, so I let that Junior shit slide. "But it came from the West Side."

"Naw it ain't," Black says, and nudges close to the woman, further from the awnin edge. "Came from up there."

"Listen . . . I seen the smoke risin up from the West Side." I'm arguin to be arguin, just for the damned sake of it, as soot smacks against my wool. The two of um look at each other, then at me, like I'm the junkie, like I'm the drunk. Like I'm the crazy one. "How you gonna tell me?"

"Mmh," Mary Ruth says. She holds out her hand, and it's bony and white, so much paler than the rest of her. "Better come on under here. Awnin'll protect you, Junior."

"Naw. Gotta get back to the strip. Parked up by Vincennes."

"Where you comin from?" Black asks, and I see Leroy's eyes in dead sockets, spinnin, feel the pipe pokin under my coat.

"Ain't comin from nowhere."

Four souls I never seen around here before run west, like they don't know that's where the cloud came from either, west then north up Vincennes. Runnin like I was runnin—they move fast, but I hear they cries still.

"What they talkin bout, makin all that noise?" Mary Ruth says, like she been disturbed from thinkin big thoughts.

"What?" I say. My eyes itch. So much soot now, can't even see it, can't tell it from nothin else.

"You ain't hear um?" Black says. "Sound like they was talkin bout a dead king. Sound like one of um said it even. 'They killed king.' "

"Ain't that yo name, Junior?"

All of a sudden, hearin "Junior" outta her red mouth hurts my ear, can't say why now, but it do hurt. Must be her voice mixin with the sound of sky droppin on us. On me, droppin on me. "That's it," I say after swallowin, "Mookie King."

"Junior," she says again, like she knows it stings and she's fuckin with me for the sake of it, "you dead?"

"No." Mary Ruth was Johnny Batiste's woman first, accordin to the pool hall cats. They say once the Cajun got all slicked-up rich off numbers loot, he set sights on mackin down this tall sweet filly from the Englewood all-girls school, this good Catholic, proper girl. They say she wouldn't give Johnny none at first, not till she saw him wearin his white suit and ridin that matchin Caddy. Mary Ruth's proper womb was all his only once she caught sight of the Baptist's clean Caddy glidin on 47th Street, the pool hall cats say.

Then, soon as Johnny moved on to big blond broads belongin to gangsters, soon as he turned Mary Ruth into a monkey addict as payback for makin him go through all that work just to get into her panties, the Baptist passed this high yellow statue on to his boy Black.

Figure Black was suppose to pass her on himself once he got through, once she wasn't fine no more; that's how niggas do the honeys on the strip. But by time he got done, she'd come to be a fiend down to her frail bones and wouldn't nobody else take her off his hands. Black didn't have no choice but to stay with her, and she ain't have no choice but to hold on to a wino; nothin better to do but keep lovin.

And here they is, under a grocery store awnin on 43rd Street, statue tall and bright like the sun protectin her slicked-up bum of a husband as soot rains. I see how she stands over him in case the awnin ain't strong enough to stay up there, and how he squeezes up next to the mother of his baby—the mother, before God took care of that sickness. This Mary Ruth who ain't nowhere near fine like the pool hall cats say she use to be, Black nudges against her and holds on like he's makin sure she stays standin in honor of that good God, holdin on so them yellow eyes don't start spinnin in sockets. I got no choice but to respect these two, cause it don't matter that somebody long dropped a bomb on this place, or that King is dead, don't even matter which side of town the smoke comes from, up or down. All that matters is once the black cloud runs outta soot, the two of um's gonna go about they drunk way, livin and lovin and wanderin these four blocks.

"Come up under here, Junior," she say. "Nice coat's gettin all dirty."

I look at the wool at my shoulders, see I'm covered in smoky gray. So I shake myself off, feel the pipe cuttin skin as I move. I grab Mary Ruth's bony hand, this hard but weak limb, let her pull me under the grocery store awnin, and I hide under Black's statue just in case.

After a while, he gives his woman a ten-spot (same bill I paid him for helpin me find Leroy—it can't be) to buy him a fifth outta the grocery store behind us. She frowns before squeezin the bill in that pale hand. "Don't worry, baby, we gonna take care uh you, too. Later." The ol man stands from his woman and pokes me. "Ain't that right, Mookie?"

I brush him away cause he ain't clear and clean no more, brush him soft enough that Mary Ruth won't notice. "That's right," I say, only cause I gotta give him respect, no matter his foolish way. Gotta, cause he's from my strip.

We share Black's fifth—Johnny Walker Red that flames the throat once you swallow—passin the bottle and waitin for the sky to stop. We don't argue about where the smoke come from no more, just watch for it to leave this place. Leave and let us go about our way, cause if the king is dead, muthafucka, ain't nothin we can do about it but what we doin right now.

* * *

Cops say they found Leroy the night after MLK got clipped. Somebody from the buildin called um cause they smelled that death seepin outta apartment nine. Ain't seen no holy negroes runnin around our way since then, none after I left Black and Ruth on 43rd Street. The cloud chased the righteous away, leavin only the rest of us.

Me and J.C. sit in the T-Bird, on the corner of 45th. The little man looks at me, coughin into the sky. He's started smokin every day again. "What we gonna do?"

"We? We bout to take care of business. What else can we do?"

"What happened to Leroy, Mookie?"

"Fuck Leroy. Them fat muthafuckas, Willie and Julius, got to him. The Banks brothers. After I said not to touch him."

"I heard he overdosed."

"That's the same thing I been told. You know it's more than a month since I put the word out for nobody to sell to Leroy. Said it to the Bankses' face myself."

"How you know they the ones who sold Leroy that dope? How you know?"

"Don't matter. They said fuck me. That's what Willie sat in my face and told me. What you think we should do?"

J.C. shakes and holds the smoke in his lungs; I answer my own question. "We gotta take care of business. You know how it is. Ain't no place for weak niggas in this thing. We can't let nobody sit up and say they ain't gonna do what we tell um to, not to our faces, not on these streets. Salvie wouldn't let nobody get away with that, would he? Willie and Julius ain't even payin the thirty-five percent they supposed to. If nothin else, we gotta take care of that. We ain't got no choice, do we?"

"Naw. What you want done?"

"We men, J.C., like you say. We gotta protect what's ours. What else do we got?"

Saturday night, and I'm sittin on Papa's love seat watchin raindrops. Been a stormy spring, the most rain I remember ever fallin here. Sky's always cloudy, ground too wet to bring growth. The little man's meetin with the Banks brothers down the block, safe from the pour. I stand and stretch my neck to make sure the T-Bird's covered. It's just fine. Somethin must be lookin out for me.

I've killed one myself—Henry the stickup man—and just called for the Banks brothers hit yesterday. Tommy Ricci and Salvie and those who clipped King, they make a livin off our end, killed so many more than my years have allowed. But, even off the death I brung, I feel less the nigga, like I'm reachin the high places where rich men sit on thrones.

Thunder shakes the ground, lightnin cuts open night, rain rocks our windowpanes, and I ain't no street-hustlin fake no more. This heart beats a true gangster's blood.

* * *

Ain't till December that Geri gives birth to the child Leroy Cross left her with. She brings me a nephew on Christmas Eve 1968, a son. We name him Isaiah.

3

9

J.C., IT'S SEVEN-THIRTY, boy. You bout to miss work." Grandma Rose woke me like that every weekday, just so I wouldn't be late to the Loop; my office was suppose to be there, downtown on Wabash and Adams. Then on Saturday mornin, she'd make sure I was outta the house by noon, cause work only lasted for a few hours on the weekend. Sunday we'd go to Ebenezer Baptist and, between worshipin, Grandma'd brag to her lady friends bout how her boy made such a good livin in the Loop, made good enough salary to afford new curtains and rugs for the crib. Told um how I'd come outta Phillips High School, even though she'd missed the graduation cause it was so late in the day, too late for her to be on our streets—her boy was drivin her round in a gold Cadillac, though. How many of them could say the same for the men in they own families? How many? Her boy sure wasn't one of them triflin niggas, scrappin and hustlin and thievin, tearin down West Kenwood. And if anybody from the neighborhood told her somethin else bout her boy, anythin bout a connin, gun-totin, dropout crook named J.C., she sure ain't believed um—they was talkin bout somebody else's little bastard child, not her boy. She'd raised me right, too good for such surroundin evil.

I ran down the staircase, pullin my suit jacket onto my shoulders. "I'm bout to leave, Grandma."

"Leave? Your head ain't dry from the shower. And I made breakfast."

"I gotta go, Grandma. Got a meetin."

She looked at her crystal wristwatch, my gift last Christmas. "It's eight in the mornin, boy. That's all. You don't gotta be at the office yet, not till nine. Come eat, J.C. Sit down."

"It's a special meetin I got, ma'am." I followed her to the kitchen.

"With your bosses?"

"Yeah, them bosses."

"Still need to eat. They can't keep you from proper nourishing."

I grabbed a piece of toast from the table spread and turned to go. "Thanks, ma'am. Appreciate the bread. Gotta go."

"Stop. Lemme straighten your collar in back."

I leaned against the kitchen door frame as Grandma Rose fixed my shirt. "Is it okay?"

"Hold up," she said. My mouth dripped crumbs. "Turn round for me to look at you."

I wiped my face and circled to the woman. Except for a head of silver-gray twists, Grandma Rose'd fought off the years. Her skin was brown and without a spot. She was little, like me, but full of good Baptist livin. "I look okay, ma'am?"

"Good," she said, her eyes showin a slow tear. She bit her lips. "So good. Go on to your meetin."

I walked off slow, didn't feel like rushin no more. "You need me to leave the car, Grandma? Mookie can come get me."

"Naw, naw, you say you got somewhere important to be. Go on to your wherever. Need to stop callin that boy Mookie. His name ain't no Mookie. Missus King named him Morris, so that's what you call him. How he doin?"

"Just fine. Told me to say hello last I saw him."

"Oh," she said, Ebenezer pride shinin in them eyes again. "You two are such fine young boys, doin good things. Tell Morris to make it to church sometime. He's so blessed: got his people to look out for him, fine home, that pretty dark-skinded sister, good job. He should spend every Sunday thankin Jesus."

Felt like rushin off again.

"If only yo mamma, yo grandpa could be round to see how you turned out, J.C. If only."

I opened the front door, ran away repeatin Grandma's words to nobody.

Tony Ricci's nails was long and sharp to cut through skin. Had to snatch my hand away and rub the scratches. I looked at Mookie. How come he hadn't warned me bout the boy's grip?

"How you fellas doing?" Tony stepped away from his Camaro and we walked to the ol Snake Pit's lot. "Ain't seen you all in what—years? You still play football, Morris?"

"Naw," Mookie said. "Gave that up after high school."

"So did I. Course, I was never good as you."

Mookie smiled. "Yeah. Gave it up, though. Don't play sports no more, except shootin craps."

They laughed and slapped each other's backs. I didn't see nothin funny, cause my wrist bled slow. "I never played no football," I said. "Couldn't make the team back then."

Ricci laughed through his words, and he talked fast, like his lips was fightin to keep up with the hustle. "What the fuck can you do in the game your size? Ain't never seen coloreds kicking field goals before."

Mookie shuffled a step to my left. "What you need us for, jack?"

"Oh, Salvie didn't tell you?" The boy turned serious and proper quick enough for you to know jive talk was just another part of the hustle. "I got a deal for you fellas. My father bought this piece of land we're standing on. He gave it to me, said I could do whatever I liked with it. I've been talking to Salvie and Joey and some other fellas who know this type of neighborhood good. They tell me the place used to be some kind of a blues club, name of . . ."

"The Snake Pit Lounge."

"That's it—I knew it had to do with snakes. Hate fucking snakes. Salvie says the joint made a nice piece of change over here, though. That's all I'm trying to do, you see, fellas, profit. So I wanna rebuild it, bring back the joint that was. What I need you two for is handling the day-to-day operations when it's open, you know what I'm sayin? I figure I can't just come over to the neighborhood nowadays and expect you people to give me your money. Those good days is gone. I'd be better off, I figure, opening a business and pushing colored faces in the front. The money's still gonna be made, you see. It's just a matter of finding two guys like you, respected fellas around here. Two guys I can trust."

Mookie bit his lip and looked to 47th Street. "You want us to manage the Pit for you?"

"For the most part," Tony said as we walked to the burnt-out foundation. We hadn't been nothin but kids way back, but we'd torched that joint real nice. "Manage it, collect my dough, keep the entertainment and employees in line. That's what you're good at—been doing it for Salvie all this time, ain't it? Keeping our investments straight over here, right, Morris?"

"So what we get outta this? You askin for somethin that's gonna take time we ain't got. What comes our way in return?"

"We know what happened to the last muthafucka who ran this place for y'all. We know," I said.

"That was a different story. That Jackson fuck, Salvie told me about him. That guy owned the joint by himself. He was hardheaded, so he got into trouble, ended up out in the Styx. He's got nothing to do with this. I'm gonna be the boss of the new place, and you'll be my faces. You're with me, so as long as you take care of my money, you'll be fine. And I don't expect you to do it for nothing. I ain't stupid—

I'm gonna look out for you fellas, that's what I'm trying to say here. The money Salvie pays you, you get the same from me. How many fucking Cadillacs that come out to? Plus you'll still get time to take care of Salvie's thing. I talked to him already. What do you make outta the deal then, that's your question—how about another five hundred change per week, just for hanging around a nightclub, listening to good music, and looking at beautiful broads? What more could you want? Ain't that the heaven all of us's living for?"

Mookie leaned on what'd been the Snake Pit door. "What makes you think people round here gonna turn out for a blues club? It's three years since the joint burned. I don't be hearin Muddy Waters tunes around these parts no more, except up in my head."

"Don't worry bout that, Morris. I'm running this thing. I know how it works. Trust me, I'm gonna update the whole setup. We'll get pretty cocktail waitresses for the VIPs and horse to sell in the washrooms and a new stereo system for the kinda soul records we like. You're right, it ain't gonna be no blues thing. This's a new day, needs a modern way, brother. What do you think, Morris?"

"Mookie."

"Huh?"

"Name's Mookie." He looked at me. "We'll give it some thought, talk to Salvie, and get back."

"Oh." The Ricci boy stepped away from us. "I was looking for a answer today . . . this morning."

I coughed loud for attention. "Now that I think hard on it, this ain't the first time I seen you these last three years."

"What?"

"You don't remember? Bout a year back, I took a chick to one of these hot-tub houses downtown, on Hubbard. We was leavin and I looked to the back room, the manager's office. And there you was, man, countin the loot for that muthafuckin dirty joint. You didn't see me leavin out?"

"No," he said to the ashes. "No, I didn't see you. You sure that was me?"

"Yeah, course I'm sure. Else I wouldn't uh brung it up. That's the kind of business you use to runnin—dirty hot-tub joints for hookers?"

"I've done a lot since last I saw you." Tony stepped back our way. "So what do you say about this here?"

"It's gonna be called the Snake Pit still or what?"

"I got something new in my head. Soul Mamma, that's the name I'm thinking about using. How's that sound?"

I laughed for the first time all mornin. "What you gonna call it that stupid shit for?"

Tony's face turned pale, white showin blanker than it really was causa his midnight-black hair. "I like colored women." Salvie'd always said Tommy Ricci's boy'd grown up to be a pitiful muthafucka—I didn't know it for sure till I saw the foolish beggin in his eyes in the Snake Pit's lot. "What do you say?"

Mookie nodded and they shook hands. But I backed off when the Ricci son held his sharp nails out for me, rememberin the hurt from before. It was only Mookie's frown that brung me to give the boss' boy my hand, lettin his grip cut me open again.

* * *

Took a month to get the Pit's shell rebuilt. The construction trucks and cement mixers came not even a full week after we'd first met with Tony. And when the workers started, there wasn't no long breaks or off days, so the new Snake Pit on 47th Street got whipped up quick that summer of '69. Couldn't tell how strong the foundation was, though, or if it woulda held up to torchin better than Jackson's ol joint.

"How's the hustle, J.C.?" The Ricci boy leaned against his Camaro hood, watchin as I crossed the lot from 47th. He wore bell-bottoms and a polyester shirt with winged collars opened enough to show pawn shop gems round his neck, and he sported a plaid suit jacket on top of the outfit. Salvie woulda shot us dead if we'd shown up to do business lookin like him. But the Ricci boy could get away with dressin like a rich clown. He was the boss' son; even with them thick red lips stolen off a Black face and afro-high hair rollin with the lake waves, he was still Tommy Ricci's son.

One of the construction rigs dropped a stone on 47th Street and the pavement shook. I stopped walkin and his mouth twisted into a half-assed grin. "Need you to do me this favor," he said. "I asked both of you, you and Morris—Mookie—to watch over my club, instead of just him, so you could check and balance the guy. No offense, but I don't trust him. Make sure he handles my money straight, J.C., don't steal nothing. I don't want nobody I'm paying to be cheating me. Need you to be my eyes inside this place, my man."

"What you gonna pay?"

Tony reached into his pants pocket—he carried a fist-sized wad of hundred-dollar bills. "Let's say two—no, one hundred dollars plus the regular per week."

"Two." The jackass was hustlin himself while tryin to play me. How could a fool get over on anybody after he'd let the world know his ignorance? I'd take his punk ass for everythin and then some.

"Done," he said, and offered his hand. His touch didn't hurt then, for it was softened with C-notes. "I appreciate this, J.C."

"Whatever, muthafucka."

Tony stepped into his ride. At my back, I heard him speed outta that lot and I looked at his two C-notes. I remembered some ol pool hall cat tellin Mookie that a clown was the world's greatest hustler once you'd bought into his fool show—trick you into handin over the last breath outta your lungs cause you couldn't stop laughin at him. All while the jokes tumbled outta painted lips, those clown eyes cut your heart into two hundred pieces. I tucked the bills away and wondered how much Tony Ricci'd paid Mookie to watch over me.

* * *

She danced round Grandma's cellar, showin her thing on Saturday night like always. Swingin it east to west till she knew my head was spinnin, then swayin north to south. Lettin that little dress I'd bought to replace her mamma's Low End rags, lettin it dangle above her knees and ride up her thighs while she moved. Then blinkin like she was ashamed, cause it'd all—the show of brown skin—been on account of some kinda accident. She got to tossin her head round, like she had a head full of hair up there, a movie goddess' full blond hair blowin round in the wind like Jane Fonda's. But when she moved the head too hard, I caught the kitchen of naps at the base of her neck, or too fast and the place round her ears where the perm wasn't holdin no more showed and that movie goddess bullshit became just that. Besides, ain't no movie goddess had no behind so big it giggled as it wiggled at you, no matter the girdle her mamma made her wear so she could pretend that the girl wasn't exactly what folk said she was.

Of course, I'd told Mookie all kindsa stories bout Christina's sweet thing, how nice and tight the womb held on, just so he wouldn't know I wasn't but a punk. Told them tales so good there wasn't no way he ain't believed it. I'd been thinkin and dreamin bout getting into that baby girl long and hard enough that, hell, I'd just bout started to believe them tales my damn self.

Believed till I'd bring her down to Grandma Rose's wood cellar on Saturday nights, fiddled with the hook on her skirts and slid my hand up her knee skin, cause the honeys from St. Lawrence Avenue didn't have sense enough to wear pantyhose unless they was headed to Sunday service. Made it all the way to the place where she got warm to sweat my palm, up to them powerful thighs that belonged to a thirty-year-ol lounge veteran, not to no child with a ghetto stupid smile. All that way after a week of spendin my soul makin Ashland Avenue gangsters rich and happy, before goin with Grandma to hear Reverend Goode preach the Word the next mornin, all that way just lookin for my thanks. Lookin for a cut of heaven. And that dumb smile'd leave from her pretty little face just as my sweat'd come, and her lips'd twist up into a tight little circle like she ain't know what my hand was seekin all along. Eyes rolled up to the top of the cellar steps full of phony drama, waitin for the door to open no matter I'd swore Grandma'd gone to the Ebenezer lady's club meetin and wouldn't be home for hours. But her eyes'd roll, and she'd yank the skirt back down over her knees, protectin that sweet pussy, and she'd yell no, loud for all 45th Street to hear just in case I'd missed the point.

Made it so bad, everybody round the strip knew Christina was a tramp. Julius Banks'd turned her out in the dope fiend temples on 43rd and Cottage back when she was just thirteen and playin hooky from the junior high school and still had the prettiest ass on them streets. Grandma Rose'd heard bout her even, warned me bout the young whore with the rear end—like how Grandma'd said it, the *bee*-hind—way up on top of her hips, who'd got with the deacon, half the cats in the choir, and Reverend Goode's oldest boy. Holy rollers and gangsters was Christina's thing.

Mookie, too—I caught the way her brown eyes'd get to peekin while we was at the clubs with him and Mora, dyin to give him what she wouldn't take cold cash to give me. Only thing kept me from figurin Mookie'd gotten into her drawers was that he'd keep a straight face when I'd tell my tales. If he'd gotten her, my pride woulda paid the price, no other point behind it. He had Mora, finest thing that ever walked the streets between the lake and State, so what would he've needed such a little tramp for if not to chop the nuts off pride?

Christina knew I was wise on her givin it up all over, too, and still didn't give a damn bout tellin me no. Claimed she ain't wanna spoil it with me, that I was some kinda special nigga who she was savin it for when I married her. Made me hold out while she was lovin Julius Banks' fat ass and every other joker with two pennies and a lollipop in his pocket. Girl was bold enough to tell that "I love you" lie, too.

Musta figured me for a straight jackass. Seein as I'd kept tryin after her for two years runnin, drivin her round town in my Caddy, takin her to the jazz and blues spots to meet the big-time hustlers on the strip—big-timers she knew too well for herself—feedin her face with Miss Nelly's cookin, showin myself with her in fronta my world. All without touchin no parts of what I only dreamed was heaven. After seein all that, what could even a Low End tramp take me for but 47th Street's biggest little jackass?

I took the needle from the Isaac Hayes record, but Christina didn't slow down, little head twitchin and body shakin like she had a groove inside her, somewhere, soul music inside of her. "Could you stop movin, girl?" I said. "Come sit down over here."

That shimmy shake didn't even hiccup; my voice had no place in the song she jammed on. Christina's head was down to the cellar floor, and her eyes'd closed, and she kept dancin with Lucifer, like how Reverend Goode said we was doin when we listened to that foul sin music. "Worldly things," he said, though callin it that made no sense to me. If Christina was jammin with the Devil, made more sense to say she was getting down in hell, not on the world.

I grabbed for her arm as she jiggled near, but she snatched herself away too quick, and flicked that holy thing in a clean circle. Shook around for bout thirty more seconds, then the song stopped, and her head came up from the cellar floor. Them eyes fixed my way, watered up like she'd just woke outta some scary dream. She came to me, heels too high for her little-girl walk clickin on wood planks, and sat in my lap.

"What's wrong with you?"

"Nothin," she said, and rested her head on my shoulder's end. I didn't have nothin else to ask her, never had much of nothin to say at all. If I wasn't tellin her I'd buy her all she wanted just if she'd give up the thing I needed, what was there left for us to talk about? All I wanted to know was what I wanted to know. So I rocked back in the chair, felt her scoot against my knee, and I went after it like always. Same tired game.

"What you want me to do?" I asked, but she didn't say nothin. "What I gotta do?"

"Bout what?"

I touched her leg, felt little hairs startin to grow round her knees. "You know what, girl. Been lovin you so long I don't know how long it's been no more. Forever, that's how long. All for what? Ain't like you lovin me back."

Christina looked up from my shoulder, lips poutin. Her hips pressed against the C-notes stuffed in my pocket. "I do love you, J.C. Every day I tell you I love you. How else you want me to say it? I love you, nigga."

"You can't just tell a man you love him. Gotta show me. It's only right. Forever's a long muthafuckin time to be lovin somebody for nothin. What do I look like?"

Her eyes was gone, little head dropped back to the cellar floor again, and my hand was at her thigh, just under it. "I do love you," Christina said.

"Gotta show a nigga, else he don't know it."

She grabbed me at the wrist, just as I was touchin the girdle linin, pushin my palm back to the hairy knee. "What happen to Julius?"

My stomach flipped so hard she had to sit up off me. "What you talkin bout, girl?"

"Don't play like you don't remember Julius. You knew him. Used to see you with him sometimes," she said. "Over on Cottage. You, him, and his brother, over there hangin out in alleys. I seen it—Julius brung you up all the time, too."

"I know who you talkin bout. Ain't say I didn't know him, did I?" I looked round the cellar, runnin from that empty little girl stare. "Just can't figure why you askin me bout him. Cat's been dead for more than a year, far as I hear. How you know what he use to talk bout, besides?"

Christina, much as everybody else on the two blocks between Grandma's crib and the strip, knew good and well how the Banks brothers'd ended up. Half the point of me doin it was so they'd know and learn from the knowin. Even if she didn't figure it out firsthand, all she had to do to get at the truth was wiggle that behind for the right preacher round there, and he woulda babbled anythin she wanted to hear. So the girl was tryin to hustle me, like I still wasn't nothin but her jackass.

"Use to tell me bout you, he did. Say how he didn't like seein me out with you cause y'all wasn't no kinda good, you and Mookie King. I knew Julius real good."

I reached to the dresser in back of us, into its cracked top drawer. The thing'd been Mamma's when she was a kid, and Grandma Rose was savin it for when she came home after all them years (let Grandma tell it, Mamma'd have to come home once she woke up from her whorin dream). I pulled the sack from inside, reached across Christina's lap, and laid it out on that dusty table I'd cleaned the Baptist's chains on top of years back. In that sack was my gift to Christina—I always brought her gifts on Saturdays.

I laughed, reached out to catch her just before she slipped off my knee. "So that's how come you ain't lovin me, cause Julius said I wasn't bout nothin? Ain't that bout a bitch. Jealous, dead muthafucka."

"Got no reason to disrespect somebody who's passed. It ain't right. Besides, I told you I love you, J.C., how many times you want me to say it?"

"Ain't bout sayin it," I told her.

She stayed far enough down my lap that my hand couldn't get nowhere up her dress, and her eyes shot round the cellar, runnin from mine, then fell to the table. "What's that you got up in there?"

I pulled the joint from the gift sack and twisted its paper wrap to make for certain it was rolled tight as could be. Lester Hooks'd sold it to me the day before, that magic love potion reefer cooked specially to get the most hardheaded colored girl's panties off. Asked him what it was exactly, and he acted like he didn't wanna tell me, so I gave the Blackstone Avenue weed peddler a extra twenty and a call on Joe Defelice's Saturday mornin number, and his bumpy lips'd got to flappin. . . .

"Topps paper dipped in a glass of Jack Daniel's, reefer grown outta the highest Mexican hills, up so high Jesus, Joseph, and Jacob be gettin blowed on the shit months before the banditos climb up there to pick it. That and a sprinkle of magic witch powder bought from the North Side, kinda powders white boys smoke to make um dream in cartoon colors and see diamonds in the sky. Just a pinch of that magic powder laced in with the reefer, cause you don't want the honey to be hallucinatin bout Woody Woodpecker while you tryin to get between the legs. Just a pinch. Uncle picked this up from off them Chinamen when he was over fightin the Ko-rea War, ceptin they used opium dope sprinkled with the powder, cause they got plenty uh that shit in China. Been usin this for three thousand years over there, since before the start. Colored twat can't stand up to this potion, cordin to them Chinamen—black, brown, red, yellow twats melt. Guaranteed to get you what you want, how you want it, else I'll give your money back. And you know I don't wanna go givin up no money I put in my pocket already. Like you cuttin me off at the

knees. That's how good this sucka is, joe. Call it Three Dicks on a Stick, cause she's getting fucked three times, by Jack, by the dream powder, then by my weed, before you even slide your black iron up in there. Twat's screamin ready for you after gettin this sucka put on it. Guarantee, I tell you. . . ."

I licked the joint at its tip, tasted the whiskey dip bitin through paper. Went into my shirt pocket for the lighter we used on Salem squares every other Saturday night and watched its flame shoot outta the silver square. Shoot and float in the cellar air till it swayed with the breath from our noses, like baby girl dancin to Isaac Hayes.

"What's that you got there?" she asked again. "Tell me."

First she'd been a virgin when I met her, then she'd loved me, then the whore child who'd belonged to the fattest dope dealer for miles didn't know a joint on first sight. I watched the fire reflectin in her eyes, turnin um brown to orange, and I laughed. "Why you ask me bout Julius? What I'm supposed to know?"

She slid to me and dropped her head against my chest so I couldn't see the eyes no more. When she spoke, her words came in a mumble.

I lit the joint, smelled the burnin of sweet weeds and the stink of somethin else, flat and poison and almost not there. "Can't hear you. Talk up, girl."

Her head rose again, and smoke'd took the fire's place, and the eyes was back to brown. "Said folk round the streets claim y'all done it, you and Mookie. One of y'all. I figure if Mookie done Julius like that, least you know good enough to tell me bout it."

"Mookie?" I swallowed hard and felt my head spinnin again. "How you figure it was him?"

"Who else?" She licked her lips. "You?"

I held the joint toward um, them thick red doors she'd barely let my own lips touch, waitin for her little fingers to reach up and take the joint like the grown-up hussy her mamma was so afraid for her to be. Wasn't tellin her nothin till she'd tasted Lester Hooks' love potion. "What if it was me?"

"You what?"

Christina's tongue played with the reefer, lickin the closed end while it rested in her mouth. "Me who put Julius and Willie down like that."

She sucked on it finally, lips draggin till the smoke puffed outta the holes in her nose and her face swole full of clouds. "By yourself?"

"Just me."

She laughed and put the joint in my hand. "Most say it was the two of y'all, if not Mookie who done it on his own. Ain't never heard no story said you did."

I held on without bringin it to my mouth, watchin reefer eat at paper. "Don't mean it ain't so."

"You did Julius like that, J.C.?"

I felt the flame crawlin up to my fingers and brung the joint to my mouth without breathin. Only had one—couldn't waste it. "What if I did? Big and bad as your boy Julius Banks was, what would you say for the muthafucka who took him and his brother out?"

"Don't know," the child said. She sucked it straight outta my hand without playin, that hungry suckin of hers.

"I'd say the nigga who took out the baddest nigga round, he's gotta be called the baddest nigga left. That's fair, only thing makes sense to me."

"If it was you, J.C.," she said, and rested on my shoulder's point, "if it was you, then you the baddest round here. If it was you . . ."

I held the reefer high to keep it from settin fire to my shirt. "And the biggest, whoever done it's gotta be the biggest, too. Only right."

"Yeah," she said. "He's the biggest."

"Okay. It was me who popped Julius and Willie."

"You by yourself?" the girl asked.

"By myself," I said, and handed the joint to her. "So I'm the biggest, baddest nigga you know, right?"

"Guess so." She sucked soft and long. "But it's wrong."

"What?"

Her head rested again, lips puffin brown smoke on me. "Killin ain't right. Ten Commandments—you be up in church with yo grandmamma enough to know that simple shit. Bible sends you to hell for killin."

"That ain't fair," I said while she choked on the love potion, no matter that it was my turn. "Up in the Bible, most folk goin to hell, not just killers. Thieves, liars, bastards, whores, they headed there, too. Devil make a place for um all. If you goin by the Bible, some of us is on our way to hell two, three times over. You think Julius ain't there? Devil built a whole new floor just to fit that fat monkey muthafuck in there with all his sins."

I touched Christina's leg and the sweaty heat at her thigh'd slid all down to her left knee. I let her finish the reefer. "So?"

"So I might's well go on and be the baddest man round here," I said. She held smoke between her cheeks, like she was scared to lose it. "Cause I am. And you might's well go on and love me."

I reached for the dress's waist buttons, skipped right over messin with her legs—could see the dead in her eyes, the jaw puffin smoke against baby cheeks, and I knew she was gone. Gone, and mine like I wanted—Lester'd said his reefer worked fast like so. When the dress was undone, and I'd touched the little pouch above her hips, I went underneath and pulled on the girdle linin. She didn't say a word as I tugged away her mamma's shame. Said nothin until, between smoky coughs, she told that Low End tale to me again—"I do love you."

"J.C." I heard her against the cellar walls, on top of Marvin Gaye moanin bout how she was all he needed to get by, and the wood floor's creak, and the empty pound of my hips hittin against her waist. I looked down and saw her dress raised up over her tar back, the naps at her neck, and that sugar hill I'd barely make it round to get into the womb, if that was where I'd made it to for real.

"What?" I yelled.

"J.C.," she said again, loud to echo outside against 45th Street, just like her no.

I thought I felt it. "Who am I?"

She laughed, so I hit against her hard till my stomach hurt. "You the biggest, baddest muthafuckin nigga."

"What?"

"Biggest, baddest muthafucka I know."

That was what I told myself, kept tellin myself up in my fool head, repeatin so many times it came to be the truth, and I did feel heaven inside a baby girl's womb.

10

SALVIE'S WRINKLED HOOK grabbed me round the shoulder. Felt like it was bout to pull me to the pool hall ground, then it rested, led me to that table against the back wall. I looked over my shoulder.

"What you doin this way, man? It ain't the weekend. Somethin wrong?"

"No. Ain't nothing wrong here, J.C. Just need you to take care of something."

"What kind of something?"

"Hear you're gonna be managing this new joint on Forty-seventh. You need to watch things over there."

"I know," I said as Salvie racked the balls. "I talked to Mister Ricci's boy. He told me what he wanted done."

"Really? Well, lookit here, kid. I got more orders coming down, straight from the man. I know you ain't heard about this."

"What's the man got to say I ain't heard already, Salvie? Bet I know what you gonna tell me before it leaves your mouth."

"Bet you don't." Salvie grabbed a cue from the near corner as B.B. whined. "Did you know the Ricci boy's got a thing for dark women?"

"I know it," I said, and chalked. "Told me so hisself."

"Did you know this's the reason he's so fixed on running this club? Figures it'll turn out as one big black cunt dream come true for him?"

"That's common sense, joe. You gonna break this eight-ball round or what?"

"Go ahead." He shrugged as balls scattered the table. "You know, I try to be liberal as possible. You gotta be an open-minded man during these open-minded times."

"Brain can't open no further than the frame God put it in."

"Exactly, kid," Salvie said. I'd cleared the table of five stripes. "So, understanding that I'm liberal as I can be, hear me when I say that a white man messing with dark women can only lead to trouble."

"Oh yeah?" I backed from the table as I missed. "Dark man and a white woman, that ain't but trouble neither, huh?"

"We ain't talking about that *infamia* right now. But you remember Johnny Batiste? You know he got caught with a friend of mine's lady?"

"Really? Think I heard bout that once."

"You see where he ended up, don't you? My point's that all of it leads to trouble—lust causing you to cross those color lines. Everybody gets curious, I know. But I can't figure why a man, a white man, would keep going over that way time and time again, chasing after these dark broads. Don't he ever learn his lesson?"

Salvie missed and stood to the side, leaving my two stripes and the eight ball. I chalked the stick again. "The Ricci boy had a bad trip with a colored broad before?"

"Bad? That ain't the word. Tony was out in Harvey, running a joint for us, you see, this club on One-forty-seventh. Cocksucker was supposed to go there, count out the dough, and bring in our cut. That's it, nothing more. So why's the *pazzo* go and find some little darkie to lay up with, huh? Who told him to get involved with this nonsense? Who? One day, the broad shows up at the pawn shop, talking about how she's due in such and such months. Think of the look on Missus Ricci's dear face when this girl walks in there telling the old woman she's got a half-spade grandkid on the way. What the fuck does she want the old lady to do? Nobody knows, cause poor Missus Ricci chased her black ass down Ashland Avenue with a pawned butcher blade—she was gonna cut the goddamn thing outta the girl herself, I'm telling you. She's a Neapolitan, see what I'm saying? Next thing you know, the broad's goddamn idiot brother shows up at the joint where Tony's at, talking garbage off the top of his head—in front of me and Angelo and Vito and our friends from out there. He wants Tony to pay for the kid, buy him this, buy him that, whatever. Seems he ain't gonna let his sister marry no wop, that's what he said—a *wop*—no more than the Riccis was gonna let Tony marry the colored broad. Beat that. He just wants wop money, you see. This's around the time you and Mook first got in this, so whaddya know, Mister Ricci sends me and my nephew over to goddamn Harvey to resolve this here trouble. Goddamn Harvey. What am I gonna do? I gotta do like how the man tells me." The balls'd stopped makin noise as they hit against each other, and B.B.'d run outta whine.

"So what happened?"

"Whaddya mean, what happened? We aborted it." Salvie's eyes beamed on the table's green, on the eight ball left. "Resolved the thing, like Mister Ricci said. No more trouble. That's what I'm talking about here. Can't nothing but bad come from it, crossing those lines. Yeah, I'm liberal, but it just ain't right."

"You been runnin round the South Side all this time, these years. You ain't never had you no Black pussy?"

He missed the eight. "I take care of business over here, that's it. All that other, messing with these broads, ain't right. What the fuck I gotta explain to you?"

Lyin. Ol muthafucka was lyin his dirty ass off. "I was just askin, man. Wonderin."

"All right. This's what the boss needs for you to do: you're gonna be around this club all the time, around Tony and the girls and whatever else goes on over here. He wants you and Mook to make sure the boy stays outta trouble. I know you can't keep him from involving himself with colored broads if he wants. Tony's a fuckup, so that's the first thing he's gonna look to do. I'll lay money on it. But Mister Ricci don't want nothing else to happen when his kid goes over that way."

"Nothin else?"

"You know these things that go on. Make sure Tony don't suffer nothing, no trouble, I'm saying. No diseases, no bitches casting voodoo spells on him, no jungle babies, nothing out of the order. This is on you, kid, coming straight from Mister Ricci. Look out for his son."

I unbent my back as the eight rolled into the pocket furthest away. "Game over."

"Yeah, I see," he sighed. "You gonna take care of this for us?"

"It's done, Salvie. Done, and I won."

* * *

The Ricci boy left hirin his Snake Pit workers to me and Mookie—figured we knew the folk round that way, so we could best choose qualified souls. The clown was tryin to convince his main niggas that we had his trust. It was the best part of the hustle.

By the second week in August, the construction people was through layin down carpet. We sat in the back office, the first room they'd finished—built over the same space where I'd busted Jackson's kneecaps with a Negro League slugger—tendin to the pitiful folks lookin to sell themselves off, grouped in the waitin area. Things was bad enough round 47th with the Jew businesses leavin and the fine souls runnin when MLK died that just bout everybody young and still livin on the strip was hustlin to slave for Tony Ricci's Soul Mamma Pit.

"Ain't that Sermon back there?" Mookie hit me as I talked to a little brown girl who'd drop to her knees and open wide before I hired her to wipe the Ricci boy's tables.

"Who?"

"Sermon, you remember . . . Carl Martin from high school. Use to carry the Bible round, tellin you bout the Resurrection while you was tryin to eat that nasty cafeteria lunch. You remember Sermon Martin. Ain't that him waitin out there?"

I looked. "That ain't Sermon, Mookie. I don't even know why you askin. He got took down in the marines, man."

"Naw, he ain't. He's standin right there. How could he be dead when he's standin in my face?"

"It ain't him. Sermon crapped out in Vietnam, I'm tellin you." I looked outside again as the girl left our office. "He don't even favor Sermon, not really."

Mookie stood from the leather chair and parted the door blinds further. "It do look like him, J.C.—spittin image."

"You crazy, man." I puffed my cigarette. "Sermon was big. Used to scare the shit outta me when we was kids, standin over you with that shadow like a elephant, readin scripture. That cat out there ain't but a two-bit."

"Don't care what you say, J.C.—that's Sermon. Watch." He stepped outta the office. "Carl! Come here, my nigga!"

The fake Sermon smiled and pushed his way to Mookie and they hugged and stepped into the office. I didn't stand up, didn't care, cause that wasn't the Sermon I knew from the Forties. He had the hard, barbecue-coal complexion, and bout the same good height—but on top of the head, that fake had a unpicked afro clingin to his head for dear life. I remembered Sermon with church boy curls relaxed and slicked down to his scalp. And his eyes wasn't smart like Sermon's, on a body fifty pounds smaller than the one I remembered—and like I'd said, Sermon'd crapped out in the war.

"How you been, Mookie? Ain't seen you since what, sixty-five, sixty-six?"

"Not for a while," Mookie said, and stuck his head outside the office. "We done today! Go home! Come back not tomorrow, but Thursday!"

"What you doin? We got people to hire."

"Sit down, J.C.," Mookie said as the door slammed closed. "You see we got a friend from the neighborhood here. Don't be rude."

"J.C? Not little J.C. from off Forty-fifth Street? That you?" The fake Sermon reached for me. "I can't figure how I ain't recognize you, man. Look the same, same as I remember."

"Who you suppose to be, joe?"

"What?" He turned to Mookie. "Look at this guy. Still crazy. It's Carl Martin, from the neighborhood. You don't remember?"

I pulled my chair to the character and looked him over. "If you're Sermon, why'd your people tell everybody you was dead, nigga? Said you took one in the swamps."

His face wrinkled like he'd been hit. "Lemme tell you." The fake rested on the wall, his nose twitchin like he smelled the brown girl's sweat, so full of sugar, hangin in the air. And he frowned, disgusted by the sweet, stinkin sin of what woulda gone down if he hadn't showed his face between the office blinds. "Helluva mixup. Went to 'Nam in sixty-six and got shot, right. You know what they did, them government folks? Went and screwed up my papers, sent word home I was dead, body lost over there. Confused me with some stiff, had my family, everybody, praying for the Lord Jesus to have mercy on my soul. What kinda mistake is that to make? I feel almost worse for the family of the cat I got confused with. They was expecting that brother—and you know it was a brother—thought he'd be home two weeks ago, and he's blown up over in rice paddy hell. I feel sorry for him, yeah, but I got outta there. Family known I was okay for six months now, figured they woulda told everybody. Guess they ain't quite sure themselves—we never did get the right papers, the ones saying I'm still alive."

I gave him my hand slow. "Sorry. You look smaller, joe. And I heard you was dead over there."

He let go my grip and hugged me full. "Don't worry, brother. Just happy to be back." Sermon's body jumped in my arms. "Watch where you got your hand, J.C. My wound's right there. Careful."

"You hurtin still?" Mookie pointed him to his chair.

"Got this wound. Shoulda turned my back on them marines when they came callin in the first place. Pain ain't but my own fault. Shoulda never gone over there. Shoulda known better."

"What happened?"

"Hell . . . happened. Took a bullet just to get outta the place." I laughed before the swamp of his eyes fell on me. "You better believe it. You take yourselves over there and do war for this country. Go off to another world, killin men's children for folk who won't do the same for you. Then you call me from the jungle, call and tell me you won't take a bullet just to get outta there. If you can do that, I'll tell Nixon to give you both medals for bein the two biggest Black jackasses God ever born. You better believe I took a shot on purpose."

"Where'd they get you?" Mookie was askin questions, but I was lost in Sermon's swamp—didn't wanna know how he'd got like that.

"Right here," he said, and pointed to the side where my hand'd touched, between his chest and kidney, wincin as his own finger jabbed through polyester. Didn't care what he said, or what Mookie said, or what jive I'd bought for a minute, that wasn't the Sermon Martin from our Phillips High. The cat I'd known was gone, took, somewhere.

But Mookie went on questionin him. "You let um get you so close to your heart?"

"Ain't have the choice. Gook was standing in front of me one minute, then the bullet was coming at me. Nobody asked where I wanted to be hit, just shot me right outta that jungle. Praise Lord Jesus."

"What if it'd gone straight through to your back and left you so you couldn't walk? Or took out your heart and killed you? What if that'd happened?"

"I'd be outta that jungle, that's what if." He held his head and looked round our office slow and calm, like his disgust was gone all of a sudden. "I'm out of it, Mookie, J.C. Give your praises to the Almighty, cause that's what I do every day. It was Him who sent me to y'all, same as the folk you just turned away."

"For a job?" Without meanin to, I found myself in his eyes and I looked away quick, bitin my lip. "Sermon?"

"Why didn't you come soon as you got back?" Mookie said. "We coulda had you workin long time ago. You ain't have to wait in no line for us."

He rubbed his wounded place. "Don't wanna work the streets. No way I can question the way y'all live your lives when I got not a cent in my pocket. Ain't my place, or my right, to be doing. But I can't be out there like that. I came for your help, and I ain't trying to disrespect nobody, but I'm lookin for real work. Just a wage, whatever you can offer. Bussin tables, washin dishes, servin drinks, sweepin floors, whatever. As long as there's pay to it. Been livin with my woman since comin back. Survivin off her, you could say. I wanna put some money on the table for rent, some food in the icebox, myself. That's what I wanna be able to do. Be like a man. I don't wanna fight nobody else's war no more. Just take care of my own folk."

"What's that the Bible say?" I let words out to stop myself from laughin at his ass. "Beggars can't be choosin. That's in the Bible, ain't it? Ain't it, Sermon?"

Mookie scraped at the desk with his pen. "Your injury don't hold you back? I mean, you feel good enough to work?"

"Course, Mookie. Wouldn't have come here if not. I'm recovered, recovered as a brother can get."

My eyes reached for Sermon's again, out of my control. "What happened to your weight, man? Seems like you a helluva bit smaller than what you was in high school. You see I ain't recognize you first off. Don't look bad or nothin, just not as big. Figured they woulda built you up to fight them woks. What happened?"

He rolled his eyes and rubbed the wound with no show of pain. "You go to hell, J.C., come back, and tell me if you ain't lost some weight. Devil's fire burned me up."

"We gonna look out for you," Mookie said, "got plenty of steady work here. Whatever you lookin to do, you got it. We open in two Saturdays, Labor Day weekend."

They shook hands. "Thank you, Mookie. I knew I could count on you. We're from the Forties together. That means something, don't it?"

"That's how white folk do it, look out for their own. They don't let their own stand in no lines. They look out."

"Better believe they do. Like I said, I'm living with my woman. I'll leave her number with y'all so you can call and let me know when I gotta show for work."

"Forget that," Mookie corrected. "Be here at eight-thirty on the Saturday before Labor Day. Wage'll be waitin on you."

"And a job?" Sermon wanted to smile—I saw the crack between his lips—but couldn't let his joy free. "Don't want nothing for nothing, Mookie. Need to work."

I laughed, spit sprayin against my hands and my pants legs, too much to hold on to.

"There'll be a job, Sermon," Mookie said, "trust me."

The marine gave me his hand again. "I owe y'all."

I breathed smoke and tried to look through him, to the gunshot hole. "It was that bad over there? Bad that you had to take a hit to get out?"

"That bad," the fake, swamp Sermon said, and walked through Soul Mamma's new back door.

* * *

I smoked a cigar, the clown sipped bourbon, celebratin the rhythm and the fog droppin from the new ceilin, the high heels dancin on corner tables and the Black folks wigglin on the floor tile. Riches were comin in, that was our cause for rejoicin. Soul Mamma was packed that Saturday before Labor Day. Me and Tony Ricci sat at the back VIP booth.

"I ain't never gonna figure why you all, the brothers I mean, always chase after white broads. Look at that dark one over there, the girl with the thick lips and juicy hips. Ain't no such creation as a white broad who can look like her, beautiful like a colored woman."

"Who told you niggas want your women? You ever seen me with a white chick? Never. Ever seen me lookin at a white chick? Never."

"I have, in the magazines, on television, everywhere. I have seen you lookin at white broads. That's all what the brothers look at. Skinny white broads."

"Fuck you." I walked to the liquor bar for rum. When I came back, two honeys sat with the Ricci boy—the one next to him was light brown with a afro shinin like she'd just sheened it, and the other was the thick-lipped, coffee-skinned honey he'd pointed out before I left.

"J.C., J.C., my man. Introduce yourself to my friends. Just met these pretty things as they walked by our booth. Lucky us, hey?"

I sat next to the dark girl, who paid me no mind, and sipped rum. "What's happenin? I'm J.C. . . ."

"We know you," the one with the afro said. "Rose, J.C. Rose. Ain't this your place? That's what we was told."

"Somethin like that." I chased the rum with cigar smoke. "I run the joint, like a manager, so you could say it's mine. What was y'all's names?"

"Joy," she said, and just bout sat in Tony's lap. The other stayed fixed on the dance floor. "And this's Ebony."

"Ebony?" I turned to her. "That your real name, Ebony?"

"No."

I watched the rum swirl and blew smoke into the club's fake clouds, waitin for somethin more. But when Tony Ricci left to dance with the one called Joy, I was alone with thick-lipped, ebony silence.

"Told you I love your women, brother," the Ricci boy mumbled before they disappeared in lounge fog.

"You wanna fuck me."

I figured liquor woulda brung her to talkin, so I'd ordered cognacs; she was on her second. There was a glaze in her eyes, but those words was the first outta her drunk mouth.

"Huh?"

"You wanna fuck me, I said. I mean, that's why you keep givin me these drinks. You want me to get drunk so you can fuck me."

"That's what you think? How come I can't just be entertainin you, treatin you nice so you'll enjoy your first time at my place, bein a host? How come I can't be doin that?"

"Cause all you know to want to do is fuck me, boy." Ebony looked in my eyes for the first time. "That's how come. That's what all y'all want, to fuck me. Nothin more. You see this black thing and that's what hits you upside the skull, all you can think about. Fucking."

I smelled sweet whiskey with each word. She was okay-lookin: nice body, a little on the dark side, but okay-lookin. She'd have to bend over, though, her bein so tall. I moved closer. "I don't just want that. I wanna be your friend."

"Get outta here, boy. You can't help what you are, I know."

"You think you look that good, sugar?"

"Ain't saying that. Ain't got nothing to do with how good I look. White cats like that bastard been fucking you so long, you gotta wanna fuck somebody else. I'm right here, easiest, blackest thing for you to get at. You ain't gonna turn around and fuck him, are you?"

"Can't say I would."

"See. So, if you scared to fuck him, you gotta wanna fuck me. You gotta fuck, right? But you know what?"

"What?"

"You ain't getting none of this."

"Why not?"

Ebony laughed and rolled her eyes as I slid away. "Cause if he fucks you, then I let you fuck me cause you too scared to turn around and do him, it's like I'm getting fucked by the white cat in the end. If I'm gonna get fucked, might as well get it straight from the fucker, not his messenger. You just the middleman—gotta cut out the little middleman."

Tony and Joy was back, laughin stupid laughter. I looked to the main door, saw Mookie walkin with Sermon. Joy's light eyes flashed—I peeked back their way before she had a chance to hide it. Didn't know the reason, didn't even give her much thought then, just remembered. Sermon, though—I wondered about the fool, whether that floor-sweeping job Mookie gave him'd healed his gunshot wound, made him feel like a real man who coulda fucked with ebony silence.

* * *

Me and Mookie spent most of our time countin somebody's money. When Calvin or Miss Nelly or Uncle Leon or the pimps or the pushers gave us their payoffs, we'd take a tally before dumpin it into Salvie's big shoppin bag. And for hours we'd sit and go over their wealth. And what was the return for our time? Five hundred dollars, chump change, every week. Five hundred dollars from men who'd made near three million cash every year since we'd worked for them. And that was just off the two South Side miles we handled. Taxes probably brung in ten million across the city, which didn't even begin to speak for the other rackets. I was good enough with numbers to know five hundred dollars wasn't nothin when compared against true bountiful sin.

We sat in Soul Mamma's back office, a week after the openin. "Eight hundred and fifty-five, eight hundred and sixty, eight hundred and sixty-five . . ." I looked over my shoulder, and Mookie stood there, gazin at me. "Eight hundred and seventy . . . what you doin, man? Why you starin?"

"I ain't. Ain't even lookin at you. Ain't doin nothin." He walked to the opposite wall and stopped by the wall safe, its door shinin silver just above the shag rug. Didn't take five minutes for him to start watchin me again.

"How much's Ricci payin you?"

"What?"

"The Ricci boy. How much's he givin you?"

"Five hundred a week, same as you."

"I'm talkin bout the loot he's givin you extra, to make sure I don't steal nothin from him."

"What? How you figure that?"

"Cause he's payin me two hundred a week to watch your ass."

"Oh yeah?" Mookie paced the square. "You held out for two?"

"That's what he's payin me." I ran my hands through the night's profit. "So you gettin less than two hundred dollars and you still standin over there spyin for that muthafucka? How long you known me, Mookie? Ten, twelve years?"

"All my life, just bout."

"So it don't mean nothin, all these years? More important for you to treat me like I'm a dirty thief for that muthafucka's chump change? Who is he?"

"You just said you took two hundred to do the same, so what difference you makin outta this?"

"Ain't nobody standin round here lookin over your shoulder. That's all you been doin tonight—watchin me like I'm a whore. I took his money, so what? Don't mean I gotta do his deeds. I'll take some more of his money, what he gonna do bout it?" I slipped a fifty into my pocket. "Go, run and call Boss Tony."

"Put that scratch down, J.C."

"Why? He ain't gonna notice. The boy made a good ten G's tonight. How's fifty dollars gonna hurt him? That's like somebody takin a penny from me and you, like nothin."

"Put it down, J.C." Mookie walked my way, his eyes swole like I'd welched and he was bout to gimme a lead-pipe beatin for it. "We got this job, runnin this joint. We ain't out on the street collectin payoffs, dealin with crooked niggas, bashin in skulls. We doin somethin you ain't gotta lie to Grandma Rose bout. How you gonna go fuckin it up, stealin somethin you don't need? That's the problem, J.C. You always lookin for a way to fuck up what we got goin good. Put his loot back."

I stuffed a twenty in my pocket. "I ain't puttin back shit. Ain't even his loot. This's what he takes from us. Nothin wrong in me stealin it. You wrong for tryin to give it to him."

"Put it down, J.C."

The alley door shook. I moved to answer, my hand near the .45's safety, protection from Mookie's lead-pipe beatin as much as from the prowler. Except for kickin the safe door closed, Mookie didn't make a move, though. And that wasn't nobody but Sermon in back. "What you want?"

"I came at a bad time," Sermon said, his eyes blinkin fast and lips shakin as the words passed. "You takin care of business. I'll come back later." He half turned to drag himself off.

"Sermon," Mookie called, always worried bout loser niggas. And there was loss in Sermon that night. "Come here. What's the matter?"

He waved at nothin and closed the back door himself before droppin into my chair. "Went home after work tonight."

"Yeah," Mookie said as I leaned on the wall. "The bartender give you the cash for your pay?"

"He gave it to me," Sermon whimpered. "Then I went home."

Beads ran from his head. "Why you ain't there now, muthafucka?"

"I went straight home. Went home and kissed my baby. I could smell her, sniffed a few times to make sure. She had a rich scent bout her, you know? And it wasn't a woman odor, not no expensive perfume. Smelled like a rich man."

Mookie looked my way before speakin. "Your woman smelled like a nigga when you was kissin on her?"

"A *rich* man's stink," Sermon said as tears fell quiet with his sweat. He looked at the ceilin, talkin to Jesus maybe. "Like she'd been with some rich cat. Last week, I walked in and she was on the telephone. Minute she heard me comin she hung up her conversation, face sweaty like she was scared I'd heard her. Every other day, she's got expensive gifts. One day it's roses, next it's gold wristwatches, then she's wearin new kinda clothes. I ain't shell-shocked, so I know I ain't bought her none of these things. I was eighteen months in a blood-filled swamp, killin for them, just so I could get back home to my baby. Said she'd be here when I came back. Now I'm here and I ain't good enough, got too much dirt on me. I ain't even gotta ask, cause I know. She went and found her a rich man, some kinda gift-giver. What am I gonna do?"

I looked up and there wasn't a damn thing above us but drywall. "So why you here for? What you want from us?"

"Don't know. I knew y'all would still be in, taking care of business. I got nowhere to be, is all. Not this minute. Gonna move to my folks' in the morning. Can't go just now, like this. This's my fault—I been getting away from my Bible ever since I was over there. Lost my way after all this time."

"You need money?" The same paper he'd been ready to beat me

down for, he could turn round and offer to a punk floor sweeper out of a alley. I thought bout shootin Mookie just then—heard that .45 trigger sing my name.

"I've took enough from y'all," Sermon said, and looked away from the drywall, gave up. "What you can do is gimme more work, so I can earn a better wage. Then my head won't be so caught in this nonsense. Besides, if I'm a man earning more, what's she gonna need with some rich cat?"

"Nothin, not a goddamn thing," Mookie said. "We got windows need cleanin. Lightin to be handled, boxes to be lifted, all kindsa work, not just sweepin floors after hours. We can pay you more to take them jobs, if that's what you want. But what you gonna do before the mornin?"

He shrugged. "Walk the streets. What else is there?"

"You don't wanna hang round here with us?"

I grabbed my suit jacket as Mookie fixed his attention on that wounded fool. "I'm done. Y'all count the rest of it. I'll get back tomorrow."

As I walked into Soul Mamma's alley, I took Ricci's fifty from my pocket and kissed its face. I glanced at the empty sky hangin above Soul Mamma's garbage before gettin into my Caddy and thankin the Lord Jesus who hadn't answered for Sermon's loss. For the seventy dollars extra I'd made, seventy bones to go with the seven bills Salvie and them paid me under the table already, I repeated it the whole way to 45th Street: "Thank you, Jesus."

Salvie'd passed fifty—so ol that the hairs sneakin from under his hats had turned gray, and his face's skin'd shriveled into potholes, cracks, and what Grandma Rose called liver scars. I could feel his age, so I didn't fear him no more. Instead of fear, I imagined the devil on his knees, beggin for his life. Salvie had sensed his fall and started bringing his stupid nephew Angelo with him on pickup night. After all them years there was no trust between us, not even pretend trust. The more a smart liar got to know another smart liar, the less he believed. That was how it was with Salvie and his street hustlers.

"How's Mister Ricci's kid?" His right hand offered the shoppin bag to Angelo, while his left was on his side, near the .38's hidin place.

"Tony? He's fine," Mookie answered from his seat behind Salvie, without a clue what the hell he was talkin about.

Salvie looked at me, waited. "He's okay, far as I know," I mumbled.

" 'Okay'?" Angelo laughed. "What the fuck does that mean, okay, far as you know?"

The ol man groaned; talkin'd come to be painful for him even. "Didn't we, didn't I, tell you to look out for the kid? Didn't I tell you that? Said them was orders straight from the man. And what'd you say when I told you to do that?"

"Said it was done, Salvie."

"That means you gonna take care of it," Angelo interrupted. "Don't it?"

"Well, don't it?"

"I said he was okay, far as I know. What more you want outta me?"

"Is he messing around with some colored girl?"

"Don't think so," I said. "Far as I know, he ain't."

"You ain't done like I told you, kid. Not like you promised you was gonna do it."

"Look, Tony's okay. I didn't ever say I could keep him from bein with whoever he wanted to be with. Didn't say nothin like that. You ain't even ask me to do that."

"Got a funny feeling in my gut, is all. But he's okay, huh?"

"Far as I know. That's all I can tell you, Salvie—he's okay, far as I know."

"And he ain't messing with no dark chicks?" Salvie turned to Mookie. "Huh, Mook?"

"Don't know. I ain't been payin him no mind like that. Has he, J.C.?"

"Don't think so."

"J.C. says he don't think so. So, I guess everythin's cool, man. J.C.'s been around him more than anybody at the club. So you can trust his word that the boy ain't messin with no Black girl, if that's what you concerned bout."

"Good," Salvie sighed, his head turnin to fix on Angelo. "That's good. None of you is stealing from the boy's take over there, huh?"

It got hot sittin in that Chrysler, hot to taste sweat drippin above my lips. "Why y'all askin these dumb-ass questions?" Angelo stared through the rearview; I frowned evil as I could back at him. "Askin these questions, then disrespectin me? You said to look out for the boss' son. That's what I been doin, lookin out for him. You ain't said to be wipin his ass, to be up in his head, you ain't said nothin bout sleepin in the bed up between him and no Black chicks, and ain't nobody told you we was stealin nothin. I been lookin out; that's what you pay me for, damnit. What else can I do? Gimme my money, Salvie."

I didn't wait for the ol man to kick me out or for Mookie to leave, just walked off with my wage. Of course I'd been lyin, didn't care nothin bout what the Ricci boy was doin with whoever, or what Salvie thought bout it, as long as I got me my five C-notes.

I caught the clown with shiny-hair Joy that Saturday, walkin outta Soul Mamma. Didn't take notice causa jealousy or fear, and definitely not from no duty to Salvie's ass. Somethin heavy just hung over the two as they left out the joint, air powerful enough for our cocktail waitress' eyes to flick over to that doorway; she'd been called by the hangin, too. But Joy and Tony was dumb to it—the two of um left Soul Mamma's locked at the arm, laughin more fool's laughter.

"How come you ain't told me bout him?" Mookie asked, squintin cause the air'd caught him finally, no matter the love that waitress offered him once her attention was free again, hips grindin to the JB's groove right against his thigh.

He nodded to the exit, figured I'd miss him stick a bill into the girl's waist belt. She hadn't brung us no drinks in a half hour—his tip was for those hips. "Bout what?"

"What we was supposed to do."

"Watchin Ricci?" My stomach turned as she ran her fingers across his mouth. "Fuck that. Salvie only said—"

"Shh!" His eyes jumped to her.

"My fault. He just said to watch him, that's all. Make sure he was okay, that's what he said. I ain't take it for nothin serious. What I look like, the boy's mammy?"

"Still shoulda told me," Mookie said. The clown and his woman was gone by then. "Them orders was from . . . I shoulda known."

"Nigga, if the boy gets into trouble, he gets into trouble. Good for him. It's what he got comin for messin with what he ain't got the right to mess with."

"Still shoulda told me."

The waitress blew kisses, licked lips, and rubbed the greasy waves on his head, all while she kept that empty tray steady in her left hand. Mora came to mind—she was the only thing he had that I was jealous of back then, just his woman and that lead-pipe swing. "You gettin fat."

"What?"

"Said you gettin fat. Need to lay off all that sauce. Salvie and them got you so caught up, you turned into a fat drunk."

"Ain't nobody gettin fat. This's good size I put on. Means I'm a strong brother—that's what it means. Fuck that nonsense you talkin."

"I'm just lettin you know." She went on offerin herself. "Don't wanna see you turnin into a fat-ass black whale in life."

"You gone crazy, fool. If I need to stop drinkin, you need to stop smokin."

"Fuck you, fat ass." I blew tobacco at the waitress—and she ain't even pretend like she was studdin me. "I like smokin."

"No you don't. I drink outta bein caught up, you smoke outta fear, fear of the same white men who got me caught up."

"Okay. I'm afraid of the white man, so I smoke. Salvie's got your draws full of shitty worry—I don't know the difference between that and my fear—so you drink. I won't get fat doin this. That's all you is, Mookie, a fat drunk. A fat black whale of a drunk."

"But them squares gonna kill you."

"What's that supposed to mean? You ain't gonna die?"

He looked at her hips, so wide and curved, and licked the skin above his mouth. "Not from fear I ain't."

I closed my eyes, sat back. Somewhere in the smoke of Salem squares and the black of nothin, I felt the thing that'd hung over the clown and his Joy. It was with us in Soul Mamma's Pit—I saw myself touchin its weight behind closed eyelids, and it bloodied my hands underneath the palms. But in that heavy darkness, the cocktail waitress did at least bring me a drink.

11

THE .45 BOUNCED at my side—I wore the holster at my hips so I could reach the trigger quick. Heard the Caddy idlin behind, but I kept runnin, tennis shoes stompin against alley gravel without makin no real sound. Just empty poundin. Hadn't even got a chance to change clothes after Mookie'd called—trash wind sliced straight through my pajama bottoms—he'd scared me so bad, I couldn't do nothin but rip to Soul Mamma. He'd spoke shaky words, same stutter-shake I used to hear in Mookie's rap when Salvie was lookin for him on the strip. A frightened boy bout to catch a whippin was the sound of him. He hadn't told me what the trouble was; maybe Ricci'd counted the take himself and found I'd been stealin twenties and fifties, decided his main niggas deserved beat-downs for the disrespect. Tony and Angelo and Vito'd whupped Mookie and caused enough pain that he'd spit my name for mercy. I was just the good little bastard nigga runnin in for my share then.

I pushed the alley door and there wasn't no whips, no Italians, just two tired cats from the Forties and the dirty cash surroundin um. Mookie sat on the desk, next to Ricci's money. He didn't say nothin, just looked at his lap and rubbed his temples. Sermon slouched in my chair like he'd took the worst of the beatin. Blood stained his army fatigues still—at least I thought it was blood. Couldn't tell for sure cause they sat in darkness.

"What's goin on?" I closed the door and turned on the ceilin light. "What you call me for?"

Mookie stood, his eyes to the shag rug. "Turn that goddamn thing off. Don't nobody need to know we in here."

I made sure the jacket covered my gat and did like he'd said. "What the hell he doin here? Ain't the floors swept up?"

Mookie looked at me—but my man's eyes wasn't beat or tired, just scared wild. He didn't answer, unless lookin at me through the scared holes on his face was his answer.

"What's the problem, Mookie?"

He twisted his mouth, and when he talked, the voice was cranky and rough like Salvie's. "Tell him what happened."

Sermon waved his hands in the air, and he cried tears I saw without light.

"This the last time I'm gonna ask. What's goin on between you two? Why y'all bring me down here? It's damn near two in the mornin."

"Tell him, goddamnit."

Sermon swallowed. "I went home tonight, after sweepin up the joint."

"Shit." I saw the plastic light dome at the ceiling, dim and empty, just before my eyeballs rolled under the lids.

"Went straight home, earlier than usual. Wanted to see my baby, you know. You understand how you wanna see your baby especially some days, some nights."

"Just tell the muthafuckin story, joe," I said. "Don't wanna hear bout your baby, don't give a damn bout the heifer. If she's fuckin round on you, it's your fault for bein a chump who be babblin bout the Bible, you Bible-babblin chump."

His tears kept fallin, quiet like he had no strength to whimper. "Went home and couldn't find her. But I smelled that stink, that rich-man stink I told y'all about before. Smelled it and heard breathin—

heavy, you know? So I chased what I smelled and heard. And where'd it lead me to?"

"Your bed, Sermon," Mookie said.

"Yeah, to my bed. And there my baby was. She wasn't alone, you know? I ain't shell-shocked crazy from that jungle, like I say, so I knew it wasn't me in there with her. And I know I don't smell like that, rich like that. So I pulled down them covers, but wasn't nobody layin there except her. I know I smelled that stank, and I know I saw the sweaty look on her face, ten times the look she got when I caught her on the phone. So I started searchin under the bed, through the closet, behind the doors, on the windowsill, cause that rich, dirty motherfucker—excuse me, Lord—was somewhere. All the while my baby was grabbing on me, lying to me, telling me wasn't nobody else there. 'Leave it alone,' she kept screaming, 'leave it alone.' The more she talked, J.C., the more madder I got. I grabbed my piece, made sure the clip was in."

Sermon wiped his eyes and I saw the .32 in his lap for the first time. "What you doin with a gat? Muthafucka. Where your stupid ass get that from?"

"Gotta do what you gotta do, J.C. That's what I learned over there. . . . When I looked up, he was running to the front door, I could smell him all the way from our bedroom, that rich stink. So I took aim, blasted without seeing him clear, didn't even know how he'd got from the room to the door. What was laid out buck naked, fancy clothes up under his arms, trying to sneak out into the world? What'd I see? A white boy, a motherfucking cracker, dropped in my home. My baby was with a white boy—you hear me? She had the nerve to be screaming his name in fronta me, yelling for his life with all this hurt in her. Cried like her soul was stabbed. I thought to shoot her ass, J.C., kill her right there for doing me like that. Only thing stopped me was that I love her like I do, even after she did me this way. So I wanted to die myself, stop this nonsense for good. Put the piece up to my ear—what happened? No more bullets. Thought there was God, J.C., even for a nigga, a God."

"Tell him, Sermon," Mookie said, "the name your woman was screamin for."

"Couldn't make it out right off, she was sounding so crazy. I listened good, though, so I'd know who it was damned me to hell. Sounded like she yelled 'Tony, baby! Tony, baby! Tony baby! Don't die, Tony!' That's when I thought to shoot her."

I slumped against the Ricci money desk and blinked hard before my laugh rolled out. "What's your woman's name?"

"Joy." Sermon looked up; Jesus'd called him finally. "Funny thing to name a woman who done me this way."

I looked at Mookie—felt my face turnin wet. Not cryin wet causa Sermon, didn't care nothin bout him right then, just funny wet from that hyena laugh. I felt the fear in Mookie's telephone voice, and I laughed at it. Two boys from down South, like them warnin stories Grandma'd told, scared of a Ashland Avenue lynch rope. Shit so funny, I wasn't wipin at nothin but crust at my cheek after a while. Eyes'd run outta water.

"What the fuck's wrong with you?" Salvie's voice cut from Mookie's mouth again.

"He's laughing cause he can't believe this. I feel you, J.C., for real. After doin all that killin for them, Joy had to sell me out for one. Crazy goddamn thing. Took a bullet just to get outta their war, now they got me right back in it. What've I done to deserve this? Crazy. Why I always gotta have their wrong on my hands?"

"Shut the hell up," I said.

"Is he dead, Sermon?" Mookie asked.

"Who?"

"This white boy you went and shot."

"Oh, not sure. Hope so. Least then I know I went to hell like a man."

"Shut up," I told him again. *Yeah*—my eyes found Mookie's, spoke the truth to him, spoke it loud for me to hear—*it's time to run, my man.* And everythin woulda been all right, forever all right, just if we'd listened and ran from that place.

"Look, this's what you gonna do," Mookie said. "You a fugitive. The cops is out for you. You need to get away from this side of the city. But don't try leavin Chicago just yet. They probably got bus stations, airports, trains, all locked up right now. You killed one of um, stupidest thing for a nigga to do just bout. They ain't gonna rest till they find you. You need to take your ass over to the West Side, somewhere like that. You say you got people over there—that's good. Go on to they place, hunker down, don't show yourself in public at all. I'm talkin weeks, maybe months. When the doorbell rings, don't go nowhere near it. Cops gonna come over there, lookin for you eventually. Only people you need to stay in touch with is us; we'll let you know when it's safe to get gone. Call, you got the number here at the club, call every Sunday. Don't talk to nobody unless it's me or J.C. We'll let you know when time is good for you to make a move. We're gonna look out for you, Sermon. I promise. All right?"

Sermon nodded and handed over the .32. Mookie gave him a fifty from Ricci's pile before takin the pistol. Damn him, and goddamnit to hell his loser niggas.

"Thank y'all. I knew I could count on you brothers, that's why I come here. Need to take time to get back into the Word. That's what I'm gonna do, get back into the Book. I appreciate y'all help. Lord musta sent me here cause we're from the Forties together."

"Don't worry, Sermon," Mookie said, "not at all. The Forties means somethin to us. We'll take care of you, brother."

* * *

"What's the word, J.C.?"

We sat in the wood cellar, smokin and drinkin on top of that ol table. I smelled cleanin bleach in the air, heard Grandma Rose walkin across the floor above. I put my finger to my lips, though there wasn't no way she woulda heard us. Mookie nodded and I breathed Salem smoke.

"Word on the street's the Ricci boy's still alive," I whispered.

"You sure? I mean, from who'd you get this?"

"Officer Dunne over on Forty-third Street told me himself," I said. "Told me yeah, they lookin for Sermon, but only for attempted murder. Accordin to him, Tony's laid up at University of Chicago. Took one to the spine. Won't walk no more, far as they can tell it."

"Attempted murder? Won't walk? That's just as bad—worse even."

"Hell yeah, that shit's worse," I said. "Cops came by the club, askin a lotta questions and all, talkin like they givin out rewards for anybody who know where Sermon is."

"Anybody bite?"

"Ain't nobody got shit to bite with except me."

"You bite?"

"Almost." I giggled. "Figured if I took a reward from the pigs, Salvie'd find out and kill my ass before I collected the cake."

"You heard from them? Salvie and them?"

"Not yet. Gotta bring in the loot tomorrow, so I figure I'll deal with that soon enough."

"We're dead," Mookie said. "They gonna kill us."

"Yup. Tomorrow. Me first, then they'll come for your ass."

"Tomorrow." His face wrinkled. "They told us to make sure the cat was safe."

"I know. I know."

Mookie gulped his drink. "They won't find nobody else smart enough to take care of they business. Salvie'll get Angelo and Paulo to beat us down. And so what? We dealt out many a whuppin before, probably got a good one comin ourselves."

"That's some silly shit you sayin. If they come over here for us, it's gonna be to kill. You know that, just said so yourself. They'll put two holes between our eyes, that's all. Two for each. They blame us for Sermon, and we gotta pay. Salvie got us to do wrong and he'll find a hundred other niggas willin to do the same for this wage. He ain't thinkin bout that."

"So why ain't we runnin and hidin on the West Side, like Sermon?"

"Live by evil, burn in its flames, that's what Grandma Rose say." I patted the .45 against my waist. "I ain't dyin like no scared pussy. If they come, they'll pay for bringin my crazy bastard ass into this shit before I go down. Only respect I got for Sermon is that, after he put a bullet in that muthafucka, he knew he could burn peaceful. Like he's supposed to burn. Peaceful. Least he knew he was a man."

"That's some bullshit, J.C.," Mookie said, and sucked away the rest of his Jim Beam. I didn't get a chance to answer him back, to curse his words or put the .45 gat to his head so he'd see my point. I didn't get my chance because Grandma'd opened the door. She stood at the top of the cracked staircase and her orange light fell on us; I had to blink and squint to see her. The ol lady didn't move, not even when she spoke; wouldn't come no closer to us. "You need to stop smokin them cigarettes, boy," she said.

* * *

I walked outta Calvin's barbershop, finished makin my rounds, when his ol dreary hand reached out again, squeezed me at the shoulder to stop the blood flow to my neck. I felt the execution in his fingers as he pulled me away, but didn't turn to look. Just let my body get drug off.

"Salvie?"

There was a steel jab in my side, then my .45 left its holster. Salvie led me into a alley's shadows; I heard him breathe for the first time as our feet crunched gravel. "Don't say nothing, kid. Just don't say nothing. We're gonna take care of this easy, go for this ride together. Just don't say nothing. Like this, it's easy."

Three waited in the Chrysler. I looked in the eyes and recognized each. There was Angelo and Paulo, Salvie's nephews, and Vito the Hack. I turned to Salvie himself—the ol man didn't seem weak from the years no more. Darkness hid his wrinkled body enough that he reminded me of the quiet gangster who'd scared the crap outta Mookie as a boy. They'd come for me first.

"Just don't say nothing, J.C."

I thought bout runnin, I did. But where to? Wasn't no place where they couldn't find me once the noose was ready. They always chased down and caught those who'd wronged them, snatched the souls and buried the leftovers. They owned mayors and presidents, senators and governors, popes and saviors. Where would I've hid myself?

The end was my safe route. And with Paulo and Vito in the car, the end was the only place they coulda took me. So I didn't fight as he pushed me into the Chrysler, as Salvie squeezed me between his ol body and the Hack's. The car didn't move, though, at least for the first minutes. Eight blue and brown holes fixed on me, whipped me with stares. But I gave back each of um, my eyes never lookin to escape. That was how they knew I wasn't studdin death, causa my eyes—I wasn't runnin, not by foot, not by eye. Had no fear in me. I wasn't goin down like no scared pussy, no sorry slave nigga. They drove on.

"Where the hell y'all takin me to?"

I didn't feel pain, just saw its silver flash. Then nothin. Swam in the stink of the end, choked on it, but I didn't drown—I knew how to breathe in it by then, like a fish. Wished I'd felt some hurt, tell the truth, but that rotten end was all they offered.

I reached up for salvation, then down, but there wasn't no God to judge or Devil to punish. Not like in the Book. Nothin at all till that second silver flash. I raised my head and spit dirt from my teeth, heard the engine hum behind and looked over my shoulder. There was the gangsters who'd brung me to my just deserts, eyes fixed on somethin above the ground. I followed them to a body lined in night. Couldn't place it right off, but it was familiar, had known it all my life. It was shaped like a man, short legs close to the ground, its head pulled to the sky. The body kneeled on the dirt, next to me, and I pushed my hands against the ground.

"Don't get up," came the voice, and its sound was familiar, too. I didn't listen—the end'd freed me from fear, I could say that for it. And without fear, there wasn't no reason for me to listen. I pushed myself to its waist and looked to where its face shoulda been. My eyes searched the surroundins for explanation, found only a field of dead crops and stale fertilizer. The smell of rot was near, but not in the wind. Rose up through that ground instead, into my pants legs as I kneeled in dirt, too. I wasn't in hell. It was the Outfit cemetery, the Indiana Styx soil, they'd brung me to. I shook, started to fall, but found my balance on the ground. "This is J.C.?"

I turned to Salvie, cause the thing'd spoke over my head. "Yeah, this's the one," Salvie answered.

"Does he know what to do?" Tommy Ricci's pale face showed from blackness. He grabbed me by the hair. "Do you know what to do?"

He had my eyes locked, held them in that killin stare. I couldn't see the sky no more, just the pulled scalp, the eagle nose, the thin lips, the tears on his jaw.

Salvie's whisper came from my back. "Better tell him you know what to do," he said. "Better tell him." And the gangsters laughed.

I tried to turn to the Chrysler and ask for understandin, but the father's tears held me. "Yeah, I know what to do."

He tossed my head loose and his face was gone again. The figure's short legs faded into night and dirt, and I had to go to the toilet.

"Get in the car," Salvie said as his jab returned to my side. I did as I was told, cause I was alive, scared as hell cause I was alive.

They snatched the coat from my head and dumped me in the money-countin lot on 35th Street. I laid facedown in the gravel, waitin for the bullets. "Take care of that by next Tuesday," Salvie said, and they sped away.

There was a knot above my neck, and my ears shook with that silver thud, left to right ear, and I did hurt then. I stood, unzipped my slacks and let go fear in a puddle on the street before stumblin south. Nobody'd said what was to be done. Not Tommy Ricci, not his four helpers durin the ride from the Indiana. But my gat'd been returned to its holster—I felt the lump on my left hip. Looked east and west, up and down, and there still wasn't nowhere to get away, just night and concrete and dyin grass and the rows of shacks that made up my home.

I heard an engine idle as I walked to Grandma Rose's door, that hum from the Styx that'd made fun of my end. I didn't turn at first, figured it was another car with its same Detroit fresh sound.

"This's where your mamma lives, hey, boy?"

I saw Salvie and Angelo and Paulo and Vito the Hack out on 45th Street, laughin in the smoke of the ol man's Chrysler. Hurt banged my ears and understandin took my throat, fast and hard to choke.

* * *

Me and Mookie sat in Soul Mamma, in the back office. There was scratches on my face and the knot on back of my skull'd swole up worse that mornin. But I tried to cover my marks by keepin the side of my face to him and usin my hands as a mask. If there'd been cuts on his face, too, it wouldn't have mattered—if they'd come for him, I woulda had no reason to hide, and I woulda still trusted Mookie. But I was scarred up and alone, so I stayed quiet.

Mookie pushed his chair from the desk. "What's wrong, J.C.?"

"Huh?"

"Why you ain't sayin nothin? What's the matter?"

"I can't be quiet when I wanna be? You always quiet. I don't be botherin you bout it."

Mookie laughed. "What happened to your face?"

I slapped my palm upside my forehead and held it there. "Ain't nothin happen for you to worry bout it."

"Ain't say I was worried, just wanna know. They came after you?"

"They?"

"Salvie and them? They came?"

"Why? They come for you?"

"You see I ain't scratched up and I ain't got no knots on my head, muthafucka. Naw, they ain't come for me," he said.

"Why you think they did me then? You're in this much as I am. They're comin for us. Come for me, they gotta come for you."

"And if they come for me, they come for you, right?"

"True. I ain't sayin that's where these scratches is from or nothin."

"What happened?"

I grunted—didn't mean to, but I grunted. "Salvie drove me out to Indiana."

"The Styx? Goddamn, J.C.—they was gonna take you out for real. How'd you get away?"

"Didn't." I pointed to the knot. "They busted me on the head, so I was out cold when they drove me there, had my face covered up the whole way back."

"They went to Indiana, way out there, to beat you down? That's it—just like I said?"

"Hell naw, they ain't took me nowhere to do nothin just like you said. Didn't say I got beat down—just busted on the skull. I told you, when they come for us, it's gonna be to kill."

"So why you still here if that's so? If they came to kill you, why you sittin here now?"

"All I said was we went to the Styx. Nothin else happen."

"Now we ain't gotta worry bout nothin? Y'all went for a joyride to the graveyard; that's all it took to square things?"

"Naw," I said, and lit the day's fifteenth cigarette, "that ain't all, Mookie."

"Now what?"

"We gotta take care of Sermon."

* * *

I was supposed to be at Ebenezer with Grandma Rose, praisin the Lord Jesus. But Sermon used Sunday mornins to check in with Mookie, always callin to share words from his Bible. So I sent Grandma to church alone that Sunday and waited for the ring in our back office. When Sermon checked in, we'd pray together, and the Lord'd forgive us both.

The call came before noon and I grabbed the receiver quick. "Hello?"

"Speak to Mookie King?"

"Ain't here," I said, and figured the voice. "This Sermon?"

"Naw. Who this?"

"Don't worry, man. It's J.C. What's happenin?"

"Where's Mookie at?"

"Takin care of business." I said. "Be cool, Sermon, it's me. You okay?"

"Yeah, I'm okay. J.C.? Thought you was supposed to be at church with your grandmamma."

"I am. Been to Ebenezer most every Sunday long as I can think. Mookie had business to tend, though—said you'd be callin this mornin. Wanted to be sure you was safe."

"You missed Reverend Goode for me, J.C.?"

"We promised to look out for you, didn't we?" I sat in Mookie's chair and looked through the office blinds, on the empty space of Tony Ricci's Soul Mamma. "Anyways, Mookie says y'all share the Word from the Good Book when you check in. Said it keeps your spirit high. Must be rough doin what you doin, hidin out and shit."

"Better believe, J.C.—it's hell. But I been here before. Been to hell in the jungles, you know? Lord brought me through then, said there was a reward in the end for my sufferin. Ain't that what He says, J.C.? You heard Reverend speak on that in Sunday service?"

"Of course I have, Sermon. What scripture you gonna share?"

"I always got the Word to speak. I'm the one in need, my man—you got scripture? I been over here damn near two weeks, and Mookie ain't no churchgoing brother. But I figure since your grandmamma raised you up the way she did, you know the Book enough to tell me something special outta it."

I looked to the ceilin light, still dim. "I think I know a passage, Sermon. But I wanna tell it to you the next time I see you, share it face-to-face."

"Come on, J.C."

"Not now, man. You gotta wait," I told him. "It's face-to-face scripture."

His breathin paused. "All right, J.C. I hear you. Lemme read this to you, see what you get outta it. A God-fearin brother like you should understand. It's from Psalms: 'He made a pit, and digged it, and is fallen into the ditch which he made. Mischief shall return upon his own head, and his violent dealing shall come down upon his tongue. Yet, in the end, he will praise the Lord according to His righteousness and will sing praise of His name most high.' He's lookin out for me, J.C., long as I bear Him witness. He's gonna take care of those who give Him due praise, let those souls up into heaven. He ain't gonna let no Satan snatch me. That's how I read it."

"Jesus ain't gonna let nothin happen to you."

"You get that from the Word, don't you, J.C.? That's what it mean, huh?"

"Yeah, Sermon, that's what it mean. I know it's true," I said. "It's a good time for you to leave the city now. Mookie said so. We pick you up tomorrow round seven. Takin you to the bus station. He got you a ticket on the Greyhound."

"Mookie bought me a ticket?" I blinked at Sermon's happiness. "Cops ain't watching the terminals no more? They're letting me leave—where's my bus headed?"

"Don't know, Sermon. Ain't seen the ticket myself. Somewhere down South, I believe. But you can go wherever you wanna after you get outta the city. You know Mookie, you know he'll slide you some loot."

"Yeah, I know him. Mookie's a good brother. Didn't I tell you the Lord was looking out cause I give Him due praise? He's working through y'all."

"You just be on the corner of Washington and Central tomorrow at seven, and everythin's gonna be all right. You gotta keep the faith, joe, cause Jesus know the way of the righteous."

"That's the holy word you was gonna tell me later, ain't it, J.C.? 'Jesus knows the way of the righteous.' " Joy, the joy of Sermon's salvation, screamed through the telephone. "Amen," he said.

* * *

He stood on the corner, green bag slung over his shoulder, the same army fatigues he'd worn the night he shot Tony Ricci coverin his body. Those stained clothes was the first thing I saw as Mookie drove near the West Side block. The second was how Sermon's bag was empty. Could tell by the way the wind made it flap against his body. The last was his eyes fallin on the shiny T-Bird as we came near. Sermon was ready, let that stare tell it.

Mookie stopped the car at his curb. "What's up, my man?"

"What's up, Mookie, J.C.? It's that time?"

"It's that time," I chimed.

"Where the rest of your things at?" Mookie opened the driver-side door and let Sermon inside. "Bag looks empty. I don't know when you gonna be able to come back to the city now."

"Don't matter. Ain't got nothin else. Wearing everything important, clothes and such."

Sermon laid low in the backseat and rubbed his wounded place till Mookie handed him the ticket. He opened the envelope and smiled. "Memphis, huh? I know folk there, some good brothers I was in 'Nam with. That's a nice place to end up in, Memphis."

The T-Bird rolled down Washington and I watched Sermon through the mirror. He sat up straight and turned to the house at the corner of Central, wavin to the family who'd protected him from white justice. When his hand got tired, the index and middle finger offered peace to his kinfolk, whose yellow palms pressed against safe windowpanes.

"What was that scripture you was gonna share, J.C.?"

I turned to the windshield, couldn't look at him just then. "Told it to you already, man. Don't you remember, yesterday, over the phone? You remember?"

"That really was it? Yeah, I remember, of course. Just wanna hear it again, that's all. Can't never get too much of the Truth."

"Oh, you liked it? Grandma Rose's favorite phrase from the Psalms, that's where I got it. 'Jesus do know the way of the righteous.' She always be sayin that."

"Jesus do know the way of the righteous—that's somethin special, ain't it?" Sermon looked around and his eyes showed doubt for the first time. "Where we goin? Ain't the bus station east way, toward downtown? We goin south."

I looked at Mookie. "Yeah, Sermon. Bus station's the other way," he said. "I just gotta pick somethin up from Soul Mamma."

"Oh, the nightclub? That's where we're headed to?"

"Yeah, we stoppin by Soul Mamma on the way, Sermon. That's all."

—

We waited for Mookie in the club's alley. The marine was spread out in his seat, not sleepin, just layin down low again. I thought of Salvie and the rest of them laughin as they drove by Grandma Rose's house. I wanted to shoot Sermon in the kneecaps, cause it was that loser nigga's fault—my fear—but it wouldn't have done us no good then. Too late for that.

"You think this's gonna work out, J.C.?"

"What's that?"

"Running from white folk," Sermon said. "I did just about kill one. Like Mookie said, they ain't never gonna let it ride till they catch me. I can't see um letting me get away with putting bullets in no white boy. Dumbest thing for a brother to do. I served in 'Nam with them motherfuckers, I know how they think. They gonna hunt me till I'm hung, J.C. That's how they are."

I watched him in the rearview mirror, his body shiftin like he wasn't comfortable. "Why'd you say that passage yesterday if you ain't gonna have faith in it? What's the point in readin scripture if you ain't gonna believe what it say bout God, right in fronta your eyes?"

"I've just been thinking, J.C. Two weeks is a lotta time to be hiding in cellars, leaves you with nothing to do sometimes but think."

"What you been thinkin on, Sermon?"

"This God we pray to, what if he ain't ours? What if he's the God of the motherfuckers—sorry, Jesus—who's chasing after me? Then his scripture ain't meant for my ears, is it? Maybe that's the case here, J.C. I'm stupid to be reading the Good Book if the God on the pages ain't even talking to me, ain't I?"

"Yeah, you'd be stupid to take what ain't holy Word for the truth, Sermon," I said, and looked away from the mirror. "But if He really is the God of them who's chasin you, then there ain't no point to runnin and hidin now, is it?"

—

"You ever look at the whole verse your grandmamma's saying comes from, J.C.?" Sermon held a pocket Bible small as his hands as Mookie drove past 49th Street.

"Huh?"

"You ever looked it up? 'Jesus knows the way of the righteous,' ever looked that up?"

Mookie frowned and poked my knee.

"Can't say I have."

"Like you say, it's right in Psalms. Chapter one, verse six exactly—'The Lord knows the way of the righteous, but the ungodly shall perish.' This's the Psalm you're talking about, right, J.C.? That there's what the Book says in full." He closed the Bible and stuffed it into his army fatigues. "Where we going now? We still ain't heading to the bus station."

The .45 holster knocked against my chest, scratchin skin through my shirt. "Goin to that stop on Ninety-fifth Street," Mookie said. "That's how come we drivin this way."

"For what? We ain't but fifteen minutes from downtown. And if we goin to Ninety-fifth, why ain't we on the Ryan? That's about the fastest way out there." Sermon sniffed the T-Bird's air.

I looked at the white bag Mookie'd brung from Soul Mamma. The janitor's hammer was zipped inside, and it clinked against the seat. That was how we was gonna do it—park under a viaduct way out south, then once, twice upside Sermon's skull with his own tool. Wouldn't have took no more than that, and it seemed less evil somehow than another gunshot to his body. Besides, he'd looked so ready standin on that West Side corner, like he understood. "Always wondered which verse that psalm came from," I said. The T-Bird came to a red light on 51st.

I didn't see the marine leave the car, just the driver seat pushin Mookie against the steerin wheel as Sermon squeezed through the door. Even when I looked to the left, all I caught of his escape was that empty bag trapped in the car window, and Sermon's combat boots poundin up 51st. My gut soured as I thought of the Hack torturin Grandma Rose before hangin her from a meat hook. Mookie looked at me, black eyes wide and wild.

"I got him," I promised—promised them all—and jumped from the car, the knot at the back of my head throbbin for peace.

* * *

"Stop, J.C. Please lemme go!"

We'd been runnin for a good two blocks, runnin so long I wasn't thinkin bout Sermon's yells no more, nor bout Grandma Rose and the gangsters, not thinkin nothin, just runnin with emptiness. But as Sermon cut north at Cottage Grove, Julius and Willie Banks did come to mind. Takin um out shoulda made me bigger than Mookie and Salvie and Tommy Ricci and, more than anybody, bigger than the fat, dead dope pushers who drowned in fronta me. But who was it that got credit when the street found them two shot up over on 43rd? Of course not me. "Wasn't no way it coulda been shit-talkin J.C. Rose," the street said, "not Esther Rose's little boy from Ebenezer, who took out the Banks fiends. Same cat who pissed his pants in Mister Manley's history class? That one, no way—he just be talkin loud noise. Had to uh been the cops or the mob, if it wasn't Mookie King."

So, just as when he'd shot that two-bit stickup man and left him on 35th Street, it was Mookie they bowed to when the bodies turned up under alley trash. No juice'd come to me through my sins, for I was just the little cat in Mookie's lead-swingin shadow. Never got nothin true outta doin wrong. I drove round in a gold Caddy, had paper in my pocket, managed Soul Mamma, fucked all the little high school girls I cared to, but I wasn't shit. Didn't even know what'd come of the gold chains we'd took off the Cajun—dug through all that garbage to find um, only so that Mookie could hawk um and

Salvie could suck us in for life. Then the gems disappeared. Nothin, that was what Johnny and the Bankses dyin did for me.

But what'd others got off the same gems? Mookie was the most feared cat on 47th Street, had the deepest pockets, Mora, and enough pull with the Outfit to keep um from comin to collect when he'd welched. And Tommy Ricci and Salvie, wasn't no tellin what profit my wrongs had brung them bastards. Ol men'd built up gold thrones from my sin, most likely, just to rest they asses in as they ruled.

So how come I wasn't at home, protectin Grandma Rose from Vito and Paulo? Sermon hadn't shown me no disrespect, never even lied to my face as far as I knew. What he had done was what I wished for the strength, hell, the stupidity, to pull off—Sermon'd cut off the serpent's tail. I wouldn't profit nothin from the fool's end; somebody else, maybe, but not profit myself at all. The only explanation for the chase was that I'd gave myself right back to fear then. Simple truth. I ran on.

Didn't turn at Cottage Grove like Sermon, went on down to Southpark Avenue—Doctor Martin Luther King Drive, they was callin it by then—instead. I knew where he was headed, so I pushed the folk out of the way and reached under my suit jacket. I didn't bring the .45 out just yet, though, didn't wanna scare nobody away on the evenin street. They had to see.

"Look out, boy!" . . . "Watch where you goin!" . . . "You see his eyes?"

Bumped into 47th Street Black after cuttin at the strip, the ol bum shufflin west to his corner, or somewhere, as I tore through the wind of him.

"Where you headed to in such a hurry, boy?"

"Shut up," I puffed.

"Better watch where you goin," Black yelled, and I slowed myself bout a block past him. Forty-seventh and King Drive, there was Sermon, runnin to me instead of away. I'd known where he was headed soon as he'd made that turn at Cottage Grove. Wasn't nowhere else for him to go but to the center of colored life. I wouldn't kill him there, not in fronta that big-mouthed bum, not before all the people. Couldn't shame Grandma Rose's Ebenezer Baptist like so.

I looked at the brand-new street sign, then at the empty buildins and beaten streets, the people still sad for the world passed on. And I looked into Sermon's eyes when the street ran out of anything else to see, saw the readiness he'd shown on the corner of Washington and Central. I found his faith—he believed, but did he understand? His arms opened for my hug, spread wide no different than that first time he'd come into our office. He looked happy, grinnin at the North Vietnamese bout to mercifully shoot his ass from the jungle swamp. I grabbed under my coat and, when I aimed the gat, it wasn't in pity or holy mercy or fear. I aimed at Sermon's stupid faith in me and Mookie, for his belief in somebody else's God, fixed the .45 on his foolishness, and fired twice to end his run. His chest opened and his body lifted from the sidewalk, hangin in red air. He'd got what he shoulda been ready for, so there wasn't no scream as he smacked against the pavement, black fish outta foul water. He had that punishment comin; from me, in fronta our people. My juice was seen. Respect shoulda been mine.

The souls tackled me and steel sprung from my hand. I tried to stand, but the weight of 47th Street Black's forearms held me down, smashed front teeth into the sidewalk cracks. I was kicked and spit on and cursed under Doctor King's sign, made to pay for stealin they world, to suffer for the men I served. But when I looked up, it wasn't Sermon's blood, the clean yellow street sign, or the folk's pain I saw. It was that T-Bird convertible in my eye, shinin against the moon as it passed. I screamed as Mookie disappeared, west on 47th Street.

12

MY NAME IS JESUS CHRIST ROSE. I was born in a Georgia swamp. My father was a mystery I couldn't even picture. My mamma was a fourteen-year-ol whore I hadn't seen in twenty years since she went off chasing free living. She brought me to the Forties when I was a baby and dropped me with Grandma Rose. Grandma was the only real mamma or papa I ever had. They buried her while I was gone. Nothing I could've done about it. Kenwood, 45th Street. That was where I started to die.

I know my history not because Grandma told it to me, but because I put the bastard pieces together in this place. Gonna hold on to only some of what's gone down behind these bars. Let the rest out. Better that way.

They took me on a murder rap second degree. Killed a nigga floor sweeper. For that they sent me to a cage. Fifteen years. That same time we used to kill when we was kids smoking squares and watching Cath'lic girls becomes everything while they got you locked up. After they take love or freedom or time from you, it seems all-important. Even if you wasn't doing nothing with it when you had it.

* * *

The cell they locked me in was a six-by-nine. There was a funky bed cot, a sink that tilted to the toilet, and paint chips dropping from the walls. And the john didn't flush good, so years of chips floated in the commode, sucking up all the shit and water.

The Decatur joint was packed to the walls during my time. So much sin going down that they had to lock us right up against each other, cage to cage way out in the boonies. Jaime Manuel was the skinny brown man in the cell next to mine. He'd come to Decatur long before the Panthers and Muslims and King, stayed long enough for the world to have turned around the sun twelve times and end up exactly where it'd started when they'd put him there. Got taken down for stealing some Gold Coast white boy's Jaguar from the Magnificent Mile. Jaime said he'd broken into the load, took it for a ride on Humboldt Boulevard for his amigos to see, then got arrested as he parked the Jag back where he'd stolen it (he'd bought some junk and blasted a Puerto Rican while joyriding, so they had him on possession and murder, along with grand theft auto and a mess of priors and suspicions). So Jaime came into Decatur as a jackass. Never said much, though, not after telling the story of how he'd ended up in the joint—just so I'd know how bad a Chicano he was—and how he'd seen many come and go out of my cage. I'd last, he claimed, if I learned who to fuck with and who to leave alone. "Don't fuck wit Manuel," he said, so I let him be.

Jamie'd learned not to be an ass committing bullshit crimes, at least. He'd moved up to selling dope, selling it and paying the guards to leave the business be. Turned out one of the joint's top chiefs was his supplier. The Decatur lockup, when it came down to it, wasn't any different from 43rd Street. And Jaime wasn't but one of the Banks brothers, skinnier and with a Mexican for a daddy.

Took months to figure out how to use the bathrooms right. Between dealing with the broken cell toilet, to trying to hustle the guards into giving me a cell that was clean and safe, to recognizing there was no such thing as clean and safe for a colored in prison, I came to understand the only change that mattered between being locked down and living free outside. I learned that, on the street, filth hid behind gold chains, haberdashery, fancy clothes, and loot, creeping out when you weren't paying it mind. But in Decatur, there was nothing for filth to hide behind, so it crawled around, surrounded and bit—*ate*—you whenever it got ready to.

The Blackstone Ranger crew from the neighborhood showed up before my second week was over. My eyes popped open in the middle of sleep, just as they'd opened on every night past: twitching nervous and without a clue what they looked on. Seeing the bars and the blackness of Block D after lights-out had cleared sight those nights before, but the bars were gone and Mookie stood over me then. Or something carved out of darkness, standing tall and bringing a shadow from the slicing moonlight, looking so much like Mookie. I blinked and made out four outlines behind him, shorter—in his shadow much as I was—and grumbling loud like mad-ass trolls, but still not loud as his disgusted breathing. I turned away from the nightmare and held my breath; the wall plaster'd stunk like piss since the toilet exploded my second day. But before I could sleep again, the tall Stone grabbed my head and pulled me from the sheets. He twisted my neck so I looked at him good, saw that he even had showy white teeth and wavy hair like Mookie's. Then over his shoulder, past his Stone trolls and the open cell door into that crack of light where the block guard disappeared, whistling and twirling a set of keys.

The tall Stone yanked until my eyes bugged wide to let go tears. "Hear you from off the Forties."

"What?" My lips barely opened for the hurt of scalp pulling from the rest of my head. "Fuck you."

"Yeah," he said. He looked like Mookie, but his sound was Mississippi, words twanging through lips like he'd just stepped off of the cotton fields. "Fuck me. You J.C. Rose from Forty-seventh Street. Hear you a bad little muthafucka. Runnin shit with Mookie King, took out a mess of cats round the strip, makin tall paper . . ."

"Down with the Talian gangsters, a pimp-ass gangster yo damn self," one of the trolls grumbled.

"You a bad little nigga," another cosigned, from the back.

"Baddest little nigga," the tall one said, black eyes shining.

"Fuck all y'all," I told them, and their grumbling and breathing turned louder.

"You J.C. Rose," he said again. "I heard bout you from off the Forties. We know bout you. Niggas been talkin."

"That ain't me."

The tall one laughed. "Too late to take it back now, jack. You's a bad muthafuckin nigga. You done the crime, payin the time, sowed the seeds, done the deeds, can't change yo creed."

"Ain't me."

"Ain't? Fuck you, little nigga," the tall Stone said, his voice soft but sharp to cut through Jaime's snore on the other side of that wall. "Fuck you."

"Yeah," the trolls chimed, "little nigga."

"That I-talian shit don't mean nothin in here. This our world, boy, you in our world now. Muthafuckin Blackstone world," he said, and the light at his back was gone. "If you ain't down with how we roll, you can't roll."

"Fu—"

"I know . . . fuck me, fuck y'all, fuck it all." Felt like the scalp'd tear from my skull just to keep him from taking the whole head. "You talk good talk, little muthafucka. Don't mean shit. You wanna roll in here, you gotta get down with us, you bad little—"

"Get down . . . get down . . . ," the back troll sang.

"Get down with the Stones. Get down with me," the tall one said. His off hand reached into his uniform pants and fiddled until it showed free holding Johnny the Baptist's rotted dick, took from under the trash in the 49th Street alley. Right there in his palm—no way such a yellow limb belonged to that tar-black Stone. The thing was Johnny's faded Louisiana color, I swore, like it didn't belong to

Blackness at all. And it'd been shined, cleaned from the mess left in the Cajun's crotch, so the blood barely showed. That was the Baptist's dick stitched at the tall Stone's waist then, and it was hard and pounding against his black hand. I saw it and knew I was still dreaming. "Bad little muthafucka."

"Get down," the back troll reminded.

I gritted my top teeth hard, my jaw fighting the pull at my head until my eyes and nose tore at the skin seams. He let go the hair, and I was free for but a breath before one of the trolls grabbed at my neck and dragged me from the bed. He dropped me so I bowed in the shadow.

The tall Stone pulled a switchblade from the back of his pants, dug its point into my throat. "If I feel one tooth against my shit, I'm gonna slice you. Open up . . ."

I chewed my bottom lip to keep my mouth shut, so they beat at me with lead pipes hard to sting the bone, gave me the whipping I'd had coming for so long. Didn't even matter—all I had to do was fix on that yellowness bopping in his hand to find the teeth strong enough to keep my mouth shut, no matter their pipes or the blood knotting just above the blade point at my neck. Fought on until one of the Blackstones, giggling instead of grumbling, caught me at the kidney with his lead—one of my old tricks—and I screamed. The troll holding my head snatched the holes in my nose to keep my face open just wide enough and that tall Stone stroked inside my mouth with his stitched-on dick, and I couldn't do a damn thing but swallow a dead Cajun whole.

They pushed me to the middle of the floor when he was done, and circled around. The back troll stepped forward. "My turn," he said, voice chiming still, repeating what nobody'd said.

I felt hot jism hanging from my lips and spit it loose before kicking my left leg, aiming for the tall one. Caught him in the crotch good just before he'd put Johnny's thing back into his prison pants.

He coughed and I kicked him again quick before they could jump me—got him better the second time, in the stomach, and he grabbed himself and fell next to the toilet. He'd slashed down with the blade, though, sliced my eyebrow and opened up my cheek, nearly cut out my eye. The rest of them pounded me, the chiming troll sitting on my neck as they racked with lead, and my body went numb as air left. The tall Stone stood and pulled me to the toilet, and I tasted blood against my lips, my own and the Cajun's stale blood, as he held me over the bowl. Looking into years of swirling shit was the last thing I remembered from that night, that and the trolls pushing my head into a pool of niggas and spics in cages, and the toilet exploding as one of the bastards flushed. I knew the dream was over because the taste of piss on plaster mixed with Baptist blood washed the rest of his jism from my tongue.

I woke in the middle of the floor—the sun's light shined down through cell bars by then. I raised my head, saw I'd slept in a puddle, looked harder and caught the block guard standing over me, twirling his keys and whistling still. My top was stank wet. I tried to move anything other than my head, but couldn't for the hurt. "What happened, boy?" Before I could curse him, he rapped the bad kidney with his riot club and giggled. "Time to get up now," he said.

* * *

Mookie sat in the visiting room with a kid slung over his shoulder. On the glass divider's free side, the young eyes (I couldn't tell at first because he was so soft-looking but, staring closer, I saw it was a boy) fell on me. The boy had black, black eyes, too, but soft and clean like they hadn't ever seen wrongdoing, knew nothing about sin and crime.

Mookie picked up the gray telephone and I lifted its receiver. "Who the hell is that?"

"What?"

"Whose fuckin kid is that?"

"Watch your mouth. He hears you."

"Who is he, muthafucka?"

"This's Isaiah, Geri's boy. Don't you remember him?"

"Yeah, I remember," I said. He didn't ask about the cut on my face, like he saw no line of stitches down to my chin, and I didn't say anything about his Blackstone twin who'd made me suck a dead yellow man's dick. No real reason behind the quiet: just loud, two-nigger silence. "Why you bring him to see me like this? Ain't run cross the boy since he was still in a muthafuckin stroller. What kinda first memory is prison for him to have, damnit?"

"Watch your mouth, jack. He ain't gonna recall nothin bout comin to see you. What you remember from when you was two years ol?"

"Muthafucka, you don't know what he gonna recall and what he ain't gonna recall. Muthafucka. Keep on bringin him up here while I'm locked up and what's he gonna know to call me except for a bastard convict? Son of a bitch, Mookie—don't bring him no more."

"What's wrong with you? Sound like you been livin in a sewer." Mookie patted the boy's curly hair. "Didn't plan on bringin him. Watchin the kid for my sister is all. He ain't gonna know nothin bout you . . . but watch your mouth round him. How many times I gotta say it?"

"You're baby-sittin?"

"For my sister. Yeah, I'm baby-sittin."

"Ain't you the puss-ass nigga these days. What's goin on on the streets while you run around baby-sittin like a bitch?"

"What's wrong with you?"

"With me?" I laughed and tapped my knuckles against the glass plate. "Look around, muthafucka. Look left and right—what you mean, what's wrong with me?"

"My fault, man. You all right?"

"Hell naw, I ain't all right. Just told you to look around."

"I know, J.C. But you get the Salems I sent for you?"

"Yeah."

"Magazines, too?"

"Bring books with Black hookers in um next time. Paula Kelly, Tina Turner, whatever. Just bring Black gals."

"You're welcome, J.C. Don't they got no *National Geographic* up in here?"

"What?"

"For naked coons."

"I'm talkin bout some good-lookin Black gals."

"I'll see what I can do. They don't be puttin coloreds in them magazines every month, you know."

"Oh—probably not. Just get as many as you can. I'm tired of peepin these naked white hookers."

"Beggars can't be choosin."

"Hear what I'm sayin, Mookie?"

"Whatever," he said. He glanced at his quartz watch—he tried to hide it, but I caught him. "Anythin else you need?"

"Nothin I can think of. Things goin good on the street?"

"Okay. Money's gettin made, you know how it is."

"No, I don't know how it is."

"You know. Same as always."

"You're takin care of my share?"

He laughed. "Of course."

"What does that mean—chuckle-chuckle, of course? What's that supposed to tell me? You takin care of my loot or what, muthafucka?"

"Asked you to watch your mouth," Mookie said. He propped the kid on his shoulder. "What you so scary for? What else am I gonna do with your share but take care of it? It ain't my money, it's yours. All of sudden I'm lyin to you? You don't got trust in me no more, J.C.?"

I laughed, saw moon shining off the red steel of a T-Bird rolling west. "Of course I trust you. . . . How's my grandmamma?"

"Huh?"

"You been goin by to check on her like you said you would, haven't you? How's Grandma Rose?"

"She's fine, she's fine." He glanced at the quartz again. "You know she don't let me in the crib no more. But I sit cross the street to make sure I see her takin walks. I think she stopped goin to Ebenezer, but she's okay."

"You sure?"

"Yeah, I'm sure. She's fine. You know your grandmamma, how strong she is. She's fine."

"All right, Mookie. Just makin sure you're lookin out for her like you said."

He didn't bother hiding the watch anymore. "I gotta get this kid to Geri, J.C. It's bout three o'clock. Gotta get back to the city."

"You're leavin?"

"Got to. They had me waitin for you all that time. Now I gotta go."

"I'll watch my mouth."

"It ain't that, man. I understand you stressed out bein behind them bars. Don't trip on that. Just gotta go."

"You leavin me alone here, you know?"

"Sorry, joe. Can't stay no more." Mookie hung up and Isaiah grabbed on his suit jacket shoulder as they stood.

The security guard took my arm, tried to lead me back into the pen, but I rapped on the glass. "You seen Christina?" I said, just knowing he'd read my lips through the divider. He frowned. "Christina?" I yelled.

Mookie stood still, like he was trying to make sense out of what I'd said. He shrugged and turned again, turned away, and walked off. But he'd heard. Isaiah waved as the guard drug me back into the cage. Three years would pass before I'd see Mookie—my man, Mookie, my brother—again.

* * *

Those first months, being connected with Salvie back home didn't mean nothing. The Outfit had pull inside, of course, ran everything much as they did on the strip. But my street ties to them brought no respect downstate. Italians never even blinked my way, just hung at cafeteria tables or their weightlifting corner in the yard, whispering to each other like Salvie and Angelo in the Chrysler's front seat. They were the strongest group in the joint, no mistake to be made about it. They were always the strongest.

Vinnie Povich was in the lockup the same time as me, serving time for hijacking a truckload of TVs and stereos with some Milwaukee hoods. I knew of Vinnie from the outside; just a small-time connected bust-out man from Western Avenue, under Salvie and Joe Defelice, way under Tommy Ricci. Just the fact that he was in Decatur said that he wasn't shit, even for a half-bred Italian. The feds could take the big-timers down for tax evasion, money laundering, rich crimes, but the state couldn't touch them. Filthy state joints like Decatur were for us and the Mexicans, because big-timers like Mister Ricci and Salvie were tied in with the Springfield political boys.

But since Vinnie was the only connected cat in lockup, he played the boss. Walking around Block D in silk pajamas, smoking Havanas, and doing no work that I knew of. All the Italians and Polish grouped around him in the cafeteria or on the yard every afternoon, so they were called the in-house Mafia. That was how they ran the joint—throw in the Latins and we outnumbered them three to one. I felt no special respect for them cats, but once they started wearing silk pajamas and talking that Mafia shit, they were calling the shots just like any other white boys.

—

I got my first big job back in '71, just after the New Year. Was mopping cafeteria floors, my regular chore, when I heard footsteps in the dark before the kitchen. No one except me was supposed to be back there that late in the day. I kicked the bucket from my front and stood still. My palms turned red and my heart jumped as the pail hit against one of the tables, bringing a splash of stinking ammonia water. The scar on my face twitched—wasn't ready for more beatings. No way whoever was creeping in the shadows was getting me then. I'd take them down as payback for those goddamn trolls who'd fucked with me. "Who's there?"

"J.C.?"

My fingernails dug into the handle's wood. "Who's callin me? Come outta the shadows."

"J.C.?"

"Who's that?"

"It's Nate, man," the figure said, and stepped from the dark.

I looked around and there was no guard near. That was the first sign something was about to go down, when the prison cops disappeared.

Frail Nate limped to the cafeteria table and rested himself. I knew the gimp from 47th Street hadn't come for anything by himself. Him I'd bash over his thin scalp, kill him with one good mop blow. "Nate? What you want? Why you hidin in shadows?"

"Wasn't hidin, J.C., ain't got nothin to hide from. Just came from talkin to the man. He got somethin for you."

"The who?"

Nate frowned and tapped his fingers three times. I swung around quick, thought he'd sent a signal for me to be rushed by the Stones, or the Disciples that time maybe—didn't matter, just knew they were coming. I wasn't about to be no niggas' whore, never again. They'd kill me before I went to my knees.

But Nate sat there tapping his fingers against the table. I mopped spilled water. "There's one man in here, J.C. You been here long enough to understand, been round long enough to know."

"Who you talkin bout, Nate? Tell me, cause I don't hear what you babblin."

"Vinnie. He got somethin for you."

"Povich?"

"Yeah, he got somethin."

"Vinnie ain't no muthafuckin body. Ain't shit but a thievin hood off the street, like me and you. Just happens to be a cracker, a half-wop cracker."

"Lower your voice. You gotta learn to whisper like they do." Nate waved his hand in the blue dark. "I ain't no muthafuckin hood. They got me on a bum rap. I told you that a hundred times. And you know how things is. Out there, yeah, Vinnie's a hood. In here, he's the man."

"Bullshit, Nate. Who said so?"

"What? He's the man, J.C., that's all. Ain't shit else to argue bout, less you wanna be stupid bout it."

"All right . . . he's the man. What he got?"

"A favor. Vinnie wants you to take care of somethin for him. He knows what kinda work you was into on Forty-seventh Street, heard how you handled business. He's got somethin special for you to resolve, brother."

"Ain't none uh your brother, nigga. Why don't he come ask me hisself? I been here most of a year. You the only vic he can holler at?"

"Shh!" A guard'd stepped into the cafeteria. "You know how they work, J.C. They don't talk face-to-face. They gotta pass word down through channels. It's how they work, through channels."

"What's he want handled and what's he payin for it? That's all you gotta tell me." I ran my mop over the clean floor.

"You gonna do it?"

"Can't say till I know the pay. Don't treat me like I'm a muthafuckin spic over here."

"What kinda loot you want, jack? Dollars don't mean shit in this place. What's to use it for? Ain't known money could buy back life, have you? All he can offer is protection, make sure don't nobody trouble you while you in here. The cut there on your face'll be the last wound this joint'll put on you. Vinnie can make sure of it, if you do as he say. How you think I made it through these years, huh? All of us don't gotta be in no half-assed gang to get by. The man looks out."

"If you do as he say?"

"That's right."

"Do like he say and be a good boy. What's he want, Nate?"

"There's a vic who do this here kinda work, moppin and cleanin up. Solomon's his name. Big Black muthafucka, wears glasses, owes Vinnie on the racket he got goin. Sellin squares outta the laundry room and whatnot. Sells whatever you can't get in here easy, got a couple guards in on it with him. You know how these things is, same type of shit that go down outside. Just take care of the business like you would on the strip."

I looked up from the mop's circles, watched the guard leave again. "How I know I'm gonna be protected if I do this? I ain't gettin no guarantees, nothin."

"I told you I'm looked out for. It's him watchin over me, not nobody else. Man's good for his word, J.C., he ain't no liar."

I laughed and wrung the mop clean over the pail. "So how come one of his own don't handle this? I see him hangin round here with his *paisans*. What he need me for? They afraid of this cat?"

"Ain't no fear, man. You know that. I'm just deliverin a message. All I can do is guess reasons. I figure when this go down, the joint's gonna know who done it. You know how word get round in here. If it's heard a white muthafucka beat a nigga—no matter that it's business—a white Polack or wop beatin a nigga, Vinnie's gonna have problems. The Stones, Disciples, Muslims, everythin Black on the yard'll come together, mad at the man. Now, if it's known another nigga beat this Solomon, even if it was done for Vinnie, there ain't gonna be no big thing made of it. You know how it works."

"Sure as hell how it works." I dropped the mop in the pail's water and rolled to the door.

"So what you gonna do?" Nate'd returned to the dark.

"Tell the man I said it's done, long as I get my protection."

* * *

They sent me to a shrink during those first months because of the murder rap, even if it was only second degree. For an hour every Tuesday and Thursday, they'd let me off from mopping and scrubbing to meet with a bearded old white lady, whose name I never thought to remember. Seeing her was the psychological part of what they called my reformation process. The only way a locked-up cat could get early parole was if he'd finished all parts of the process: psychological treatment, education, and reintegration. Staring fifteen Decatur years in the face, I'd play their game, anything to get out of that six-by-nine in half time.

So we'd sit in a little prison room, me, her and the thick bush of red hair under her chin like goat fuzz. Nate claimed she'd been a nun back in the day, before she'd got too crotch-hot for her habit and God'd defrocked her. Whatever, we spent that hour looking at black ink spilled on top of white paper and shared—her word for it, "sharing"—what I saw in the pictures. During my first visit, I told her the butterfly-shaped spot looked like somebody'd got his head split open and bled all over her note cards, and if she was going to buy cards big as that she might as well've sprung the extra dime for cards with lines to keep her bloodstains straight. Her beard bunched way up to the bottom lip and I knew she didn't find me too funny at all.

After a month or so, I'd look at her spots and get serious, try to at least, just for the sake of tricking off the time. Looked at one picture, ink shaped like a little boy riding a donkey, and said the sight of it made me think of dark men who wanted to think clean thoughts, do good things, live right lives, but couldn't because they were dark men trapped on a blank, flat nowhere. Beard touched her top lip and I knew for sure she didn't find me one bit deep or funny. No-habit-having nun sentenced me to an extra month of ink blots.

When I was done with her, the reformation process passed me on to a social worker. Meant I'd graduated to the next treatment step—the only locked-up bastards who didn't have social workers were vics who were behind bars for life, without a phase to finish or a life to reintegrate into. The guy they sent me to was named Loomis, a blond-haired Anglo nebbish, as Salvie called the Outfit paper accountants and lawyers. It was Salvie who'd taught me how to tell the difference between the kinds of white folks; his Italian people were oil-skinned with dark hair and noses big and sharp as crow beaks, "king noses" he called them; you knew the "nappy Jews" because of their skin, colored cream and clammy from two thousand years of nigger-loving blood mixing, and the shamed eyes sunk into their faces; Irish were lily white sprinkled with freckles until you'd made them mad, when the freckles took over and turned them red like the old nun's goat hair; and those Anglos had faces that were round and flat at the same time and teaspoon noses with no lips, and their skin was white and they were so proud of their whiteness that they couldn't help but glow in that pure, clean, showy, blank color. Like Loomis—Salvie was full of it mostly, but he had that nebbish pegged right on.

Loomis didn't like looking at me when he talked, better for him to fix his rim-covered green eyes on the paper under him, nothing but a pale bald spot staring me in the face while he scribbled against paper loud and hard until his desk wood squeaked. He'd ask questions, then cut in before the end of my answer with a breath heavy and hot to burn across his desk, dragon puffing to find out something else new that was nobody's business. Then he'd write out the part of the answer he'd heard, *rat-tat-tat*ting on no matter how stupid the shit I'd told him, like nothing mattered except that he needed my words. Words, if not my soul, to fill up his forms.

Over his bald spot was an American flag, a picture of the governor (the Outfit sent that cat an even thousand cash stuffed in fruitcakes every holiday and election night—I wondered what glowing Loomis would've thought about that), and a framed picture telling that old Christian tale, the one with the set of footprints trailed out to the sea water. Called it *Footprints,* in fact, that tale about Jesus picking up his disciples and carrying them through rough times. Grandma Rose had the same wise picture hanging from her kitchen wall. For all the Bible reading she'd made me do up at Ebenezer, that story was still stupid as stupid could be to me—Jesus carrying a nigga when things got tough on the beach. On the beach? Next to the flag and the governor and Loomis' pale head, though, *Footprints* wasn't bad to look at while the nebbish poked.

"So what does J.C. stand for?"

I found the place in the wall hanging where footprints disappeared in shore waves, and I wanted to spit. "Stand for? Don't stand for nothin. It's my name—J.C."

"That's two letters or one word?"

I laughed. "What?"

"The prison file shows you as 'J.C. Rose.' But is it really like Jacy Rose, like J-a-c-y Rose? Some kind of a nickname?"

"J-a-c-y? What'd that be short for?" The sky in the wise tale opened, shining on the beach and bringing light to Loomis' shady office space. "File's got it right."

"You don't understand, Jacy," he said. "Hear my question—what's the name on your birth certificate? Your God-given, real name?"

"J.C. Rose," I said, and tasted the salty wad drying in my gums. "That's the only name I got. Just J.C. Rose."

"It's got to stand for . . ." The bald spot rose to the ceiling, and he put those green soul-sucking eyes on me for a quick second. "Why do you fellas want to give me such a hard time? Always with the hard time."

I twisted my face to match the thin-lipped sneer showing on Loomis'. His pen *rat-tat-tat*ted across the paper and the cheap wood squeaked loud and high like a woman screaming, and I held my knees together to keep my feet from tapping his floor. "Have you always had that scar running next to your eye?"

I touched the line of bubbled skin on my right cheek and felt the switchblade sliding down my face, traced the dig from the end of my forehead to just next to my top lip. By the time I'd reached the tip, I saw Mookie's shadow hanging over me and tasted the Baptist stinging my gums. "What you mean, always—like it's a birthmark?"

"Did you have the scar before you came to Decatur?" Loomis stopped writing and looked up, looked through me still, but I swore his eyes turned pitiful and teary.

"Yeah," I said, quick enough for his face to twist in doubt. "I'm from Forty-seventh Street"—not talking to him really, but to myself, or to the footprints in the beach sand, running hustle on Jesus as he disappeared in sea water.

"What did that to you?" His pity even sounded real.

"Switchblade," I said.

So Loomis shrugged and, just like ol Mister Manley the Phillips High history teacher, the little bit that he'd gave a damn left both his eyes and his face, and that blank, cocksucking disgust was back. "So what're you here for, Mister Rose?"

"Reformation," I said. "They sent me here to finish reformin."

Loomis' mouth showed yellow teeth as it turned into a shady smile, like I was some kind of a joke. "That's why you were sent here," he said. "But why are *you* here? What do you want from our meetings?"

"To get reformed." I laughed before the bastard pointed his scalp back at me. "What the hell you want me to say, to find out what J.C. stands for?"

I heard his breathing against the desk. "You're not engaging this seriously, Mister Rose."

"Engagin? Yeah, I am. This's what I've got to do to get out of here—what, you think I want to be in this fuckin place fifteen years?"

"Language, Mister Rose." He looked up then back down, quick so I couldn't tell if *fuckin* really bothered him or if he'd said so only because *Footprints* shined on us.

"They tell me I can go about and get reformed, do it right and get out in half. What you want me to say, joe?"

His breathing turned into a hum. "Changing your lifestyle is the purpose of reformation. Altering the way you see the world. You can't go through the motions and get it done the right way. What good would that do the society? Or you? That's what I tell you fellows all the time."

"I'm here to learn somethin better to be, then," I said. "See different ways of goin about life. I want to know what reformation means."

"Still giving me the hard time." He leaned back in his chair—cheap leather on wheels instead of the painful wood scraping against floor tiles that I sat on. He played with his pen, and the hum turned lower, into a moan. "I'm here to help, Mister Rose. But you have to do the work to help me help you. Otherwise there's no point to this, and we're wasting each other's time."

"I said I want help. I'm ready to listen to you tell me how to be a good citizen. I ain't stupid. I know there's somethin for me to learn in here." I tried to look Loomis in the eye so he'd buy my shit, but his head'd dropped to the desk again. He didn't write anything, but he wouldn't look up. "You hear me talkin to you?"

He laughed again. "You want me to teach you what J.C. stands for?"

Anglos tended to be, what were Salvie's words, "sarcastic, cock-sucking fucks," cracking their taunting jokes. "That ain't called for. That's how come niggas don't bother with y'all shit. We tell you to go to hell, y'all get mad, insulted. Y'all tell us to go to hell, we take our stupid, trustin asses right on down to the Devil's throne and stay till he's done burnin the shit outta us. But Devil ain't never done once he's started—muthafucka got fire forever. That's how come he the Devil. We say we need y'all help to get out of his hell, you laugh and snatch your hand back and leave us dropped there with him. So why should a nigga've fucked with y'all's bullshit in the first place, if we end up with our asses on fire one way or the other? Don't matter for a nigga."

"Mister Rose," Loomis said, his forehead wrinkled, "please change your use of that word. It insults me."

"*Nigga?*"

"Yes, that word."

"Bothers *you* for *me* to say *nigga?*" My chair tipped to the door—if my feet hadn't been at the ground, I would've crashed into the sharp corners at the edge of Loomis' office. I saw in his blank face that he wasn't trying to be sarcastic, not sarcastic at all, just cock-sucking. "I'm insultin you?"

"Yes," he said without smiling. "*Negro, Afro-American, Black,* even *colored* is a more proper word for what you are than that. It's 1971. I can't stomach that word today, and certainly neither should you, no matter whose mouth it's coming from."

"*I'm* insultin *you?*"

"Yes. *Black* is a more proper term to use today." Loomis wrote on his form, but his eyes bounced around the walls. "Your file says that you shot a man dead on the South Side of Chicago."

"Yeah. Cat was chasing me down Forty-seventh Street, trying to attack me in broad daylight, so I protected myself. File say that?"

"You shot him, that's what's here. Your representatives argued self-defense, but you happened to be carrying a forty-five handgun when this gentleman attacked you. In the light of a public street. Why'd you have the gun, Mister Rose? Were you robbing the gentleman?"

I let go my own laugh. "Gentleman? What'd I need to rob Sermon's ass for? Rob him of what? That nigga—Black mu—that nigga swept up floors for me. Rob? I kept paper in my pocket. Always."

"The gentlemen you killed worked for you? You were a dope pusher?"

My chair fell back again, and my head tapped the wall. "So if a nigga—"

"Please, Mister Rose."

"If a Black has people working for him and he gets paid good, he sells dope? What you want me to stop saying *nigga* for, if that's what I am?"

"That's what you think of yourself?"

"That's what you think of me, damnit."

"You care what I think?"

"Naw, I don't give no shit. I'm just trying to get out of this place. Fuck you." He scribbled quick to catch whatever my face showed before it sputtered off.

"Go ahead, Jacy."

"You were talking."

"I was," he said, and stopped writing finally. "All right. I've lived in Chicago. I spent years in the city, long enough to know that if one fellow is walking down Forty-seventh Street and another fellow attacks him, and the first fellow pulls out a forty-five-caliber to protect himself, both of these characters—whether they're black, orange, green, blue, purple, or crimson—both of them are criminals. The color doesn't matter unless you want to make it matter. Period. I worked in

Cook County, and I'm no fool. Now, I'm just asking you to help me understand here. Were you a pimp?"

I straightened the chair on level ground. "No, sir. That's how much you know—hookers don't even work Forty-seventh Street. Pigs won't let it go down. Who could I pimp?"

"Okay, you say you weren't intending an armed robbery, you weren't a dope pusher, and you're not a pimp because you can't be. So what's that leave? Were you one of these shakedown fellas?"

I held on to the splintered wood arms to keep myself from jumping out of the chair and bashing his scalp bare-handed bloody all over Jesus' footprints and that goddamn red, white, and blue stitching.

"So what were you, Mister Rose?" Loomis put the bald spot on me one more time, bracing himself to scribble.

"Was what I am. A ni—a Black man looking for reintegration." Loomis wrote God knew what and I looked over my shoulder at the cracks around his door, saw light fading in the prison world past his little office. Our time had to be running out, had to be—mopping and scrubbing had to be done in the common area before I collected Vinnie Povich's cut of the cigarette racket.

13

HADN'T HELD LEAD in more than a year. No welchers to squeeze, no money to count in that place. Hadn't even thought about how I'd loved watching Mookie's swing. I used to practice on Salvie's welchers, wishing I had juice to swing my lead like his, to crack a skull for doing wrong. I couldn't remember missing it, though, not until I stood outside that basement laundry room. Figured living on the other end of a beating had caused me to believe in mercy, turned me soft. But that rod (not a real lead pipe, but a cracked-off bed leg) felt good against my palm, gave me a little juice. I waited, wished Mookie was there to see.

The guard appeared at my side, winking and juggling through his keys. He smiled as his badge sparkled silver, smiled like evil, and opened the laundry room door. The fingers on his right hand flashed twice—ten minutes, he was telling me. I tiptoed into the room and the door was closed at my back. The guard left us, whistling his lights-out song.

Solomon's scalp shined like the floor tiles as he let go his mop. I didn't know if he'd figured why I'd come, didn't risk it, so I hopped across the room and snatched the fool by his shirt collar. Gripped the rod in both hands and jammed its metal under his chin to strangle breath, but Solomon was strong as concrete. He slammed me into the industrial dryer, headfirst—no matter, the street'd taught me how to hold on to a welcher. Solomon's strength didn't mean a thing if he couldn't breathe, and long as I had his throat in that bed leg hold, his air was mine. Even after my skull'd bumped against that metal door, he could only swing his arms and gasp.

"What the fuck?" I yelled at the pain. On the strip, welchers didn't fight back. Any nigga with the balls to put his foot in your ass had the cash to pay his debts.

I saw the big man's wire frames twinkling on the tile and crushed them under my shoe, jammed the rod into the apple of his throat until he groaned. "Why you treatin me like a whore? You owe. Didn't you make some kinda agreement, said you'd cut us in? Didn't you do that? Where's our piece at?" Solomon stopped flailing his left arm and pointed to ten cartons hidden underneath the clothes-folding table. "I'm gonna let you go, muthafucka. You walk over to them boxes and bring me what you owe. I'm trustin you, so you be a good coon." I let go his throat and Solomon fell to the tile. He coughed until I popped him on the shoulder. "Come on, muthafucka. Let's finish this shit. Gimme my cut. Fifty packs. Count um out slow so I know it's here like it's supposed to be."

Solomon tumbled across the room and sorted the cigarette packs, stuffing them into three cartons. When he was done, he offered the cut with his left hand. I peeked the shank shining in the right before he could stand. Wasn't me swinging on him then; no, that rod just crashed into his jaw on its own. He slumped, dropped with the cartons. I grabbed his collar again and red trickles dripped as lead beat into his scalp.

"What's my name?"

"What, muthafucka?"

"J.C., damnit. That's my name. Say it!" The blood turned black as it trickled over his skin. "What's my name?"

"J.C."

"What's my name?"

"J. . . . C."

"What's my name?"

"J.C., damnit."

Like Mookie's, my arm swung, and the bed leg cut that laundry room air hard and with rhythm, bringing screams from the welcher. My mind flashed to 47th Street, Willie and Julius, Soul Mamma, Tony Ricci, Christina, Sermon, Black, Grandma Rose, then the face of a girl I didn't know really. Sweet young face. Seeing her, backed by Mookie's T-Bird on the corner of King Drive, brought me to dragging Solomon across the floor, slamming his head between my shoe and the laundry room wall. "Trusted you, muthafucka. You said no funny shit."

"Didn't say a fuckin thing . . ."

The security whistle sounded as his head bounced against concrete once more. I took Solomon's stash from under the table, stuffing extra into my pants. Snatched what I could even if they weren't Salems, claimed them for myself because I didn't fear no goddamn body.

They stormed the room, flashlights on his bloody head, then on me. The whistling guard snatched my arms as the other put me in the same sleeper I'd used on Solomon.

"Block D, cell two!" he yelled.

They lifted me by the throat, but we were on the same side, so they wouldn't take me to solitary. They were doing their job, putting up a front for watching eyes. They dropped me in my cage and walked off with the cartons—Vinnie Povich would get his cut. We were on the same side, so they didn't take the squares I'd stuffed in my drawers.

I sat on the cot, rocking north to south, thinking of the faces from the Forties, Solomon's blood on my shoe and hands, the bed rod I'd lost. I heard a whisper from the next cage. "What happened?"

"Go to sleep, muthafucka."

Wasn't long before the sound of Jamie's junkie snore took the place of his whisper. I thought to bury myself under the prison pillow, but there was no rest from the faces. So I kept rocking.

The man's word was good. Vinnie gave me his protection like Nate promised, and my stay in the joint was smooth after the Solomon job. Came about more work through Nate—the Block D nigger collector, they called me. Vinnie took over Solomon's cigarette racket, sent thanks through Nate, and I never mopped another cafeteria floor. No Stones or Disciples bothered me, no guards looked my way cross-eyed. Solomon never tried revenge (at least not on me—shanked up the whistling guard real nice, though, sliced him left ear to throat then back to the right). Crazy Jaime even offered a piece of the dope action to keep the guards from squeezing him. True, when I traveled the yard, I was alone. And nobody came for Sunday visits, but that was all right, cause I didn't need any faces on the other side of dividing glass. I'd found profit inside my cage.

* * *

I took GED classes in the prison library during my education phase. I remembered Grandma Rose bragging to her lady friends at Ebenezer about how I'd graduated high school. More than the job lies or lace window curtains or any gold Cadillac, it was schooling that made Grandma sound proud, proved that she'd done right raising me. After breaking her heart (old woman found out everything at my trial—how I'd run from Phillips High, and beat, and killed, and stole, everything), I figured to at least come home with something to show for those years. To prove I wasn't a waste of the woman's blood and time, I'd bring a diploma back to 45th Street.

Every day for six months, between ten A.M. and noon, I went off to the "Decatur Information Room," which was what the liberal warden called his library, and listened to folks talk on about the same nonsense they'd been talking on about since before we'd left Phillips. I listened and I wrote and added and subtracted, and I read. That Information Room was something else, held more books than any of the other Illinois prisons—sign at the door said so for proof. More books than the Kenwood neighborhood library Grandma Rose'd took me to on her cleaning rounds as a boy, more than our Phillips High library far as I could remember. By the time six months had passed, I swore I'd read half of them all, read enough to pass their test flying and prove I was what they called a "functioning literate." Showed them all, yeah, got my GED diploma on September 13, 1972. I prayed to Jesus the night before graduation, asked Him to tell Grandma about me finishing school. The Lord said He'd do it for me, too, said Grandma Rose was proud, whether she'd be there to say it or not.

Me and Jaime smoked a Sherm stick in the furnace room that morning, got high as the sky above, so high I was the last man alive. Just me and my GED and an old woman's pride. It was worth it in the end, I figured. By the start of graduation I was up so high all I could see in the crowd was Grandma Rose. That was her for sure, my smoked-out brain told me. Sitting there with the rest of Block D, right between the whistling guard and Nate Hill.

Liberal warden let us GED graduates visit the Information Room much as we liked after graduation, seeing as we were his reformed inmates, all educated and shit. Took time to get the hang of making sense of so much writing without coming on a headache, though—Salvie'd never put much business on paper on the strip, and what he did was second-grade stupid. But I ran across a few books on famous Blacks that kept my attention, seeing as I'd never heard the names before: Garvey, Du Bois, Robeson, Washington, Wright.

Read a book on slaves, by Frederick Douglass, talking about how Black folk dropped to their knees and ripped crops out of the ground in that southern sun, and if they didn't get down fast enough or rip up much as master expected, he'd whip them till their backs bled; how that was all they could do to keep themselves from dying off. Only place they could hide from the sun burning on those whip slashes was close to master's big house, in the shade it cast down from master's hill. But if he caught you too close to his big house and you weren't a house nigga, then he'd chase you down—and you'd be running fast, because you didn't want to feel no more parts of his rawhide whipping. Master'd keep chasing, though, until your legs had no more run left and you'd fall out at the end of his field, where he'd string you to the nearest tree. Take his whip to those old black scars healing on your back and tear them open. Teach your no-good ass better than thinking you were about to get too close to him, then try to get away. "Fool nigger," he'd scream as rawhide cut fresh rips and left a puddle of your mamma and daddy's blood up under swollen feet, there in the tree shade.

Then, when he got tired of fucking around with you, he sold you on to the next field; if you didn't care for your new master, figured him for not treating you good as the old, you could always run. Try escape again. Such was the slave's life in that southern sun: running, getting chased, searching for free life, only to find there was just so far to go until you were tied against the tree with a Mississippi lesson slicing up your skin. But in the end, Douglass said, Black slaves would come up and reach that shade they was looking for, away from master's big house and his hill, because they had no choice but to find it if they kept running. No choice, in the end.

When I finished that book, I moved on to what I knew something about already: Grandma's Bible. So much scripture between those covers, Sermon would've loved it. Holy this, hail that, alleluia. Didn't learn much of anything there that I didn't already know, but it wasn't bad all in all. Functional literacy helped pass the time between collections on Block D.

It was the security of the man that'd saved me from prison's forever, though. I was supposed to be serving hard time. Please. The months became like blinks of the eye; the years, breaths took while I slept. Sometimes the days went on and on, but so what? Eventually, the sun went down. I had Vinnie to thank, because with him, my sentence didn't mean a thing but words on paper. Nowhere to go, nothing to fear, just living somewhere between the scripture.

* * *

I'd took on a liking for Loomis—not a fairy, hard-up prison liking, just dug talking to the cat. We were meeting once every other week by then, our hours cut down by half. In fact, it was around the same time I'd started to look forward to sitting in his funky little space that he shortened up on the meetings. Nate said the cutback was a good thing, meant the process'd figured you to be in need of just a bit more socialization, and well on the way to freedom.

Loomis'd learned to put up with me using that word, *nigga,* even. Said it was because the only way reintegration could help was if it dealt with me in the way I chose to see myself, in the words I used to talk about myself, and went from there. Any other way and they'd be trying to change somebody who didn't exist, some nursery rhyme negro who the process'd dreamed up for itself. If I called myself *nigga,* then that was how I saw myself, and the only person who could change me was me, whenever I got ready to change me. What, I wouldn't walk, talk, think, look, and get looked at like a nigga anymore if I didn't let *nigga* slip out of my mouth? Not where I was from, no sir, not back in the Forties, not even inside a Decatur cage did that hold true. Loomis had to respect me for the real me then. I liked him more for putting it that way, even if he'd took that acceptance shit out of a book he'd read at the university.

After those first few years, meetings came down to once every six to nine months, which was fine if it meant I was on my way. As long as I didn't forget it was a con in the end, no doubt, no matter how much I liked talking, an evil con because it was all part of their prison hustle. We met because somebody'd said it had to be, not because it was true. Nothing was true about the hustle: socializing criminals so they'd come right back to the state pen as educated hustlers who'd committed bigger crimes after learning the skills without integrating into freedom. The game was simple. The psychological part went on until they were done fucking with you, education until you were done fucking with them, and reintegration ended when fucking time in the cage was up, which was never.

"Figured out what my name stands for."

Loomis' face showed those doubt-filled wrinkles. "What?"

"My name. Remember you asked me what the letters stood for? Long time ago?"

He flipped through my file, found the page he wanted, full of ink turned black against faded paper. "You know how long it's been since we talked about that? Back then, you told me J.C. didn't stand for anything. Just the two letters. What happened?"

"Been thinking," I said as my eyes ran from Loomis' wall. "It does stand for a real name. Got to."

"So what is your name, J.C.?"

"Was looking up at the sky one day, out in the yard, man, and something I saw up there"—the nebbish scribbled—"told me that the nigga who laid my mamma twenty-five years ago came up with my name, gave it to me because he knew what he wanted his son to do in life. Knew what I was gonna be. He named me Jesus Christ. Grandma Rose was such a Baptist, she couldn't ever twist up her lips to say it, though, didn't want to go about blaspheming her Lord. Grandma couldn't even believe the daughter she'd gave birth to'd took to such sin in life herself. So it was the old lady who started calling me J.C., short for my true name."

"Jesus Christ?" The words came from Loomis' lips squeezed through a smile. Not his sarcastic Anglo sneer, but pitiful smiling.

He'd figured me as more crazy than conning. "What'd you see up there that told you Jesus was your name?"

"Nothing," I said. Loomis couldn't send me back to the goat-haired shrink unless there was some kind of an emergency—if I'd threatened to kill myself, maybe or, better still, kill him. Too many cats waiting for the process in cages to worry about starting me over at step one. "Looked up there and couldn't see a damn thing. No clouds, no heaven, no God, just a clean sky. Then it spoke, that nothing, told me the truth—my name is Jesus Christ Rose."

Loomis scribbled so hard, I swore the pen'd crack. "The sky spoke to you?"

"The nothing up in the sky. It did."

His smile blinked away. "I don't know if you're playing games, pulling my chain or what. I don't know—I usually can tell, but I can't right now." He took the glasses from the round face and rubbed his eyeballs. "You need help if you're serious about what you're telling me, and I can get it for you if you ask. Nothing but a matter of filling out the right forms."

"What help?" I sneered, and my lips cracked, stretched thin like so.

"I can get you into clinical therapy, the kind of counseling you'd have trouble accessing outside these walls. Now, if you're just clowning around, then your grandmother is correct indeed. That is blasphemy, Mister Rose."

"Blaspheming?" I laughed at Loomis like I never laughed at Grandma Rose—would've caught one of the old woman's Arkansas beat-downs for making such a noise—deep from in my stomach and loud to fill up his office space. "When'd I say I don't believe in the man? Didn't even say I don't worship or respect him. All I said was my father named me after him. What blasphemy?"

"You're taking His name in vain, Mister Rose. I'm going to assume that you're just trying to get a rise out of me," because everything was about them in the end, those Anglos. Just then all the liking I'd felt for Loomis disappeared. "Going to assume you don't mean what you say in a serious sense. To speak of Jesus in jest is sinful."

"That ain't true, man," I said. I'd come up with questions by 1973, and time led me to some kind of answers. Enough answers that Salvies and Loomises and Manleys and Decatur guards, none of them could outhustle me. "Taking God's name in vain is a sin, not Jesus'. Nowhere in the Good Book does it say talking of Jesus in vain is wrong. Because it's not. So I ain't doing anything, and my father—maybe he wasn't shit but a bastard motherfucker in every single other kind of way, but he wasn't doing no wrong by giving me this name. No different than naming me Washington or Jefferson or Lincoln or something."

"It is different, sir," and his sneer turned higher, more hateful, than I'd seen it before, high up into his cheek. "Jesus is God. That's in the Bible. Perhaps you need to read a bit closer. I can let you borrow my King James edition if you're in need of a proper translation."

"God is God, too far gone to even question, and ain't nobody else Him. Jesus was just a nigga, like me and you." He squinted—I'd shot all his acceptance of the word *nigga* to hell then and there. "Just like me."

"That is sacrilege," he said. Loomis spun his chair to the flag so I was looking at the side of his head. "Your grandmother is Baptist, you say. I'm Episcopalian. Your talk rings foul in our ears, Mister Rose. I'm sure she wouldn't want to hear you speaking these things."

After the W, the P was the most important part of being WASP, according to Salvie—not a close second, because that skin was mighty above all things. But God was no joke to a Protestant. They had to show thanks to Him who'd given them all their W. "I never said I wasn't a Baptist, man. Grandma took me to church every Sunday. I ain't saying nothing bad about Jesus. His name is the same name as mine, is all."

"I've seen a lot of young men, young colored boys, coming under the influence of Muslims behind bars. It's true across the nation in our prisons. That's where they get you, when you're locked up. Have you joined the Black Muslims, Mister Rose?"

It'd took me almost three years, but I noticed at the front end of Loomis' Christian tale, right before the frame border, a second set of footprints. Just two marks in the sand. I hadn't seen them before because they didn't fade or trickle off, just ended at the edge before the main prints marched alone into sea water. "I ain't no Muslim—told you I was raised Baptist."

"So explain it to me. Tell me why you're Jesus Christ."

"You're not listening. Never said I was him, just said Jesus is my name. I ain't like him yet. I can be, but I ain't."

"Oh really?" Loomis turned my way and burned.

"I read the Bible, man, I know what's really written there, not what some preacher pretends to be there for his own good. Old Testament doesn't say a word about God sending a son down to open up the gates of heaven; all that was made up in the New Book to explain Jesus dying early, before he'd really done shit but some magic tricks. Savior was supposed to come and save God's people from living foul lives on earth, but the Jews killed Jesus before he could do a damn thing about that. Besides, if God closed the gates of heaven Himself, how come He had to send His own son just to die and open them back up? Why didn't He just swing the gates opposite the same way He'd closed them up, save his own son the trouble of hanging on that cross?"

"I don't know," Loomis said.

"Only great thing Jesus did before dying was bringing up that one cat: Lazarus. That's what a savior was supposed to do, save niggas' lives. Old Testament says so. He pointed the way for Lazarus right out of that cave. Cave wasn't but a tomb, Jesus knew, and everybody else knew—except for Lazarus. When you're up inside, it's too dark for you to see one way or the other where you're at. So old boy needed Jesus to show him out of there. You've got to give the nigga his credit—he *was* a special nigga, that Jesus. No way I'm blaspheming him."

"You're serious?" Loomis put the glasses back on, soothing his stare's green burn.

"Yeah, I'm serious. Wouldn't say it if I wasn't. J.C. stands for Jesus Christ, no doubt. You about to write that down or what?"

Loomis didn't speak for a minute, just tapped his pen against wood. "That's my job. Is this your way of seeking out help?"

"Help me save a nigga? You can do that?"

When I'd sit with Loomis afterwards, a third picture hung on his wall, between *Footprints* and the new governor and just above the American flag. He'd found himself a framed portrait of Jesus—Jesus with Hollywood blue eyes and a flat face with no lips, no lips but a mouth turned up into a proud smile. And the same sun that shined on the office from the *Footprints* beach shined behind his Jesus, so the outline glowed. Loomis hung that picture on his wall, I figured, there in the blink of his lamp's shadow just so I'd understand what it took to save a dead man from forever in the darkest cave.

14

GRANDMA ROSE IS GONE." It was Mookie's first visit in years, but I couldn't see his face anymore. His words took away sight, soaked my eyes until I was blind. I dropped the receiver and banged my head against the glass divider until I could see again. And I looked into a hole. It wasn't in front of me, didn't have anything to do with Mookie, or the Decatur guards, or the poor folk who'd come to see their cousins locked in cages, or the divider, or the sight of my face reflected in glass. Heard words coming from the hole, but I didn't speak back. Couldn't tell whose words they were even, barely heard what they said. I looked up in the hole and paid mind only to Grandma's smile, the pride dripping from her eyes. She fixed my prison collar, kissed my scars. I thanked her and bit my lips so I wouldn't cry too, bit until I tasted blood, but it didn't help. Tears came anyway.

"You need me to leave the car, Grandma? Mookie can pick me up."

"Naw, boy, you go on. You got somewhere you in a rush to be, gonna need your car to get you there."

"You sure, ma'am?"

"Course I'm sure, J.C. You got somethin to do."

Mamma gave me birth in south Georgia, when she was fourteen years old. She'd ran down there with a man who claimed love for her, some little nigger who left her in the swamp once her belly poked with new life. When she decided she couldn't raise a baby boy on her own—not between drinking and sexing—she spent her last spare change to ride a Greyhound back to Chicago, where she dropped me with Grandma Rose and went on her way. That was 1950. I hadn't seen the woman, my mamma, since.

But Grandma Rose brought me up good, good as she could've working for the Board of Education. Not a teacher, just scrubbing floors and serving up hot lunches. She did teach me how to take care of myself, how to worship the Lord on Sunday, and to be as nice a colored boy as I could. But I'd always known she would leave one day. My daddy spilled his seed and split the swamp, Mamma brought me to the Forties and dropped me off before booking out, so Grandma Rose would run, too. And she did, left me twice; never came to visit in Decatur, then dropped dead before they let me free. I'd known it.

"Naw, boy, I ain't gettin into none of your car. I know what you do now. I know what you is, boy. You the Black devil, like Reverend Goode talk bout. Down in hell. That's how you afforded that fine car, how you got these curtains and rugs and this crystal shackle round my wrist. Take these things hence, boy, make not mine house an house of evil. I know what you is. Don't waste your blasphemous tears on me, just keep walkin on your sinful path and know I ain't never gonna be beside you. Leave me, boy, I belong to God. I ain't gettin into none of your car."

"But Grandma, I'm not the devil anymore, I got my GED. I know my name's Jesus now. . . ."

Grandma dripped away and I saw Mookie on the glass's free side. I didn't know what he was saying, couldn't pick up the phone receiver.

So I read his lips. "What you want me to do, J.C.?"

I wiped my eyes and shrugged, turned away. I cried again as I left the visiting room, because no matter what she said in dying, Grandma Rose hadn't raised me to be no Black devil inside of a hole.

* * *

My secret place helped get me through. Of course, since the secret was on their prison yard, it really wasn't hidden from shit—I was still locked inside those walls. I called the yard's far end mine only because it was the one place where the sniper guard couldn't put his scope on me. The secret place was behind his tower, at an angle too steep for a clean shot. If I didn't have squares to smoke, I'd sit there and forget the place around me, just stare at the sky.

Every other Decatur corner was closed by steel or cement, except up high; liberal warden didn't have the building blocks to make a ceiling blocking the sky. So I looked up there and saw freedom. The blue—which was heaven, Jaime mumbled at night between snoring—the clouds, the sun, the rain when it drizzled, the snow when it was cold, I saw all of it. The state'd fucked up giving me a place to peep free life, especially while I sat where their rifle couldn't take aim. Hadn't run across one peaceful thing about Decatur, but up there I found security. If only He'd gave me wings so I could escape to the blue and the clouds and the sun, I would've known good enough to use them, flown right past the man. I saw clear, too, and Nate'd spoke the truth years before. That was Vinnie Povich in the sniper tower; he was the man. But what could Vinnie do about an escape on wings?

I laid on the ground, wondered how long I'd have to fly to get away from that place. I whistled when I thought of it, not because there was forever between me and freedom, but because I was near the end. I saw God in those clouds, far above Povich. Heard Him calling my name, too, so I sat up and reached for glory. But all I felt was the wind blowing against fingertips. And when I looked again, only the man on high peered back. He didn't put his rifle on me, didn't have to. Just caught my eye, and held it to make sure I knew he stood between the prison yard and His blue heaven.

* * *

Loomis still tried to find me help after Grandma passed. Worked it out so I could take college courses through the university's Adult Continuing Education Directive program. ACED was an optional experiment, which meant they couldn't force me to go, and there was no penalty for quitting. The university just wanted guinea pig convicts in search of higher learning. So Loomis signed us up for Saturday classes taught in the commissary: me, a couple of Irish sharks, a biker heroin pusher, and some Jew-boy fences (because we were the cons with the head smarts). He said that I'd connected education with Grandma Rose, so continuing the process could only bring me to heal from the grieving. Plus, college was the highest form of socialization, and what better could a bunch of jailbirds get out of Decatur than high socialization? It was the last step of his process hustle, but he was trying to look out the only way he knew how to look out, and if college learning took away time I otherwise spent thinking of things I couldn't do a damn thing about, things too far beyond me, then it was a good thing.

I took three ACED classes in the commissary: algebra, preindustrial American history, and English composition. Algebra, I quit after three Saturdays. Arithmetic'd always been just fine with me, I'd liked messing around with numbers back at Phillips. But once that foreign exchange TA from the university got to adding and subtracting letters and lines, math stopped making any kind of good sense. How could such claptrap be put to use in the socialized world? And history was slow as ever, kept me no more interested than the hum inside Mister Manley's classroom walls. Better to not know the how, when, and why behind the world and instead live in it for what it was, in all its mighty funk. Quit preindustrial American history six weeks into the thing, just before the midterm test on emancipation.

I did finish English composition. Reading and writing had purpose in the world—couldn't be socialized if you weren't a fully functional literate, like the liberal warden said—and, because it had purpose, it mattered. The shit was hard; wrote a new paper every other Saturday, and on the off weeks, we'd rewrite the paper we'd just done, or plan an essay for next class. The first few class meetings, I'd come about headaches like to kill me, worse than ones I'd get reading in the Information Room. Too many words, not enough space in my brain to hold on to them without pain. Headache would stay with me for two, maybe three hours after class ended. Only thing to make it go away was catching a nap under a corner stairway or in my secret place. But then I'd dream and all the words would get to jumping around inside my head, and the hurt'd come right back.

Would've quit English on the very same Saturday that I walked out of Algebra, but the teacher had us debating in class and I was arguing with one of the fences, and I used a word on him from my dreams. The blank look on his face and his mumbled comeback let the whole class know that I'd whipped him good, just by using that word: I'd called his argument "mendacious." Wasn't even sure what I'd said—and neither were the rest of them, they just tripped off the way the shiny word rolled from my lips, "men-DAY-shus"—until I looked it up in the Information Room dictionary later. The root of *mendacious* was *mendicant*, which was a poor man, and the word itself meant "full of lies."

Loomis was big on talking up English studies, too. Reading and writing were the end-all of being human. The act of swallowing information and spitting it back out made people more powerful than the animals and fishes, creating civilizations in words and announcing their rule over the land and sea just as it was written in Genesis. And for me, having language to read and write would let me finish the thoughts I bounced through the darkness and against bars. Language would make my thoughts real thoughts. He gave me a journal to carry around Decatur and catch those notions, catch and record them so I could reflect on the time once I was free.

During our next two meetings, he asked if I cared to share my writing. But I hadn't put a damn thing down, didn't even know where to start, so I told him he couldn't see nothing; my writing was private, I told him. The third time he asked, more than a year after the first, he told me to set the journal on his desk during our session, and he opened the cover and flipped through those clean white pages while I looked away, or he hypnotized me so I wouldn't know he was checking through the book right in my face. Whatever, Loomis hustled me somehow, because at the meeting's regular ending time, he stood from his chair and walked around the desk. Said that I should stay in his office for a half hour by myself to think and write—"continue my entries," he said, sneering in his WASP way. Then he sharpened two pencils and put them next to the journal, and left me.

For fifteen minutes, I stared at the dingy walls, then the growing mess of papers in his corners, and at *Footprints*, looking for something else new in the wise tale. Five minutes passed, and I'd tapped the pencil against cheap wood, bringing those *rat-tat-tat* noises with each hit like a frustrated nebbish, until the lead cracked. Then I looked at the governor and the flag and the pencil sharpener on top of Loomis' black file cabinet, and at the Hollywood Lord, though I knew there was nothing new in those things, and I thought about animals and fishes and civilization and the Good Book and Grandma. I put Loomis' second pencil to paper and wrote, *My name is Jesus Christ Rose. . . .*

15

THEIR EYES MADE ME WORRY. Had the lawyer paid them? He said he did, but I saw no freedom in those stares. Four judges sat peering down from a bench and across the wooden wall separating me and the counselor from the set of windows high above us. They'd shoot me if I made quick moves, like the sniper tower guard, kill me if I tried to escape. That was their message. I sat in front of the kin of the same bastard who'd sentenced me to live behind bars in the first place, begging them for parole. Sat there knowing I'd serve the rest of my seven and a half years, and have no choice but to be happy about it. And when they let me out in September of 1984, they'd keep a cot hot for my return. My black ass would be back, see, and none too soon.

Living around 47th Street hustling had taught me to pay attention not to the words coming from mouths but to those from eyes. The ice in the judges' stares left their talk empty, said that they hadn't come to grant free wings. There was no heaven for second-degree murderers, payoffs or not. My lawyer had delivered my ten G's from the stash Mookie was holding for me. And? Did they give him a receipt for my parole? What could we do when they said "no chance, nigger convict"? Complain that we'd come up with the right amount, greased the powerful palms, so what was I doing behind bars still? Ask where my justice was because, hell, I'd paid cash dollars for it?

Who would we file our complaint with? With the same clan I sat before then, of course, to those who'd convicted, jailed and conned me already. Where else was there to turn for freedom?

"Do you place value on human life, Mister Rose? Have you learned to respect another's right to live?"

I caught the only female's gaze, held it like I'd held Salvie's and Angelo's and Paulo's when they'd driven me to the Styx. I wasn't afraid, wasn't about to run from any of them. "I give nothing else on earth more worth than life. It's God's greatest gift. Only He has the right to take it from us."

"So you have remorse for your actions, Mister Rose?" Twenty-five hundred dollars apiece had kept the others' mouths shut. But the beige, gray-haired lady—definite Jew—with the see-through righteousness, she gave me some kind of a fit.

"Remorse?"

"Yes, remorse, Mister Rose. You're sorry for committing murder, taking God's greatest gift, as you call it, from another human being? You regret your crime?"

I turned to my lawyer, David Peters, to his banana-peel skin and curly hair, his blue single-breast with the plain silk tie and rich handkerchief creeping from the breast pocket (it'd been so long since they'd let me dress proper). "Tell them you're sad about taking the life of another man," he whispered. "Say you're sorry, mention God again. You're asking Him for forgiveness, what have you."

"Yes, remorse. Great remorse. Didn't understand the words you used, is all," I said, though I did understand her. I did. "But yes, of course I'm sorry about killing that man. I think about it every day, wished I'd never raised a gun against anybody. I just pray God'll forgive me, have mercy on my soul."

"May I humbly enter into the record, to remind the esteemed panel," Peters interrupted, his voice swallowing the fog in the hearing room, "that this man whom Mister Rose was convicted of murdering was himself wanted for an attempted homicide. That the individual presented a threat of bodily harm to Mister Rose, was publicly attacking my client as the weapon was discharged. May I remind the board to take into consideration this evidence from Mister Rose's trial?"

"The facts of Mister Rose's conviction have been reviewed prior to this hearing, as have the files from the state's psychologists and social workers and the transcripts from his continuing education," the judge said. She pointed to the reporter. "Record that."

I leaned to the lawyer, whispered at the side of his face. "What is this going down here? This ain't what I bought, joe. Did she get her cut or what?"

"It has to look legitimate. Play the game, J.C."

"Mister Rose, we've heard you mention the word *God* several times," the fourth judge said, voice wheezing into my ears. "Have you found religion during this period of your incarceration?"

I smiled the good-negro grin me and Peters had been working on, full teeth and all. "Definitely. That's been the biggest gift to come from my time in prison, that and my education. I've had the chance to think of God, read the Bible, become a strong Christian, a schooled Christian"—*between shaking down cigarette pushers for the in-house Mafia, jagging myself off to white women in* Playboy, *and paying you people kickbacks*—"I mean, I've always believed, but Decatur has given me time to understand Him. I have a good relationship with the Lord now. He has a plan for everybody, and a plan for me. I know that."

"Good, good," the fourth judge wheezed. "Faith is an important thing. It gets you through the dark times, having faith in something."

"Amen," the judge to his left mumbled. "Amen to that."

"How are you going to live?" Who'd lied to the woman, told her she was the virgin motherfucker? "You have an idea for employment? What kind of future has your God planned for you, Mister Rose?"

I glanced at Peters out of the corners of my eyes without turning from her. "It'll be rough, I know that much. Finding work ain't an easy thing for an ex-convict. That's the way of the world. If justice fails, you don't get caught for doing wrong, and you keep a pearly smile on your face, piles of cash in your bank accounts. If justice works, you serve your due time, then you go around begging for work without a nickel in your pocket, no food, nothing. Problem is, justice fails more times than it works—that's how it seems where I'm from." Peters hit my leg and I went back to the script. "I've looked into the different ways out there for me to make a good living. For a while I'll sweep and mop, poor man's jobs. But I got my GED during my time, and I'm going to learn how to use these hands in the world, pick up a trade. There is good work there, you see. If Jesus can cut wood for a living, I'm not too proud to do the same as a man, am I? That's what's laid out for me, ma'am. God'll balance the scales in the end. . . . I took nine hours of college classes during my time, you know?"

"You enrolled in nine," she said. "The record reflects that you completed three."

Her words slammed the hearing room walls once they were done setting me straight. They were the one answer needed to all questions asked: killing, beating, gambling and thieving didn't matter. Dropping algebra and preindustrial American history told all the story that needed telling on me.

"But I finished English composition," I hustled, "the hardest."

She looked confused. Figured I'd stomped her, broke myself free, but the second judge, the cat with the pointy mustache, picked up where she ran dry. "Your sentiments are encouraging, Mister Rose. You sound like a better man through your reformation. But what we're concerned about this morning, what's most important for the well-being and safety of the people of Illinois, is for us to establish whether you understand your specific wrong deeds, and whether you'll repeat them. Why, then, did you kill in 1969? And what's going to stop you from killing again in 1977?"

Bastard'd got me. Ten G's gone to waste, seven and a half more years to be served. God'd balance the scales, but what about my life? I'd burn in prison flames, and they'd make sure of it. Garvey and Robeson, those cats I'd read about in the joint's library—much better niggas than I ever was—they'd sent them to hell for knowing truth.

I'd believed fate offered me something different because I'd paid up front? Who was I? The Block B Muslims said it—the man only cared for us as slaves, running and sweating in the southern sun, or tied to a tree waiting for the slice of master's whip. I wasn't acting like I knew that truth myself. Acting like another know-nothing, hypocrite negro instead, hoping against the way it was since back in Exodus time. Blue eyes spoke, told me how stupid I was for believing years served and a few dollars made me educated and reintegrated, a man ready for freedom. They'd reformed me instead into a nigga who paid master to let him escape from the fields, a nigga who wrote it all down in a journal as he ran. A bribing, conning, hustled, educated, literate slave chasing his own ass back to master's hill. I tried living it their way—Rose's, Manley's, Jesus', judges' good way—I tried, but found no sense in such life.

So fuck it. What am I gonna do if you parole me? What do God have planned for me? Lemme tell you, you and missus judge over there. I'm gonna ride up and down 47th Street in my gold Caddy all day, dawn to dark, wavin at the tramps and laughin at the losers. And, when the night comes, you'll find me at Soul Mamma's VIP booth or at Miss Nelly's best seat, blowin smoke at the employees and wavin my new .45. And I'm gonna laugh, cause everybody in the joint, everybody on the strip, every muthafuckin body on the South Side'll fear J.C. Rose. When I'm done with that, I'm headin to my new pad, rent paid outta my cut from the policy and street shakedowns we pull for Salvie's Outfit. Little Christina'll be waitin for me there. And I'm gonna bend that fourteen-year-ol whore—naw, it's 1977 like you say, so she's grown-up by now, knows all the tricks—over, gaze on her beautiful black ass. And I'm gonna take it out on her, go into her, cause she left me to dream about pictures of white Playmates for seven years, take it out on her even if she ain't fourteen no more. She's learned to scream by now, just like Mookie said Mora use to do, and it's makin me smile again, her screams. I'm gonna be thinkin bout you though, missus judge, thinkin of you as that little Black girl hollers. I'm so used to dreamin bout white cunts, I won't be able to help it. But in the end, this ain't bout you or Christina, 47th Street or Soul Mamma or Salvie's Outfit. It's bout me, just me and my cash stash. There ain't even no more Mookie, cause soon as I get out, I'm killin that muthafucka. That's how much worth I put into God's greatest gift, this life you asked me bout. That's what He has planned for me in free blue heaven. Don't worry, I'm gonna make it all right in this world of yours. I know the hustle.

"God, sir. He'll keep me from repeating my crimes in the free world. It was because of my lack of knowledge of Him that I killed before, you could say. I didn't know the Lord back then. If I had, I would never have taken a life. My faith wouldn't let me get away with that."

* * *

They gave me freedom. I didn't care why, figured ten G's overpowered the judgment behind the eyes. "My client thanks you with all sincerity." Peters, the same jive turkey ambulance chaser who'd bought my reduced sentence and conned the state out of pressing weapons charges on me years back, jumped from his seat in praise. "We have true gratitude for this justice."

"Mmh," was all I said. On the strip, a hustler kept his game face on until he'd put the dice down for good and left the circle with his winnings. Salvie'd preached that.

My last day in Decatur, I stood next to a gray door. I'd taken inch-by-inch steps through that same door back in September '69. But I paced left to right at the end, took the longest stretches my legs would allow, and between each, I giggled. I'd wanted to talk to Loomis before leaving, tell him goodbye or to kiss my ass or something, but the guards wouldn't let me near his office. Said he was busy starting some cat from Block A on reintegration.

I didn't move too far from prison yet. The further I was from the building, the better the man in the high tower could aim his rifle. They wouldn't get me, I couldn't let them, not after our deal'd been made, "consummated," like Peters said. Too late for welching. I looked at blue heaven and the sniper peered back. "Fuck you," I mouthed. He didn't aim his rifle, though. It was too late, so he peered on, and I waited.

As that fancy white car—not the T-Bird convertible that'd left me on 47th Street, but a new, funny-shaped ride—rolled to the gate, I ran from the cage. Too fast for the man to shoot me down, I ran. Like the football hero I'd always worshiped, with young girls cheering in the stands happy for my freedom. The gate opened slow, gave Mookie time to step out of his car and show me what he'd become over the years. He looked fine, rich suit and polished steppers, with a crisp handkerchief triangle like my lawyer. He'd moved up in the world.

The gate was open. I ran to him, hugged my brother, my man, for he was all I could touch to feel new freedom. His body was too warm for killing just yet, but I looked over his wide shoulders as I held on, at the sun hanging above us. From there came warmth, not from Mookie, that was what I told myself. I hated it. So, so much I hated that warmth.

4

16

THIS LIFE'S still all about countin. Ain't never come across nothin like the feel of bills between the fingers. Twenties and fifties and C-notes so smooth. Look at um, the gray faces passin by, gangsters in their own right, gangsters in their own time. I hear these crackers countin with me—"nine thousand eight hundred and twenty, nine thousand eight hundred and seventy," we say. Smooth bills. Look at the numbers. Ain't never been good with math, not unless I was countin my own loot. And this money ain't even mine no more, not with J.C. comin outta the joint today. All these years of wages from Salvie and Tommy Ricci, all these bills. "Nine thousand eight hundred and ninety."

Sure ain't no thirty grand here, though. That's the kinda scratch the little man's gonna be lookin for, knowin how good a head he's got for keepin track of figures. I know he been tabbin five C-notes on the first of every month since they locked his ass up. Countin careful, too, like the bills was right there between his thumb and fourth fingertip. But hell, things come up, he's gotta understand. Cash's gonna get spent when it's sittin around for seven and a half years. What else it's supposed to do, collect dust in a office wall? Some jive fool from the strip woulda stole it by now not for my spendin. What good would that've done him?

Most of what's gone got spent on J.C. in a roundabout way

anyhow. When Grandma Rose passed, I had to flip the cost on buryin her. Ain't no chance Mister Shipp's funeral bill was comin outta my own pockets, no chance. And when that shady lawyer came shakin me down for cash to get J.C. outta the pen, I paid him all of fifteen G's. Yeah, that muthafucka was shakin me down, I saw it in his beady, bourgie eyes. I paid him off, though, had to. What else was I gonna do, let J.C. rot in there for another seven years? That money definitely got spent on him, nothin he can argue about.

Maybe I woulda left J.C. in the joint if I'd thought I had a chance to get away with it. But 1984 was still comin and they woulda let his little ass outta there, and what did Black use to say about what go round and all that? "Nine thousand nine hundred and forty."

The rest, I don't know where it went to. If so much of Salvie's loot had disappeared while I was handlin it, where would I be? Silly question, silly enough for only Willie Banks, Leroy Cross, or tall Henry to answer. I do recall buyin mirrors for Soul Mamma's office. Don't know how much they cost for sure—a lot, that's all I recollect. Ain't like I had to run to a bank account and take out my own loot to pay for um. Spin sixty-six, thirteen, eighteen on the wall safe and it's been here for me. Easy cash. And yeah, I used the money for some miscellaneous nothin over the years: a few suits, took Mora to Vegas, handled Geri's rent, got winter boots for Isaiah, a lotta miscellaneous nothin far as J.C.'s concerned. So his share wasn't spent all on him really. Can't even lie to myself no more.

But it was my right to spend, shoulda been my loot any goddamn way. Been me handlin business at the club, handlin shit on the street, by myself all these years while the little man's sat on his ass behind bars, gettin fed and livin for free off the state. Shoulda been my loot, goddamnit. If he hadn't been in the joint, would he've spent all these cents on himself? Scratch woulda ended up goin to miscellaneous nothin somehow, cause that's how niggas is, buyin and sellin themselves for nothin. He should be a happy ex-con, should feel lucky. Most come out the joint with no stash at all, like Nate Hill. Come out and the only thing waitin for um is a slug to the skull on 43rd Street.

Hell, J.C.'s been blessed—I only spent most of his scratch, not all of it, and he's still just about rich for a cat from these Forties. "Nine thousand nine hundred and ninety."

I look at myself in the office mirror before I leave out. There's a long drive to Decatur ahead, so I gotta make for certain I'm lookin good. Got on the best European-cut money—mine or J.C.'s money, I don't recall—can buy. Gained a bit of weight, not too much considerin I'm gettin up close to thirty now. But they tailored these threads perfect, just right to hide the belly. That's good, keeps me from lookin fat as I am: I come to expect it, cause them Europeans know it all when it come to threads. I pat my head, let my hand roll with the waves. Like the flow of the Ricci boy's black afro, my curls look. But he's a gimp now, so I really want my do to look like his ol man's, like a European crown. That's what I want. I straighten my tie, fold the handkerchief into a triangle, and slide it into my coat pocket. Remember to pull it out enough to show before I leave the mirror. Smooth bills. I watch my fingers dance in the office safe's silver shine, watch in these mirrors, before I shut the money box door. Then it's just me in this reflection. I look good now, I'm sure of it, good enough to go get the little man outta the joint.

It's warmer downstate, especially for March. No buildins to block this sun out in the country. So warm I wanna put the top down once I'm outta the city. But I ain't ridin in the T-Bird no more, ain't had that ol ride for three years now. Traded it for a '74 Mercedes beamin as white as J.C.'s ol Caddy shined gold. I see the jealous glances as I pass on the strip—gone from empty waves to evil peeks the higher I climbed. They claim to love me still, but the eyes is green. Don't matter, cause there ain't one of um who got nothin for me to care about.

I've rose from a T-Bird convertible to a Mercedes with a sunroof, so who is they to hate me? I'm the baddest nigga, bad enough to be known as the original gangster, since don't nobody remember Johnny the Baptist these days. That's who I am, the original gangster from 47th Street, just drivin through the hot flatland in my white Benz.

There's the joint. Don't know how J.C. made it for seven years behind them walls. I hated to see him livin like that, hated it so much I couldn't visit no more. Drivin these miles to sit and talk to him was too hard, specially as he wasted and shriveled up like my papa. Trapped on the other side of thick glass, cussin through a gray telephone. And that bloody mark down the side of his face.

He's mad I ain't visited since comin to tell him Grandma Rose passed, I know. Been since '74—I remember the year. It was around the same time I traded in the T-Bird.

All these bars and wires scare the hell outta me, I gotta say it, make me think of how close I came to lockdown myself. Coulda been me back there right alongside the little man if I hadn't kept drivin down 47th, left J.C. to get stomped by Black and them. That thought alone is enough to tell me what I done was right. Drivin away from the scene and not comin to see J.C. for most of seven years, they was both the right thing I did.

The gate opens slow, like it ain't ready to let J.C. free just yet. I see him comin close, runnin to my Mercedes. Looks excited, frantic, so I get outta the car. I don't want him to scuff the paint job, and the way he's runnin, it don't seem like he's got enough time to stop. His color's gone bad, changed from gold to this sick beige like he ain't been eatin good, and his bush's all dirty and napped-up on his head. Stitches left a scar on his face, too, so dark against this vomit skin it shows from here. He looks like a 43rd Street junkie now: crusted, thin, and faded. Don't know what else I shoulda expected after these caged years. Guess it just shakes me seein him as less than the J.C. I knew. You think you ready for anything on this earth, but truly facin what you call yourself ready for is a whole separate trip.

The second thing to mind as the gate creaks is how J.C. chased Sermon down 47th Street. Goddamn maniac. That's what seein him reminds me of—a little maniac bastard is all the little man's ever been, tell the truth. I glance at the sky, and the clouds tell me to get back in the car. I look at J.C. and see the .45 wavin in his right hand, but I know that smokin gat got left on 47th Street for the pigs to steal. *Run,* the clouds say. Before my mind can set my legs to sprintin off to the crop fields, the prison gate opens. The little man's free to wrap his arms around me and squeeze away my air, squeeze hard like I welched on Salvie. So tight I can barely raise my arms to protect myself. *Too late,* the clouds say now. When I loosen my arms a bit, I squeeze J.C. back, hug him cause I can't do nothin else. This prison watchtower hangs over us, though. Its shadow, leanin with the downstate sun, is all I feel as I hold on to the little man.

* * *

"You mind if I smoke?"

"What you mean, mind if you smoke?"

"In your new car—mind if I smoke in here?"

"You like the car?"

"Yeah. It's got a nice paint job. Can I smoke in here or what?"

"Why should I care? You used to hit squares in the T-Bird every day without askin. Don't you remember?"

"I remember," J.C. says, and puts the cigarette between his lips. "This ain't no T-Bird, though, this's some new kinda fancy foreign ride."

"A Mercedes."

"Yeah, right, one of them. Just figured I had to get permission first. You got a light for me?"

I point to the knob above the radio. "There it go right there, the one closest to me."

"Which one?"

"Said the one closest to me, on the left." I point to the dashboard lighter again. "The knob with the smoke cloud on it. Just push it into the socket and it's gonna light up for you." J.C. reaches for the circle and presses. "Now wait for it to get hot."

"I know how to use a lighter, man. Ain't been that long. How much time it's gonna take for it to get hot?"

"Seconds—five or ten."

"That fast?"

"That fast. When it pops out, it's caught a flame. Just take it outta the socket and stick your square on up in the part that burns."

"I said I know how to use the thing." The little man lights his cigarette and whistles.

"Now put the circle back in the socket."

"That's a mighty fast flame." He whistles again. "Time passes, things change. That's how it go, no?"

"Just keep gettin better is all."

"Maybe," J.C. says, rubbin his hand across the dashboard. "What's that down there, up under the radio?"

"What?"

"That slot." He slips his stubby fingers into the cassette deck.

"That's my stereo. You put a cassette up in there and it plays music through the speakers."

"Not making eight-tracks big like they use to, huh?"

"Got a whole new kind out these days." I reach cross J.C. and dig the Isley Brothers tape from the glove compartment. "See?"

"Ain't that a muthafucka? Suppose it has been a long time. Put it in there, Mookie. Let me hear how this joker sounds."

I turn on the Alpine, pressin the Dolby stereo buttons till J.C.'s tongue licks cross jealous lips. The song plays: *Driftin on a memory / Ain't no place I'd rather be / Than with you. . . .*

I wait for the little man to speak. "This is a mighty fancy ride," he says. "What happened to Miss Nelly's, Mookie?"

We drivin north on King Drive, but I ain't givin no thought to the world we pass, the life that's changed durin J.C.'s time. Just thinkin about my white Mercedes and its stereo speakers. I look up as we pass 49th Street and the boarded-up joint that use to be Miss Nelly's. The little man gazes on the strip where we found Johnny's stiff years back. "Things," I say, and hear air chucklin through my lips.

"What?" J.C. looks away from 49th, taps his fingers on the door handle, in time with the Isleys. "Where'd Miss Nelly's go?"

"Moved," I say. "Got a brand-new joint further south, further east. On Stony Island, that's where it's at. Opened a place three times bigger than the ol one. Been over there for bout five years now."

"It's a nice joint?"

"Course it's nice. Why would she move if the place she was goin wasn't better than where she was at? What point would there have been? Gotta take you over there, J.C. It's somethin else, I'm tellin you."

"Mmh. Guess everybody has moved up in the world."

"Naw, most of um just stayed where they was at, ain't moved a lick while you was gone." I turn left so we won't pass 47th and King. Ain't ready for that just yet.

Till these last few minutes, not much talkin has been done durin this ride from the clink. The little man feels comfortable, I suppose, now that he's back on our side of the world. Just hope he ain't comfortable enough to start askin no lotta real questions. We been on this trip for a good two and a half hours and J.C. ain't made no mention of his stash or Christina. Good thing, too, cause I ain't lookin to get into them conversations. Time for that's comin soon enough.

"Your uncle's store move over to Stony Island, too?" He's lookin out the window again, at the block between Wabash and State.

"Naw," I say, and make another turn, at State. "Leon's store ain't gone nowhere but to hell."

"What?"

"The store, I mean—it's gone. Kept losin money, no more customers and such. Niggas round here won't shop less they at the big markets these days. Leon had to shut down last year, ran his fat ass back to Kentucky. Only way somebody move up round here is if somebody else get worser off. You know that."

"Thought you said things got better." We rollin back on 47th. "How come you're driving in a circle, Mookie?"

"No cause behind it. Wasn't a circle no ways. Just did a square."

"Mmh. Where we headed? Thought you'd drop me off at Grandma Rose's place."

"Gotta run by Soul Mamma's first. Business to tend."

"Soul Mamma's?" J.C. nods as the music ends. Damn questions comin quick now, shootin off the little man's chapped lips. "That's where you got my loot hid at?"

"Yeah," I mumble, "that's where it's at."

"Good. I need my scratch," J.C. says. He points to the sidewalk as a red light stops us at Wabash. "What's up with that old fool Black?"

"He's still on the corner of Michigan, if he ain't wanderin around drunk. Still got no place to go. Always somewhere near, maybe back on Forty-third Street."

"Still hangs over there?"

"You know how it is, how Forty-third gets to a nigga. You know."

"Yeah," J.C. laughs, "yeah. Don't figure that for changing—there, pull over, Mookie."

I roll the Mercedes along the sidewalk, to the ol dark man underneath the straw hat. Don't he remember Black jumpin his ass, the bum and all the rest of the strip folk, holdin the little man down till the cops came to clean Sermon's blood?

"Black!" The little man hangs from the passenger window and yells now. "What up, fool? Remember me?"

Black looks over the car, then turns like he about to run off. Then he remembers he ain't got nowhere to go, so he stops and rubs larger holes in his pants pockets without speakin.

"What's up, man?" I brake our trip against the curb. "It's Mookie and J.C."

Thoughts of runnin flash behind his eyes' haze again. He spits without turnin away from us. "Yeah?"

J.C.'s damn near fallin outta the car window, waitin for somethin more from Black. "Don't you remember me, man—J.C. Rose? Don't you remember, back on Forty-seventh and Southpark?"

"Yeah," Black says. His voice is low, like his mouth's fightin with his mind over talkin to the little man. "They let you out the joint already, boy?"

"Just today," J.C. says with pride. "After seven and a half years. Not holding anything against you either, Black. I'm out, and I'm free, and what's years passed by don't matter now."

"Best be careful," Black says. Ol man ain't even got no clue what the little man's talkin about. "You hear what went down with Nate Hill?"

"No."

Black laughs, looks at me for the first time. "You ain't told him?"

"Didn't get the chance. I was bout to."

He spits again. "First day he was free, first day he was outta the goddamn joint, somebody shot his ass over on Forty-third Street. First day he was outta there, dead. Wasn't even meant for him—Frail Nate just got caught by a bullet flyin bout. Forty-third, that's a bloody street these days. Since Mary Ruth passed on, I stay away from that strip much as I can, I sure do. Just be careful, boy."

J.C. peeks my way, then watches the cars passin on 47th. "Careful," he repeats.

Black's still spittin on the sidewalk. "I'm surprised Mookie's lettin you ride with him these days. Don't got time for nobody else round here. Don't speak no more, don't wave, nothin. Got so high, he's too good for the dirt the rest of us walk on. Hides his rich ass in leather as he travels these streets. Don't try to stop him and ask for a ride, he might just run you over. Got too big, Mookie, way too big for Forty-seventh Street."

"What you babblin bout, jack?" What kinda gratitude is this he's showin for all I done for him—but hell, what else should I expect but the trash talk of such a nobody? "I always been there when you was in need. You disrespectin me, ol man, like I'm a punk."

He ignores my words, reaches for J.C. "And you know what this muthafucka, your boy here, done worst of all? You know that fine, shiny T-Bird he used to drive round in? Remember how he said he was gonna let me have it once he bought a new car? You remember that? You was there when he used to say that to me, wasn't you?"

"Yeah, I was there."

"You know what he done? Instead of livin true to his promise, he went and gave that fine ride to some crackerjack car peddler out in the suburbs. I don't know exactly where—out there in the suburbs somewhere, though, I know that for sure. Bought himself two cars since then. All while I walk round here on these same dusty feet, waitin for a colored man to live up to his word."

J.C. looks to me again and, much as I can't believe it, he shakes his head. "I don't know what you talkin bout over there, Black," I say. "You see I'm still on these same streets. You must be lettin that Johnny Walker Red Label speak for you instead of your own good sense. What you need, man? I got it for you—whatever it is." I take a twenty from my billfold and reach across the little man's body. The bill's dancin in the wind as it waits for the thanks of Black's fingers.

"Keep your loot," the ol bum says. He walks off to his corner.

"What's wrong with him?" J.C. asks. "Told him I'm not thinking about Forty-seventh and Southpark today. Holding nothing against him—what's he evil about?"

I drive on to Soul Mamma. "Ain't evil with you," I say. "Folk round here just mad at the world. Don't be fooled, J.C. Like I say, everything that was here ain't all better. Same souls was on these streets back then's still here now—in the same place they was before then, same place they gonna be after now. You just ain't seen it is all, can't see it after this long. All of um got anger, though; you feel they anger even if you don't see. Look at these streets, point to one thing worth somethin. White man ran scared with all his loot and storefronts before you even went into the joint. Miss Nelly's restaurant and Mister Shipp's funeral store both set up better shops out south. Calvin's is on Seventy-ninth Street—even the barbershop craps is gone from here. Look round, J.C. What you see worth studdin? I don't see nothin. Gone wherever, if it ain't gone to hell. Time's come to get outta here cause, I don't know bout you, but I ain't lookin to spend life in no place like this here. When it's over, there ain't even nobody round to bury my ass. Time passes, shit change, ain't that how you just figured it a minute ago? Shit don't change for the good, time's gonna stop passin for us. Don't you figure?"

"Maybe," J.C. answers. I think he's gonna say more, maybe ask another fool question, but he stays quiet as I roll the Benz into Soul Mamma's alley.

* * *

Gotta get over this. I feel J.C.'s shady eyes as I flip through the files. I feel, but I don't say nothin, let my mind drift. I see only the words and numbers on the pages in fronta me, on these contracts, not knowin exactly what they mean. Salvie's got final say over all club business, see. It's been like so, ever since J.C. went to the joint and the Ricci gimp got put in his wheelchair. I just run employees—personnel, like Salvie says—and it's important work. Bossin the cocktail girls and cooks and bartenders, important work. The words and numbers is Salvie's thing. I'm lookin at these files only cause I ain't ready to face J.C.'s music then, so fixed on this nonsense that his voice scares me when it comes. "How's Geri?"

"Geri?"

"Your little sister, how is she?"

"Ain't little no more, ain't been for some time. Big as I don't know what, J.C., eatin much as Mamma do. Just like her. Girl's doin fine though."

"She married?"

"Married to who? Naw, Geri ain't married, nowhere near it."

"Just asking," J.C. says. "Figured her little boy needed a daddy, that's all. They had shrinks in the joint, preaching about how most of us locked up had no male figure at home. I never knew my daddy. Figured she mighta got married to give the boy what he don't have."

"He do got a daddy—Leroy Cross, you remember. He's dead," I say. "How you gonna come about a father other than the one you born with?"

"All right, Mookie, he don't need no father. How's the boy doing, though?"

"Isaiah's good, livin like a little man. Him and Geri moved from my folks' crib a while back. Got their own pad on Yates."

"Oh yeah?" J.C. smiles, like he gives a goddamn. "How old's the boy now?"

"Seven, eight, somewhere round that age. Think he just made his eighth birthday this past December. He's in school, I know that—third grade, I think."

Never seen a smile phony as this on J.C.'s mouth. Nigga even sounds different. Bein gone so long, locked up like that, changed him up—somehow. "What about you? You still on Forty-fifth?"

"Me? Hell naw. I crib with Mora in Hyde Park, been over there for the longest time. Gonna get us one uh them condos on the lake."

"You still with her?"

"I look like a fool? Get mine on the side, yeah, but show me where I'm gonna come across a dime piece better than her, better overall, to sport round here. You show me."

J.C.'s quiet for a bit and I turn my chair his way. "Ain't one," he says. "You seen Christina around?"

Wish I wasn't lookin at him now, cause I can't turn again till I answer. "The young girl you used to fuck with? I see her sometimes. Think she's married."

"To who?"

"Don't know. Can't recall his name. Been married awhile."

"That's how come she stopped visiting?"

"Suppose so." I spin my chair to the opposite wall, hustled outta that bind. "She's gonna be by on Saturday night, J.C. Saw her this week, told her to bring her ass to Soul Mamma this Saturday. We throwin a party, chief, celebratin you comin home. Everybody in the neighborhood's heard you out the joint."

"I don't know, Mookie. Wanted to go early Sunday morning and visit Grandma Rose. Didn't get the chance to say goodbye right, just wanted to give my proper respects, put nice flowers out there."

"Sunday?" I spin just enough to see myself in the mirror now. "I forgot to tell you, we got a meetin with Salvie this Sunday."

"Salvie? Salvie who? Fuck Salvie. Ain't seen that old muthafucka in seven years. What, I'm supposed to not see Grandmamma in her grave because I'm running off to kiss his greasy white ass? Fuck him after all this time, Mookie, I've been telling you that for years. Can't even believe the old son of a bitch's still on these streets."

"He's still here, J.C. And we meet with him and his people on Sunday mornin. It's big-time, not no money-collectin bullshit. Suppose to get together at Tommy Ricci's pawn shop. Big-time."

"Big-time? Do me a favor, Mookie. While you're up at your big-time meeting with your big-time crackers, you give Salvie a message from me. Tell him I said fuck his old, greasy white ass. Tell him, before this's all said and done, I'm putting a gun to his head and he's begging me for life like I'm his Lord and savior—big-time, greasy, gray, wrinkled muthafucka."

"So you ain't comin?" I pour a shot of Captain Morgan from my desk drawer bottle and swallow it away. "Think they might got somethin for you."

"Fuck Salvie and everybody else with him. I keep telling you that, Mookie, all these years. You hear me? Gonna see Grandma Rose on Sunday."

I smile like J.C.'s stupid. "Ingrateful, that's what you always been. A goddamn ingrate. You rest for a few days, J.C. After you rest, you tell me if you wanna meet with Salvie or what. Tell me then. Take your time and think bout it. Early Sunday mornin, like I say."

J.C. chuckles as my lips get tired of stretchin to smile. "Where's my loot? They got it at Tommy Ricci's pawn shop? I'll meet with Salvie then—where's it at, Mookie?"

"Your loot? Right here. Got it locked in the office safe, waitin on you."

"That's what I want to hear. Been looking forward to this day for seven and a half years. Safe's still in the same place?" J.C. walks cross the office, squats at the panel between my two wall mirrors.

"Yeah, right over there."

"Got the old combination from back then?"

"Had the lock changed after all this time," I say. J.C. opens the wall panel and metal shines off the mirrors' edges. His fingers fiddle with the dial. "Wanted to make for certain your stash was protected."

"Good looking out, Mookie. That was a smart thing to do. I appreciate it—see, I ain't ingrateful anymore. What's the combination?"

"Gotta look it up. Don't recall it right off the top of my head." I shuffle through the desk drawers. "You know I ain't never had no real head for numbers. Can't keep um up there." I stare at the blank back of one of Salvie's contracts. Ain't no point in comin up with lies to cover my ass now, but that's all I know to do. Tell lies. "The combination—it's twelve to the right, twenty-four to the left, sixty-eight to the right."

"What'd you say?" J.C.'s workin the dial quick, bought into my word. "Twelve, twenty-four, sixty-eight, that's it, right?"

"That's it. Spin it right, then left, then right again."

"I did." The little man groans. "Ain't working. Twelve, twenty-four, sixty-eight?"

"That's the combination. You took it clockwise, then counter-clockwise, then back clockwise again? That's how it works."

"I know how to open a safe, muthafucka. Right, left, right, you said. That's how I opened it every night back then. I remember how to open a safe, Mookie. Unless this's some bullshit lock you put on here." He pulls at the safe door until the walls shake.

"Been usin it all this time, it's a good lock. Try again, J.C." He spins the dial and my fingertips swell with blood. I remember where the lead pipe sits (behind the office coatrack) and the .38 (middle desk drawer) and I swallow the salt leakin between my lips. "Did you spin it past zero? Supposed to do that before you run the combination. Else it won't work."

"Done that. I know how to work a lock. This one's not right." His eyes ain't turned to me since fixin on that safe. "What the fuck's going on here?"

"Guess it's broke, like you say."

"What was the old combination, Mookie?"

"You know I don't recall. Can't keep numbers in my head like that. Ain't got no head for figures. It was you who was good in arithmetic."

"I remember the old combination," J.C. says. "Shit, gotta remember it—need my paper. What was it? Sixty-six right—"

"Ain't gonna work, man. I changed the lock."

"Thirteen left—"

"That ain't it, J.C." But he pays me no mind.

"Eighteen right." The lock clicks and J.C. snatches the safe door open. He turns to me before he checks what's left of his stash. "Damn. After seven and a half years, I recall a number that easy. Genius. Coulda been an accountant with a head on me like this one here. Clockwise, counterclockwise, clockwise, just like you said, Mookie."

He looks into the metal box and the shine disappears. Ain't no sound neither. Two of us ain't even breathin. I'm sittin, but I feel dizzy, no oxygen makin it to my brain. But as my pupils spin I see the pipe layin in the office corner. Four good steps and a wide reach, that's all it'll take for me to get to the lead. There ain't no way for this little bastard to get to me before I grab it and bash his skull open.

"You've got me looking in the club's money box, not mine, Mookie," he says. "My safe is the one with the twelve–twenty-four–sixty-eight combination you was talking about, right-left-right. Where's it at, Mookie, the safe with my stash up in it?"

"Ain't no other safe," I mumble. I blink, ain't dizzy no more. "That's yours, right in front of you, that's it."

J.C. reaches into the silver box and pats the smooth pile of bills just like Salvie does, countin by touch. He chuckles, not happy or evil, just lets air out of his lungs.

"Ain't no more than ten thousand in here. That's all I feel. Missing another twenty-some G's. Cash money gone, Mookie. Where is it? Where's the other safe where you've got my loot at, damnit?"

"Twenty G's?" I got the cool coon act goin. "What the fuck're you talkin, twenty G's? Your math ain't good as you think. Salvie, the same man who you was fuckin off left and right a minute ago, been givin me five hundred a month since the year you went into the joint. I buried your grandmamma, and I paid to get you outta prison. What the hell'd you expect? The loot I spent for them things came outta your stash, not a penny more. That's what you got left there."

I don't see the little man spring across the room, don't even know he's moved from in fronta the safe till I feel the sting of starved knuckles against temples. My ears ring and the dizziness returns. I swing, swing at nothin cause my world spins so fast. I'm lost again, till the little man's fists beat against my back and sides and I fall from my chair. I grab the leather, use it to protect myself till the dizziness leaves and I can grab the .38 Special. But J.C. lifts the chair, slings it against the back-alley door. He drags me to my knees and beats me for Tobias and Henry and the Banks brothers and Sermon, gives me what I got comin. Eardrums don't ring no more, but chime in my brain, chime before they burst. I feel my mind drippin down both cheeks, and I close my eyes, hope to pass out for the pain. But there ain't no such peace comin my way.

J.C.'s fists don't let up till he pulls me to wobbly foot and spins me square into the mirror. I feel glass breakin around my face, slicin skin and soilin my European suit. Don't matter, cause he's fucked up, givin me a chance to get to the pipe. I push myself from the glass and grab the metal from the office floor. Now I'm ready for him to spring cross the room again. I wait, cause I know he's comin. I'll split his little head ear to ear when he jumps at me—next best thing to a bullet to the brain is one of these lead pipes to the skull. I see him this time, jumpin from the ground like some kinda jungle cat, movin so fast he looks like brown wind in the office air. But I got the lead gripped in both hands, like Papa learned playin ball back home; my eye is on this maniac comin at me, got him measured good. So I swing only when the wind is close enough, hard, to knock the prison-rotted teeth from his mouth, to kill his flight and lay him out on the carpet at Soul Mamma's ground. Swing so hard that, when I miss, the pipe flies from my hands, crashes next to the leather chair. J.C. lands and, in one swoop, bends me into a choke hold. I feel my throat close on breath, can't beg, can't even give up, just grit my teeth and wait.

"I got you, punk muthafucka."

My left hand pounds the floor and its skin is torn on mirror glass. Can't scream for the air caught below the choke of the little man's arm. I hear death, or sleep at least, it's near, so near. Rumblin cross the ground, ready to take me off to heaven, where I'll sit on the beach and watch the lake's waves crash as white girls in bikinis and Black girls who look like Lena Horne dance on the sand around me. That's where I'm about to get took off to.

But it ain't death comin my way—ain't worthy of a dream so fine. I look down as J.C.'s hold gets weaker, and the pipe's rolled cross the floor, stopped under my fists. I reach for it, get a good grip on the metal. Don't even look over my shoulder, cause I can't, just knife the pipe through air, anglin for J.C.'s right leg and stabbin the side of his knee. The little man lets out a seven-year scream, and my throat is free. I cough and let go the pipe—lead falls from his leg as he stumbles the office, hoppin to keep his balance. Why does he fight his fall? Don't he see I ain't even tryin to get up from here, no matter how much broke glass surrounds? Don't he see?

He's down finally and, when he's on the ground, the lead rolls next to my cut hand. And J.C.'s leg, I see it twitchin with his loss, before sleep comes for the both of us.

"Why'd you stop visiting, Mookie?"

I blink, come to, and the little man's sittin against the office desk. I'm too tired to move from this floor, so I don't try. His leg's bent funny, like it ain't never gonna work right again, restin about a inch from my face. I look at myself in the one unbroke mirror plate. Cheek is torn from the poundin of fists, the slicin of glass. The cuts is gonna heal—ain't gonna form no scar like his, ain't that deep or black to last—but I ain't lookin too pretty right now. I look into the safe, this empty silver box. "Huh? What you say?"

"Seven and a half years I was locked up. All my life before that we was like brothers. Why'd you stop visitin? I was alone down there."

"If you like my brother, how was I gonna come and look at you locked down in a muthafuckin monkey cage? How you think that made me feel?"

"You? I'm locked up and how you feel matters to somebody?

How's that sound, Mookie? I was in the joint. What difference your feelings make? You some kind of a bitch? That's what you sound like right now, a punk-ass, weak bitch. It was your fault I was in there."

"Don't start that shit."

"It's truth. It was your fault. Seven and a half years gone, your fault."

"Ain't told you to chase nobody down no public street. Ain't told your ass to shoot nobody in fronta half King Drive. Who told you to do that? Wasn't me."

"That was your black ass driving off afterwards. Left me, that's how you played a nigga. Like you didn't know who I was. Your fault."

"Who sounds like the bitch? If I'd pulled over and we both'd gone to the joint, everything'd be proper with you? What kinda fool logic?"

"Fuck you." The office's silent for a long minute. Feels like somebody ripped holes in the walls to let the March wind beat against me. Blows so hard, I still can't stand. "Know what?" J.C. says.

"What?"

"You stole from me, sold me out, left me alone in prison since I was twenty-one, all that. Fine—I know what you are now. This ten G's you didn't get a chance to take leaves more profit from my time in a cage than I got from a free life of knowing your ass." J.C. pushes himself to foot and limps to the alley door. He stops and ties closed a garbage sack, one with fifty-dollar bills pokin from its plastic—the little crazy muthafucka's about to walk down 47th Street with ten grand in a Hefty bag—and he kicks me in the kidney with his good leg. "Tramp, motherfucking slut, welching bitch," then he's gone. I think to grab my Saturday Night Special from the desk, chase after him—I do got two legs to his one—kill him and take the rest of what shoulda been mine all along. Just can't move for this wind holdin me to this ol shag rug.

* * *

Christina ain't married to a man. That ain't but a lie I told J.C. so we wouldn't have to get into the story. I figured we'd deal with the loot thing, knew he was gonna bring it up soon as time was good. Figured that was enough truth for his first day free.

She ain't no little girl no more neither. Looks older than I do for certain, older than the joint's turned J.C.'s scarred skin. Can't be over twenty-five, but she got enough wrinkles and rips to make you believe she's in her forties. That's what years of fuckin with 43rd Street will do for you.

I remember the last time she was supposed to ride to Decatur with me. Called a hour before we was set to leave, talkin about she had a family emergency at seven in the mornin, beggin for fifty dollars. Told her to meet me at Soul Mamma, gave her some of J.C.'s stash—no way his young slut's woes was ever gonna get paid for outta my own pocket neither. She took the loot and disappeared through my back door, said she'd come back after handlin her troubles. Thirty minutes, she said. A month passed before I saw Christina again. She started poppin back up at Soul Mamma, screamin out my name in the alley or on the dance floor. If that didn't work, she'd send some junkie fiend after me in Hyde Park, or follow me as I drove the strip, anything to get holda some of that stash. Soon as she ran outta lies to tell, she offered herself. And I turned her down first off, thought about the blink J.C. used to get in his eye when he talked about the girl. I did think about him. But time passed, and the memories I didn't care for died, leavin behind only how tight he claimed she was set. So I went on, gave her what she wanted (my dick just as much as the loot and dope cause, hell, I remember how she peeked my way when she was a kid). Didn't turn out to be worth it, though, sellin the little man out for his woman. No matter how much I let myself forget, it wasn't worth it. Bad as sin I felt for whorin Christina like that, specially seein as she wasn't tight like J.C. claimed no more. Wasn't worth it at all.

I figure, after these six, seven years, we both hooked on this wrong. She screams these days, says she ain't never felt nothin like me before, that nobody—not J.C., not nobody—got what I do. And I like her cause no matter how fine Mora is, ain't much sin left to us. Mora's screams is sighs now, her moans mumbles. But Christina, she's young and married to the junk on 43rd Street. She ain't the only tramp I cheat with, of course. They all love me. Ain't even the youngest. Just acts so damn hot from all that junk pumpin through her blood. That's how come she's hooked on me. I make her scream and my—J.C.'s—stash keeps her high in Fiend's Heaven.

She looks good tonight, though, not beat down as usual. Got on a pretty dress, hair done up nice and straight like it usually ain't, brown face painted pretty. And she's still got heaven's holy temple hangin high between her back and thighs. Years and poisons ain't had no effect on that yet. I admire it especially as she comes close causa the short dress and high heels, makin a show of her hips risin with the cigarette smoke's pull.

She creeps to the bar, looks around before she rests on the stool to my right. "What's up, lover?"

"What's up." I stare at my drink, can't look her in the face because it's her fault, me sellin the little man out. It's her fault. "What you want?"

"Just came by to say hi, baby. Ain't talked to you in a while. You don't call, don't knock on my door, you're not even thinking about me no more. I know, because I use to feel it when I was on your mind. What's wrong? You don't like me, lover?"

"Stop callin me that shit—'baby,' 'lover,' shit like that. Don't be callin me them names no more."

"Why?"

"This day's for J.C." I sip the rum, can't even taste no Coke mixer—they know how I like my drinks these days. "You oughta respect the man. How you gonna talk to me bout 'baby' and 'lover' and all this when we suppose to be celebratin him tonight? That's shady as all hell."

"What?" I feel her frowning, but still can't look her in the face. I smell the perfume I like, though, strong and sweet to cover that junkie funk. "A month ago, when you was knocking at my window, back when his ass was still locked up, you wasn't talking about respect. That's some two-faced shit on your part, Mookie. What, you scared of that little jackass or something? I thought you were the big Willie around here, ain't that what they be saying? You afraid now he's free?"

"Ain't afraid, just two-faced," I admit. "Respect the man cause he's outta the clink, that's all I'm sayin to you. Treat him like you supposed to, all right?"

"He ain't even here. You say respect this, respect that, and that motherfucker ain't even got the good sense to show up for his own goddamn party. Shit, you're just scared of his ass. . . . What happened to your face?"

"Accident."

"What kinda accident?" Her words yell in my ears, loud over Soul Mamma's smoky noise. "Not a car accident? You didn't wreck that pretty white car, did you?"

"Not no car accident. An *accident* accident."

"So how come I can't show you love?" Christina puts her arm around my shoulder. "What's wrong, baby?"

I push her away. "I told you, don't call me them names. This's J.C.'s day. He's your man. Act like you got some muthafuckin sense. You need a drink or what?"

"Don't want no funky drink. I miss you, Mookie."

"Miss me? Must wanna get lit." I remember I ain't got J.C.'s stash and wish I hadn't opened my mouth. I gulp the rest of the rum. "Call me later."

"In the office?"

"Yeah, call me in the office."

The little man walks into Soul Mamma and I choke on Christina's stink. I walk away from the bar. Ain't afraid, just don't wanna argue about it no more.

He's got on a fresh suit and overcoat, neat haircut and enough jewels and oil to cause him to shine in the club's lights, like his gold color's back to regular. He looks at me from across the room, stops for less than a second, then struts to the VIP booth. I hear clappin here and there on the floor, folk givin praise to the little man. Didn't nobody like J.C. back in the day, nobody in the Forties. But he shot a cat on the strip in fronta fifty witnesses and survived the time served for it. Goddamn, he deserves respect. I ain't never took nobody out like that, ain't spent a day in the clink, so who am I to question somebody who done both?

Besides, this's J.C.'s day. I just figured him for not showin. Thought the crowd'd get caught up with the wine and funk records and forget why they'd come out. But he's here. The folk from my streets, my folk, line up to welcome him home, and the waitresses, these gals who claim to love me, they go to him now. Christina's left the bar, wiggled to the fronta his line. He's on top tonight. That should be fine with me, after bein the man for these seven years, but I don't like it. I touch my scratches, lean against the wall.

As the crowd breaks and it's just J.C. and Christina in his booth, I walk his way. Of course, Christina runs off when she sees me comin, disappears long before I'm too near. I don't care, ain't worried a bit about what she been tellin him. My wrong's been done already; what am I supposed to do to change it?

"What's up?"

The little man grumbles, laughs as he looks at the glass cuts. "What you want?"

"What's up with ol girl?"

"Who?"

"Ol girl, Christina."

"I don't know. Came over here talking about welcome home and she missed me, shit like that."

"Oh. That's it?"

"Mmh. So what do you want?"

I sit. "Nothin, nothin. Just to say the same—welcome home."

"I've seen you once already and heard those words a thousand times. You've got nothing else to tell me?"

I know this bastard don't think I'm about to apologize. "No, nothin else."

Christina watches from the bar. "I don't care for her anymore," he says. "Looks like she's on that shit."

I groan, sound more like my ol man, let Mamma tell it, with each day passin. "She does."

He looks my face over again. "I did that to you?"

"Yeah, you did," I say, without expectin him to apologize neither. The little man laughs again and I don't speak until he's done. "You comin tomorrow?"

"What?"

"To meet with Salvie in the mornin. You comin?"

"Fuck you."

Now I snicker. "Fuck Salvie or fuck me?"

"Fuck Salvie, and definitely fuck you."

"Told you they got somethin for us. Why you gonna cheat yourself after seven years?"

"Don't say nothin else to me, Mookie." His words is calm, but his shady eyes pop, and his color turns sick again. "Don't need to hear what you're talking about. Didn't ask for whatever they've got for me. Don't want nothing but my loot."

"You not with me no more?"

"Ain't been for years, joe. You can have whatever they're trying to give me, if that's what you're worried about." He lights a Salem.

"Tomorrow's Sunday. I'm going to see my grandmamma. I'm through with the rest."

"So what you gonna do with yourself? Who gonna put food in you? Can go see your grandmamma's grave all you wanna, but she ain't leave you no money to set you right, did she?"

"Got no reason to worry about me. I used time to get my GED. I'm good, far as that goes. Got a step up. Taken care of."

"Your what?"

"GED. Like I finished high school. You finish school, nigger? I did."

"Oh, so you got schooled in the joint. Educated, like one of them Ebenezer folk? Is that right? That mean you ain't shoot no nigga dead on the corner of King Drive, and you ain't just spent years in the clink? Somebody gonna see your little ass step into they place with your muthafuckin G-E-muthafuckin-D and hand over a job to put food on your table? Then they gonna let you up and keep that job the rest of your life? You gonna be one of them paid, schooled negroes like at Ebenezer, cause you got a G-E-muthafuckin-D, nigga?"

J.C.'s eyes flash again and I think he's come to his senses and he's back with me. Where he's supposed to be. "I'm goin to see Grandmamma's grave in the mornin."

I stand from the VIP booth. I wanna kick him in that wounded leg, but from the square bubble at his chest, I believe he's packin a new .45 gat. I walk away, done with Soul Mamma for the night. I grab Christina's arm, pull her off with me, and leave his party. Ain't got no more respect to show this little bastard.

17

THIS'S YOURS NOW. South Shore to Ashland, Forty-third to Ninety-fifth, it's yours." I don't believe the words. Best not to. This way, I won't show no reaction. I look around the pawn shop office, don't see much other than the surroundin stares. There go Joe Defelice's cat slits behind Tommy Ricci's desk to the right, Salvie's forever circles to the left. And, at my back, I feel the blood in Vito the Hack's beady pebbles and the stupidity of Angelo's empty holes. I sit in fronta Tommy Ricci's desk, try to fall into the gaze of the man himself, but the shine of his orange lamp hides his eyes.

"Maybe you should cut the little fella in."

I know they see my frown. "J.C.?"

"Yeah, the kid who came in here and tried to sell me those necklaces. You remember that? From what they tell me, your friend did a favor for us some time ago, deserves our thanks. So maybe you cut him a piece of your cake. Say you take South Shore to the Dan Ryan, give him everything west to Ashland. Or you Forty-third to Sixty-seventh, him on down to Ninety-fifth. However you decide to share, it don't matter. It's your neighborhood to play with."

"Where is J.C.?" I see no lips movin, but it's Salvie's voice in my ears.

"He went to his grandmamma's grave. You know she passed while he was in the joint?"

Salvie groans. "No, I didn't know, Mook. Terrible things—deaths, funerals, seeing your family put in holes—terrible things. Tell him I said sorry, would you do that for me?"

"But first you take this message to him," the man in the orange haze says. "Let him know that, like I say, after how you all have served us, showed that we can trust you, we're giving you this place. Profit is in the neighborhood, Morris, big profit. I've done a good business over here for thirty-five years. But this ain't the place for me no more. Business'll always go on, we know that. There just ain't nowhere comfortable for me to hang my hat in this part of the city."

"It's time to move on," Salvie says.

"Move up. That's what's best for all of us. Time to go someplace where it's okay for a man to hang his hat. And, see, I gotta take Salvatore with me. Been at my side so long, I wouldn't know what to do without him. Just like you and the little fella when you come in here to sell them necklaces. Peas in a pod. How long you been with me, Sal?"

"Thirty-one years."

"Thirty-one years, you hear that? I gotta take him with me, what can I do? The South Side belongs to you all, Morris, you and that little kid. It's yours to cut up how you like it. Joey's the man you check in with. It's him, really, who's taking my place over here. That's on paper, as far as the higher-ups is concerned. We gotta have somebody for the big shots to check with, see. But you're our man on the street, running whatever goes on around this side of town. We got nothing if you don't run things right. You'll be fine. You and the little kid have shown us good things these years. Good lieutenants, you'll be. Army can't run without lieutenants, can it?"

"Course not, Mister Ricci," I say. "Gotta have people you can trust out there."

"That's my point, what I'm trying to say to you. If you control the streets right, keep doing what you've been doing, just on a bigger scale, this thing will be fine. The business'll run on, keep all of our pockets full of cash. The first thing I expect for you to do is move away from Forty-seventh Street. I know that's where you know best cause it's where you came up, over there. I understand. But it ain't the center of this part of town no more, ain't really been for years. What you need to do is set up shop on Stony Island. That's where action's good these days, toward the lake. Start a little trade on that strip, keep it for yourself. You ain't even gotta pay us a cut. Car wash, liquor store, barbecue joint, whatever'll do good for you. That's where our big money is, Stony Island. You gotta be in that neighborhood to do business."

"What about Soul Mamma?"

Tommy Ricci's frown does show in orange. "Soul Mamma?"

"That nightclub," Salvie explains before coughin. Air leaves stomachs all around me. "We're gonna take care of the dump. Not for you to worry about, Mook."

Mister Ricci rises, his face creepin from haze. "Everything else—Angelo, Vito, your action—stays the same, except that you deal with Joey. That's who you bring your concerns to from this day. Otherwise, your operations, your cuts, they stay like they is. Same for Paulo, Vinnie, everybody else in the street. Let em know." He disappears again. "Any questions?"

"No questions," Joe Defelice says. "Just like to offer congratulations, *padrino*." Mister Defelice steps his thin frame into the man's space and they hug, not a long, trustin hug, but a passin touch given the look of truth by wet kisses placed on both cheeks. Salvie follows, shares the same with Tommy Ricci, then Angelo, and Vito last. They stare at me, waitin. I don't believe I'm to be part of this here Italian love, but they expect some kinda sign.

I stand and offer my hand. "Congratulations, Mister Ricci," I say. Don't got a clue to what it is I congratulate, and his touch is cold no matter the bright orange that surrounds him. "Thank you, sir."

The ol-timer lets go my palm and steps away from the lamp, followed by his crew. "It's still morning, and it's Sunday," he says. "Who ain't been to church yet?"

* * *

Miss Nelly don't serve chitlins no more. Don't know why; folk eatin at her new joint look the same as those who came to the restaurant on 49th. And I figure they hungry for her soul food still, even the stank chitlins. But Miss Nelly's place is too fine-lookin for the cookin and servin of pig bowels now. No chitlins, no ham hocks, no grits here either. Closest this palace on Stony Island gets to 49th Street is yams and pumpkin pie, vittles sweet enough for rich folks' stomachs.

I don't care that she got rid of them dishes myself, don't feel it's right for a man to get dressed for a night out, a restaurant dinner, only to pay good money for slave food. It's Mora who's always complainin about how the menu's changed.

"This joint's long sold out, Mookie," she say, then, "I don't want to come here anymore."

"Sold out to who?" I keep askin. Still ain't but Black folk who eat at the new restaurant, the same highfalutin coons who came to Miss Nelly's ten, fifteen years ago. Only difference I see now is that dreams came true, so much so that proper talk, manners, and good clothes ain't part of no phony show. This's the only change I see, that the highfalutin is real. Still the same folk sittin at these fancy tables, still pictures of her with the world's big-time negroes on the walls—Cosby, Walt Frazier, Chamberlain, Dick Gregory, Poitier now—alongside them ol shots from 49th Street.

"Miss Nelly's is sold out," Mora repeats. "There's no chitlins on her menu these days."

"To who?" I ask again. "Who she sold out to?"

I look around the gold glory of the dinin room. Miss Nelly's been closed to the regular public this evenin and is filled instead with those who make a livin in the hustle, on my side of the city; Lester Hooks from the Forties, the Blackstone Ranger who took over the 43rd Street junk trade after the Banks brothers got clipped; Nicky Stokes from 79th Street, who runs the gamblin and dope over there and not only pays Tommy Ricci a piece of his action but collects for the man south of the strip since long before I came into the business; Frankie Ray, the top man on Stony Island, an enforcer who peddles pussy outta the motels toward the southern end of that place, down near the Fun-town carnival park. They all come together this April Friday to find out who's been made the area's top lieutenant, the man who's gonna crack the whip over nigga backs. We all know Tommy Ricci's been moved up in the Outfit—no longer just the South Side boss, he's number two over everythin in the city now. So it's time for one of us to take over our own streets. The others brung along armies of shady soldiers wearin Superfly suits—hidin pistols and scared hearts—not for protection, but to show how much muscle they got, how many fools there is who'll kill and die at their word. We're here, every wanna-be big-time South Side hustler, just waitin on the word.

Mora's to my left. I watch her chew, still so soft and proper-like, and I smile. Smile cause, as I look around the restaurant again, I see not one of these wanna-bes, these pimps, these pushers and hustlers tryin to be God, got a woman who look near good as mine. She don't scream no more, and she ain't gave me no son of my own, but she's the finest dime piece in our world. What army I need when all these cats know I'm fuckin her? They see my muscle.

I look one last time, and there's one missin, one wanna-be I forgot about. J.C. ain't here, ain't even been told about this meet. I was the one supposed to let him know, of course—ain't seen the little man since that night at Soul Mamma, though, so I ain't had a chance to tell him how the Forties and everythin else around it's ours now.

He don't know that we true gangsters, reached the place pointed out the day we found the Cajun's body in a garbage pile. J.C. deserves this much as I do, true, just ain't seen him to let him know. So it ain't my fault. Bastard claimed he was done, told me to keep whatever Tommy Ricci was givin him. That's what I recall. It's his own fault for sayin that shit before he knew what was bein offered.

Besides, Tommy Ricci won't care if it's us runnin things or if it's just me. All he did was say maybe I should cut the little fella in. Long as the profits reach his hands in the end, what difference do it make to him? So, hell naw, I ain't chased J.C. down to tell him what he don't need to know, what he asked not to know. I'm gonna take care of the little man in due time, outta my own pockets.

The wrinkled man in the gray hat walks through Miss Nelly's eatin room, soft-steppin like he don't wanna be here. Salvie said he'd show at eight-thirty, and he's on time like always. Lester, Nicky, Frankie all rise, dreamin in ignorance, as Salvie passes without lookin their way. This man who showed me how to get rich off the hustle walks to my table, his hands hid in trench coat pockets. His grip don't even show till I stand up. Then Salvatore Fuoco, who's been the word on the South Side streets since he came back from fightin white folks' last war against white folks, hugs me. That same passin, unlovin hug I saw in the pawn shop's back office it is, no eye contact, just a cold touch. But he don't kiss my cheeks, just grabs my right hand so those watchin know it's for real, grabs without lookin in my face. "Take care of things," he says. Then Salvie soft-steps outta Miss Nelly's—soft but squirrel quick, cause he do hate bein in this place.

Ain't till I sit that I feel the eyes on me. It might be shock they feel, me bein the youngest of Tommy Ricci's South Side cats. Logic said that Frankie the Pimp or Nicky Stokes woulda ended up runnin these streets, cause they veterans. Besides, I ain't built no army of my own like them, ain't had the chance. Could be disappointment in these stares. Bossin the strip means I'm gonna be rich like nobody's business, have say over the politicians and businessmen in this part of the city, even if I do gotta answer to Joe Defelice. I'm in the spot they been wantin for life. Maybe it's envy they feel, the kinda painful envy you get when your dream comes true for somebody else. It don't matter, cause they armies, they rackets, this world, is all mine. I'm the king of all black-faced gangsters now.

* * *

After all this time, I know the left side of J.C.'s mouth good. Spent years lookin at the cat in my passenger seat, at the fuzzy naps lined down from his ear and cut into his face where the afro bush on top becomes a beard and covers his lips. Always had these crusty lips, too, especially just under the place where his sideburn turns into mustache. Then there's this puddle in the crack between the top and bottom lip, like he can't help himself from baby droolin. Never understood, if he's got so much spit in him that he can't keep it from collectin in this pool, how come his lips is the driest suckers I ever seen. Used to watch him as he reached up to clean the corners with his shirtsleeves, smearin slime across the front of his face. Little nigga'd turn my way when he was done wipin, and them damn lips'd still be cracked and spiderweb dusty. More than once I seen his grandmamma take the spit outta her own jaw, rub it into her hand on top of greasy Vaseline and swipe his mouth with the whole palm of her hand. Wipe so hard she cupped the bottom of his head and squeezed the lips into a circle before lettin him go. When she was done, tears dripped from his eyes cause the ol lady'd snatched into some soft nerve, shame wrinkled all across his nose and forehead, and ash gray streaked into the chapped end of J.C.'s frown.

Twenty years gone by, maybe more, and this's all I see as I walk up on the little man in the 47th Street pool hall: a drip in the slice of these thirsty lips, twinklin against the faded lamplight over Salvie's favorite table. He's talkin loud for me to hear him a table away, but the words and the voice ain't his really. They sound familiar in my ear, just not like they suppose to be comin outta this mouth. I'm close enough to see his left eye slimy and shinin like the lips' corner. A conk-headed punk from 43rd Street stands tall on the back end of the table with the red six in his fist. Ain't till I spot him that I know who the little man's talkin to.

"No sense to cryin like a bitch about a shot you already missed," he says. "You put the ball off the table. Yeah, it's dark in here. Joint's never had good light. And? Only fucking up your next shot crying about light that's never been here from day one. You missed, it's done. Got too much juice in you, chief. Fuck it. Nothing else to come out of the thing. Just put the ball back on the table, close to where it was as you can get."

The boy don't move. I seen him before, over on Indiana Avenue shootin craps against brick, runnin with the rest of the wanna-be Blackstone snot-noses. He spins the six in his fingers and stares at the space between me and J.C. The little man looks my way, puts those beady eyes on me, and I peep his pool stick, still in his right hand but restin against his hip like he ain't in no hurry to shoot.

"What's up, J.C.?" I lean on the empty table in front of theirs, waitin for the little man to get over his starin fit and say somethin, but his lips twist, corners touchin the shamed wrinkles lined from his nose. Like a smile, but bush nappy with that beard and foul in place of happiness. He taps the stick against the pool table, like he's either nervous or checkin to see if he's got wood long enough to reach across this space and crack me upside the head.

I squeeze the jacket to my body, feel the package hidin in the chest pocket just above the .38 scrapin my armpit, and I take a step back so his stubby arms won't reach me no matter how long his stick. "We've got a game going," J.C. says. He reaches to the ashtray at the table's rim and brings the square—Salem, I guess—to his lips, smoke and dust floatin my way when he breathes.

"I see."

The 43rd Street boy stops watchin long enough to put the six in the opposite corner, up against one of J.C.'s stripes. Then he's fixed on the nothin between tables again. I close the space as the little man bends over and puts his stick to the green, chokin the cue. He slides it past his ass three times—stick woulda gone straight through my skull and still had plenty wood left over to come outta my backside, if the bastard'd the heart to put it there—before lettin the cue loose.

"What's been goin on?" I ask him.

"Shit." The white ball bounces the ten stripe clean of that six, off the wall, and to the far pocket's cup. "Shit. What the fuck's up?"

"Ain't but a thing," I say. The kid's eyes cut to me. "Heard you been hangin round in here. Wanna holla at you is all."

"Got a game goin," the boy says, and I flinch at the sound of J.C.'s words from his fresh mouth.

"Watch yourself. This grown-nigga business," I tell him.

If Salvie or the Baptist, or even Clean Willie, said boo our way back when we was his age, I woulda had the good sense to haul tail quick as a blink, shit in my pants and a smile cross my face cause the real players recognized I was livin. Can't speak for J.C., he always been a hardhead, but that's what I woulda did. Wouldn't have stopped runnin till I was safe on 45th Street neither. But this cat stands across the table, and he's got the gall to stare me dead in the face. "Better watch yourself now, Freddy," J.C. lets him know, spit smirked cross his face. "This's Mookie King you talkin to."

But the kid knows me—they all recognize who I am in his crap-shootin corners. He just ain't seen nobody drug down the strip hangin from the back of a Chevelle, or no lead pipe poundin on a back just for the sake of makin right somebody's disrespect. Not yet, he ain't seen it; or if he has, maybe he's heard them back-in-the-day stories about J.C.'s crazy ass. Been told that the little man popped one of God's best street preachers on 47th and King—in broad daylight. Thinks the little man'll protect his silly ass. Must not know the difference between a bastard and a fool, that J.C.'s all of the first yet ain't nowhere near none of the second.

"He's top dog over here now, Freddy," J.C, says, just about gigglin. "He's the man. Better watch who you talkin to like that."

The kid wises up and looks down to his own ashtray, where he's let a cigarette flame out with his hard-core act. "Be gone, shorty," I say, and he drags off, leavin behind his dead square, the pool stick, and a bunch of singles, fives, and tens sprinkled about the table.

The little man stands from his crouch puffin the Salem, his eyes fixed on the empty corner where the boy stood. He counts the table's chump change and giggles clear and evil before stuffin loot in his pants. Don't matter that balls is still scattered all around the green—J.C.'s eyes jump around the hall, checkin to see if the boy's lesson is learned, but Freddy's gone off somewhere where little eyes can't find him.

"What's up, J.C.?"

"Told you—shit, joe," he says, and lets his stick drop to the ground, spinnin to darkness. "What the fuck you want over here?"

I walk to the boy's end of the table, starin at the smokeless square and touchin the table. I can't see his left side drool over here. I listen to my own grumble.

"Congratulations," he says, bendin to grab the stick or to keep from lookin at me, or both.

"What?"

"Heard you got promoted." He shoots without bendin and his cue taps the ten into the pocket, soft and sweet. "Word's on the street."

"Don't believe all the bullshit niggas' talk," I say. "You know better."

"Mmh," J.C. moans. "Hear you've got half the city on lock now, don't even got to bother answering to Salvie. Hit the jackpot, joe. You made it. Big-time."

"Come on now, J.C." I reach into my coat, for the package, not for the .38: J.C. don't flinch no ways. "They gave it all to me, huh? I'm the big boss nigga now? Got last word, makin all the paper? Sound like somethin Salvie and Tommy Ricci would let go down to you?"

He laughs and squashes his square, crumbled ashes flickerin in the tray as just one line of white smoke rises to the lamp. "Sound to me?" he asks, and his laugh turns back to that empty giggle. "My word matters?"

"I'm askin." I step toward him, fix on his eyes as he wipes um dry of slime. He rubs the corners of his mouth with the same hand. "Ain't I?"

"Don't know," he answers, and chalks the stick. "How'd the pawn shop meeting go?"

I laugh now, tickled at the little man for real, and drop the white package on his table. "There."

"What the hell?" J.C. says. "Move that shit. I'm trying to shoot."

"That's your cut."

"What cut?" J.C. bends so low I don't see nothin of him except the stick strokin past where his ass should be. "Move that shit."

"Took care of collections yesterday," I say. "There's your cut."

"My cut wrapped in a envelope?" He slams the cue, and the 43rd Street punk's five ball bounces against the wall, then back into the pocket at J.C.'s left. "For seven years? Twenty G's up in there?"

"Twenty-five. That's what you got comin—twenty-some G's."

"You figure?" J.C. says as the cue bounces the eight ball off his package. "Told you to move that shit."

"It's what you got comin."

"Had one hell of a meet with Salvie and them, didn't you?" He stands, and both his mouth's corners and his eyes is shinin wet again. Powder's still at his stick's tip, but J.C. chalks—he's grinded the nub to dust by the time his mouth opens. "Told you before to keep whatever they were giving you, don't want any parts of it. In the clink, after they've took everything from you, stripped you bare-assed like a whore, all you've got left to stand on is your word. And if you ain't got that, you ain't got shit. So what I say means something, joe: I told you, that's yours. Move it off my table."

"You move it."

"Don't play me, nigga," J.C. says, and his words bring stares from the cats hangin in the hall's other corners. Even Freddy watches from the Royal Crown machine by the door. "You're giving up what you know you owe me in that envelope. But you're saying it's my cut on collection day. I look like a jackass or what? Got double coming now."

Decatur's got his head harder than it used to be, turned him into a sick muthafucka. I'm givin—hell naw, I ain't gotta be doin this—givin him twenty G's plus, in payback. A cut, payback, whatever the fuck, and he's talkin nonsense. Didn't have to come here and offer him nothin. "That's your piece, J.C. I'm tellin you, it ain't mine to move nowhere."

"Told you to keep it. They put it in your hands, you keep it. That's how it goes. Possession's ninety percent of the truth."

"Muthafuckas told me to bring it to you," I say, hopin he'll shut up about it. "Your cut."

J.C. drops the stick back to the floor. He grabs the package and squeezes it in his little hands, his eyes shinin in the dim, and rips the envelope at his sides. Two and a half stacks of hundreds poke out for him to flick with a chalked thumb. "Twenty-five G's." He smiles what I figure for a real smile. "My cut of the action."

"Told me to pass it on to you," I say. "It's yours."

"No," he says, "it's not." He tosses the package back to the green and the top stack slips out for Ben Franklin's gray face to fix on us, dry and crusty as J.C.'s mouth. "Got double coming."

"Are you crazy, nigga?" I feel warm salt swimmin behind my own teeth and spit into the darkness. "Don't fuck yourself for pride's sake."

"Not fucking myself for nobody. Fuck you. I know I've got loot coming to me. And?" The voice ain't his again—its sound is old and barely there, but all around us in this hall.

"And what?"

"This's payback for what you took from me, or it's my cut of the action?" His eyes dry now cause his lids don't blink, eyeballs locked on me. Searchin every hole in my face, for the sweat, or dribble, or drool, for a answer. Tryin to find the punk in me as he chalks the cue stick with the tip of his thumb.

But I never saw Salvie or Clean Willie or Johnny the Baptist break. Real players don't never break. "It's your cut, J.C. Take it."

"Fuck you. One last time—fuck you, Mookie," he yells to bring the pool cats' and conk-heads' stares again. Yells, then spins his stick to the floor before disappearin somewhere in this dark, the only thing left of him a trail of smoke from another Salem he's fired up.

And these stacks of C-notes, gray faces with eyes winkin under the fizzle of the ceilin lamp that swings over Salvie's favorite table. *You a gangster in your own right, in your own time, my nigga,* Ben's dry lips say between blinkin in and out.

Freddy from 43rd Street stares, sippin on his RC and watchin like he's tryin to figure what I'm gonna do. I wanna tell him to mind his own, cause this here's grown-nigga business. But it ain't. I push the stack of bills into the torn envelope, stuff it back into my coat pocket, and walk into the pool hall dark, opposite the rise of J.C.'s smoke.

I feel his shadow as I roll on 47th Street. East, to Hyde Park, I'm headin in the Benz, but it's behind me. I know. A Kentucky spirit, floatin there like the black mountain ghosts Papa use to talk about before his head went bad, floatin far enough back that I can't smell the prison funk or cigarette burn, close enough to let me know it'll catch up once it's ready to. Don't matter when that day will come, cause I won't know till it's too late and my soul is already snatched, my heart left on the corner of King Drive right where J.C. dropped Sermon in '69. That ain't even the little man back there, really, not in whole, not yet—just his shadow, trackin my steps down this strip that was once ours. Followin just so I know this ain't done, and it won't be till his shadow gets ready for it to be done. Goddamn bastard's shadow follows me all the way down to Woodlawn Avenue, close enough by then that it covers the Benz's window, blackness breathin on my neck.

So I swing the sedan around, chase this ghost back west on the strip just to teach the bastard who the fuck I am, let his goddamn shadow know I ain't no Low End punk. And it runs, clears out so quick that sun shows on 47th Street again, orange rainin on the intersections at Vernon Avenue, Ellis, Drexel, Cottage, and on King Drive down to Prairie. Bastard's bookin, baby, lettin that warmth free and loose on this place, shinin like I don't remember it shinin before, cause it's the punk, this evil thing, not me. Tryin to bring some kinda fear? Don't he understand who I am now?

The shadow thinks it's got away, too, that it can fool me by cuttin into a alley just west of Prairie, figures me for not followin in my pretty white Benz. Hah—that's what this stupid Kentucky spirit gets for thinkin without knowin who it's fuckin with, thinkin too hard for its own damn good. I push the pedal to the carpet, watch the Benz's dashboard dial kick up to seventy as I swerve through 47th Street souls, rag-heads and shorties, honeys and bums crossin in the middle of the strip, tear through um, cause I'm gonna get me this ghost. End this shit now. Shadow's been after me too long already. I swing the ride into the alley, rippin one-handed down gravel, cause I got the .38 in my left. And I see it—him—stopped up there near the alley's end, spit shinin in the left corner of his mouth somewhere in that black mountain shadow. Waitin on me. The dial swings up to ninety, and the .38's tappin against the windshield, cocked and ready to finish him and his muthafuckin (if he even had a fuckin mother) shadow, and the garbage bins tumble against my car door, rats and mice and stray cats and dogs jumpin over fences to get outta my way, most of um just in time.

And I catch the bastard, reach the place where his chapped lips shined, I swear, at the end of this path where I saw J.C. waitin on me, ready. But I'm at the alley's end and the little man ain't here, and the sun shines down warm on me even between this brick. I look over my shoulder, at the garbage scattered about this alley and dust still risin from the ground, what's left of my chase. But he ain't nowhere to be found, not with the garbage, not up in light. I put the .38 under my armpit, and I think I see somethin twinklin wet and silver down 46th Street, and it is spit in the corner of a mouth.

But that ain't nobody but the mail delivery man, slippin a message under the door of a Kenwood flat. I drive all the way outta the alley, into this spring warm, and I know Salvie and Tommy Ricci told me truth now. It's time to leave this place. Even with the sun shinin down warm, this strip and everythin around it ain't nothin but dead to me.

* * *

Don't stop for the red lights on 47th no more, don't feel I got to. I remember how the big cars use to roll west on the ol strip, ignorin the lights. Red or green didn't matter, cause them cars stayed on their path. They gave me power now, so I don't gotta break my stride on these streets neither. Ain't like the police's gonna pull me over. Who I gotta answer to? They know I'm the big man around here, that I control the back-alley loot that makes their job a good job. Faster I get where I gotta go, faster I can make sure our money's made and their cut protected. Ain't no reason to pull me over in this nowhere place, no profit to be made from writin a ticket for Mookie, hasslin the King, these days.

"Mookie! Mookie!" I look to the south, to the tired voice, and here is 47th Street Black callin me from his corner. The ol man waves and coughs smoke, his bloody eyes leakin tears—lonely tears, scared tears, sorry tears, don't know. I stop and press the power button for the passenger window to fall.

"What's up, Black? What you want?"

"Nothin. Hear you goin away."

"Goin away? Where I'm supposed to be goin away to?"

"Don't know. Just that you bout to leave, this's all I been told."

"Ain't goin no place," I say.

"You not?" The drunk rests against my car. "Where you headed this minute, then?"

"To Soul Mamma. Gotta pick up some business papers."

"Where you goin to after that?"

"Home, Black. Just goin home."

"And you ain't leavin these parts no time soon?"

"Naw."

"Never?"

"Never? Can't say never. Everybody gotta go away sometime, don't they? Ain't no point to life if we forever in the same place. Who'd wanna spend their years like that?"

Black wheezes. "Where you goin, Mookie?"

"Nowhere, I ain't goin nowhere." His spit gets near the car. "Just to Stony Island, that's all."

"Stony Island? What's over there?"

"Everythin. You ain't noticed all of what was here's gone? Where you think it went to? Everythin's on Stony Island Avenue now, Black."

"Naw it ain't. It ain't all left," the ol man argues.

"What the hell you talkin bout? You see how the strip looks?"

"Yeah, I see. I see everythin ain't gone. I'm tellin you the truth, Mookie. I'm still here, see?"

"All right, Black, you still here on Forty-seventh Street. You stay here. I'm movin to Stony with the rest of the world."

"What's over there so big like you say?"

"That's where Miss Nelly's is moved to. Calvin's Barbershop is on Seventy-ninth Street, right off the strip. Even Mister Shipp's funeral joint's there. It's a new world, Black, where life lives. On Stony, that's where a young nigga like me's gotta be to make his scratch."

"Oh yeah?" Black's tears is dried. He spits again, closer. "Well, this spook knows better than fool talk like that. Now maybe, like you say, you see life on Stony Island. Bout fifteen years ago, I saw it right where I stand. Accordin to you, that life's gone away. Fifteen years from now—mark my word, cause I won't be round when the day comes—but fifteen years from now, you gonna look round, wonder where the life you once saw over there went. If you mark these words like I'm tellin you, you gonna figure out that what used to be is run off to some new heaven, maybe north, maybe further south. Fifteen years later that place's gonna die too. Killed, strangled, whatever. Life'll run off again. One day, all the new places to run is gonna be used up, and that life will end up right back on Forty-seventh Street. Where else it's gonna go? And guess whose ashes'll be layin on the corner of Michigan, waitin for that fool to come home."

I put the window up halfway, feel the wind off the ol strip. "You should move to Stony. That's what you need to do, Black, move with me."

He laughs. "You don't listen no more, Mookie. You use to be such a good listener when you was a boy."

"I'm for real, jack. Bout to open up a business there. You come work for me, ringin up customers, sweepin, whatever you wanna do."

Black's spit smacks against my tire and I think bout drivin off. But

I ain't gonna see this man no more, so I swallow anger, forget it. "You know I came up on Forty-seventh and Ellis, Mookie. Raised myself on this street ever since it took away the rest of my people. This's all I know. You tryin to get a dead man to rise up from the grave, askin me to leave Forty-seventh. This's it, the forever I been left with. . . ." He stops and smells the air.

"What's wrong, Black? You sick?"

"Can't you smell?"

"What? I don't smell nothin."

"Where'd you say you was headed?"

"To Stony Island."

"Right now. I'm talkin bout now, where was you headed?"

I frown and sniff the air for myself, still don't smell nothin. "The club. Gotta pick up some business papers."

"Naw you ain't," he says. Black spits, onto the pavement this one last time. "You ain't goin to no club, ain't no papers to be picked up. Soul Mamma's burnin."

I smell again, and flames is in the air. I see black smoke risin further west, up from the strip. "You sure that's Soul Mamma?"

The ol soul laughs, cause I'm stupid. "Soul Mamma's burnin down. I know fire, and I know what a woman burnin smell like—just told you how long I been on this street. Twas damn fire that put me here."

18

STONY ISLAND AVENUE STRETCHES for five miles. It ain't no forever boulevard like Western or Cicero Avenue further west, or no lakefront highway like South Shore Drive. In fact, Stony's just this dark strip that cuts through Hyde Park's glory into one slum—the no-name ghetto east of Englewood—then Vernon Park, the purgatory in the valley of rich Pill Hill (where the negroes hide themselves when they ain't high-steppin on this strip), before Stony becomes the Calumet Expressway and takes you into the south suburbs, far away from this place. It's dark over here, like I say, no matter the rows of streetlights shinin their orange on the pavement. They call Stony a island, I suppose, causa the slab of concrete floatin in the middle of the street, separatin the north traffic from that headed south. Here, on this unbreakable divider, grass lives, even trees; it's green. Don't nothin else real grow on the street.

Other than the traffic, the concrete separation that allows grass to be, and the five miles of pavement, the strip is full of shops where broke folk spend their last cent on poisons they don't need—barbecue joints, greasy chicken shacks, liquor stores—poisons that's gonna sneak up and kill um. There's a hospital, just north of the Skyway overpass that slices the strip in half. They bring the bodies here. And, of course, there's God, just like on 47th. Stony worships at First Fellowship, Second Lutheran, Missionary this, Methodist that. There's even a mosque, on 74th and Stony, with a five-point star trapped inside a moon on the roof. These places is where they bring the souls.

I'm gonna open a car wash right near the mosque, on the other side of the strip. All the other businesses that came this way have profited. This's why Mister Ricci told me to move here. Besides, there's so much traffic on the street, so much dirt, I should make riches, my own legitimate riches.

At the strip's southern end, between 90th and 94th Streets, you got the filthy motels which Frankie Ray uses to hawk colored whores. And Fun-town, the broke-down amusement park, is on 95th Street. Here, Stony dies a all-of-a-sudden death at the expressway out to the south burbs. The five miles before that belong to me. That's why I came all this way, all this way south, just to end up on another cracked strip—I came, and it was worth it, cause this strip is all mine.

* * *

Now I see how Salvie's Outfit's been able to control everythin around the city—the world?—all these years. From where I'm sittin, on top of Stony, I can understand and appreciate. It's all about services with the Outfit, just like with the government. Uncle Sam can make sure you get electricity, water, gas, legal protection from the coons and spics, army protection from the Cubans and Russians, all that, or Uncle Sam can see to it that you don't get jack. So you pay Sam his taxes to keep yourself and your family and your block all bright and safe and clean and warm. The Outfit controls a different set of services: the city garbage trucks and dumps, the liquor license board, the restaurant unions, the street cops. So if you don't pay, or listen, to Salvie's mob you lose your benefits. Maybe all your chefs and waitresses and cleanup crews start takin sick days durin the weekend rushes, or your garbage dumpsters get to overflowin with a month's worth of rotten shit, enough to cause the neighborin businesses to call the health inspector (whose cousin's an Outfit guy) and get your joint shut down till the garbage's hauled off. Or maybe you gotta turn your liquor lounge into a fountain joint, offerin water and ginger ale to the winos lookin to spend their money and souls on drunk bar stools. Street cops come in with the illegal rackets: the gamblin joints (the ones that ain't ours), the whores, and the dope. Some need police protection, some need police ignorance, and some need both, which is how come we can take such a huge chunk—30, 35 percent—outta they money. Gotta pay the pigs somethin and still see a profit ourselves, else it wouldn't be no point to it. As long as you go with the flow, pay up a nice cut, do like we tell you, everything's okay. Otherwise, we gotta fuck your business up. And if you keep bein hardheaded, you gotta take a beatin. Or maybe your trade's worth more than your life, and we clip you. Like how Salvie and them done that Snake Pit Lounge bastard, Jackson, years ago. Just like Uncle Sam's government, this Outfit I work for.

The Stony Island folk know where I stand. They recognize I ain't really in the mob myself, know it ain't me they gotta please in the end. "How could this Black boy ever be a true mobster when they don't even really let in white cats who ain't Italian?" the Stony Island folk say. They know, but they gotta respect me still. Ain't no other choice, cause I'm the middleman between Tommy Ricci, Joe Defelice, and the survival of their businesses. That makes me the most powerful goddamn Black boy around. Better know where I stand, else I'll fuck your little shop up. Might as well be in for all the power I got over here, you see.

One time, the righteous fools who ran from 47th Street after Doctor King got clipped jumped on some ol preachin podium with me. Got to tellin Frankie and Nicky's boys they wasn't payin taxes no more. Had to call um in to one of Frankie's joints for a meetin. "What the fuck is goin on over here?" I asked um. They whined and cried some cockamamie pro-Black bullshit, askin how can I do this to them—takin away all they hard-earned paper for the white man. Blah and blah, yimmin and yam. So I laughed, though I wasn't happy a'tall, and took my money clip from my pocket (the solid gold one with *KING* engraved on the face). Snatched free the first bill—think it was a C-note—and I said, "Brothers, what color is the face on this here piece of paper?" "White," they said. Then I snatched a fifty. "And brothers, what color is the muthafucka on this here bill?" All at once, they told me "white." I snatched bills till I was at my last twenty, heard "white" for the hundredth time, and I said, "Brothers, what color was the muthafucka sittin in his bank who gave you this here hard-earned cash I'm takin from you?"

"White," they said, voices low all a sudden.

"Well, my brothers, that's why I'm doin this here to y'all. Find me niggas who print up money showin Black faces, and I'll be right next to you talkin bullshit. Till then, I ain't takin a damn thing, I'm just givin whitey back what whitey gave unto us, like the preacher say, and y'all stupid muthafuckas need to go on and reach into your pockets." Bastards got my point, and they paid me. Simple business. Those who got a problem with it is just mad cause they ain't seein a piece of this action.

They catch me before Sunday service. I go to church now, not cause I worship or even cause I believe, but cause it's the best place on Stony Island to do business. New Ebenezer Baptist sits in the middle of the strip, on 79th (there's Calvin's off to the east, I can see it from here—on Saturdays, they shoot craps in the back room for ol times' sake) just after the Skyway. Church is the perfect joint to meet with the strip's business folk, or with this bloodsucker alderman of Stony Island's, cause it's right in the center of everything. I stand at the top of the church staircase, near the entrance and above the worshipers, easy for them to find me. From here I look on everything north and south.

Jimmy Moore is my age. A dark cat with a hairy face, he wears black shades over his eyes and shinin pimp suits over a pole-thin body. I could break him in two if I wanted, but in the time I've been on Stony Island, I've found that he's big-time on this strip. In 1979, junk means more to folk than hookers and numbers, so Jimmy's bigger than Frankie Ray and Nicky Stokes, all without connections to the Italians. He runs the Blackstone Ranger gang—five hundred boys who kill and die in the name of this sorry-lookin bastard and his street religion. They control Stony, sell the strip's heroin, take kickbacks outta whatever else goes on (includin Nicky and Frankie's rackets), got their own shops on the strip. A little mob they are, strong and crazy enough that Tommy Ricci ain't never even tried to shut them down. So, since they sent me over here, I gotta get this wild bunch under my control, do what gangsters, police, mammas and daddies ain't been able to do in twenty years. I got a five-mile street to run and no more J.C.; somebody's gotta enforce my word.

"You handle that cat or what?" Jimmy's voice stings like rocks against the ears. "Our shit straight?"

"He's handled. Y'all ain't got nothin to worry bout." I watch the alderman leave the staircase, watch as he disappears inside New Ebenezer. "So our deal's done?"

I can't see Jimmy's eyes, but his forehead shows insulted wrinkles. "I told you I'm gonna look out for your honky friends."

"What?"

"Don't want to or nothin, but I said I'm gonna look out for um. Told you everything's cool. You must ain't got no faith in the Black man, just believe in these honkies you run with."

I laugh. I know he don't expect me to be punked. *I* punk *him,* see, not the other way around. Where's his fear?

One of Jimmy's boys reaches across the stairway railing, hands him a gold walkin cane. "You ain't doin for honkies, and I ain't got faith in honkies. This's between me and you, my brother. "

"Ain't yo brother. You don't know nothin bout what I'm ridin on, chief, so don't call it out."

"My fault." I'll play his game, let him think he's the big man with his Low End bullshit. "But this's our business. You only helpin me, Mo. This ain't about nobody else."

"Say that in Tommy Ricci's face." He walks to the church door but never turns his shades from me. "I been on this strip for years, doin whatever the fuck—excuse me, Jesus—I wanted. Got this place protected, the other nations runnin scared. Ain't had to worry bout no pigs comin over here, takin my racket and puttin none of that ready rock junk in its place. Ten years I kept this up, joe, you hear me? Ten years—that's somethin else. After all that, I ain't tryin to slip up and let no devils on Stony to take us down. Too many go out like that, fuck up by lettin niggas with black skin and white thinkin sneak near."

"That's what you say I am?" I look south, then north, up the strip. "A devil? Didn't I tell you I looked out for you with that alderman?"

"You say you did."

"I did."

"We'll see."

"I'm true to my word." The staircase is empty now, except for me and this man in his Easter bunny suit. "And what'd you promise to do in return?"

"Said I'd look out for you, some shit like that."

"Have my back, that's what you told me—help me run the strip, let your Stones muscle for me round here. Long as I got City Hall outta your pocket, you'd get outta Ray's and Stokes' business. You'd work with us. We had a deal, that's what you told me, Mo."

He laughs. "We'll see."

"We'll see? We got a deal, Mo. You saw me talkin to that muthafuckin rat alderman, saw us shakin hands right where you stand."

"Watch your mouth—house of God, chief."

"You saw me."

"I saw. But who you with?"

"You know damn well who I'm with, else we wouldn't be havin conversation. Ain't nobody tryin to take over your thing. We just gonna make our own money here, that's all."

"Now it's 'we' again, what 'we' gonna do," he says, and laughs. "You need me to help you run this Stony Island for them, Mook?"

I'm gonna play his game, like a true player should, until I get what I want. "Yeah, I need you behind me."

"So we partners? I help you protect their thing and keep my business. We'll run the strip together like that, be partners: me, you, and Tommy Ricci?"

I look at the church—service is about to start. "Everybody wants to be the boss," I say, and hold out my hand.

"And it's my turn."

"What?"

"To be the boss, my turn. Black man's turn, brother."

I laugh. "Long as we got a deal, we're partners."

Jimmy Mo grips my hand and we walk into church, runnin the strip together. I'm gonna clip him before too long, just so he knows Tommy Ricci gave this strip to me alone. Just gotta help him understand who runs the hustle on Stony Island today.

I don't pray durin service, don't figure there's cause for such a thing. Got this far without askin God for shit, so I figure life'll go on just fine if I don't start beggin now. Can't do business durin service neither, and I sure ain't about to listen to Reverend Goode's rantin, not this Sunday. All's left is to sit and think in this pew. It's Jesus I wonder on. Don't much understand the cat, to be honest. I remember Reverend Goode—durin one of them long-ago moments when an empty skull left me nothin to listen to but his preachin—talkin about Jesus hangin on the cross. The son of God prayed for his father's help as he bled, accordin to the preacher. And after his prayers wasn't answered, Jesus turned angry with the father for abandonin him, then died. But how come somebody who raised a man from his grave had to ask God for freedom from wood and rusty nails in the first place? The Reverend woulda argued some nonsense about how the son was a man sent to earth, a man who got soft from the pain of hangin there and called out for his father's help in that weak moment. Reverend wasn't sent here to explain nothin to me, see, least not the truthful way I'm lookin for it to be told.

I figure Jesus musta been a lie—either that or he was stupid as a coon. Simple logic says a man that powerful don't need to beg for nothin. If the Italians and the Jews got together to crucify *me* (and that's what happened to this Jesus, how Reverend tell it) and my father didn't come to help, I'd get down from that cross myself and use all that fish-multiplyin, sight-givin, grave-raisin power to snatch Him off his throne. Then I'd take over and run shit just how I wanted to run it. Sure wouldn't stay up on no slab of wood, whinin about why ain't my daddy here for me like this sorry bastard did as he died.

"Amen," Mora says to the Reverend's babble.

I look at the woman to my right, remember how fine she used to be, how she screamed. But Mora's in her thirties now, into her thirties good—thirty-four, thirty-five—and time, not even a lot of it, has brung her to hard age. Chunks of fat show under her chin, and her skin's turned such a pale yellow that veins streak in green along her arms and neck. And she's got a sick womb, frozen solid with blue ice. She ain't the trophy she used to be, ain't the finest gem on our side of the city no more. So I'm about to get rid of her, maybe even after church, I'll do it. But this's too cruel, nothin she really deserves—I'll wait till the Easter season is done, then. Next week I'll cut her loose. Ain't no thing, I can always find someplace else to live, been lookin at the high-rise condos over on South Shore Drive. I won't have to strain to see the lake from there either, just look out the window each mornin, down on the miles of water, on how far

I've come. Besides, if I move to South Shore, I'll be closer to the strip. That's where I need to be.

Findin a new woman ain't no problem neither. So many of um claim to love me here on Stony Island. Even when I walk outta Ebenezer with Mora today there'll be at least one winkin her hot brown eyes my way, offerin a white-stockinged leg. They got no respect for who I'm with, won't even see nobody standin next to me, especially not this high yellow, faded queen. When the white Benz or gold Firebird drives these streets, it ain't no desperate bum who calls out my name, it's the love of ladies ol as Mamma and younger than Geri, some young enough to be my child. This strip is my stage, I belong here. Where else would they worship, who would they swoon for, if not for Mookie King?

I know the faces, the important ones, in Ebenezer's congregation. There's the alderman, and the gravedigger Mister Shipp, who makes riches off the blood of Stony's rackets, and in the corner, that skinny Black pusher whose dope spills on Stony long as we walk the concrete strip together. And in front is the Reverend, preachin his holy babble in God's house. They scared of me, yeah, so scared I notice a wince in the eyes as they fight not to give back my stare.

But there's a set of eyes that don't run when I look back. I see them, feel them, in the very back row of Stony Island's new temple. Low to the ground, these eyes is, cause they belong to a small man. His glare winces, true enough, but not in fear. The short, shady eyes wince cause they hate what they see. As poison, death, faith, and lies fear me, I fear his hate.

So it's me who runs to look away. I hide in the pupils of little Isaiah, not so little no more, truth be told. He sits beside his mamma, to the right of my mamma, and there ain't nothin but love in him. The hate in the back of this church won't never get me, cause I got the innocence of these clean eyes to run to, the blessin of my nephew's quiet watch. This is true love, see, not the love of Mora's lust, or that of the strip's greedy tramps, but that of a ten-year-ol who believes in me. I don't gotta worry about Mora not bearin children, as long as I look into Isaiah's eyes and call him son. In return, I won't never let the boy dream a lie. Isaiah'll know better than to waste his life with crippled years or die in a swamp of his own blood and shit. The boy will get down off the cross before it's too late, I'll make sure of it. I have to, cause I'm all the father he's got.

"Ebenezer Baptist Church owes great praise and gratitude," Reverend Goode tells them, "especially to the blessed support of one of our own during this season of the Resurrection. It is because of his contributions—great financial and spiritual contribution—that our congregation worships in the magnificence of this new temple, blessedly built in less than twelve months. To this one man we offer thanks. Brother Mookie King . . ."

I stand and turn to the congregation, look into the eyes of those who owe me, feel their respect. The applause rises from the front of the church, carries on through to the back rows, in waves up to the balconies. It's loud, so loud—ain't never heard such praise in this life. Not when J.C. came back to 47th Street, not when Isaiah's real daddy played that Black, sad song, not when I was the quarterback, not even when Papa swung at them fastball pitches, never. These holy folk clap for me long and loud enough to drown out the hate in New Ebenezer's back row. I feel nothin but warmth against these walls I built. They do love me.

* * *

The house on 45th Street's still got its hobbled odor, even as they pack to leave. Mamma, she's ready, even likin the idea of getting outta the Forties. Me and Geri don't live nowhere near, so ain't no reason for her to be here. Maybe she still coulda found herself some kinda happiness if I wasn't bringin them to Clyde Avenue. Maybe she was all right in Papa's funk, didn't think nothin of brick two-flats next to negroes on Pill Hill. But this is what my riches is for, givin my people what they didn't think about havin, wouldn't uh never had otherwise.

But Papa ain't moved from his love seat. As this place he's limped in for twenty years gets snatched up around him he stares out these barred livin room windows. No painful mumblin come from him since I been here, nothin, not even the nods and grunts I'm use to. Papa just sits on this love seat like the wound that took his legs and words finally stole what was left of him. Mamma's harassed him about not liftin a finger to pack, me and Geri and the boy greeted him, but the ol man ain't stirred—not till Isaiah, clumsy with age, trips into his feeble knees. Papa groans, then his stare loses its blink and he's more silent than before.

"Where Grandpa and Big Ma goin, Uncle Mookie?" The boy speaks from behind a cardboard box that hides him from his granddaddy. He's afraid of the ol man, always seemed so.

"Near the Hill," I say.

"Why?"

I laugh at his voice's squeak. "Cause it's a better place for um to live."

Isaiah peeks at his granddaddy as the ol man starts to move, but drops his head's tight curls behind the box before Papa can turn to him. "How're they getting there, over to the Hill?"

I lift the black rockin chair over my head and set it on the porch. "You mean if they goin by car or truck? That what you mean?"

"Yeah. How they getting to the Hill?"

"By truck," I say. "I rented one to move all these boxes, all the furniture on the porch, everything, to the new house."

"They got a new house?"

"Yeah, of course they got a new house. Where else they gonna move to but a new house? A better, bigger, safe place right off the Hill."

"How?"

I frown, tired of the boy's game. Wonder if I asked so many questions when I was ten years ol. I think to ask Papa, but he don't know. My fault. He do know, just won't say so.

"How, Uncle Mookie?"

The boy's whinin now, so I reach cross the room, drag him from his hidin place. He cries fake tears as his jeans-covered knees scrape the tile.

"Stop, Mookie!" Geri's voice yells from the upstairs. "Stop messin with my child!"

I drop the boy beside the kitchen table. "Shut up that cryin, boy," I say. "How come you ask so many questions? Ain't nobody ever told you bout questions?"

"No." Isaiah pouts.

"Well, questions, see, you ain't supposed to ask um less you already know answers, else you find out somethin you really don't wanna know. Ain't nobody ever told you that?"

"That don't sound right, Uncle Mookie," Isaiah says, swallowin snot. "How am I ever gonna find anything out unless I ask somebody? What's so bad to know? You just don't wanna tell me the truth."

"That ain't so," I say. "I'm lookin to save you heartache, is all. That's what answers bring, heartache. But you go on, ask all you want if you think you know so much better than I know. What was your question?"

Isaiah pauses, like his little mind rethinks the thing. He smiles. "How're Big Mamma and Grandpa moving to a new house on the Hill?"

"Number one, it ain't on the Hill, their new house," I answer, unrollin my shirtsleeves, "it's just off the Hill. Number two, I got your grandpa and Big Mamma the place, bought it for um myself."

"You did?" The boy stands from the floor's dust. "What do you do, Uncle Mookie?"

"Goddamn. This's the last time you askin me, right, boy?"

"Maybe."

I hear my mother's and sister's feet poundin heavy against the empty second floor and J.C. blinks across my mind. Can't figure why. My eyes shoot to the livin room, to my ol man strugglin to push his love seat out to the porch; worn thing ain't movin though. Don't know why I'm lettin um take this furniture to Clyde Avenue. Such funky ol chairs and sofas ain't but fit for a shack in the Forties. I gotta buy um a new set soon as can be, pieces good enough for this house off the Hill. I button my shirtsleeves . . . yeah, they need furniture fit for a slick new crib.

"What do you do?" The boy's voice whines again.

"What do I do?" I sit on the kitchen table, that same table Mamma used to tear through the *Daily News* and *Defender* on top of, lookin for only God knew what. "What do I do? What you wanna be in life, boy?"

"Huh?"

"When you grow up, what you wanna be?" I chuckle. "You been runnin your mouth off, askin all these questions. I figure, outta the sake of fair, I can ask you at least one."

The boy laughs, wise. "Wanna play for the Sixers."

"That's what you wanna do?"

"Like Doctor J."

"No you don't," I say. "You don't wanna be no goddamn basketball player. I wanted to play baseball when I was ten, least I thought I did."

"So how you figure playing for the Sixers ain't what I wanna do?"

"Cause baseball was what I wanted till I found that was somebody else's dream. Can't grow to be a man tryin to live somebody else's dream. Don't get you nowhere but crippled, can't get you nowhere else. So I gave that up for football, till I found out that belonged to somebody else, too. So does shootin hoops. All I got left now is what I do."

"So what do you do, Uncle Mookie?"

"Just told you, boy. I do what I do. I work."

Isaiah groans, tired of me. I watch him run to Papa, watch as he tries to help the ol man push his seat to the porch. They give up and drop to the cushions after a minute, the boy in Papa's lap. I hold my head, wishin for a bottle. Wishin, cause I realize I ain't never had no dream of my own, not one that was worth a goddamn thing. This answer I ain't asked nobody for, and I need cheap rum to forget about it.

19

I MEET WITH SALVIE durin his mornin walks these days, or in the Greektown shops, or maybe along the lakefront beaches (never the South Side 31st or 57th Street beaches, but the stretches of Gold Coast sand up north, under the shadows of high-rises), like today. We meet where it's free to talk without worryin about spies. The big-timers respect me that much now, respect enough to whisper secrets with me in corners. They're into everything now, Tommy Ricci and Salvie, more everything than back in the ol days. They got a chunk of the unions, the Vegas casinos, the trash collection racket, most all the restaurants through Illinois, Wisconsin, and Michigan, and the politicians all the way to the White House. Tommy Ricci's over damn near all of Chicago, but Tommy Ricci's still from the South Side, so me and Joey Defelice got more power than anybody else runnin a city territory. Mister Defelice's got more say-so than I do, true. I understand that. But we all got moved up big-time. I ain't just a loot-collectin coon no more.

"I miss it sometimes, you know. Wouldn't uh figured it to be, but I do. Miss it . . . how're things over there, Mook?" We sit on the Oak Street Beach, right under rich folk and just back from the water; I never gotta look far at all to see the lake these days.

"Fine, everything's fine," I say. "And you? How's things your way?"

"My way? Best I could ask for," he says, and watches a young white girl jog past with her dog's chain in hand, both her and the mutt starin. In this pretty place, we look out of our element—a thirty-somethin Black man on a park bench talkin to a sixty-somethin gray man who sits under a beat-up hat. There's gotta be some type of crime goin down, some sickness, so they stare. The ol man gazes back at them, twists his lips like he wants to spit. "Best I could ask for. Moved to the suburbs, you know?"

"I heard. Out in Olympia Fields, right? That's what I'm told."

"Yeah, Olympia Fields. It's a nice place. Nice, quiet, comfortable place. Good town to end up in, Mook."

"To end up in," I repeat. "I moved my folks a few weeks back, off of Forty-fifth Street."

"Oh yeah?" He frowns again. "Where to?"

"Clyde Avenue. Right by Pill Hill."

His face relaxes. "That's a good place, too," he says. "Use to know some people over there. Me, I moved where I ain't gotta worry about nothing. Even off the Hill, your folks can't walk too far east without endin up in the middle of hell. Where I am, the only place I find hell is in the Bible. Or when I turn on the TV set."

"Mmh." I look into spring sun. "They'll be all right. I put bars on all their windows and doors before they moved in. It's safe."

"Don't get me wrong, that's still a okay neighborhood over on Clyde. At least right off Pill Hill, it's still halfway decent. I just can't live behind all those bars myself. Makes me feel like a animal. Don't need bars out in the suburbs. We ain't nowheres near hell. But don't get me wrong, that neighborhood just off the Hill ain't too shabby yet." Salvie moves toward me, lightin a cigarette as he closes the space between us. "So, what you need to meet with me for, Mook? What's the problem that Joey couldn't handle it?"

"Ain't no problem, Salvie. Told you, everything over there's just fine," I say as the ol man's smoke stings my eyes. "Just bringin a business proposition to you before I bring it to anybody else."

"Whatcha looking to do?"

"You know a pusher named Jimmy Moore?"

Disgust crosses his face, and his lips twist without spit. "Can't say I do. Don't think I'm familiar with the name."

"Well, Jimmy Mo's the leader of the Blackstone gang over on Stony. Don't expect you to know about them neither, cause it's a South Side thing. But they deal the dope around there. The strip's theirs, Salvie, they run it much as I do. And when I say they run it, I mean he runs it. They kill in this mutha's name."

"Years I was over there, Mook, saw all kindsa garbage. So what you telling me about this particular buzzard for? You trying to tell me I'm a fool for missing it? Better to let an old man stay romantic before you remind him how things really was."

I look away, to the water. Salvie's makin no sense to me. "This heroin business they do, it's the Filipinos that supply um—crazy dope. I'm talkin millions, multimillions a year they make. Jimmy Mo's rich as all get-out, and he ain't never paid a dime in taxes, not to y'all. The way I look at it, he owes big-time. You ain't never let nobody I know of get away with sayin fuck y'all. You wouldn't be a rich man out in Olympia Fields lettin too many go that far."

"Watch it, fella," Salvie says. "We ain't let nobody do nothing. You point out to me one somebody who can muscle this cocksucker you talking about. I know who he is, this cocksucker . . . know a hundred no different than him, like I told you. Snaps his fingers and he's got em crawling from under the rocks over there, spilling blood. Their blood, their brother's blood, their mother's, whatever, it don't matter. They'll kill white, Jew, Hispanic, Black over there, anybody, long as that bastard snaps for em to make the move. You point out to me one somebody who can fuck with that."

"So he's bigger than your thing, that's what you tellin me?"

"Not at all."

"That's what it sounds like you sayin, Salvie. Sound scared—this

Jimmy Mo's bigger than the Italians. You tellin me your thing ain't shit no more."

"Get outta here, Mook. Fucking cocksucker."

"If you strong as you act like, why not muscle this character, take a bigger piece outta his action? It's millions he's makin on the strip, probably more than that. Thirty-five percent outta what he's got should come out to a hundred K per month by itself."

"How the fuck much is too much, Mook? And what do we do about this bunch of bastards who kill for him? How do you squeeze a operation like that one, mister goddamn genius?"

"We get rid of him," I say, and feel mighty at the sound of my words. "Clip him and make sure those at his back think some other street-corner gang did it. Stupid muthafuckas'll be so set on killin everything in this other crew, they ain't gonna be concerned bout us. Then we take over."

Salvie coughs. "Take over what? You know goddamn well we don't mess around firsthand with street dope. I thought you was trying to muscle the thing, not take it over. We ain't no pushers, Mook. I can't help you with that."

"You ain't gonna be pushin no dope, so you ain't gotta worry bout soilin your hands. It's gonna be me doin it, my thing. Y'all just get your thirty-five percent cut, like anything else, and let me be the man with dirty hands."

"Years ago I told you, you don't fuck around with that stuff as long as you work for us. It's too much dirt."

"I was a kid back then, Salvie, in a different world, you see? I ain't gonna be usin the shit, I ain't stupid. This's my business, man." I breathe his smoke, take in the burn. "Shit changes."

Salvie nods, holds another cloud in his lungs long as he can. "I thought you'd made peace with everybody over there, had a good agreement."

"We got a agreement," I say. He's turned soft, this onetime killer, in his late years. "But what's peace without a piece? We ain't controllin nothin long as Jimmy Mo's around. Junk runs the shop on Stony Island. Ain't gonna lie to you, Salvie—that strip is his. But if he's gone, ain't nobody else who got the connections to put the whole thing behind them, keep it strong like it is now. It don't matter what agreement we got, cause he's makin millions and we ain't seein jack."

"What're we working with over there? We got the motels?"

"Yeah, Frankie's still got that locked up."

"We got the gambling?"

"Nicky's runnin that, the bets and numbers—what's left."

"The streets is paying taxes?"

"Of course we got that. I'd shut the strip down if we wasn't seein our cut like we supposed to."

"So what's the problem, Mook? How much is too much? Why do you need to mess around with this Moore character and his dope? You're talking about starting a war between your people over there. All this Black blood's gonna interfere with everything. Peace is a easier way to do business, Mook, easier than shooting. You hear me? It's the blood of your own that'll spill if you go about messing with this bad business."

Like I say, the ol man's got weak on me. "What'd you tell me, Salvie? Years ago, what was it you told me? Wasn't it you who said that the only people I got is those who know not to get in the way of my livelihood? Didn't you say fuck um if they keep me from makin loot? It was you who told me that, Salvie. These people is messin up profit over there, keepin me from my cut."

"So what you come to me for?" He sighs. "You know I don't believe in killing nobody."

"What?"

"I don't believe in killing, Mook," he repeats, his eyes on the beach sand across from us. "I ever told you to kill anybody? In life, I ever told you to do that?"

I search my mind, not for an answer—Salvie's too smart to ever *tell* me to kill—but for his point. "No."

"Exactly. This's cause I don't believe in it. Killing ain't a good thing. God's the only one who got the right to clip a man. Me and you, we can steal, gamble, screw, beat, but we shouldn't be out here killing nobody. It's up to Him when it's time for a man to leave this place, not us."

"You're in the wrong business to be believin such bullshit."

"Watch your mouth, fella . . . I ain't saying I ain't clipped nobody. I had to do it to get far as I've got in life, to get into this thing even. I had to. I'll suffer for that, when my time comes to suffer. That's up to God too, my fate. But you can't never say I told you to clip a soul, led you down this same way. Sure, I had you collect from this one and that one, bust up this or that cocksucker. Sure I done that, but that's different. It ain't like taking a man from the earth. God's work, that's what that is."

I drop my head to my palms, cause it aches. "So, you sayin I shouldn't move against him? I can't get this bastard took care of?"

His smoky chuckle fights off another cough. "Alls I'm saying is what I said. What goes on over there, that's up to you. Those is your streets, your people, that's what you was told years back. Long as we get our money every week, no less than what we expect, as long as we get that money, you do whatever you like. Spill as much blood as it takes to make you happy. But you're gonna have to answer for it in the end, cause it's wrong. And don't lead nobody else down this path. That's your only chance, Mook, that's all what I'm saying to you."

I bite my lip, feel poundin inside my head. "It's late, Salvie, late for that."

"That's rough," he says, and smashes his cigarette underfoot. He lights another. "You do what you gotta do then, fella."

The old man pats me on the knee and walks off, away from the lake, beat-up hat disappearin in the water's shine. It's too late to save myself, so ain't no reason not to tend to business on the strip the way I see best fit.

* * *

My new office's got bigger mirrors than what I had at Soul Mamma. It's in the car wash's far corner, tucked off so I ain't a part of this joint, but close enough that I hear when brushes don't scrub against cars. I watch through the office window, at an angle, keep an eye on whether the shiftless street punks is dryin off the cars good. If they ain't, I fire um. I've learned that there ain't room for laziness in business, not even in the car wash racket. But when they do like they suppose to, I buy um a bottle of E&J or Seagram's, somethin extra, at week's end. I still got a place in my heart for bums, see, even now.

This's where I wait, in my office, wait and listen to the rumble of the brushes, the clean scream of the soap machines. I look at my reflection, feel the scars on my face. Didn't figure mirror glass for leavin marks but some of the cuts is here still, tiny enough that they can't be seen by anybody but me now. I only notice them rubbin a hand across my face, carefully against my cheek. I don't hate the little man for my wounds—touchin don't hurt no more. I wonder about him, though, where he is these days, what he does. Ain't talked to J.C. in two years, just about two years to the day, in fact. I hear he's around 47th Street, know he's still alive, just ain't talked to him. Ain't missin the little bastard or nothin; just wonder what's come of him, is all.

The cleanin machines go silent, no cars bein washed. My heart drops—sinks like this whenever I ain't makin money, when I ain't doin somethin that's gonna make cash in the end. It ain't often, cause my heart's usually doin exactly like it's supposed to be, beatin in my chest as cash rolls in.

The bald head of one of the car wash workers pokes into the room, though they ain't suppose to be disturbin me without knockin. "Somebody's lookin to see you, Mister King."

I stand as my heart jumps into place. "Who? Let um in."

The door swings open all the way and the head is gone. Jimmy Mo's boy steps into the office, the one who carries the gold cane around for that clown. He's dressed in white like his boss, but his hands is empty. I look into his pockmarked face, and my heart don't move. "Close the door."

"Done," the boy mumbles once we're behind walls.

"What?"

"Got him by the ol Regal lot this mornin."

"You sure?"

"Jimmy's gone," the boy promises. "Three times to the forehead, enough to take him out for sure." He don't show he's sorry for it, don't even step toward J.C.'s chair, just leans against the office door like he's ready to go. Loaded .38 Special sits in the desk's right-hand drawer, like at ol Soul Mamma. Just in case some fool wants to show his little ass. "You gonna look out for what we got on Stony, make sure things flow like they been flowin?"

"That was our deal. I'm good for my word," I say. "Disciples did it, right?" My eyes run from the mirror to the back lot, where the workers is supposed to dry cars. It's empty of business still.

"That's the word we got on the street—Disciples did it," the boy's voice squeaks, and the cleanin machines scream against the walls, shakin the buildin. "It's gonna be war. Gotta start takin um out to make it look good. Takin somebody out for payback. Ain't got no choice."

I'm rich. I reach into my desk, pour a whiskey shot—hit it and smile. "You do what you gotta do, brother. Do what's right."

* * *

Mora keeps all the televisions on in the apartment, always this foolish noise. The Holy Ghost came, stopped me from breakin up with her months back—at least that's what Geri said after I told her about it. I couldn't do no wrong to the woman with this jive spirit runnin through me. It ain't fear, cause I don't feel no fear for a broad whose veins show through chunks of ol fat. It's just this stupid goddamned Ghost runnin through me, tryin to remind a nigga to be scared of livin his life. Makes it hard, but I'm lookin to end this still. All this goodness just keeps me from doin what I know is wrong: hurtin a woman who use to look just like Lena Horne. But she ain't fine no more, not at all like how she used to be. So soon as this Holy Ghost goes about its way, this is over.

"Yap, yap, yap," the TV screen says, "yap, yap, yap."

I run across the apartment, slam the power button on the livin room box. For a moment, quiet. Then my ears pick it up—this noise from the bedroom. Mora's got a television in there even. No more gospel songs sung to me in the mornin, just the silver screen's lies. Had a set in there ever since she stopped screamin, I swear. Or maybe she got the television, then she stopped screamin. That's how I wanna think it went, cause then it was the lies that iced her and not my dick. We been together for twelve years now—how far did I expect our thing to last? Was God gonna keep us like we was, fuckin loud enough to drown out her educated words and my strip jive forever? If I'm bored of her dyin body, then she's bored of my fat, bored of how I've become less the young coon as the money rolls in. We ain't done bad; twelve years is long enough to be common-law back down South, and that ain't bad. But I don't need her to see the lake and, since Hyde Park's gone mostly Black these days, she don't need me to feel nigganess. I wonder when this goddamn Ghost is gonna leave.

"This morning, reputed Chicago mob underboss Gaetano 'Tommy' Ricci was indicted on twenty counts of violating the federal Racketeer Influenced and Corrupt Organizations Act. The indictment alleges that Ricci is not only a head of the Chicago syndicate but its representative on organized crime's national ruling board, the Commission. The United States Attorney's office expects . . ."

"Did you hear, Mookie?"

I drop to the couch and turn the livin room set back on. I've forgot what I was thinkin about. "I heard."

Mora says somethin more, but I don't know what it is. I can't understand her cause what's before me—the tale of livin this life, told in the words of babblin fools—burns at the edge of me. All I can do is moan.

"What you gonna do?" the woman's voice comes from the bedroom. I do hear her now.

"Don't know." Lost track of how long it's been since last I moved. "What can I?"

"Nothing," Mora—or this sweet voice that once belonged to the finest woman south of Roosevelt Road—says. Then there's quiet, a long quiet that really ain't quiet cause it's filled with yappin and breathin. "What if they send you away?"

"Me?" I look through the bedroom door frame into this empty square, find myself in her rich ol mirror. "For what?"

"They got him. How long will it take for them to get to you?"

"Girl, I don't know no more bout Tommy Ricci than what they sayin on the TV station. Know no more than you know. What's he gotta do with me?"

I hear her breathe hard. "You know, if they send him away for fifty years, they'll get you for one hundred fifty."

I move finally, walk to the window and look east, toward the lake. Still can't quite see it from here, so I sit back on the couch. "For once, they're after one of their own, instead of chasin us, and I'm still suppose to be scared?"

"What'll they do with the nigger soul that's owned by the devil they're chasing after, Mookie? Once they catch it, what do you figure?"

"I ain't owned by nobody, goddamnit—and I ain't no nigger. Stop calling me that. " My voice's louder than I mean for it to be—echoes in the ceilin. "I don't but own a car wash on Stony Island. What'd I do wrong?"

"Lower your tone." I hear her feet, those feet that were so soft once, stompin to the bedroom door. "All I'm letting you know is to be ready when they come. Tar and feathers they'll bring for you. And you aren't getting away."

"Don't worry, baby."

"I'm not."

"One hundred and fifty years? You fuckin around?"

"At least—read about a New York guy they gave one hundred to, a year ago. Snuck a bug on him, heard everything they needed to, and put him away for a lifetime. That's how they do their own."

"Mmh." I flip stations without meanin to. "Would you wait for me?"

"What do you mean, wait?"

Channel five's talkin about Tommy Ricci, too. "For me to come home, would you wait?"

"One hundred and fifty years?"

The story's done burnin at me, made its point twice, so I turn the television off. "If you love me, that's what you suppose to do. A good woman who loves her man waits, don't matter how long he gotta be gone. Wait for me to come home from work, wait for me to come off the streets. Back from war, from jail. That's how the women did back in the day, waited for niggas. If they loved um."

"If."

I listen for her to finish, but ain't nothin else comin from her lips. "Like in the song, the one on the radio. How's it go? . . . 'Always and forever.' That's how it's supposed to be."

"Oh yeah?" I see her now, her reflection in the TV screen, standin in that space that was black a second ago. She leans on the frame, and she's beautiful—if I don't look too close, what I see *is* beautiful.

Much younger than reality, causa the distance between us. So fine and young that, if not for the fool babble of the world outside, we could be back in the ol days together. More lies. "Would you wait one hundred and fifty years for me?" she says. "Forever?"

I wanna tell her, tell her that not so long back, I loved her cause she was the sweetest thing I ever laid eyes on, and cause she screamed when I was in her, made me feel like the man I wanted to be. Like a king, she made me feel, and I did love this girl. Without blinkin about it, too—not like J.C. used to blink over his young Christina. My baby shined too bright for blinkin. Couldn't do nothin but stare with wonder at such a high-bright angel whose face was righteousness. Then, yes, I woulda waited. Now I can't love her. I can't and I don't, but I did. I wanna tell her, I swear, but I see this reflection lyin to me, and it's got me.

So I sing back to the sweet angel standin in the TV screen's blank place. "You ain't goin nowhere, girl," the jive song goes, hustlin Mora into believin that we ain't dyin. But we is—me and her both is just dyin away.

20

DON'T EVER TRUST NOTHING that's got good sense, Mook."

"What?"

"If it's got sense, you can't trust it, whatever it is: a broad, a business partner, a waiter like that kid over there." Salvie points across Zorba's dinin space to the four-eyed cat who served us. The ol man, believin that I'm lookin at the waiter, loses himself in the coffee below him. "Take this cup of coffee. I'm about to put it to my lips because I can trust it. You know why?"

I follow the waiter to the hidden kitchen. "Why, Salvie?"

"Because it's stupid, this swirling coffee here. If it had any sense about itself, it'd stay too hot for me to ever put my lips to it. Then I couldn't swallow it up, and it'd live on. Ain't that what you'd do if you was a cup of coffee, just stay so hot that nobody could ever drink you up? Wouldn't you?"

"The coffee ain't got say-so over that. It cools off by nature, Salvie, nothin it can do bout gettin drank."

"Sure it is. Coffee lives, the liquid part is alive. I was reading this book about molecules, atoms, and shit—they're all alive, these things. This cup of coffee's full of um. It lives, same as a man lives. What does a man do to keep himself from dying? Eat good, stay away from too many cigarettes, too much booze, the wrong type of women, exercise when he can. That's something alive, full of molecules and atoms and shit, fighting off death. So how come this cup of coffee, full of the same things, can't stay hot and keep me from drinking it up? Cause it ain't got the good common sense to think like that, maybe?" He raises the cup to his lips.

"How you know that coffee ain't hot right now, then? Just cause there ain't no smoke don't mean it won't burn. That foam cup's so thick, maybe you can't even feel the heat inside now. Coffee's waitin up in there, gonna sneak up on you, singe your lips."

Salvie drops the cup against the table without drinkin, black drops splashin on wood. "See, that's why I can't trust you no more, Mook. You do too much thinking for your own good. When you was a kid, you come to me and you was stupid—high trustability. If you'd come to me like you is now, I never woulda let you handle my dough. That's what I'm trying to tell you about brains and trust, they don't go together. You remember your friend, the fella with the stupid name? What was it, B.G. or something?"

"J.C."

"Yeah, him. Never trusted that kid, always took him for too smart. Not ambitious, really, just too smart for his own goddamn good. You can't trust a fella like that. What ever happened to that kid?"

"Me and him fell out a few years back."

"Over money, a broad, what?"

"Somethin like that."

"See, you can't trust no smart guys. That's what I'm trying to tell you." Salvie sips the coffee and nods. "Nice and cool. You know who the only fella I've always trusted is?"

"Who?"

"Angelo. You know Angelo, right? My sister's kid—dumbest cocksucker I ever met." The ol man looks through the shop's window. "High trustability, that Angelo . . . now what're you gonna say to the feds if they come to you?"

"Nothin, Salvie. If I don't know nothin, how can I say nothin? That's it, ain't it?"

"That ain't it. Questions—you come to me talking nonsense weeks back about some dope-pushing cocksucker over in your neighborhood. This kinda shit. Don't go trying to pin no kinda spade dope dealing on us if they come asking, Mook. We ain't no street pushers, and you know it. They know it too, but don't try pinning it on us. That's your fucking thing, you said it to me. Right?"

"I said it, Salvie." I stop, bite my lips. My eyes follow the ol man's through the window, out to Jackson Street. "This cat, Jimmy Moore, the guy I mentioned to you. You know he got clipped?"

"Clipped?" Salvie don't even bother showin a smile. "So what? Don't you try pinning it on us."

"I know."

"This guy, he was a pusher, wasn't he?"

"You know Jimmy to be in that business."

"What do I know, you motherfuck?" Salvie's quiet as the waiter passes our table. "*Babania* is what they're gonna wanna hear from you. They ain't got nothing real now, and it's bullshit what they do got, this case. They put some dope on the spoon and it starts to sound like something. It's all bullshit, all of it. I told you to stay away from that dirty business, didn't I? I told you."

I sip. "You told me, Salvie. I know."

"You know shit. The feds is gonna use a whole lotta different kinda words to get into your head, confuse you, get you babbling at the lip. Threats, offer deals, convince you to put on a wire maybe, these things. It's a hustle, just a fucking hustle's what they're running, all about trust and character. This's a fucking government for you. Got *melangianos* and spicaroons running around here robbing and doping, raping little girls and killing, spilling their fucking blood all over what use to be clean streets. And these feds wanna come after me? What kinda world?"

"What?"

"You heard me—it's bullshit." He finishes the coffee. "They're fucking with an old man's time. What do they want? I've been here sixty-two years, and what am I, a fucking dope dealer? What're you telling me about what's-his-face getting clipped for? What's it gotta do with me? I read the papers."

"Just lettin you know bout the cat."

"Some kinda fucking wiseguy, Mook. What's-his-face's got nothing to do with me. You know it—they know it. That's a bad business, I told you to stay away from it. You just do like I tell you, and keep your trap clamped."

"Don't got nothin to unclamp it for. What do I know?"

"Damn right, you know nothing. Let us wait this bullshit out. Just looking for them to make the big move with their cocksucking cases and subpoenas. Nothing you can do, nothing for none of us to do. Can't run, ain't like there's nowhere to run. This's federals I got after me. They're everywhere. What am I gonna do, leave the country?"

"They're there too, the bastards. In country, outta country, all over."

"Damn right. But you ain't got nothing to worry about, Mook. The feds ain't looking for you, just maybe they might come squeeze you, that's all what could happen." I look into Salvie's eyes, the forever of his wrongs. He blinks, turns from me.

"Yeah." I sip tea again—Mora used to drink it to calm aches—and rub my forehead. "What if they ask me bout To—Mister Ricci? Do I know him, why I know him, did he do this, did he do that? What if they try to get deep into that subject?"

Salvie laughs quick, scared. "You take the Fifth. They can't make you incriminate yourself. Don't let em treat you like a spade. You got rights, too."

I ain't figured out the point to this sit-down Salvie called me to, not yet, so what can I do but answer his bullshit questions? Answer his questions careful and listen. "All right, Salvie, all that's gonna come outta my mouth is takin the Fifth on whatever they ask, everything."

"They're just trying to come up with something, see, Mook," the ol man says. "They got Vinnie the Polack on a murder rap and the bastard's making things up, telling em what they wanna hear. He cut a deal: he sells us out, he don't go back to the pen. This don't even affect you. The feds'll mess with your brain, try to come up with more than what they got now. They're looking to make a case, so they got Vinnie. They say they got tapes, too, but who's to believe em? What's said on the tapes, who's on there, nobody's telling. Cocksuckers, whatever, this thing's coming down, Mook. They gave us a pass all these years, and now they're coming for their piece."

"What do we do?"

"What we? This ain't about you, Mook. I just told you that—nobody's concerned with you. It's going down, the thing, nothing anybody can do about it. If I come after you, you ain't gonna stop me, cause I got more power. The feds's after us, nothing I can do. The smart guy's gonna run and make a deal with them instead of going down with the thing. What else do you expect? A smart guy wants to keep something of what he's got in life. You blame Vinnie, hell, what's the odds he's working with? Either you know you're caught up with or you worry about somebody maybe clipping you for talking. What's a smart guy gonna do?"

"Make a deal, that's what you say, Salvie?"

"Me? I ain't saying a thing. I'm one of the ones they're after, what can I do?" He looks around Zorba's again, smiles, and his words come in a whisper now. "I remember learning about Greeks when I was a kid. They came before Italians, before us. Without what they started, there wouldn't uh never been no Roman Empire, no pope. You gotta admire um causa that. You people, the WASPs, the Jews, the Polish, everybody else wants to be Italian causa Rome. Same as that, I wanted to be a Greek causa what I learned in school. You're always gonna look up to who's on top of you. Now they're coming to get me for trying to be them. What deal is there for me?"

"But you said a smart man makes a deal."

"Yeah, if he's got the chance, that's what a guy with sense does. I'm not gonna sit here and tell you Vinnie's dumb for what he's doing, is all. Just a bastard, that's what he is." Salvie drops two bills on the table. "You've got that tea covered, right?"

"Lemme understand what's comin outta your mouth first: a smart man will sell you out if he can, so don't trust him. You called me down here to tell me that?"

"Yeah," he says. I drop a five on the table. "Don't make no deal, Mook, don't go lying at the mouth is what I'm saying. Cause it don't matter—one way or the other way, you gotta pay."

The waiter swipes our empty scraps and the money away. "You know I won't say nothin."

He stares at the space between us. "Of course, Mook. It's only me you take down if you make a deal. You don't got nothing on Tommy Ricci. It's only me," he says. The ol man huffs into the restaurant's air. There's nothin between us now. "I liked you better when you was a stupid kid. I could trust you back then."

* * *

I ain't never cared for Mister Joe Defelice. That's what he likes for you to call him—either that or Mister Defelice. I seen him slap Nicky Stokes upside the skull once for callin him Jo-Jo, back when I first came to Stony Island. Don't know if he just plays that tough-guy game with us, or if he slaps Vito and Angelo around when they don't call him Mister So-and-So, too. I doubt it. Ain't never seen Salvie act like he's got much respect for this skinny, empty-eyed cat. Ol man always calls him Joe or Joey, at least to my face. I suppose it's his Black boys, then, who Mister Defelice saves the head-wop-in-charge act for, just us.

Sweet dresser he is, though, better than all the other members of Tommy Ricci's crew. Looks like a gangster from the movies, like the Godfather maybe. Suit shoulders always tailored just broad enough to make him look strong, but not so strong that he's top-heavy. Silk pants pleated above the knees and cuffed at the ankle to hit the top of his loafers, showin a slice of linen socks. Ties knotted in the thinnest, tightest knots at his crisp shirt collar and, on special days, a handkerchief barely creepin from his jacket pocket. When I grew up wantin to dress like them, it was Joe Defelice's threads I had in my head.

Defelice use to head the lottery racket, back when that was a big-money thing. Sometimes I'd go with J.C. to drop the numbers loot off at his doorstep. Mister Defelice would stand on his porch, waitin for us, and there'd be this look in his eye, sound to his breathin. Can't say I've noticed anythin like it since. I been puttin up with white folk thinkin we ain't shit my whole life: teachers at Phillips, coaches, cops, Salvie, just about everybody else in Tommy Ricci's crew. But that's one thing, easy to ignore cause, one way or the other, most of the coons I've known in life *ain't* been shit. Besides, I always had J.C. whisperin in my ear, tellin me that white folk ain't shit themselves. But Joe Defelice hates Blacks deep in his heart—I see it in them eyes. I can respect, even look up to a man who knows we ain't shit, cause I know the same about him. For one to hate us though, not care that I know he hates us, and look so damn fine while he hates us, that I don't care for.

This's who I been deliverin the Stony shakedown loot to for the last two years. I drop the shoppin bag on his Chicago Heights doorstep and turn to leave, but his heavy voice calls out for me. "It's all here?"

"Yeah," I say. I stop and look back at Mister Defelice's house.

The skinny man stands on his porch, weighin the shoppin bag by hand.

"You in a rush?" I shake my head. "Come up here, up to the front." I climb the stone steps, stand so I bring a shadow over Defelice in his shiny red shower robe. I ain't used to holdin no conversations with him. Even when he's waitin outside for his loot, I just drop the bag off and leave cause I know I ain't wanted here. Can't think of ever sharin a friendly sentence with the cat, not even a phony nice word, in the past. "The feds come to you yet?"

"No," I say, and sit on the porch swing. He stares like he wants me to move, but I ain't stirred. "I spoke to Salvie already. Told me they're gonna ask about things, about a few people: him, Mister Ricci, Angelo, Vito, you. Nothin serious. Said to take the Fifth all over the place, nothin to worry about. Salvie told me everything."

Defelice sets the bag inside his house and pulls the door to. "Get up! Stand up when I'm talking to you, and stay offa my goddamn furniture." I jump from the bench and his voice drops to a mumble. "Salvatore's about to make a deal."

"What? Naw"—Mister Defelice's eyes cut away from me as he spits on the lawn—"he's one of the cats they lookin to get. That's what Salvie told me hisself. Like he said, the feds is gonna ask bout him . . . naw. Never."

Mister Defelice smiles. "They don't want him or me. Whose name is it you see in the papers, on television, every day—Tommy Ricci's, right? That's the only name anybody knows, my *padrino*'s. The game the federals play is that they build a guy up to be big, bigger than what he is even. Then they tear him down, make a show of it. That's the government's racket."

"Salvie ain't gonna sell out. That ain't like him. Last I talked to him, he was tellin me not to make a deal. He ain't bout to go that route."

"Would you stop talking to me about it?" he snaps. "Just listen to what I'm saying here. I mean, you're fucking talking, but what do you know? Not a goddamn thing. Salvatore's an old man, an old, weak man. He ain't looking to do no jail time, not now. If things go like they is, the feds won't even be able to get Mister Ricci, not with the weasel as the only one telling them a goddamn thing. Who's that leave as their big fish? If Salvatore makes a deal, on the other hand, he gives them exactly the man they want and saves his own ass doing it. But, when he talks, he's taking us all down with Mister Ricci, believe me. Salvie knows it all from where he's sitting. They'll make cases off his word for the next thirty years. They'll get to you, too, down the line—don't think Salvie won't put you on the cross to save his ass. Remember the last time you talked with the man. Did he sound like somebody ready to go to the poke?"

I think of Zorba's, then chase it from mind and walk to the porch stairs.

"Every morning, I gotta have this guy come in and sweep the house for bugs. Every fucking morning. And every night, the FBI's parked two blocks down from here, taking pictures of me and my wife and my kids, coming and going. They're everywhere, these guys. All so they can get at one man, make big fucking headlines. What kinda life they got me living? I ain't going down with the thing, they ain't getting me—not Vinnie, not Salvie, not the FBI. If I gotta get my house swept till the day I die, they ain't taking me. The guy found two bugs in the upstairs bathroom just last week. What was they gonna hear in there? It's illegal for a guinea to pee or what? They gotta be stopped."

I start down the stairs. "It's a goddamn shame what they're doin."

"Problem is, they watch and listen so hard, can't nobody get to Salvatore." Mister Defelice steps back into my shadow, so I stop moving. "There was a young guy who I brung into this thing years back. Found him over there where you're from—from Forty-seventh

Street, over there. Johnny, they called him. Stupid kid in the long run, but he had some good in him. He would know, without me saying anything to him really, what I needed taken care of. You can't ask for a boy better than him. If a guy's knees needed to be busted, Johnny'd swing the bat. If a joint had to be burned down, he'd light the match. Never had to spoon-feed him, that Johnny. He was a stupid kid in the end, like I say, couldn't help it. But when I think of him and look in your eyes, I see. You coulda been brothers, the two of you. Understand what I'm saying?"

I step down from the porch stairs, onto my getaway path. "Yes sir," I say, "Mister Defelice."

* * *

I drive down 47th on my way from the suburbs. Ain't been to this ol strip in forever, missed all of what's gone down. Lester Hooks, the ol Blackstone Ranger, runs the dope between here and 43rd Street from what I'm told, and that's the only action still jumpin in the Forties far as makin cash money go.

I'm lookin for Black.

Them that stayed on 47th long after King died, too dumb to get while the gettin was good, they've settled into the strip now. Feet sunk into a place so low that they trapped. Ain't no runnin, way too late—dumb niggas swallowed by a stupid place, eaten alive till concrete teeth chomped on the part that was mostly dead already, the wanderin part where ankles ended legs. But they still alive.

Most of um is still alive.

Waitin for a bus ride or for the swallowin to be done or for King or Jesus or some muthafucka to come and save um, starin and waitin. Some lean on the buildins, like Black used to do, usin this tilted brick to keep from fallin or to rest a back cause they ain't really gonna fall no ways. Can't fall, can't do a thing but stand, stare and wait. Just restin they backs on bricks; ain't goin nowhere but where the brick tilts them, and these buildins sure ain't about to collapse, not now. Somethin's gotta be here to bring this shadow, after all.

The strip is black now.

I roll the Benz west, against the curb at Michigan, Black's Michigan, cause I know this's where the bum'll be. Only place he known since 47th Street ate his people whole, let him tell it. Years gone by since I been to this place. Two, maybe three years, since '77 at least, long time since I came after Black, or he followed after me. Been so long, I forgot that's how it use to go around here—he'd hunt me down to beg and spit and mumble and talk and talk and talk, till he'd got to his point. Cause if Mookie King wasn't told the point, it hadn't been told. That's how big-time I was in this place, and Black knew it best of all. He was *47th Street* Black. He found me in my red T-Bird; then, after I got rid of the Thunderbird, he ran after me and my fine white sedans and gold coupes, just to share some new truth that wasn't new no ways cause he'd already told it to me seven times the week before.

Wasn't he the fool who said life'd make its way back to this 47th Street eventually, that it worked in a circle like that? What life? I'm here now, finished the last turn, and I don't see nothin but what anybody with good sense woulda figured to be here if they'd left when I did. Buildins tiltin over, souls half ate by concrete, and a blind sky hangin over. We all saw this comin—that's why we ran.

So Black wasn't nobody's Bible prophet, I only gotta lower the car window and look out on 47th Street to know he couldn't see the future good for you. But I'm lookin for him no matter; ain't too shamed to admit it, followin after him cause I wanna know. Need him to tell me about the day Johnny the Baptist got his dick and his head blown off, why Black started jumpin up and down on 47th and Michigan when he heard the news, and how come he ain't gone nowhere since. Lookin for the man cause I'm gonna ask if he woulda jumped higher, screamed louder or cried longer if he'd been the one to put the Cajun in the Styx himself, and could he've forever left this corner if it'd been him? And I'm gonna tell Black, after all these years, that we, me and J.C. Rose (you remember J.C., Black—bushy hair, crazy little nigga, shot Sermon Martin dead on King Drive, the one you jumped on afterwards, remember?), it was us who found Johnny on 49th Street back in '66, blood leaked all over the shoulders of his sparklin white suit, so much blood it smeared against them necklaces hung around his neck. Gonna tell Black, cause him knowin I first saw the Baptist dead—first, after them who killed him, and J.C.—should finish the circle, make this last turn worth it. If the 47th Street circle's finished, then Black was right, and life can come on back to this place, and the ol man really is a prophet just like in Reverend Goode's Bible sermon.

I look to his corner, but he ain't here. Ain't a soul on Michigan just now, in fact, cept for a fat ol brown woman in a coat too thick for June and a knit cap pulled down over her ears. She sees me starin through the dropped window and she smiles with fake teeth, too pearl white and even to be real, and only when she thinks I ain't payin her mind does she puff on a square and lean back on the wall.

"You know Black?" I ask. Her body jumps from its restin point, like she ain't figure me for speakin.

"Huh?"

"That nigga, Black. Always be on this corner. Use to." She hides the square behind her left thigh, but she don't move close to the car. Just watches me from his place.

"Oh," she say. "He ain't here."

I'm about to ask her somethin more, till I figure she don't know nothin to tell me. Besides, Black probably strolled over to 43rd . . . but Mary Ruth's gone, been dead about five years now, got her high ass hit by a CTA bus over in Fiends' Heaven long before I left. Black ain't got no cause to be in that place. He's a drunk, see, not a junkie.

About a month ago, somebody told me J.C. was around 43rd anyway, sellin horse for Big Lester in a alley—that's what came of the little man after he got let outta the joint. I sure ain't lookin to be over there then, no sir.

"Thanks."

I drive west on the strip, still lookin. I see two, three souls on each street who could be him—torn pants, straw hats, paper bags—could be, but ain't. Truth is, I don't know where I'm goin now. Was lookin for Black, but I can't find him so that he can tell me the honest, 47th-and-Michigan truth. Only thing I got to follow is my own way then, in fronta me in the windshield, this place where bricks bring shade, bums sip wine, and cats use to play songs, ol blue jazz songs, to get by. This's what I know—back on the ol strip, hustlin means you do what you gotta do so you can keep standin, pretendin like you ain't been swallowed already. Do what you gotta, cause the only cat who knows a God or a honest truth here is a fool—a stupid, drunk fool—and the only thing I see in front is a shadow black to blind.

21

SALVIE'S GOT A WIFE. Ol man don't wear no rings, except for the one on his left pinky, and he ain't never brung up the woman to me in thirteen years. She's a stooped-over broad, gray and ol as him, wearin earrings that sparkle off the mornin sun (bright enough I gotta blink from half a block away), jewelry too rich for her raggedy purse and polyester pants. First thing to mind is that the troll's his sister. Wouldn't know otherwise if they hadn't kissed on the mouth as the ol man opened the Chrysler's passenger door for her. Always took Salvie for nothin but a twenty-four-hour gangster, figured he went home and counted the riches outta shoppin bags from the city's blocks, then slept next to hustlin thoughts. But since there's a wife, he's got kids somewhere, young Salvies and Mary Margarets or whatever's her name. And they got grandkids, ol as they is. I wonder if the children came out as mobsters and trolls, too.

I shake, not causa Salvie's woman—that's set in. I shake now in the stink of this abandoned Buick (beat-up Skylark, left in the car wash lot weeks back) cause this wife fucks up my plan. The design was to catch Salvie on his mornin walk, take care of Mister Defelice's orders through a open driver-side window, and speed on. I was gonna push the Buick's engine so hard, so fast, I'd be a blink on the Olympia Fields street, nothin a witness could identify. But she's shot that plan down—cocksucker ain't even walkin this mornin.

Every other Sunday, he strolls past the ivory castles and green lawns to the local park, then back to their brick ranch spread. Some mornins I've walked with him, just to talk business.

Either that or God ain't on my side, not for this crime. But fuck Him—He's forever with them anyways. What can I do? If I don't follow Mister Defelice's order, Angelo, Paulo, and the Hack visit the car wash and ride me out to the Styx. Ain't sayin they won't show up one night anyways, even if I go on and do like he told me. Only a matter of whether I'm livin on a calendar or on a stopwatch. That's how it is when He ain't on your side. Just figure it's best to put my ride off, gimme a chance to earn grace. I ain't ready just now.

Salvie gets into the Chrysler and turns the engine on, but they don't go nowhere. The wife's door opens, and her polyester leg's outta the car. She's forgot somethin: checkbook, cigarettes, somethin. I sigh, then groan. She's slow-walkin back to the house, much slower than her years shoulda left her, but that's good. Means she'll take this long comin back, and I got time to do what I got to.

I step into the June air after the woman's inside the house. My eyes drop to the concrete—steamin causa the sky's burn—and never rise as I walk close to Salvie's Chrysler. It's spring hot, just that clean spring hot, but so much of it the Lord's sun gets to speakin to me, not soundin like the holy babble of Reverend Goode, but like the mighty voice of Jesus Christ. *Why you doin this, Mook?*

Ain't got no choice. I was told this's what's gotta happen. If Salvie talks, I'm goin down ventually. The ol man put me in this, true, but I sure ain't about to let him take me out. Besides, Salvie's gonna cause trouble for Tommy Ricci, wants to bring the whole Outfit down. They need him gone, and won't nobody else handle him. This's my chance. After Salvie's quieted, Tommy Ricci cleared, they'll be thankin me outta their rich asses. They paid J.C. five hundred a month after he clipped Sermon. What they gonna give to me for wreckin a federal case? The least I expect is more territory. That's the least. But after this deed, they might's well go on and put me in their thing, make me a real mobster. After so many wrongs I done, all this money made, blood spilled—why not make me the first true Black mafioso?

The mighty Son laughs. *Admit it,* he says, *you wish J.C. could take care of this. You wasn't ever the best enforcer, Mook, that was always J.C. Besides, he was the one who wanted to see Salvie beg for his life. Don't you wish you could go off to a beach somewhere, drink Bacardi, and watch women dance in the sand while J.C. sheds this blood?*

Fuck you, man! I've clipped just as many as J.C. has.

Clipped?

I've . . . killed just as many as J.C. Blasted tall Henry when I was just eighteen, had Jimmy Mo hit two months back. Without me, without my word, the little man wouldn't uh never did the Banks brothers. That was me who gave the order, not him. That was me. And I ain't never done no time for my wrongs, not like J.C. Stupid muthafucka. The little man ain't smarter than me, cat's dumb as fuck in fact, dumb enough to get caught. I always been the smarter one, just knew it was best that a nigga not let his brains show in this world. That's why I'm where I am now, and J.C.'s in a alley. So fuck him. I'm gonna handle this business. This's my time.

You're walking into a trap, Jesus promises. *You'll burn for this.*

But it's too late to change the way, I say.

I knock on the back window of Salvie's Chrysler. The ol man looks over his shoulder and I see that he's ready. Of course Salvie knows, of course he understands, he's been in this business for more than thirty years. He ain't no fool like Sermon, runnin from what's gotta happen. He's a better soul than that, got too much pride. I imagine tall Henry mighta had this same knowin in his eyes before I shot him on 35th Street. Can't say for sure, cause that spook was too good to look me in the face. But I imagine he did.

The ol man reaches over his left shoulder and pulls up the lock. I get into the cushy backseat of his money-countin Chrysler, a trade-in version of the same ol money-countin car. His eyes follow me, not over his shoulder—ol bones lock that stubby neck in place—but in the rearview mirror. There ain't no fight in him, no anger as my body rests behind his seat. Ain't no sign of weak surrender neither. Salvatore's just ready for it to be done.

"Mornin, Salvie," I say.

His eyes light with hope, hope maybe cause they see the doubt in me. "What you doing here, Mook?" I hear, for a moment, the anger of a Salvie ten years gone. He coughs. "You don't call, lemme know you're coming, nothing. I'm about to take a ride with the wife. You see this is a bad time."

I look away from the reflection—hope left him that quick, and I don't wanna see just now. I check the house, think maybe his woman's comin, that I won't have the time. But she ain't nowhere to be seen. The hour is mine, Jesus's givin me His grace now, wants me to do this. I reach under my sweatshirt, pull the capped .38 from my pants, and look back to the mirror. Salvie watches still; I remember the ol man tellin me that he don't believe in killin, back on that lakefront park bench. And I remember thinkin he was talkin bullshit. Maybe that was his way of repentin for the sins of his life, maybe he figured the end was comin soon. If so, God knew his words was shit, just like I knew. But I hope the soul's been forgiven. He at least gave heaven the respect of a desperate lie in the end.

I press the silencer into the back of Salvatore's wrinkled neck, where it meets his head. "Thanks, Salvie," I say, cause the man made me what I am—I owe him that. I return his stare through the rearview now. This's the right thing to do, eyein him in the face. But Salvie's lids drop over the holes, his way of tellin me he don't forgive. But this's my hour, too late to change my way. I watch the gray wrinkles of these lids till they're gone from the mirror. My finger rests from the trigger and I look at my sweatshirt. I didn't hear nothin, not even the pop of a muzzled bullet. Didn't feel the kickback of the shot either, not a goddamn thing. But the Chrysler's windshield is smeared red and my shirt's covered with red bits like the ol man spit death at me as I shot him, and his reflection is gone. I look to the house—his woman still can't find her goddamn cigarettes—and stuff the pistol in my joggin pants.

The door is heavy steel, much heavier than it was when I got into the car. But I push hard and I'm free. I walk fast without runnin, my eyes on the burnin pavement, ears listenin for buzzards soarin above. I hear um, so I walk faster. It's hot still, but the sun ain't speakin. Like Mora, it's got no more concern with me. This's what a gangster asks for, what a true one deserves.

It's a forever path to the abandoned Buick, even with my feet movin quick as they is. My mind leaves, drifts to '66, to findin Johnny the Baptist's rottin body in that alley. That was the first stiff I'd ever laid eyes on, ol Johnny. I remember takin gold necklaces from that dead fool. You gotta do wrong, you see, shed blood, to ride in wealth before you die. This's the hustle, and this's the truth I stole off of a dead Cajun.

I open the Buick's driver door and step inside the burn of this abandoned car. The bloody sweatshirt is torn off my body, tucked below the passenger seat, the silenced .38 hidden under its filth. I drive, cookin in the heat of salvation's fire. As I speed from the money-countin Chrysler, I barely hear a ol woman's screams for my own shitty tears.

* * *

The cops come in the mornin, show no respect, fear, or couth. I sit in the mirror, tyin silk into a sharp knot around my neck. My toes dance in the carpet's white bush. It's here in my naked feet that I feel the pigs tearin up the stairs outside our apartment unit. They're so mad that they growl, louder as they come closer. They want me that bad, like they've been chasin my ass forever.

The door shakes and Mora appears in the mirror, calm like she hears none of this commotion. I watch her walk to the entrance as the door shakes again. "Who is it?" Her voice is calm as her walk.

"Police," the pig says. "Open, please."

Mora don't glance at me, don't check what's best to do, just parts the door for them. I finish my tie, sure that it's sharp.

"We're looking for Mister Morris King junior," the cop says. "We were given this as his place of residence. We're at number seven, right?"

"Yes," Mora says. Her words shake a bit now, like they use to get before the scream of her cum. "This's number seven."

There's four cops at the door—too many to take out on my own. I glance to the bedroom window to see how much backup they got. Ain't like it matters; this hole is too narrow to climb through with me carryin so much weight now. They can't pin Salvie on me no ways. Did it too quick, too smart, for them. They got nothin. Don't they know who I am besides? I look at their reflections, recognize the faces. They know Mookie King, know better than to trifle with me about that ol man. As much as anybody, I own these pigs.

"So, this's the address," the head cop grunts. "You know this King? Is he here?"

"I . . ."

I put on my silk socks, my leather steppers, walk into the room outside. And I wait for the eyes to fall on me, the pigs' and Mora's. "What you want with me?"

"Mister King?" The one who talks, I don't recognize him. The other pig faces belong to me. "Morris King junior?"

"Mookie," I say, and grab my blazer, cause I know they about to take me in. "I'll ask again, what you want?"

"We need you to come to the precinct. Need to talk to you," he says, "about this matter. . . ."

"This big street player," the one Black cop says. I breathe and feel myself blinkin hard, a bit piece of Salvie's death swimmin in the right eye.

"This dope pusher. We need to ask you some questions about this dead guy."

"Jimmy Mo," the Black pig says, like he's proud. My eyes stop their blink and I bite my lip to stop a laugh.

Two pigs walk across the livin room like they gonna beat me down cause they caught my smile. "I ain't talkin to you till I get a lawyer. I can make a call, huh? Ain't that my right to do?"

"Of course," the head cop says and, for the first time, I notice how his badge shines silver, brighter than the rest. The Black pig grabs at my arm, touches me before I flinch away. "But you can, uh, make your call at the precinct, so we can get outta here."

The coon grabs for me again as his partner whips out handcuffs. So when I jump, they're ready to lock me up good. "Thought you was takin me down to talk. Ain't that what you just said? To talk? Why handcuffs?"

"This's just for your protection, pal. Don't worry about it."

"Protection from who?" I look at Mora, and her face is worn, tired of this livin. "How many cops you got here, how many of y'all? One, two, three, four blue pigs. How much backup's downstairs? Three more cars? What am I bein protected from?"

"Don't worry, Mookie," the coon who helped shackle me whispers. "This ain't nothing."

I flinch away again, try not to relax, cause that's why they brung this Black pig with them. To relax me. "Y'all gonna read me my rights or what?"

"You ain't being arrested, just protected until we get you down to the precinct. Protective custody, that's what we call this here," the head cop says. "Besides, you knew your rights good enough to ask for a lawyer. We don't gotta tell you what you already know, do we, Mook?"

I watch Mora's eyes as I'm pushed through the door, and see that I ain't gotta worry about no Holy Ghost gettin outta the way before I end it with her. It's over now. She liked my way when it brung her screams, when it made me a rich, skinny dark boy. But seein these fat hands in shackles is too much. She's gone—ain't enough goodness runnin through this woman to keep her with a blood killer. This's what I want, what I asked for, so it's fair. It's good the hustle taught me to always be prepared, good I made plans to move on before pigs came growlin. Woulda been caught naked in the wind otherwise. Mora's eyes, once so fine, tell me I shouldn't never bring my ass back here.

The cops push me, but not before I see one of them sittin on my livin room couch, talkin to her. I watch my aged woman and this pig, as long as the hands at my back and the handcuffs' grip allow me to see. Watch the end of what's been my home, free home, until the door she let them through closes, and they take me away.

* * *

"Appreciate you comin down, man. Muthafuckas got me locked up all day just cause they tryin some kinda new shakedown or what? What the fuck can I do?" David Peters—the same lawyer who squeezed me to get J.C. outta prison, cause the best kinda counsel to have is one as corrupt as the justice he works for—this bastard smiles in that way fine negroes got of smilin at niggas from 47th Street, remindin us where we was born. I look at the lawyer, wait for him to answer my jive as we stop at the sedan. "How much?" I ask.

Peters laughs, chuckles more than laughs. "What does the CPD care about Jimmy Moore? Did they think twice when he was alive and hustling on Seventy-ninth Street? So why should they give a damn that somebody shot him up? How many pushers do they find splayed on the streets with holes in their heads every day? Saves them the effort of doing their job, chasing and arresting them, in the first place. Like a public service. They're trying to scare you into giving up whatever you know to help them get Ricci, nothing more. But, as far as their Sal Fuoco talk goes, they can call you fool, can lack all the human respect for you in the world, but nowhere in any part of their blue brains do they believe some b-boy in two-tone shoes drove from Stony Island to the suburbs and put a slug in the back of Salvie Fuoco's head. Who in the hell are you? That's Italian business, and they know it. Until they come up with a subpoena, you know nothing, because they've got nothing. Even if they do produce a subpoena, you take the Fifth. That's if they want to press this matter."

Salvie already told me not to let the pigs treat me like a spade, so for what do I need this cocksucker and his bullshit talk? "I meant how much are you shakin me down for showin up? What do I owe you?"

He laughs again. That's all the answer I'm about to get now. "Where you headed?"

"I don't know," I say. I think of Mora and know that I got no place to be free, like J.C. when he came outta the joint. Fuck that—I ain't nobody's nigga loser. "Take me to my business, over on Stony Island."

* * *

As I drive south on the Calumet—far, far from the Island—out to the boondocks where I'm torchin this abandoned Buick, I shake. I smell the hobbled funk from my parents' livin room, left in the Forties. Then it's gone, no smell at all, no wounds, and I know time is up. God, the same God who came with me to do Salvie, has swooped down and ended the pain, judged that Papa's waste is done, and took away life. Took it and swooped off, soul in His right hand. I blink, slam on the brakes as a black car cuts in front of the Skylark. The shakin stops and I remember that He's a killer just like me, this God. Ain't nothin mighty about snatchin souls and flyin off to judge them though. So good riddance to the bloody muthafucka. Wasn't never no real father to me no ways, just somebody else's dream.

5

22

THE FIENDS USED TO WAIT for me in the alley off 43rd Street, especially after five o'clock—big-money time. After five on until eight o'clock the next morning, I took care of business behind that boarded-up temple Leroy Cross'd once lived in. Before the workers returned to their bosses, the students to their teachers, and the rest of the chumps to their nothing. Big-time business.

"What you need?"

The yellow man stepped up with crusted lips and shaky fingers. "A half dolla blow, half dolla. Gimme."

His hands reached for me as I pointed to the alley's north end. "Slow up, goddamnit." I felt for the gat against my chest, made sure I was safe from his lust. "Show some respect. Step back and pay me."

"How much?"

"What? You've been coming over here for years buying this shit. True? You know goddamn well how much. What'd you ask me for?"

"A half dolla," he said.

"Gimme half-dollar money then." He slipped two twenties and a ten into my hand and I slapped his rusty palm twice for big Otis to see at the alley's far end. Thin tears ran the yellow man's cheeks as he looked into my eyes. He wanted to kiss me; he'd done it before. I pointed to Otis again. "Go on now, damnit. I got business. Go on down there, get your half dollar, muthafucka."

"Hey, J.C., how you doin?" The brown girl stepped up, tripping over low heels. She caught her balance against brick and ran fingernails through Jheri curls.

"What's up, girl? I'm good, doing just fine. How you been?"

"Missin you."

I laughed. "What you need?"

"Blow. Got a quarter for me, J.C.?"

"You know I always got what you need, girl." The years'd taught me to be smooth at the game—as good a hustler as Mookie and Salvie'd ever been.

She showed me a wad of cash stolen out of her sugar daddy's wallet, showed it for less than a second, then stuffed that cash on deep in my pocket. A bony hand rubbed against my thigh before she took her walk without me pointing the way. "Thank you, baby."

I flashed a fist, like the old Black-Power/Black-Is-Beautiful cats, at Otis. "Ain't no problem. You take care of yourself, girl."

I watched her bones switch down the alley until the car horn sounded. "What you doin over here?" Lester Hooks hung from his Lincoln's window, teeth shining in gray clouds.

"Business, making loot," I said.

"You need to take this shit off the main strip before police come botherin you, tryin to cause trouble. Just so many we can have out here at a time. You know better, J.C. Go on to another alley, or a off street. Police gonna come over here hasslin you soon as you know it."

"All right, nigga. Just lemme make this last paper."

"Hurry up, J.C.," Big Lester said as his head disappeared inside the Lincoln. The words faded down 43rd as he drove. "Hurry before police come around. Take that business to a off street, where it belong."

"There go my man! That's him! There he go!" I didn't recognize the honey as she stepped into the alley, nothing familiar about her. She had a ashy black color to her face, sweaty though she wore no coat in the 43rd Street December. I looked into her eyes and there was no soul, no soul and little seeing, in them. "This's my man, girl." She brushed against my arm. "I told you he was fine, didn't I?"

The second woman mumbled words I didn't understand. I stepped away from them and searched the fiends in the crowd, checking whether the two were part of a setup. Had to be careful for thieves on the strip, so much loot me and Otis were holding down.

"Who are you?"

She laughed such a crazy laugh. "Lookit here, girl. He trying to act like he don't know me. What, one of your other heifers out here, J.C.? Which one is she? I'll beat her little ass. Where she at?"

"For real, woman, who are you?"

She came close again, and her breath smelled like hot rot. "We been together these years, and you gonna sit up here and act like you don't know me. Why you disrespectin me, J.C.? I oughta slap you upside your pretty skull for treating me like this out in public, in fronta my girl."

Her palm cupped my cheek's naps and I looked into the eyes again. Her stare wasn't dull anymore, just young, and her touch turned warm. I pushed the hand, stepped further away from her because, for all the years that'd scraped her skin, I did recognize its feel. Too well, I knew the little girl hiding inside that bare tramp. "It's Christina," she said. My back fell against the building and she snuck her hand into mine, hooked our arms. "See, girl, I told you this was my man. You didn't believe me, but I told you."

"Mmh," the other grunted.

"Otis!" I turned from the child to the gym shoe boy—youngsters'd long figured that the smartest shoes to rock while hustling were Converse or Adidas, not Stacey Adams, best for running when need be—who protected my bin stash at the 42nd end. "Get over here!"

"Yeah, J.C.?" Otis' sneakers cracked the frozen gravel under us as he walked the alley. "What you need?"

"Come here and do some work. Take these two away from here. They're bothering me."

"What you want done with um?"

I looked into Christina's face, saw scars reaching under her skin. "Nothing. Just take them out of my sight, Otis, far from over here. Do your job, man. Get them out." He pulled Christina and the other by thin arms, drug the pair down my alley. They kicked and screamed and laughed more crazy laughter, but there was nothing they could do.

"What're you, J.C., some kinda faggot?" Christina's voice bounced. "I offer you heaven for a little bit of what you got, and you turn me down? You must've let um make you into a sissy."

I laughed my own crazy laugh and lit a Salem as they faded. Christina was my fault—I'd brought her into the life years back, gave her that witch powder so she'd believe she loved my ass. What else did I know to do with a baby girl but scar? Scar her face one hundred times, then blow her into the sky with the clouds. What else?

A college boy stood next in line. "What you need?"

* * *

I'd tried, for Grandma Rose at least, I'd tried. All that Good Book pounding, Ebenezer Baptist living she'd done, I knew the old woman was looking down from heaven. So for the sake of her and not so much for my own soul, I'd worked hard to be a hero, like the names on old Mister Manley's blackboard. Stayed away from 47th Street, looked for a real job, took care of her crib. I'd started going to Ebenezer every Sunday again even, before they moved it to Stony. Hooked up with a nice Baptist girl up there, one from 35th and Vernon who wore frilly Sunday dresses and carried a little Bible in her white-gloved palms to Reverend Goode's services. Grandma would've loved the look of her, loved the backwoods geechy "yes'm," "no suh" sound of her even. Charlotte Humphreys was her name, chocolate dark and untouched as she could've been; Charlotte got me my first job out of Decatur, sweeping and mopping floors at her cousin's beauty salon on 51st and Cottage. Cleaning up after folks like I was still in the joint, or wounded and just back from some goddamn rice-paddy war. I hated living like that, felt like a chump every waking day. But old Charlotte'd get to talking about how proud she was of me for making it through, how I'd survived all that'd come my way. Talked all that righteous-sounding, sweet garbage while she rubbed the bubbled switchblade cut on my skin, soft like her sugar words would soothe.

Not even close. Shit, since she wasn't giving me any ass unless I gave her vows under God, the only manly thing I could do back then was go home, lift up Grandma Rose's mattress, and count the stash I'd took from Soul Mamma's office back when I'd come out. Never spoke a word to Charlotte about my loot; for all her Sunday purity, I couldn't trust the girl. Not with that ten G's in Salvie-crisp Benjamin Franklins I hadn't spent any more of waiting for me there under Rose's bed. Long as I could come home, count that paper, and be reminded I wasn't a chump, that I was Jesus Christ Rose, not Sermon Martin, that stash was going to its proper use.

Charlotte and the floor-cleaning job lasted almost a year and a half, into the middle of '78. Sweet girl, but once I'd figured her spending all that time with a convict, rubbing my wounds, getting me a gig in the beauty salon, calling me her man—once I understood all that was part of a pitiful holy mission she'd took on to save my soul, her "project," I dropped her. She talked a good game, and I wasn't sure I had her pegged right until the Sunday I let her know I was done with her game, up at the church. That blank-face mask came over the girl when the words "fuck it" flew off my lips. Old Charlotte sat in Goode's pew, staring at me with no life in her eyes, just like Christina the fiend years later. No life anywhere in her except for in that little nose twitching like she smelled skunk; hurt not so much by the loss of a pet, but by the insult of the stink. Feeling a fool for breathing when she saw me running past on all fours, black tail wiggling about.

I went into the salon to quit the floor-sweeping job a few days later and got to hollering back and forth with the girl's cousin. Heard the wrong thing come out of her mouth (something about me being the criminal, bastard son of some street-corner hooker) and I told her she was the hooker and threw the broom at her point first to dot her between the eyes. All of them—the cousin, the old ladies in their curlers and smocks, and Charlotte—chased me north on Cottage Grove, Charlotte twanging about how ashamed she was of me, how she was "never gon be side me no mo," and throwing that broom after my "no goot, monkey ass." Kept running and twanging and cursing and throwing until they'd chased me clear back to 47th Street.

* * *

"Hey, little man, where Mookie at?" Black still yelled like so whenever he'd see us on the strip. He stood on the same corner, but closer to the street, just about as close as he could've been without the cars running him over. Black had to be closing in on the short side of sixty by then; not a bad living for a bum surviving off the crumbs of poor folk, not a bad one at all. But that was just my guess on his age, a guess made believing that Black had once been born, and that he would die. Maybe the man didn't have age, though, like Grandma's Good Book said about God—the truth and light forever—maybe he had no years like that, and had been standing on the strip where it met Michigan Avenue since always.

Me and Otis stopped at Michigan, turned to the dark bum under the straw hat. "What'd you call me, old fool?"

"Little man. I called you little man. And yeah, I'm speakin to you, J.C. Sure ain't talkin to that fat-ass welfare baby standin next to you. That nigga ain't nobody's little nothin, less you a fool blind as midnight. Where's Mookie at?"

"Huh? I ain't seen Mookie since I don't know when, man. What you askin me where he's at for? I don't know. He's gone."

"You don't know where he at, little man?"

"What, are you deaf? I just told you I ain't seen the cat. Don't ask me no more."

"My fault, J.C., my fault." I could smell the Mad Dog on his breath still. "Hey, when you do see him, tell him somethin for me. Tell him . . . tell him I said he needs to come on back here to Forty-seventh."

"Ain't gonna be able to tell him shit. Like I said, he's gone, Black. Gone from this place."

"*If*, little man. *If* you see him, you give him that message for me." Black's swollen eyes laughed as they floated to Otis. "I mean, I don't miss him or nothin. Just figure it's time for him to pass that fancy red car on down to me. Maybe he come to his senses, J.C., remembered what he owe me."

"Oh yeah? I don't know, man. Don't think I'm gonna run into that cat anytime soon." I thought of all the life we'd spent up on 47th Street. "You need anything, Black?"

"Yeah, little man. Tell that welfare baby next to you to move outta the way. He's blockin the sun from me. Don't you know it's cold on this sidewalk, boy?"

"Move over, Otis," I said. The gym shoe boy stepped down to the street. I nodded. "Anything else, Black?"

"Naw, nothin else. I'll be all right. Long as I can feel the sun, I'll be all right." Black squinted as he looked into what December light there was. "How you been doin, little man?"

"I'm fine, Black. Just taking care of my business."

"You still go to Ebenezer?"

"They moved the church away from here, Black. Been gone. Got so much juice flowing in your head, can't tell what you do know from what you don't. Ebenezer's on Stony now."

"I didn't know, little man. For real." But all knowing was lost somewhere behind the old man's yellowed eyes. "How long it's been gone? Mookie took it all with him, didn't leave nothin behind for us, did he?"

"I'm not saying all that. Things were leaving long before he moved over there, at least far as I heard—I was in the joint when it started. That's what I heard."

"I remember. How's your grandmamma doin?"

I turned, spit on the street, figured it best not to fight his foolishness. "Grandma Rose's been gone so long I don't recall when exactly it was she died. Was in the joint when that came about, too."

"Oh yeah?" Black's stare dropped from the sun, to the pavement. "Gone up to God, you say?"

"If that's what you believe in."

"What else is there?" He stood tall from the sidewalk. "You can do all kinda wrong in this life, or do nothin good or bad with your years at all. God'll forgive, take you with Him in the end, long as you got faith."

"If that's what you believe in."

"That's what I believe," Black praised. His dirty hand brushed my arm. "Real nice coat you got there, little man."

I reached into my pocket. The twenty dropped from my fingers and twisted as it fell next to his dusty shoes. "We gotta go, Black."

"Thank you, little man," Black said as he bent over for the bill. "Where you headed?"

"Business to tend." Otis stepped up to the sidewalk and we moved on.

"Can I go with you?"

"Business, Black."

"Come on, J.C. . . . Damn. Give that message to Mookie for me, would you? Tell him I don't miss him or nothin. Nigga owe me that red car, is all."

"I will, Black," I said. But the east wind iced my promise. "If I see him."

* * *

Hadn't recognized I was breathing it for years, not since Salvie'd drove me out to the Styx. But the wind swallowed me as I drove along Indiana Avenue. I stopped the Caddy at the corner of 47th, had to—that stank air took hold and blew me from the car. I was the one pulled by the arm then, not a junkie whore. West it took me, to the place where I'd stood with Black the day before. Wind smelled worse than the alleys of my boyhood, worse than the Styx graveyard, bad to choke tears free from my eyes. But that wind didn't give a damn, just pulled me down our strip.

"Leave me alone!" I yelled, and, for a bit, the wind did let go.

There was a crowd, a group of 47th Street souls standing at the alley entrance where I'd been dropped. That was where the rot ran, into the alley; I'd caught its escape. I pushed past the souls, chased after the stink—or did it pull still? No, I wanted to know what'd rotted out like that on God's earth. So I chased, no different than when I'd dug the garbage filling from a Cajun's grave. No one fought as I pushed past, either, no screams as my hands pressed against the bodies. I looked into the faces, saw that they didn't smell the rot waves themselves. Those strip folks just moved to the side because it was me they'd waited for, the skunk bastard about to catch the invisible rot he'd chased forever.

There was 47th Street Black, legs spread out on top of gravel, back still halfway propped up against the building. His eyes fixed on the winter sun, no squint, no blink, cleared whites shining. Teeth hung from his mouth, browned with the spill of his last wine. No thieves'd ripped over the man's body, for there was nothing left to take. Folks gave Black his peace. Their eyes, blank as the bum's, weren't even on him any longer, but on me.

"What happened?" I turned to one of the junkies from 43rd Street. "What did him?"

"He was ol. Jesus took him on."

"Jesus," I said.

Wondered if Black'd spent my twenty before he went, or if they'd lifted the bill from his pockets. I turned to the crowd, about to question, but the wind swooped down to take hold again—strip folks wouldn't have told me the truth besides. So before I could bend over and rip Black open myself, rot pulled me back to the Cadillac.

* * *

Chicago Sun-Times—December 13, 1980

Chicago syndicate boss Gaetano "Caesar" Ricci, 68, was found guilty on ten counts of racketeering and conspiracy Monday, more than a year after the original indictment was filed against the mob figurehead. The jury, the second to hear the government's case, delivered a guilty verdict against Ricci after less than one hour of deliberation. Allegations of jury and evidence tampering, and the murder of potential material witness and Ricci right-hand man Salvatore Fuoco, were blamed for extending the proceedings. According to federal prosecutors, sentencing . . .

I laughed. When I was in the joint, the Muslims'd preached about the white world training us as criminals to commit wrongs against our own people; kept their hands clean that way, ready to count the profits of our crimes. Clean to get away with living life by their backwards holy law—Salvie Fuoco could yell all day about how he didn't believe in touching dope, but still collect a 35 percent cut of the sales on every bag of heron hustled by black and brown hands in the city. Funny that the boss, Tommy Ricci, had been done in by fool's justice, then. We'd been hustling so many years for him that we didn't want him around, didn't even need him there to direct us in the game. Without the man taking his cut, the backwards pie was all ours.

"You got business on the telephone, J.C."

I rolled the newspaper into a globe, watched it tumble the strip as I took the pay phone from Otis. "Who's this?"

"J.C.? Little J.C. from over Forty-seventh Street way?"

The voice cut through my ears, sounding like it belonged not to Tommy Ricci or Salvie, but to somebody else from that place west of Ashland Avenue. I blinked for the pain in my left knee. "Yeah, who's this?"

"You don't remember me, J.C. It's been a long time."

"If you ain't talking about something, then ain't no need for you to be talking to me. This's a business telephone, joe. Business. Who is this, and how'd you get my number?"

"You did a favor for me years ago, J.C. Remember?"

I looked across the block, then down 47th. Soul Mamma's ashes lay there, piled on top of the Snake Pit's. "I remember."

"I never got the chance to repay you. I owe you, brother. I got a deal for you. That's the business I'm calling about. You interested?"

He was a ghost. But Sermon hadn't killed him, not even close, just left him without legs. He wasn't dead—Sermon was dead. "Tony?"

The voice shook as its groan became a laugh. "You interested or what, baby?"

Serving the Riccis was what'd brung me to shooting Sermon down that street, landed me in Decatur for seven years; serving Riccis was why I'd ended up making my living selling dope in an alley next to a damned temple. That was the boy's voice, all right—Tony Ricci, the jive clown. "What's the deal you're talking about?"

"Meet me in Hyde Park, J.C., at my home. Fifty-seven-oh-one Cornell, the high-rises, number twelve twenty-eight. Come by tomorrow night. It's a good thing I'm offering. I owe you, brother."

I thought of the thick lips pouting on his pasty face, the wavy afro, the polyester bell-bottoms, the secondhand jewelry dangling from his neck. Tony Ricci's birth into a family of Italian gangsters was a lucky thing for him. Tony Ricci was a nigger in any other life. "I'll be there," I said.

"You be there," Tony said, "and we'll do this business together, me and you."

I hung the receiver on its hook as a gust caught me, blew me across the concrete. I watched Soul Mamma as I was carried away then, watched her ashes wiggling with December on top of our strip.

23

SHOULD'VE FIGURED RICCI for finding himself a Black chick. What did Salvie used to say about the boss' son? "Tony's a fuckup, so that's probably the first thing he's gonna look to do." So when that smooth caramel face showed through 1228's cracked door, no shock came to my mind. And I should've expected her to be nice-looking, seeing as Tony had high taste in his colored honeys. At least the one I'd seen him with was fine, Joy, that trick who'd sold Sermon out and landed me in the joint. The girl in the crack even looked like Joy from years before—hair sparkling curly like a Puerto Rican's, bright candy skin, with eyes that forced you to believe in her name. There was no shock caused by her color then, no shock because she was an angel. Surprise belonged to her alone, showed in the twitch of her mouth, the wrinkled frown of her forehead. For her to belong to Tony Ricci was nothing, but for me to come knocking at their high-rise brought crazy fear to her eyes.

"Hello," she said, safe behind her security chain. "Can I help you?"

"Yeah. I'm looking for the guy who lives in here. Is he home?"

"Are you sure you have the right apartment?"

Her words were more proper than Mora's from years before, sounded from heaven's ladder, way up there, and dropped my way only in pity. "Is this number twelve twenty-eight? That's what your door says."

"This is."

"Tony Ricci live here or what?"

She looked over her shoulder. Through the security crack, I could see the paintings, the bushy carpet, the full wall mirrors. I didn't hear her speaking, didn't see anyone for her to be talking to. When she turned back to me, though, a smile showed from up high. "What did you say your name was?"

"J.C.'s my name, J.C. Rose. Tony Ricci's expecting me."

"Oh, you're expected?" the woman said, and let loose 1228's chain. "Come inside, Mister Rose."

Ronald Reagan's voice hit the mirrors, hard for my reflection to shake as I passed. That evil empire jive got louder as the caramel woman led me through china and porcelain, shaded by the gray sky showing through plated windows. Tony Ricci sat in front of the evening TV news. And Ronnie was right about that place with its gangsters and fancy decorations and phony Joys pretending to look down on colored souls from up there, and trolls shaking in mirrors—5701 Cornell was a evil empire. Old man didn't see what I saw in the mirrors, and he couldn't speak my language, and his jive rained from a phony ladder all his own. But he had it right on about evil in Tony the Gimp's home.

A cloud of cigar smoke circled Tony's wheelchair before floating to the screen. "Ah, J.C. Rose, my main man," he said. "Come here."

I walked to the son as he pushed his upper body from the chair and held out his right hand. "What's up, Tony?"

He supported his weight with his left arm while his legs dangled against the metal braces, and he hugged me. "I'm doing real good, man. Take a seat. Honey, this's my main man, J.C. Rose. . . . Did you meet Janie?"

I sat at his side and looked over my shoulder for the woman who'd showed the way. She was gone, disappeared behind walls painted pink. "Janie's gone."

"Where'd she go?" As his eyes searched the room, I checked out all that fat his body had put on since the Soul Mamma days—his face was thick enough that his lips sank into his cheeks. And he filled the wheelchair with swelling, too much to hide in those baggy clothes or behind shiny jewelry. The cigar was held in the same chunky left hand that pushed him from his cripple's chair. "You saw her, though, huh, J.C.? Fine woman, ain't she?"

"She was all right." I nodded, smiled.

Ricci patted my scarred knee. "How you been? I ain't seen you in years. Like what, nine, ten years? It been that long? Talk to me, my man. What's been up with you?"

"Just taking care of business."

"Just the business?"

"Just the business, nothing more."

"That's what I wanna hear." The words from his lips still came slick and quick, chasing after his hustle. He blew a sweet stink into the air. "You're a smoking man, right, J.C.? You ever had one of these babies straight outta Havana? These is the motherfuckers Castro smokes on. Uncle Sam won't even let you bring em into the States no more, not since Fidel put his dick up our asses way back. But you smell the smoke. There ain't nothing like putting your lips around one of these babies. You know you're in business when you got a Havana in one hand, blue steel near the other, and some sweet brown sugar to take care of you."

The Ricci boy slipped another cigar from his shirt pocket and handed it to me. He offered a light; I had my own. His teary eyes fixed on me through smoke. "How's that? Taste good, don't it?"

"Tastes real good," I said, and it did.

Janie walked across the room and cut through our smoke before she was lost again. "I could always be honest with you, J.C.," Tony said, "tell you the truth of what was on my mind. That's what I liked about you back then, what made you my main man. You know, most of the brothers is sensitive. Gotta watch what comes outta your mouth to em. Might hurt the pride speaking too truthful, you know? But you and me, as long as I didn't call you a nigger, we could talk together. I can be truthful like that with you still, huh?"

"Course," I said, high on burnt air. "Say what you've got to say."

"All right, my man. I just wanna know, you see—I ain't never been able to figure something out. If the brothers is as smooth and cool as you make yourselves out to be, how come we get the cream of what's yours and you all can't do no better than living out of our trash? Why is that, bro, if the brothers is so smooth and cool?"

I laughed loud enough for him to know his shit wasn't funny, then looked for his brown woman over my shoulder. She didn't pass. "What'd you call me for, Tony? You said you were talking business."

"Don't mean nothing bad." His hair wasn't as tall and wavy as it'd been when he had legs; thick curls held tight to the skull instead. "Thought I could talk to you like that, tell you what was on my mind."

"No insult. Just got business to tend to. Time is everything."

"Right, J.C. Business, I understand. Time is everything. Like I told you, I called to let you know I ain't forgot nothing. I know you're the one who clipped the *pazzo* who left me in this chair. I know I owe you, J.C., big-time. I got this opportunity, you see, to profit. Things have opened up since my father got caught up with the feds. You heard about what they did to my old man, didn't you?"

"Read it in the paper." I swallowed a smile. "How long they putting him away for?"

"Long time—the rest of his years, probably."

"Heard somebody clipped Salvie, too. That's what was in the *Sun-Times*."

"A year ago they got him. Just when all this court shit started with my father, Salvie's wife found him in the car, shot up like a dog. To this day, nobody's said who it was that did him. He was like blood to me, like my own uncle, you know? These's been rough days." He stopped on his cigar. "But I got this business opportunity, a chance to bring in some paper. And I wouldn't have never come about this if not for making it through the bad times. You interested?"

"That's why I'm here, joe."

"Good, I knew you'd wanna listen. I got a guy, see, this friend who flies planes, wrapped up in some kinda government shit. Honduras, some Mexican shit. Flies over mountains, into jungles, across the world, everywhere. And this friend always brings me something back from his trips. He's the fella who came in with the Havanas, right? He's a good guy. Calls me the other day, says he just got back from South America. They got some beautiful broads down there, on the other side of the border, J.C., so I'm wondering what my guy brung back for me. I ask him where he visited: Brazil, Argentina, Venezuela, where? Guy tells me he didn't go to none of em, says he's just come from Bolivia . . . and I'm wondering why this clown's wasting my time telling me about some jungle joint I ain't never heard of before, right? I'm thinking what the fuck, until he says he's got a key of pure coke with him like I ain't never seen before. Now, I don't know what makes him think he knows what kinda blow I've fucked with in life. How's he know what I've had and what I ain't had? So I say to bring it in to me, cause I don't like nobody questioning my taste. This friend comes with the key, to the pad, sat right where you're sitting now—you know how much a key is? He's gotta carry it in one of them tote bags like he's packed to go see Donald Duck in fucking Disneyland for a month. He shows it to me, lets me taste a little, right? And sure enough, it's the cleanest shit I ever come across. I don't tell him that, but it is.

"Of course, he didn't fly it all the way back here for no kinda token. This guy ain't stupid. He figures I got connections with a lotta people, wants me to help move this thing. So he says to me, 'Tony, who do you know can come up with the dough for what I got, put it to use?' I say, 'I know a lotta motherfuckers who can do a lotta things, motherfucker.' I gotta play the tough-guy role, see. I'm still shit-faced from him questioning my taste—anyway, this's a friend I'm talking to, but I come across tough. I tell him, 'You know about my sister, Annie, about how the dope fucked her all up, and you know how my old man is, that he don't approve of this kinda business causa her, don't involve himself with it.' So this friend says how much respect he's got for my family and what have you. But he says he's looking to make these trips a long-term thing, going back and forth to South America, if he can find somebody to move it for him over here consistent. That's all he needs. Now, me and you know it ain't nothing to find somebody with the loot and the will to make a smart investment. The trick is finding a motherfucker with the know-how to make the thing work, and keep it working. So, my friend says he came here even though he respects my father, cause he believes if anybody can find a guy to move his gift, it's me."

The Ricci boy blew above his head and I let go laughter. "How much?"

"How much?" He pushed the wheelchair closer to the television. "Coke's been a rich drug as long as I remember, most of my life. These Jew *pazzos* who live around here, it's been their thing. That ain't who you're gonna be working with on Forty-third Street. If you was dealing with the rich bastards over here, I'd say no less than fifty-five G's for a key clean like this one. I'm telling you, it's so fucking clean, J.C. That's remembering that you'd be dealing high-quality shit over here, shit that ain't been stepped on too hard. But over where you're at, over in the ghetto where everybody's on junk anyway, you got a whole new customer. Nobody there can tell the difference, nobody cares. So, since we're trying to get this thing off the ground, let's say fifty G's."

"I can't come up with more than forty-five now."

Janie smiled that fake, up-high smile in the corners of my eyes—she sat in the dining room, holding her head and looking at the lake with one eye, watching me with the other. "Forty-five?" Tony moaned. "You can't do no better? I thought my father and Salvie gave your partner loot to hold while you was in the clink. You was supposed to get near fifty when they let you outta there. Figured you woulda put that loot on the street and made a mint, smart guy like you. What the fuck happened? You ain't spent all that dough in five years? What can a motherfucker do to make fifty G's cash go in that kinda time?"

"It was thirty-five," I tell him. "You stick a stamp on a box and give it to the mail boy to send, don't mean it's gonna end up where you meant for it to go. You gotta trust that messenger—delivery's on his ass."

"What about the junk? I know it's booming. You got everything Black and the mother of everything Black running around the South Side strung out. I watched you parking that new Caddy downstairs. What about that?"

"That's money spent to live. Ain't saved none of it. You know how things is."

"Forty-five, huh?" The medallion around Tony's neck shined yellow with his teeth. "If that's the best you can do, it's the best you can do. Figure that's more than the money we paid you first off, so you give it right back to me, right? The difference on the real worth of the key, the money my ol man paid your partner, and this forty-five wipes the slate clean. Nobody owes nobody. You can get it to me by the end of next week?"

"Of course," I said, and shook the Ricci boy's hand. Clown still had those sharp nails. "You wouldn't have come to me if I couldn't get your money in a week's time."

"Good. We're even, then, bro," Tony Ricci said. Reagan came back on the TV, talking about cutting taxes for big business—to stimulate the economy, he said. "This guy, this new president, I love him. Would've voted for him till my fingers fell off. I love this guy," Tony said. "Ronnie's going to be good for business."

"Good for fucking business," I repeated, and watched myself nod in Ricci's mirrors. "That's what we're doing here—fucking business, right?"

* * *

Junk had ruled 43rd Street long as I'd known, made the Banks brothers, Big Lester Hooks, and their supply guys into fat cats. But our racket, the coke racket, exploded back in the beginning of the eighties. Made me the man on 47th and 43rd Streets, bigger than any who'd come before. We cut our keys down with everything, flour, baking soda, rat poison—whatever white powder we could get our hands on cheap. And, just like the Ricci boy said, junkies were anything but choosy. Some, like the yellow man from 43rd, were already so strung out they went on shooting melted coke into their blood. Others picked up on snorting, dug it because up the nose was how the rich folk got their high. But our best clients were the base-heads, those who bought Lester's junk sugar and cooked it with our dirty snow until it was burned smooth, then smoked the base out of homemade pipes.

In the end, it didn't matter how they got the sickness into their souls, because coke took over. By the summer of '81, the beginning of Reagan's black depression, I was dropping ten G's a week into my safe at Grandma's house. If she'd seen all that cash piling up, no way she would've been able to hold back pride.

Not long after I made my first deal, I came off the street. Otis and his younger brothers took over handling the day-to-day of packaging and handling the product. My life became rolling the strip in the Caddy, feeling the love and lust of the fiends. No more 47th Street honeys turned on me, not after I became the man slinging coke rock. I had the riches, so it was for my eyes they wiggled.

But Big Lester made a call to my business phone at summer's end, crying about how he needed a piece of our backwards pie if I was gonna keep dealing on the side. Claimed 43rd Street was his by right, that no money could be made on that strip unless he let it be. Our trade was independent, so we'd be shut down unless he saw his fair piece, he screamed. How he figured on keeping me from making money in a trade based on addiction to depression, who knew? Back then, Otis and his brothers were the only coke hustlers around 43rd Street. Lester'd been in the game so long, he had to know that a fiend would get to their pusher hell or high water. I could've been six feet underground, and the yellow man would still be at the front of my dust-piled casket, the brown girl still on her knees in front of my hole. Lester'd been on 43rd Street too many years not to understand that. I laughed, all I could do, before hanging up on his dumb ass.

Stupid me for giving a coon too much credit, for figuring his eyes were open all those years. I was checking on Otis, making sure my paper was being made (a lesson learned from Salvie—had to keep on top of those handling your loot, always), when a beat-up Dodge full of knuckleheads from the strip rolled to my alley. The fire came, tearing up the Caddy's paint job and slicing new cracks in the gravel. Forty-third Street bled that day, not with my blood, and not Otis', but with that of junkies waiting on a fix. We survived, while losing some of our best customers. Lester'd made his move and shut us down, for twenty-four hours at least. Fiends lined back up after the pigs took away the yellow crime-scene tape the next day. But the 43rd Street trade wasn't the same for a while. The junkies came, but spilling blood wasn't good business. Salvie wasn't even around to know it, but he'd taught me that lesson, too.

24

THE RUMBLE OF CLEANING MACHINES beat against my ears, drowned everything: the Stony Island voices, my sweat, fear. Still I wished for a pipe at my side, not for protection, just to hold on to. I wondered if his lead swing was the same after all the years, or if time had made it no different than my own. That was what I decided—that his swing'd gone weak with time—as I knocked on the management door. Felt safe, believing we were equal.

"Come in," that voice I hadn't heard in so long yelled over the noise. I stepped into the office and mirrors surrounded me. I found Mookie King of Stony Island first in the reflection, the king and his boy. They counted crisp green hundred notes and stacked them on a makeshift metal desk with wheels. I didn't know the child, not until I noticed the softness in his young eyes as they blinked up from his job. Those pupils said that he knew me; Isaiah Cross remembered Uncle J.C. the bastard convict all too well. Mirrors bouncing light against walls had taken the place of bars and glass, caging us. I winked at the boy so he'd know that I remembered, too.

"Sit down," Mookie said.

I walked across the office slow, felt his stare as he looked away from the loot. The seat was bad leather, like the one he'd tried to hide himself under in Soul Mamma's office, and gray to match the desk that separated me from man and child. I sat and forced myself to look him in the face, swallowed his smooth skin, rippled hair, hawk nose, dark lips, and the new bills. Twenty K sat in front of them, I knew without counting, without touching. I hated him still. "What do you want, man?"

"I don't want nothin," Mookie said. "Lester Hooks calls, says you lookin to speak to me. What the hell would I want from you?"

I glanced at Isaiah as the boy counted out loud.

"This a business meeting or what?" I asked.

"You're lookin to talk in private?" He sipped from a plastic cup. "That's what you tryin to say? You got no tact, after all this time, no tact."

"Just thought we were about to talk business—only reason I came here."

Mookie stood from his throne. "Excuse me, Isaiah. I'm gonna be outside with this man, tellin him some things. Sit in my chair and keep countin."

His shadow covered me as we left the office and led me to a window that looked out on cars rolling through soapy rain. His black eyes watched over the business, waiting for me to speak. But it took time for courage to come, just like when we were boys. Back in '57.

"What'd you mean, sending them niggas to shoot up my alley? You damn near killed me. Took out folk who weren't doing anything but looking to make a buy, innocent folk. What'd you prove?"

"J.C.," Mookie cooed, still a cool player, "you gone foolish since I saw you last? When you ever known me to make moves like this, shootin up the streets? You do good business, I hear. What should I wanna shut that down for? I ain't against you, chief, no way. You need to go on back and talk to Lester, or whoever it is you got troubles with. I don't make moves like that. Can't these days."

"Lester says come to you, you say go to Lester. Y'all are running scared from what you've done, like pussies. The blood's been spilled.

Might as well go on and fess up to your shit. Who's running this shop?"

"Who you think's runnin it?"

"It's you who's got the Outfit in back of you, Stones in front, following your word since Jimmy Mo got blasted. At least that's what the street says."

Mookie laughed. But I heard no joy in him, not for the noise of those machines. "When you ever known me to be wrapped up with gang bullshit? I'm a respected businessman now, the owner of the ground you stand on. Remember that." He turned to the cars, hiding his face. "You need to handle this problem yourself, pay up a piece of what you got to whoever you supposed to pay it to, get outta that alley, do whatever it is you gotta do, before you get hurt."

"By who?"

"Whoever you got the problem with."

"You?"

"What you askin questions for? Like this's a kid game or somethin. Told you, I got nothin to do with gang bullshit. Dealin dope, none uh that. That's your business."

"My business? So why Lester say go talk to you? And why're you telling me to stay out of that alley?"

He put the tar of those eyes on me. "Just get outta that place, J.C., with your goddamn stubborn head. Before you get hurt."

I nodded, paused before speaking again. I was a fool, a bastard fool telling lies to himself—I was nowhere near equal to the hustler he'd become. Thoughts drifted. "You hear what happened to Tommy Ricci?"

He rolled those eyes. "Of course I heard. Know all bout it."

"And Salvie, word is somebody clipped him."

Mookie's soul sank—I felt it drown from him. "They got Salvie, yeah, clipped him a long time ago."

"World's gone mad when even they ain't safe."

"Anybody can be got, you know. You said something about Jimmy Moore gettin blasted a minute ago?"

"Yeah?"

The eyes sliced past mine. "You heard how it went down with him?"

"Took out in front of the old Regal. Some gang shit—a war, something. Disciples got him, that's why they've been shooting back and forth over here."

"Disciples? You believe that shit? I told you a long time ago, J.C., back when we was kids. You gotta listen, listen and learn from what you hear. Salvie use to tell you, too. Remember?"

"Yeah," I said, and watched mist fall on a Buick. "Salvie use to say that."

"The shots you hear on Stony, where they comin from? Blackstones still run junk much as they ever did. Killin that cat ain't do nothin for a Disciple. Jimmy's dead is the only difference between then and now far as dope go, cause he was a stubborn bastard who wouldn't cut the right folk in on his money. He was gonna slip and fall one way or the other, the route he was takin. Ain't every stubborn bastard you ever known on these streets gone down like so?

"Now they understand on Stony Island. Certain people gotta get a piece off the top to keep the business right, then your trade can keep turnin its wheels, no problem. Shoot up as many niggas as you like, no problem."

"Mmh," I moaned, like Mookie had my mind working, but there was nothing left to think about. "What'd Salvie use to call them? Hardheaded cocksuckers?"

"Something," Mookie said. "Two of us ain't been tight for years, but hear me when I say this: we learned better than them. The only way cats like Jimmy Mo and Johnny the Baptist can come about good sense is the hard way, J.C. You ain't gotta learn like them. You know."

Quiet fell over us for a bit, so hard I was scared to lift it. "It's a mad world. The things we do to make it in this place—craziness."

"Ain't nothin crazy here." Mookie's eyes reminded me of the judges' stares at my parole hearing. Except that his pupils flashed between natural black and a puke green like the cash the boy stacked in the office. "This's progress. Who's makin the dough? You see what we holdin down in there. Tommy Ricci's locked up, Salvie's in the ground. It's ours now."

"This's what the world's come to, who gets to do wrong to the other?"

"That's what we always been doin. Long as this nigga gets you before you get me. . . ."

"Everything's cool," I said as Isaiah stepped outside the office door. "You ever had a Havana cigar before?"

"One of them thick, sweet ones? Them kind?"

"Yeah, the rich cigars that burn the good-smelling smoke."

"Not for years. Not since God knows when. Salvie use to smoke um sometimes, back in the day."

"Oh yeah?" I brought one of Tony Ricci's fresh rolls from my blazer's inside pocket, offered it to him. "We've got peace?"

Mookie took my gift and hung it limp from his mouth. I lit the tip, watched smoke lift from black lips. "Yeah, we got peace, long as you can take care of those troubles, do what you gotta do. Long as you understand, we got peace."

I shook his hand as sweet clouds bounced against the glass, and Mookie smiled, teeth barely creeping through his lips. "I understand," I said. "That's what the business is."

His smile twisted. "What?"

"Doing what we've got to do," I said, "that's what. I do understand our business."

The end of my thing with the virgin Charlotte Humphreys hadn't meant living a hero's life was done for me. I'd come too far for that, had too far left to go. J.C. still stood for Jesus Christ, and I was on my way to being good as Him. Only difference was Jesus'd made it out of the valley of his own darkness by then, where I hadn't even come across Lazarus to show him from the cave.

Went about finding a bunch of no-account, legal jobs around the Forties, though. Painting houses, fixing on cars, day labor, moving furniture here to there, driving cabs there to here for Black folks headed to places where the foreigner cabbies wouldn't take them. Never worked any of those gigs more than a month or two at a time. Chump jobs weren't to be held longer than that. Niggas just bounced in a circle in the legal hustles, not here to there or there to here, but around and around.

I went out to the new Ebenezer on Stony some Sundays, though. I didn't feel as much of a chump while I was in church, praying to God. Cats at Ebenezer connected me to the day-labor circuit, in fact. That was how we made it, you see; while honeys like Charlotte went downtown every day in their long-dress, black-stocking, flat-shoe bests, to file papers, type letters, pour coffee, mule for the big company in its big building, or up to the schools to teach the little nappy heads their ABC's, 123's, like whitey-we-wished-we-could-be's; while the honeys made the loot in that world, niggas stooped down to the ground in the hot sun, trying to find shade from the heavens burning us. We scrounged for our scraps—food, drink, the feeling of being men. And at the end of the week, we were up at Ebenezer next to our honeys, begging God to lead us to that peaceful shade.

My GED, the college ACED courses, none of my time in the clink made much of a difference. Those Ebenezer cats making it the same way I made it hadn't done any time behind bars, never for a second thought about pulling off any real crimes. Too Christian and weak and scared; they were just born to be chumps, living up to their God-given potential without anything else special to do with their lives. Just hustling, low-end hustling, to the end.

I was fixing on Reverend Goode's Oldsmobile when I ran across my gold Caddy from back in the days. Out looking for parts at a Back-of-the-Yards junk lot, just outside Salvie and Tommy Ricci's old neighborhood, I saw my steel baby there, crushed in the middle of a trash heap. Somebody'd been driving it in the nine years since me, for sure—Grandma Rose'd sold it to a joker from the Low End, I'd heard while I was still locked up—and its gold was rusted and dusty from the years and waste. Trapped from the sky, dead cars on top, dead cars up under it, just holding it there. I'd thought I'd seen the Caddy rolling around the Forties since I'd come out of Decatur, but there was my gold baby, hanging high to remind me the place I'd fallen from. The lot's owner caught me staring at that heap on the far end of his Back-of-the-Yards. He held the transmission I'd come for in his dirty left hand, offering it and asking if I needed more help in his Vinnie Povich accent.

"Naw." I paid him with Reverend's money. "I'm good."

"Good? Mmh." The old man held his chin to keep his head from shaking, and he dropped the gear shifter in my hand. "Carry on, boy."

The 43rd Street alley wasn't the first time I'd come across Christina over the years, either. After I was done with Charlotte's game, I'd gone to the Low End to look for young Christina, not to bend her over like I'd promised myself in '77—Grandma Rose was watching still, I knew—not for any sinful reasons at all. But I'd heard stories around the Forties about how the sweet tramp was long gone, strung out hard on that horse since back when they'd locked me up. Heard that Mookie was one of the players feeding her hunger, that double hunger for dope and dick. Taking care of her good, the word on the street went—one of many players, they said, but the biggest of them all, old Mookie.

Like he needed the girl, with all the honeys chasing after him on Stony Island, with Queen Mora still by his side, so they said. Mookie had to be doing Christina because of me—had to be his way of reminding me how much of a fool I was for living the life of a Christian hero while he got paid in loot and pussy from the game we'd chased for years. Sitting up on the high shit like I should've been sitting, because it was my right to be sitting there, and he knew. *I'd* found Johnny. Fucking my sweet little mamma, killing her all the while, was nothing more than Mookie's way of telling me the worth of saving souls. I was the fool, sick and stupid as the rest of the losers, hustling myself into believing anything but the truth was true.

But I went to check on the girl. She looked like trash, nothing like the low-lidded baby girl I'd run across my first week free at Soul Mamma, not as bad as she ended up in the alley a few years later. Getting there slow, though. But she remembered me, even smiled when she opened the door. Those first few visits, I'd sit in her St. Lawrence Avenue apartment, watching as she shot up. Shot that shit, then turned away and mumbled words that didn't make sentences to the flower wallpaper peeling from her walls. Minutes'd pass before Christina'd move again; she'd make me promise to wait on her then, put on a ratty coat to cover the holes in her skin, and run out of the apartment. Come back in less then a half hour with a bottle of Boone's Farm wine, swallowed most of a pint herself, then offered a sip before she finished shooting up and mumbled off. After a month of that, I'd take Grandma's Bible with me and read to her from Psalms. She would say amen at the end of my verses, after pausing to show her full understanding of God's word, then turn to her wall and pick up that conversation with her wallpaper right where it'd left off.

I'd tried hard, and I was about to stop myself from all of it anyway, when I dropped by one February day in '79 and Christina answered the door wearing only her girdle and a pink bra. I heard Grandma Rose, warning me about the tramp who'd been with the Reverend's boy and fat Julius Banks and Morris junior, and so many more, heard the old woman praying for my soul—but that *bee*-hind was still up so high on Christina's hips, squeezed holy into the girdle, and she had the apartment lights dimmed just so we were in the shadows, and she offered me wine. As I was about to pull the girdle down past her thighs, she stopped me with that screeching no—put us right back in Grandma's cellar on 45th Street, that one word did—like the Holy Ghost'd taken the place of her heron high. Said she didn't have time to waste with no "buster-ass, punk nigga who can't do nothing for me but fix up my wallpaper, read some Bible, and lick my shit. What else, nigga?" No mumble from those lips, either—Christina screamed it clear for my ears. Pulled her girdle up over that *bee*-hind and told me to go on back to my grandmamma. I tried to tell her Grandma Rose'd been dead for so long, but she threw the Bible at me and slammed her splintered-wood door against my forehead.

I had a dream that night. Saw Johnny the Baptist's dick, throbbing and bopping and sewn onto something I couldn't see, held in the dirty left hand of that Polish junk man, and my gold Caddy hanging over me, not about to fall because it couldn't fall trapped in that trash hill. The junk man put Johnny's thing next to my lips as I kneeled under him.

"Need any more help, boy?" he asked.

"Naw," I answered. "I'm good. This all I need."

So one of the Stone trolls jumped from the trash heap shade and grabbed me at the throat, squeezing so my mouth opened, and the Polack put Johnny between my lips and stroked until I felt sticky mess on my jaws and teeth. He took the thing from my lips, and I spit black blood on the alley gravel. And I heard Charlotte's twanging:

"No count, chum, busta nigga," she said in her dreamy backwoods echo. "Lick me shit."

—

The original Blackstone Ranger, Big Lester Hooks, owned a piece of the gypsy cab company I drove for sometimes. That was how he turned the big-time loot he made on 43rd Street into clean dollars. I called him the morning after my dream, sun shining on Grandma's living room as the phone dial spun, told him I had ten G's to put on the street—cash to turn into shining gold. I wasn't that much of a fool, not like Jesus Christ dying to get niggas into heaven. Didn't take more than a dream to teach me a lesson I should've learned as a boy, watching Mookie after he threw his last touchdown passes—stars floated in the sky, not down low, and we couldn't be the heroes on Manley's blackboard. How hard or how long we'd tried, no matter, because much as Decatur Penitentiary was just like free life, free life was just like the joint. All a hustle played out in the filthy bighouse shade.

25

I'D NEVER BEEN to a Catholic church. Tell the truth, Ebenezer Baptist was the one and only church I'd stepped inside in life, unless you counted the Decatur chapel and the trips I'd made to New Ebenezer on Stony Island. Never saw those places as the house of a real God, though.

I waited for Tony Ricci on St. Boniface's steps at 64th and Ashland Avenue, and I searched the church crowd for signs of the Ricci boy, saw men who could've been with the Ricci crew themselves, dressed just like Salvie—tweed trench coats, gray haberdashery, plastic shoe heels. And I heard their voices, cranky mumbles, like the old gangsters'. They watched me, too, from the corners of gray eye sockets, wondering what blackness I'd brung to the steps of their Lord's house. Would I grab a purse, pick a pocket? Or was I true evil, looking to kill one, take their women and children? St. Boniface's congregation tore me apart as they walked past on those Catholic steps.

"J.C.! Come here!"

There was the Ricci boy, wounded fat resting in his wheelchair. The man pushing Tony looked like Angelo Palermo, Salvie's nephew from years before—tall enough to block the sun from shining on the ground, with pupils dense and simple. But it had been '69 when I'd last come across Angelo, so long, and the shadow in front of me stumbled with time. Maybe he was Salvie's ape from the Chrysler's front seat, I wasn't sure. Not even when I caught the thick gray hair crawling on top of his lip, not even then was I sure.

I walked down the church steps slow, watched Ricci and the ape tearing at me too. "What's up?"

"We got troubles," Ricci said, his voice as quick and cranky as the street around us. "Let's walk."

My shoulders shook with the wind as I followed them away from St. Boniface's, north on Ashland. "What troubles you mean? Everything's good on Forty-third Street."

"I bet. This *pazzo,* the one you're lying down with over there, this *melangian* . . . you know who I'm talking about?"

" 'Mulin-ian'? I don't know your language, man. Speak in English, so I understand what you're saying. What's that mean, I been lyin down with somebody?"

"Means what it says. Sleeping with him like a whore. Your friend, this guy you do business with," Ricci growled, "this King fella. You made a deal with him? I know that's what you done over there, made a deal to get in bed with this *melangian*. I know."

My heart beat against my .45. "So? I do what I do to protect my loot. So what? I'm not in bed with nobody, just protecting what I've got."

It was the stupid hate burning through the eye holes, same as the stare in the rearview mirror when I was a boy, that confirmed that cat pushing Ricci's chair as Salvie's nephew. We reached the block's end and Angelo spun Tony south to face St. Boniface's steeple. "Remember who gave you what you got, friend," Ricci said. "This King guy, he's done us wrong, committed what I call an egregious error. You know what that means?"

"No. What the fuck?"

Ricci looked at Big Angelo. The nephew paid him no mind, too busy watching me through Salvie's rearview mirror. "Like a sin.

You're in bed with him, and if you're gonna stay in bed with him, you're gonna end up paying right alongside this guy for his sin. You know what I'm saying, J.C.?"

"Damnit—try speaking it in English again, would you?"

He growled again. "What'd you used to call him—Mook, Spookie, whatever it was. The one who got you into this thing." Tony pointed down Ashland, and I could see the Ricci pawn shop's sign from there, just barely. "You know what I'm talking about. Angelo, you remember Angelo here, he tells me it was your friend who clipped Salvie, put that bullet in the back of the old man's head. You don't know nothing about this?"

I remembered truth drowning from Mookie when I'd asked about Salvie, and I wondered if the old man'd begged for life before getting clipped by a spade from 47th Street. "I don't keep up with him anymore. Haven't been close for years, not for me to know what he's done or hasn't done. Told you how he stole my loot while I was in the joint."

"Not for years, huh?" Tony watched the last Ashland folk walk into St. Boniface's as we returned to the steps. "Tell him what you told me, Angelo."

The ape cleared his throat and his eyes rose to the clouds. "I go to see Mister Ricci, all the way in Florida where they got him locked up. I just wanna know how he's doing, right? If he's getting taken care of good. While I'm down there, he tells me Joey put all this together—after Vinnie turned rat, Joey ordered Salvie clipped. See, Joey was putting it out how the old man was gonna make a deal. But Sal wouldn't do a thing like that, never, not even if the feds had him on their bugs. Mister Ricci believes Joey was trying to get rid of Salvie because he knew what was gonna come outta all this, that Salvie'd be the only one left to keep him from moving up. So Joey went to the top to get cleared, then had this cocksucker friend of yours whack my uncle. Joey was too much of a faggot to do it himself, and he knew none of us would make a move like that unless we heard the word from outta Mister Ricci's mouth—"

"All right, Angelo." Tony raised his hand for quiet.

"I mean, I didn't ask Mister Ricci for none of this. He just got to talking to me, like he was in confession. I ain't no priest."

"All right, Angelo." Tony smacked the wheelchair arm with that free hand. "You say you don't know nothing about this business, J.C.?"

"Nothing. Me and Mookie've been on our own since I came outta Decatur."

"What about this deal you're doing with him? What's this I'm hearing?"

"Just Forty-third Street business needing straightening out."

"You sure?"

I looked at the fat gimp, then the ape, whose eyes wouldn't fall on me again. "Yeah, I'm sure."

"Good, good." The Ricci boy smiled and patted my leg as the wheelchair stopped at the stairs. "I told Angelo you didn't have nothing to do with this, told him you were my main man." He coughed phlegm into his fist, wiped it away, and lit a cigarette. "You gotta help us make right outta this, J.C."

"Right?"

"We can't have people coming in here and killing our own. What would this thing be to let that go on? What would we be? A man don't let nobody come in and hurt his own people. Not in this world, no way. You gotta help us clip the guy. Who in the fuck's he think he is, some kinda special fink?"

"Mookie?" I laughed, at Mookie and at Tony the Gimp—funny, backwards clowns. "He's special."

"Setting this straight's gonna take doing, I know, cause he's connected with Joey. We'll handle that on our end, we'll talk to Joey. Spookie's got the street behind him over there, too. You take care of that on your part of town. Do whatever. Just make sure this *pazzo* is handled. We can't let nobody get away with this. Can we, J.C.?"

"No," I said. "Not at all."

"Good. He stole all that dough from you, anyway. That was our money, meant to reach your hands. Wasn't for him to take. He's got this coming, you see. For years, he's had it coming." The Ricci boy sighed. "You been to church today?"

"Me?" I frowned and glanced at the Jesus-less stone cross above the doorway. "Can't say I have. Ain't been to church in a good while."

"What's wrong with you? You gotta take care of the soul." Tony rolled himself past the staircase. "Come in, J.C. Come to mass with us. This's Sunday. What's more important you gotta do on Sunday than go to mass?"

"I ain't Catholic," I said. "Don't know anything about mass."

"What is you?" Tony Ricci sneered, the cigarette balanced on his bottom lip. "Some kinda Baptist?"

"Yeah," I said, and tried to sneer back. "Baptist. That's what I was raised."

"Whatever. God is God. A Catholic worships, a Baptist worships, so long as you worship. Ain't that what we're here to do?" I wondered how they would lift his wheelchair into the church. "This's Sunday, man. Besides, my honey, Janie, is getting baptized today. She's about to become a good Catholic girl right here at St. Boniface's, the same place where me and Annie was baptized when we were babies. That's the only way they'd let the two of us get married here, you know, if Janie was baptized Catholic. She was brung up a Baptist, too."

"You two are getting married?"

"She's my honey. Of course we're getting hitched." Angelo watched the clouds fly past, and he shook. "Mamma always told me to make sure I found myself a good Catholic girl. That's what Janie's about to become here, a good, baptized Catholic. Mamma's soul can rest now."

"What about your father's soul?" The empty simpleton in the nephew's voice was gone: those words were filled with vomit.

"My old man? Forty years, ain't that what the feds gave him?" Angelo's eyes dropped to Ricci. "Forty years with no parole. What's his soul got to do with this here? As long as I'm married to a good Catholic girl, Mamma can have peace. Are you coming in or what, J.C.?"

I cared nothing about Janie's stuck-up ass. But I stayed, wanted to know how those Italians, who praised Jesus by hanging crucifixes on their walls and around all their necks so the dying was near to remind them, got baptized into their religion. "Yeah, I'll stay. You need help climbing the stairs?"

Tony laughed. "They built a ramp around back for me to get inside easy. All the money we give here, they better find a way to get me into mass." His face turned wet with giggling. "I'll meet you inside."

"Yeah, inside," I said, and walked up St. Boniface's steps. I hadn't ever been to a Catholic mass before, but I stayed for the whole service. Stayed and watched them baptize Janie—damn, she looked like Sermon's Joy—into the Ricci faith.

* * *

My life, lived in an alley just off 43rd Street—

Otis snatched the Lincoln's driver-side door open, and Big Lester the junk man smiled and paused counting the business in hand, his white teeth sparkling against gravel. He tossed the bills into the passenger seat's green mound. "What's up, J.C.? Otis? Y'all just go head and drop my piece right here in my lap. Just drop it and y'all can go bout your way. I trust y'all."

Otis grabbed the fur-lined neck, pulled Lester from his car. The cash from the front seat floated in stank air until it dropped and made a circle around Lester. He pushed the junk man's head into the alley and I stood over them, waiting for tears. I pulled the gat from my coat only when Lester's fists pounded the alley like he fought the devil underneath, and I touched Otis' shoulder so he'd let the junk man go enough to breathe.

"You ain't shit. You know that?" I forced the .45 into his skull and tears flowed. "Muthafuckin fat, pea-headed bitch. You and Mookie can kiss my black ass, understand? The both of you together . . ."

Lester nodded and his fingers dug at the ground. Spit ran from his mouth.

"I want you to do something for me, since you're my bitch now. That's what you are now, my bitch. Or you want a choice? Bitch or bastard? My bitch?" He nodded. "Don't want to be no bastard?" Spit showed in his fur as Lester's head bounced against the gravel. "Which one? Can't be both. Bitch bends over, bastard bends down. Try again. You a bitch or you a bastard?"

"B-b-b-ba-," he spit through Otis' hold, and I heard the trolls singing, somewhere, those Blackstone trolls from my cell.

"Get down . . . get down," the song went.

"I like bitches better. Can't stand no bastard niggas. You make a good bitch." Lester's eyes switched to the shadows and he nodded again. "Stop that nodding, you muthafucka. This's what we're gonna do. The Stones with Mookie on Stony Island, they don't know it was him who took out Jimmy Mo. Start telling them on the street, Lester. Put the word in their heads. You can do that for me, can't you? Don't nod, don't you dare nod again. I got faith you understand what I'm saying. That's what I need from you, my bitch."

"Yeah . . ."

"You the baddest muthafuckin nigga," the trolls chimed there in my alley—I knew their grumbling voices still.

Then the one in back yelled, on top of the song, *"My turn,"* and I felt Johnny the Baptist throbbing ready in my pants.

"You're a bitch, but don't you even think about sending nobody to shoot up my alley while I'm over there. I know it was you who made the call before. Mookie told you to, but it was you who made it happen. Don't do it again, Lester. Try some more stupid shit like that and I'll hunt you down. Hunt you, find you, and fuck you like the fat bitch you are." He nodded and coughed more spit, so I pushed the gat deeper into his skull. "Told you not to do no more nodding, goddamnit. Remember everything I told you. You don't want me to come back here, Lester. Just be a nice, pea-headed, fat bitch and do like I say and everything'll be all right."

I undid my zipper with the free hand, grabbed the Baptist's dick, hard and pounding in my palm, but rotted so it'd turned from Cajun yellow to my brown after all that time, and dripping ready to bust a seed in Big Lester's bitch mouth. I held it over him, jism dropping to his fur, heard the trolls singing about how I was the biggest, baddest muthafucka they ever knew.

"What the fuck . . . is this? What you doin, J.C.?" The gym shoe boy's stutter drowned out the song, and I looked down, saw Otis'd let loose Big Lester's neck so my cum wouldn't touch his fist. And that was *my* cum, *my* dick hard and beating with *my* heart opposite the .45 in *my* right hand. Lester's top lip flapped over the bottom, jaw locking his mouth closed. I looked up as Otis tapped me at the shoulder; his eyes were wide, panicking like he knew I'd put it in his mouth once I finished with the junk man, and there wasn't a goddamn thing his Converse sneakers could do to run him away from it. I let go—the troll's song faded, took the throbbing and the jism with it and left me with that junk pusher and my 43rd Street muscle staring at me, limp in the alley. I zipped myself and breathed.

I shot Lester in his left leg, just so he'd know my word was to be heard and followed as gospel. Like the priest when the Catholics baptized Janie. "This is the word of the Lord, black bitch," I said. Not the trolls, not the Father, but *me,* I said it.

The kneecap exploded, sprayed on the money and on his pretty fur, and on the front of me. Lester screamed in pain, screamed for help, screamed through foul air. But he'd been on 43rd Street so long, he had to know nobody would come for him. Otis stepped out of the circle as the pusher rolled around in his mess of blood and paper money. Lester screamed on until gravel piled inside his mouth, covering the white of his teeth.

The cop, Frank Dunne, stood at the alley's end, staring at us until he saw the junk man squirming and heard his screams—he walked on when he knew Big Lester would live. "Remember to do like I told you. You better." I took the package from my coat pocket, feeling the special pinch of cash protected inside before dropping the envelope in his circle. "There's your piece," I said as we walked to the 43rd Street opening, away from the junk man's screams, and the Baptist's rotten thing, the trolls and their song, and the devil underneath gravel.

* * *

Sermon's blood streaked up 47th and King Drive still. I saw it after all the years, the specks of red dirtying the busy street corner, leaving red cracks in the pavement. I'd search the sidewalk through the passing feet of 47th Street, and there the dried drops of marine blood were—part of the street. Nobody'd bothered to clean his mess after the body was carried off, nobody'd noticed. But I saw the stains, tracking a path from Ellis to King Drive. And whenever I passed that spot, the shiny Thunderbird was there, too, driving west in the corner of my eye.

I remembered coming out of Decatur, how revenge was the first thing on my mind, the mission of freedom, revenge and bending over young Christina. But Mookie'd climbed high above me and young Christina far below by then—a Black angel and a whore junkie, a whore gangster and a burning angel. The mission I'd come up with behind those bars was lost, and only the coke hustle let me forget.

But it all came back to me after Lester's Blackstones'd shot up the strip, hate more than anything else. Mookie left me so he could take over Stony Island, steal my loot, take my honey, but for him to crucify me because he wanted a piece of my trade? I would've never believed it if I hadn't been standing on that corner as bullets ripped the fiends. Tony Ricci'd only created a excuse to move against him, gave me the strength and way for revenge. With the gimp at my back, Mookie wasn't too high for me to reach. I hated him still—he left me alone on our strip.

Sermon's blood was under my feet, on that corner, twelve years after I spilled it. I looked to the sidewalk and saw the crimson pools—not tracks anymore, but pools. And, of course, Mookie was in my eye, riding in another fancy European ride that floated to the corner. Black'd said how fancy leather upholstery hid Mookie from the filth on our street years before. Shooters'd already been sent for his life, but he'd survived. It would take the most familiar fire to catch the king of Stony Island.

Mookie's passenger-side window dropped for him to speak, but not for me to touch him. I saw the lead pipe below his steppers. "What's goin on, J.C.?"

I kneeled in Sermon's pool. Mookie's eyes twitched as I touched the door, and I backed away. I remembered driving the strip together, just me and my man way back. But I wasn't good enough to lean on his fancy sedan anymore. My time would come. "Shit. Same old shit. You know ain't nothing changed round here, joe."

"Oh yeah?" He switched his hazard lights on, but no cars passed. "I hear you're the man on Forty-seventh these days. Got muthafuckas bowin down round here."

"That's what you hear?" I smelled Sermon's rot, heard fat Lester's screaming. "Where you get that from?"

"Don't know. Don't matter. That's what I hear," he said. "So what's up? You the man now or what?"

"If that's what you hear . . ."

"That's what I hear."

"I can't argue with it, then. Must be true."

Mookie groaned and smoothed his tie. "Goddamn shame."

"How so?"

"You the man over here on the same street we used to run together. Me and you, you remember? But on Stony Island, I can't step outside and be safe. Thought I was runnin shit. Guess not. Goddamn shame."

"What's happening on Stony?"

"You ain't heard?" He frowned, like he couldn't trust my word. "I can't drive up and down the street, *my* own street, without some sons of bitches sprayin the car, tryin to take me out. God's with me, that's only why I'm still here. Was comin outta New Ebenezer Sunday before last and they shot up the fronta the goddamn church. Got a lead pipe under me, a thirty-eight in the glove compartment, and a thirty-two under the passenger seat. I'm ready for whoever comes at me. What'd your grandma used to say? 'Live by evil, burn in its flames'? Ain't that what she said?"

"Those was her words."

"You best believe I'm gonna take some of the bastards with me when they come, then."

"But what they shooting at you for? Why?"

He wouldn't buy the hustle; a frown cut into those black eyes. "Word's goin round I had Jimmy Mo killed. You ain't been hearin it?"

"No. They say it was you who blasted him in front of the Regal?"

"That's the word. Muthafucka had a whole nation behind him over there, now all of um's after me cause somebody put it in they stupid skulls I had him clipped. After all the loot I made for them, after all the years, they're after me. What kinda gratitude?"

"None. Ain't no gratitude at all, " I said. "What're you gonna do?"

"Protect myself. What more?"

"That's it, I suppose." Sermon's blood soaked my pants leg and rose up to my waist. "Just protect yourself."

"So what you need, J.C.? What you call me over here for?"

My mind'd left the man, gone from his sedan, even from the red pool. Gone to where—55th, 49th, 47th, 43rd, to the Styx—I wasn't sure. "Huh?"

"What you call me over here for?"

"Oh—Tony Ricci. I spoke to him a while back and he was talking about you clipping old Salvie. Said his people was mad as all hell about it, wanted you took out. Just looking to let you know. But you've got closer fires burning after you from what you say, so take care of what you gotta take care of, joe."

He looked at the blinking hazards on his dashboard. "Always gonna catch up. Ain't no use to runnin." And 47th Street was quiet—no screams, no wanderers, no smoke, no Black—quiet, just listening. "Tony Ricci ain't nobody with his ol man in the pen. Besides, I got Joey at my back, so I'm all right far as they go."

"You sure?"

"Yeah, course I'm sure," he mumbled. "Course."

"Cause I was gonna let you know that I got a kid running for me, gym shoe boy named Otis. Been handling things out here for a while. Looking to take him off the street. He deserves better: big nigga, make a good bodyguard if you needed one. That's all I was going to tell you."

I swallowed salty sweat and Mookie looked me over. "Oh yeah? This guy ain't wrapped up in no gang shit?"

"Not at all," I said. "He's a good kid. Been working for me, pushing and whatnot. Take a bullet one day, scare a angel out the sky the next. That's why I say he could be a bodyguard for you. More protection."

"Protection's a good thing," Mookie said, nodding. He looked around 47th Street. "You remember Black?"

"Who?"

"Forty-seventh Street Black. You remember the ol man?"

"Yeah, yeah," I said, "of course I do."

"Wonder what ever happened to that bum. I been gone from over here so long, I don't know what's been goin down."

I thought of Black laid out in the alley with his eyes locked on the sun for the last time. Mookie didn't deserve to know. He'd left us. "Don't know. Never see him around no more."

"Never?" he moaned. "Probably dead, then."

"Probably so. Been a long time, you know."

"Yeah, that's what happened. Black's dead." Mookie's eyes wandered. "Remember when we was kids, me and you, how we used to play stickball in the street? Used to skip school and go sit on the curb across from the girl's school, watchin the honeys. Remember?"

"Yeah," I said. "We thought we was sharp, smoking on them nasty Salems."

He smiled real joy for the first time in so long, far as I'd seen. "You know we used to do all that shit only cause there wasn't nothin better for us to kill time with."

"But we moved on, tried to be like them—Salvie and them," I said. "Got to drive fancy cars and wear good clothes without nobody bothering us. No police, no white folk, nobody. Thought we was moving up in the world, didn't we? Got with some fine-ass women, made a lotta muthafuckin paper, Mookie, a helluva lot."

"Sure did. And we was movin up, we was. Movin up big-time. Me and you was on top of this place, ran Forty-seventh Street right before you went to the joint." He turned off the hazard lights.

"Don't peek over the shoulder, just slows you down. Now we ain't no more than Julius Banks and Lester Hooks. Two half-assed dope pushers—ain't moved up, ain't gone nowhere."

I looked at Forty-seventh Street, then at Doctor King's street sign. "Guess not," I said.

"I'll take that protection," Mookie said. "Just send your boy to the car wash. I'll talk to him."

"Good. We got peace?" The sedan wasn't a fancy BMW no more, but a red convertible. Mookie's greedy fat was gone, too—he was only eighteen years ol, too young for such rich weight. And 47th Street wasn't dead, not in 1967. I heard craps bouncing off the barbershop's back wall, right there on the corner of Southpark Avenue.

"We got peace," Mookie said as his passenger-side window dropped all the way. A soft hand hung from the car. "We got peace."

I slid my palm against his before the Thunderbird floated off. Disappeared west, became a fancy sedan in the cool sun, my man a fat gangster. And 47th Street was a graveyard for broken bricks and loser niggers. In front of my eyes, hate returned and took away our peace. I rested on the sidewalk, sat down in Sermon's blood to bathe in the cold light of winter's beginning.

* * *

Time passed, and I had a dream. Just voices and noises, that dream. Mookie spoke to me in the nothing behind my eyelids, said for me to watch over Isaiah. "*Make sure the boy grows up right,*" Mookie said, "*make sure he don't become a weed, grows up a tree and not a mushroom, not like us.*" He gave orders, like we were twenty years old and still over in the Forties. I listened, though I was the smarter of us, listened because Mookie sounded like he knew what I couldn't know. There was no argument, just the promise that I'd do like he told me.

Then the noises came—that sound of a monster rising out of Lake Michigan to roar and burn. I was dreaming, but I felt pain. There was one flame, then another, then so many that my mind lost track. I thought to scream, but held myself. When the monster's roar faded it took away the burning, too, left only an echo—then quiet. Free to think in that black hole, I wondered what thing had called for me with such a noise. Judgment, damnation, what? Didn't matter, because whatever it was, I wasn't ready to answer. I swam off in the water bordering my hole, but the thing roared again, louder. I turned, swam in the opposite direction. Stupid me. What escape?

I made it out of the lake, though, somehow made it into the sweaty covers of nighttime, but the earth shook on. Monsters were everywhere. As my head fought through sleep and my eyes opened, the noise became that of fists pounding against Grandma Rose's front door. I pushed away the bedsheets and ran to answer its call. "Who is it?"

"CPD."

"Who?" I touched my chest for safety. But my heartbeat was all I found, and the heart offered no protection.

"Police."

Through the peephole, Frank Dunne's frame tilted on the porch. I opened the door, then the barred screen, and two cops stood with him. Clouds of cold air breathed out of their lips and noses. "It's two o'clock. What you want, man? This ain't your beat even. What're you doing over here?"

"Come to tell you your pal is dead," Frank grumbled. "Put up a good fight, but he croaked just thirty minutes ago, over at South Chicago."

"What?"

"Your pal," he repeated, and coughed without covering his mouth. "Mookie King, that's your pal, right? He's dead."

I felt only what a bastard was supposed to feel when fate came about—no pain or no joy, no relief. Felt nothing. I swam in the red pools again, nothing good or bad about me. "I need to call my lawyer or something?"

"What for?" Frank leaned against the porch railing. "We're just letting you know what happened, in case you wanna protect yourself. These is violent days in this part of the city. Wouldn't want you to end up like your pal."

"Thanks." I tried to touch my heart again, but couldn't find the beat. "Appreciation."

"Can we come in or what?" The cop at Frank's right turned red, his face full of icy blood. "It's cold as shit out here."

I stepped back from the screen, shaking as raw air cut through. "Yeah, yeah, come in."

They crept into Grandma Rose's house, looking around, suspicious. The red-faced one peeked up the staircase. "You alone?" He smirked.

"Yeah, ain't nobody else here," I said, and stepped toward Frank's crooked weight. "What is this? You sure I ain't gotta call my lawyer?"

"No, everything's fine. We're just checking on you, is all," Frank said. He pointed a crusty finger at the Christmas tree across the room. I'd put the thing up, with decorations and all, because that was what heroes did. We raised trees for Jesus—to the end, I tried. "That's real, ain't it?"

"Course it's real."

"That's a nice fucking piece of timber. Never had a real one myself." Frank walked to the tree and ran his hands through its pines. "Merry Christmas."

"Yeah," I said as the shakes ran through me. I stepped into the living room. "So, Mookie's dead? What went down?"

The red-faced cop laughed as he looked at a framed picture of Grandma Rose. "What always goes down over here?"

"He was over on Stony Island, coming outta some joint, a car drives up, and whaddya know? Somebody puts nine holes in him." Frank squatted beside the tree, found the cords for the light decorations, and plugged them into the wall. The Christmas colors—green and red and yellow—filled the room. "Like he said, ain't that what always happens over here?"

"Mmh," I said. The third cop, his skin without color, without white, stood back from them, staring at the dancing decorations. I laughed (at the cops, at Mookie's end, at the lights of Christmas, at myself for trying not to be the chump still—be a hero, not a chump who peed himself because walls trapped him in. I didn't know. But I laughed). "Y'all want somethin? Something to drink, I mean, something?"

"Don't worry about us. Just making sure everything's kosher over here," Frank said. "As kosher as can be. You know, when I heard it was this Mookie who killed Sal Fuoco, I wanted him myself. If I woulda caught him in a dark alley, just me and that fuck, he was mine. It shoulda been me."

"Shoulda, coulda, woulda," the red-faced cop mocked. "In a dark alley—shit, how do you sound? It's over, Frank. Whoever got him took care of him good, no?"

"More power to whoever it was," the third cop mumbled.

I sat on the plastic-covered couch, watched Frank and the red-faced man peek into each one of Grandma Rose's corners, peek and snicker at their own fake investigation. The third took a seat on the staircase, lost in colors. Every evening after sunset, the rhythm of those Christmas bulbs trapped my mind, too. Like warning lights on an ambulance they looked, speeding from near death and shining on the strip. I lit one of the cigarettes from the old cocktail table and breathed clouds as I followed him, let the colors race me into their show.

"You sure you're gonna be all right here?" Frank patted the third cop on the shoulder, stirred him. "You don't need me to leave some guys?"

I blew smoke as they slithered—just like Grandma told me the snake came out of the apple tree—slithered on from her place. "Naw," I said, and found my heartbeat again. "I got protection."

The colorless cop looked at me as those lights let him go. "More power to you," he said as they walked through her door.

6

And by the sword you will live and serve your brother;
and it will come to pass when you have the dominion,
that you will break his yoke from off your neck.

—Genesis 27:39

26

MY GUT RUMBLES, loud and heavy till it hurts. Stomach turns like this whenever I ain't fed it in a bit. I rub my hand over the mound of skin and it rumbles again. Hunger's painful.

I push the woman, no, the child, from my side and look for the time—11:30 A.M., the nightstand clock says. I stand and blink, not at the mornin sun; clouds got it hid good. So gray, this winter day. It's at the sight of my own reflection that my eyes flash, so much shinin in these mirrors all around me. I've woke to these silver visions for two, three years now, however long it's been since South Shore became home. Looked at myself in this glass so many times, from so many angles, I'm often turned sick by what I see.

But I blink this mornin, like somethin's new to be found. Got rich fat on every inch of skin, enough for my body to sink—ain't nowhere else left on these bones for weight to grow overnight. And the slashes J.C. put on my face is part of me, so no matter how the sky shines off me, I ain't never gonna be surprised by their mark. Everythin else, I was born with.

Stomach rumbles again and I rub the fat at my gut without soothin it. I turn away from the reflection, to the nightstand. Time's still here, showin in hot red, but that ain't what I've come for. This clock's had its way already. I reach to the telephone and dial Otis' number from memory, run my hands through the child's bushy hair as I wait for a ring. I would sing to her, if I could—such a fine child.

"What's up?"

"Otis," I say. "This's Mookie."

"Boss?" Phony—I know it's phony—joy rings in his voice. "What you need?"

"Come get me," I say. "I'm at South Shore. We got business to tend before it gets too late in the day."

"What's up, Mookie? What we got to do?"

I frown. Guess nobody ever told Otis about askin stupid questions. Sure ain't about to let him know now. Nigga's gotta learn on his own one day; he's got time. "Just bring yourself, man. Bring yourself, the Caddy, and a gat. Be here in twenty minutes. I wanna get this took care of."

"Sure, boss . . ." Sounds like he wants to say more, but I hang up.

I get dressed quick, run from seein what's in these mirrors, hard as it is.

"Where you goin, Mook?" The child sits up on my bed, sheets fallin from her naked brown.

"Out," I say. "Goin to work."

"Oh." Her smile, the sweet smile of a lie, makes everythin okay. "Bring me back—"

I reach into my wallet and drop a C-note on her thighs. The child frowns and tosses the bill away. She lays down, coverin herself again.

"Goodbye," I say, and walk from the bedroom. Ain't got nothin to stay here for, nothin to say to her, no argument left in me. Besides, she don't sing, and when she screams, the noise ain't true.

"Where we headed, boss? What business we gotta tend?" I look on this strip passin us, Stony Island Avenue. It's so cold this December day—not thinkin of nothin but the air breathin against my window, cloudin the glass, so caught up I just about forget his question.

"Goin to get somethin to eat, Otis. That's our business. I'm hungry."

"Hungry?" Otis moans. "I thought we had somethin needin handlin before it got too late. That's what you told me, Mookie. Said for me to pick you up in twenty minutes. Ain't that what you said to do, man?"

"Sure is." I chuckle. "And you made it in good time, Otis, good time. Now I need food, got pains in my stomach from bein hungry." The Caddy floats through the red light at 75th Street. "What you doin, Otis? Slow down. We got time. Stomach ain't about to kill me."

Otis moans again. "What you tell me to bring a gat for if we just goin after food?"

I look at the big man for the first time. "Dangerous for me out here, man. Specially on the strip. You know this—you seen it. You can't ever be sure no more, can't never trust. Ain't no tellin when they'll come, or from which way they comin."

"Can't be sure," Otis repeats. He wheels past the early afternoon traffic. "Where you wanna eat at, boss?"

"Don't know." Miss Nelly's is to my left, to the east. I breathe, smell the slave-food stink from my first visit to the joint, more than fifteen years back. Now my picture hangs on its wall, up there with the big-time negroes from these years. J.C. and Mora and Christina is in the photo too, but it's my picture. I'm the face in the middle.

Otis sees me gazin at the restaurant. "You wanna eat Miss Nelly's, boss? You want?"

"Naw," I say, not carin to look at no funky pictures. "Just drive, Otis. I'm thinkin as we go. I'll let you know when I come up with somethin."

"Sure, Mookie," Otis says. "Take your time. Ain't no rush, is it?"

"No rush." I look down the strip, south, to the end I can't quite see. Just past 87th is far as eyes take me, just off Pill Hill. Clyde Avenue is in the opposite valley, between Jeffrey Boulevard and the lake. "Mmh," I say. "Remember to stop by my folks' place after we eat. We need to check on Mamma, make sure she's all right."

"Sure, boss. That's all we doin today, runnin errands? We ain't takin care of no real business?"

"You got somethin better to do with yourself?" Otis shakes his head without hidin the fear in his eyes. I smile, likin the fact that I got this scary power over such a big nigga. "I just finished sayin how these is dangerous times, didn't I? How I'm gonna go without checkin on Mamma, then? She lives by herself, you know?"

"My fault, Mookie," Otis says. "Didn't know."

"Yeah, she's alone by herself. Ol man's been dead."

Otis drifts, like I lost my power that quick. He stares through the Caddy's windshield as we sit at 87th Street's red light. There's a boy walkin cross the intersection slow, starin at the clouds and breathin cold air.

"Did you hear me, Otis?" The big man turns from the boy, looks at me as the light becomes green.

"Y-Yeah, boss," he stutters, "I heard. You said your ol man's gone."

"Dead," I correct, drawin the line between death and desertion. Don't want Otis thinkin I ain't never known my father, like I'm one of these who ain't never even seen what his papa looked like. God-damned bastards. But I ain't them. My ol man wasn't shit, but I knew him; too good, I knew him. "I said he's dead. Not gone, dead."

"What's the difference?" I laugh at Otis, keep laughin till he understands he's both stupid for askin and that I ain't gonna answer him. "How long he been dead?"

"Years," I say, "two or three. He was a baseball player, you know?"

"Oh yeah?" Otis laughs now, like he don't believe me. "Who he play for?"

I think of Papa in the ol Negro League (the nigga league, as Mamma use to call it down in Kentucky), swattin home runs and runnin bases with the other colored ballplayers. He was a hero on his team, my father, one of the best in that dyin game. So good that the major leagues heard about him and sent this white cat from New York, wearin a suit and matchin hat, to watch Papa play. I remember that game specially, how he hit pitches and dove for balls, all for the man in the stands. World belonged to Papa—crowd cheerin, the man beneath his black hat smilin with dollar signs in eye—until this tree trunk of a third baseman, this jealous bastard, kicked Papa above the brow as he slid headfirst down the line, stomped his foot into the soft part of Papa's skull, tore shoe spikes straight through to the brain. Crowd was quiet, a quiet like I ain't never heard quiet since, as my ol man laid there, bleedin dreams on the diamond. New York man didn't say nothin to us, didn't even stay to see how Papa was, just left the place to its end. That's why the ol man limped into the grave. He never was the same.

"Who he play for, boss?"

"Nobody," I say as a black limousine cruises past the sedan. Ain't seen one like it in some time, not one bad as this shiny limo. "I use to watch them things ride up and down Forty-seventh Street, Forty-third Street, wherever, when I was a boy. Back when I lived over there. Used to wonder where the rich folk was goin. Always wanted to ride in one."

"Why was anybody drivin round Forty-seventh Street in a limo? How you figure they wasn't headed to the cemetery? Them limousines you was watchin was part of a funeral march, man, carryin some ol dead fool. They all look the same, black limos."

"Maybe so. I never thought of it like that," I say. I look to the west, catch Harold's Chicken Shack in my glance. "That's what I want. Turn round up here, Otis. Go back to Harold's. That's what I wanna eat. You like that joint, don't you?"

"Of course, boss." Otis turns at 89th Street, just past the library.

"Good, good. That's sure what I got a taste for. Ain't no place better round here." I watch the limousine's taillights disappear in the strip's southern end. "You right, Otis. They was headed to the cemetery. What else was a black limousine doin over there except headin to a funeral?"

* * *

"Mookie! Mookie! Where you goin, man?" The bums still call out, still love me after these years. We can't even make it cross the lot between Kenwood Liquors and Harold's without hungry men beggin for attention.

"What's up, brothers?" I show my toothy grin, the one learned from the lawyer David Peters. He's got a office on top of the Sears Tower now—that's how high we've all rose in this life. "Always good seein y'all, always. How's life over this way?"

"Cold," the hairy bum says.

"Cold?"

"Yeah, cold as all hell," the other, skinny and dark, agrees.

"Hell ain't cold," I say as the second bum shakes. "Ain't been there or nothin, but I never heard nobody say it was cold. Hot, that's what most claim, hot enough to burn the insides. That's what I been told."

"You don't know, joe," the second snaps. "This hell we standin in right here is cold. I don't know nothin bout no nother hell, but mine is freezin. You can't feel it like I do."

"What y'all muthafuckas want?" Otis steps between me and the bums. He's a good bodyguard, but these two ain't bout to cause me harm.

"Don't want shit from you," the second says, and spits near the big man's shoes.

"Mookie, would you look out for us?" The hairy one stands on his worn toes, looks over Otis' shoulders. "Bring us some food outta Harold's—a wing, a breast—whatever a brother can spare?"

I cover my mouth to hide mean laughter, fight to swallow it.

"What you gonna do with a wing or a breast, man? There's two of you. Y'all will go through that kinda food in a minute and still be hungry. Who you gonna beg then? I ain't gonna be nowhere round. A wing and a breast won't do nothing for hunger." My stomach rumbles, more hurt than before.

"Bring as much food as you like, then," the second says. "Whatever you feel is gonna feed us, take care of this hunger, you bring that. You the man, goddamnit. Knock yourself out."

I nod, remember Christmas is comin soon. "Ain't got no lotta loot on me," I say. "But I'll see what I can do, take care of y'all best I can."

Otis' eyes turn shady as he touches my shoulder. "Come on, Mookie."

"Take care of us, man," the hairy bum begs. "Member your promise."

Me and Otis walk on to Harold's. "Y'all watch my Caddy while we in here," I yell over my shoulder. "I'll throw in somethin extra from the liquor store to go with your food. Keep you warm. Just make sure don't nobody touch the car. Y'all know which one it is?"

"Course. That fine Sedan DeVille against the wall."

"That's the one," I say. "Watch it for me."

Otis laughs as he holds the chicken shack's door for me.

"What's wrong with you?"

"Don't know why you care so much for nigga losers," Otis says, but it ain't him in my ears. My mind can't place the voice just this second, cause it's from years ago. It scares me, this voice. "I can't understand it."

* * *

What else could the gym shoe boy be doin on the pay phone all this time—can't be nothin but the obvious. J.C. told me this cat was wrapped up in dope when he recommended him. He mentioned it, but after I set eyes on Otis' swollen shadow, I figured bringin him in as a bodyguard would keep him from pushin. As I wait inside the chicken shack, though, wait for these fifteen minutes to pass, I can't figure what else the boy could be doin but handlin dope business, what else but settin up a sell or a pickup or drop-off. That's how they do it, these hustlers, I seen um—Willie and Julius used to handle their entire junk operation from a phone on 43rd and Cottage Grove, back in the day. Ain't nothin changed, not far as pushin the product is concerned.

Like I always say, it don't matter to me what a man do with his years. What should I care about somebody sellin junk or caine or whichever drug it is these days? He ain't puttin nothin in my blood. So long as we get our 35 percent, I ain't concerned. But I'm a respected merchant now, own a business that makes legitimate profit. I keep company with aldermen and ward committeemen and the business folk from the strip. I even know select white folk with loot invested on Stony Island. It's a highfalutin circle I walk in. So I can't very well have my chauffeur, my personal assistant, my—what is it Reverend Goode calls Otis?—my "valay" out here makin dope deals while he's with me. How do I look bein near such gutter crap?

I look away from the shack's entrance as Otis comes close. He walks to Harold's counter. He's watchin me, though, I feel his eyes: sneaky, maybe guilty, definitely shady, the corners of these eyes. "You bout to get somethin or what, Otis?"

"Yeah, boss."

"Hurry up. I wanna get outta here. No tellin what them muthafuckas is doin to the car out there."

"Lemme get a order of catfish. Hot sauce to the side, extra fries." I pound my hand on the table tiles, look around for scared glances fixed my way. But ain't nobody in Harold's just this second, nobody but me and Otis and the folk in the kitchen.

"What the fuck is you doin, man? How you comin into a chicken shack orderin fish? What you think this is? Catfish ain't they specialty. This's a muthafuckin Harold's *chicken* restaurant. You got fried fish joints up and down the block. It already takes um forever in here, how long you think it's gonna be for um to cook what ain't they specialty? What's wrong with you?"

"Can't help it, boss. That's what I got a taste for, catfish. I can't control what I wanna eat."

"We bout to be in here forever," I say. I sigh, feel as tired as I am hungry now. "Fuck it. Come sit down, man."

He looks around as he walks to the table, looks at nothin, and his eyes turn more goofy than anythin else. "What's up, boss?"

"I saw you on the phone out there, holdin that conversation. Fifteen minutes you was out there. Who was it you talked to all that time?"

"I called my wo-woman." This cat couldn't be no gangster. How can you big-time hustle if you can't tell a lie without a stutter? "Just checkin on her."

"Your woman?" I smile. "Didn't know you had one special. A whole month you been workin for me, and I didn't have a clue. How's she look?"

"She's straight, a good-lookin honey."

"Straight? Good-lookin? With the money I pay you, you should have the finest lady on the strip. Don't you figure?"

"Don't wanna brag on her like that. You know how it is, Mookie."

I laugh. "So what you sayin? She's fine as rich wine and you too bashful to tell me bout it?"

"She's a good girl, boss."

"That ain't tellin me shit. She a sweet mamma or what?"

"Just good-lookin."

"You bullshittin, nigga." I smell Harold's day-ol grease. "How was she?"

"Huh?"

"When you checked up on her, how was she doin?"

"When I called just now? She wasn't home."

I frown and look away from Otis, don't wanna talk about this no more. If he gets caught dealin around me, I gotta kill him—I mean, I gotta find somebody to clip the big man. Don't dirty my own hands like that no more.

"Forty-eight! Number forty-eight!"

I look at my ticket and smile. "See, Otis? See how quick they come with my chicken? We'll be here another hour on that fish, you watch." I walk to the counter and take the six wings soaked in mild barbecue sauce. My stomach screams hunger, so I steal a french fry from the package. I ain't gonna eat the rest just yet; this empty pain can wait till we get to Mamma's house. Long as we leave this place soon as possible.

I look into Otis' eyes as I sit. Nothin worse than the look of a stupid liar. Stupid liars' eyes ain't just full of ignorance themselves, they look at everybody around them like we all got their same ignorance. Shows in these pupils laughin at me. I don't like the idea of Otis takin me for ignorant. That's all right, cause he's dead if I catch him. Who would I get to kill this bastard? Who—who else but J.C.? He put this gym shoes shadow on me. The little man was my enforcer in the ol days, besides, and I ain't never come across another bloody as him. "You ever heard of this ol corner lounge called Soul Mamma, Otis?"

"What was the name?"

"Soul Mamma, that was what they called the joint."

"Can't say I'm familiar with that spot. Never been there."

"How ol are you?"

"Twenty-one."

"Twenty-one? Seems like you should recollect this joint. You been on the South Side all your years?"

"Yeah," he says. "Lived in Ida B. Wells since the day I was born."

"The projects?" I glance behind the counter, frown at the cashier so she knows we waitin here. "Wells is over on Pershing Road, ain't it?"

"That's Ida B. on Pershing, yeah. That's where I came up."

"Then you should know the joint I'm talkin bout. Soul Mamma was this here nightclub on Forty-seventh Street, down near State. Ain't but a empty lot now. Burned down in seventy-seven, I believe."

"Oh yeah? Seem like I should remember this joint. What about it?"

"Nothin, nothin. It was a nice place, is all. Don't find many like that around here no more, not on the South Side."

"They had some good fish?"

I don't bother laughin. Instead, I take heed that Otis' eyes ain't lyin to me no more. His pupils is blank now. "We ain't serve no lotta food. Me and J.C. used to run it together. Managed, handled the loot, all that shit. It was our thing. We didn't own it, I can't say that, but it was ours. That's what everybody round here . . . I mean, everybody on Forty-seventh Street used to call it. Me and J.C.'s spot. We was tight back then, the two of us."

"Y'all ain't like that no more."

My head takes his words as a question, but my gut knows they ain't meant to be. My gut knows. "Naw, we ain't been close like that for years. Time passes, things change. It ain't the same," I say. "Sure ain't the same."

"What happened?"

I think about this without havin to. "Loot, women, dope, years. Shit happened."

"What you expect?" Again, it ain't Otis' voice I hear, just his lips movin. "Ain't that how it always goes over here?"

"Number forty-nine! Come get your catfish!"

The big man looks at his ticket, noddin. "It didn't take that long, boss. Can you grab that for me? I'm gonna go on to the car, make sure them bums ain't done nothin to it. I'll have it warmed up by the time you get there, it bein so freezin today."

I walk to the counter, holdin the wings to my chest and starin at the girl behind the register. I ain't frownin no more—she's done her job and we about to leave this place. I take the catfish (goddamn, it stinks—all fish smells like it's floatin upside down in the lake, far as I'm concerned) and catch the girl's eye. She looks angry with me, so I flash my toothy lawyer grin. "Thank you," I say, but she don't speak back. Just rolls her loveless eyes and turns away like she don't care whether I ever come back in this place. I forgive her, though. She's too young to know who I am.

Goddamn, I forgot the wing and breast for these bums—what am I gonna do? Fuck em, like Salvie use to say. Otis'll take care of um. It's damn near Christmas, though, so maybe I'll give up the change from my own lunch. Five dollars and some cents. Gotta eat whatever they can with that. Bastards should show me gratitude. "Merry muthafuckin Christmas, Mister Mookie," they should say. They won't though, cause they ain't but two wanderin fools. What better do they know, what gratitude they got to show? Where's my bodyguard? There he is, leanin his big frame against the Caddy, waitin. He'll take care of um if they start trouble.

The clouds split as I step on the lot's gravel, lettin the sun beat on this cold place. Warmer than they got right to, orange rays shine on my strip. Clouds keep tearin till this sky is filled with only blue heaven and hot light. And I hear it, I hear it and see the dark marsh where Leroy Cross plays his song. The souls, not as many as before, run from the flames and the ashes of those who been burned already. They blink past me, through the marsh and away from the light. It *is* hot, this place, but I don't speed my pace a'tall. Why should I run with poor souls? This's my strip, my world. What is it they call me around here—king of Stony Island, ain't that it? See, the clouds parted for the heat to surround me, right to left, front and back. So even if I did run, where would I run to? "Alabama," that's the name of this sad Black song. Leroy Cross told me so himself.

The bums, the hairy and dark one, even they run off to their alley. But they ain't nothin, the two of them. What they gonna do but run from the sun, what better do they know? Otis, he don't move. The big man is with me, so he understands you can't escape. The sun's all over, surroundin the soul, burnin whenever it gets ready to. Otis knows. A nigga who runs from the sun, what would J.C. call such a fool? Stupid coon? Muthafuckin loser? I sure ain't neither of these things, and Otis is with me, so he knows not to go nowhere. Look at him, the big man, look at his eyes—patient smarts is in place of stupid lies now. Orange light's shed knowledge on a Black bastard. This is the sun's power.

The strip is empty of traffic, no people, no cars. More than three years I been over here, and I ain't never come across Stony Island deserted like this. Not at five o'clock in the mornin and definitely not just past noontime, never seen nothin like it before. This blazin star in a cloudless sky's scared everybody away. Losers, that's all it is on Stony Island. These Black souls who call me king, they ran. Losers, the whole goddamned bunch of um.

The angel roars from heaven, no, from nowhere. He screams, whoops, and hollers, bearin witness not to me, not to God. Why's his wings so beat-up? It don't make no sense a'tall first off. But this angel is from 47th Street himself, bronze like dawn with cracked lips and lyin eyes. I think to tell him all the losers ran from the strip, but I can't speak just now. The clouds close up again, bring back the gray, and the angel stops in front of me, blockin my path across the lot. He don't scream and holler no more, just stares.

I hear the song, louder, this blue jazz song. Gotta scream just to drown out its music. Then his fire rains on me, catches up after all these years to set me free, and I scream in pain now. Hunger is gone—heat is all I feel, and the burn of justice hurts worse than hunger. I'll know all soon.

"I ain't ready!" I yell, but the angel can't hear me. Yes he do—he just don't care. I drop to the gravel, but I been here. Fell to this ground long ago and never got up. My feet is gone, then my legs. And it's dark. I'm caught in the marsh, my soul twistin in hot funk. I hope he leaves somethin for Mamma to bury proper. This is all I ask.

I ain't ready—my body trembles, seizes, and my eyes is snatched open. I see the sun shine on the strip again. This sun is still warm, but it don't burn like before. Otis nods to the angel with his battered wings, and my cough is thick and wet. I know for sure whose words it was comin from the Otis' mouth, couldn't have been nobody else tellin me the truth. Metal presses against my temple and a shadow hangs over me, the short, black shadow of a man. I can't close my eyes for the dreams seepin through these two holes, so I gotta forgive him. Unlike Salvie, I ain't got no choice but to understand why justice came for me.

"Jesus, J.C.," I say before meetin my ol man in hell. "Jesus Christ."

27

WAVES ROLLED AWAY as I sat in the chapel's corner. The back alley rot let go, just for a bit, to look on Mookie resting in his fine casket. The box's platinum handles, the body's silk suit, the grin on his face, happy with the taste of his end; even the flowers, all those pretty flowers decorating his box, red and green and purple and pink, so many I couldn't see God at the front of the chapel anymore. All of it floated off, left me to live.

"Uncle J.C.!"

I turned to the exit, past the crowd of worshipers, the fashion-fair queens tripping over heels too high and tilting under furs too heavy, and the chumps just stepped out of jail or down from the pulpit, to the young voice calling for me. The boy stood next to the chapel's open doorway, looking more like his uncle, his real uncle, with the years gone by. "What's up, Isaiah?"

"I'm about to leave," the boy yelled.

"Leave? Where you going to? Service ain't over just yet."

"Got business up on Forty-seventh, J.C. I'll be at Mamma's place after the graveyard. You'll be there?"

"Of course," I said. The lights in the chapel flashed and dimmed. "How long you going to be?"

"Don't know. Won't be too late. I'll see y'all after I finish."

I frowned, wanted to ask more questions—Isaiah was my

responsibility, according to the dreamed promise I'd made to Mookie. What business did a thirteen-years boy have on 47th Street? I should've asked, but we yelled across the room, bringing stares. None of their eyes were bold enough to match mine, though. When I stared back, all of them darted to the casket. I smiled. "Take care of yourself."

I watched him walk off with a half limp I'd never noticed before. He met another boy, dressed in all black and waiting outside the main parlor, and they left the Stony chapel. Back when I was thirteen, Grandma Rose would've whipped me till I bled blue tears if I told her I had business on 47th Street with some cat dressed in black.

The lights flickered back to full power and Mora stood next to Mookie's casket, not crying phony like the rest, but shaking her head, like his passing was a waste. He wouldn't have agreed, not with a dead face pretty as his and a body heavy with rich fat. There was nowhere left to rise, nothing left to regret, I would've told Mora if I'd felt the energy to stand from that corner. She finished pitying his body and her hand came to her head as she saw me in the pew, and she waved. I didn't return the greeting, just nodded like I was too busy grieving. She didn't come to soothe my phony pain, though, didn't walk nowhere near me, just rolled out of the Stony Island chapel with the waves. I remembered envying Mookie because of her years before. There was no more of that, no more coveting—the Decatur Information Room's word for my sin, *coveting*. True, she was still so fine, far as my eyes could see it. But I'd already taken everything from him.

How could a nigga use death to free himself from death and call it justice? If I committed a sin to destroy a sinner, what made my hypocritical sin the better of the two? Mookie didn't answer the question, didn't understand my dictionary words, so I breathed, and the alley came back to me. That was all justice offered; damnation for J.C. Rose was forever swallowing the stank air I'd been swimming in for more than fifteen years. There was no peace, just a life of rot in the wind. That was fair.

Big Geri stood next to her brother as the worshipers left the service, off to follow the parade down Stony Island. I stood from the corner and walked past her to look on the body. That was the closest I'd felt to the man since long before the end, since we'd fought in Soul Mamma's office years before. Even dead, Mookie's face was beautiful. Mister Shipp'd smoothed over the glass cuts on his cheeks, his hair shined, curly and long like it grew on. And his lips—I lost myself in that smile, lost thoughts until I couldn't hate anymore. I didn't say it for Geri to hear, but I wished him heaven.

"They're about to close the box," she said.

I bent over into Mookie's casket and put my beard's naps beside his smile. Felt the rubbery skin and tasted the makeup of the death racket. I held on to the casket rim as my mouth touched the boy I'd spent so many years worshiping. And, as I leaned near his ear, my hand brushed against his thickest ring. There was Johnny the Baptist's jewelry melted down, I knew, shining on my man's index finger. Any gold I'd ever seen glowed orange like the sun after it'd been shined, but my eyes told me that shine was the true remains of Johnny's gems. The stale blood from the Cajun's stiff reflected the years. There were my chains. "Peace," I offered, loud enough for Geri's ears. I stood straight and looked at her.

"You gonna be at the funeral, J.C.?" She touched my shoulder like I needed comforting.

"Yeah," I said, and shook. The chapel turned cold, so I walked on. "Of course I'll be there."

* * *

The gravediggers used machines to rip dirt from the ground. I could see Mookie's casket, its handles spotted with snow, sitting on the metal rise as the crane dug away at his grave. Like the closed box was being offered, in fancy wrapping, to God—the king's last chance before he was buried under earth. The Lord wouldn't change His mind, though, wouldn't even take the time to think on it. Mookie was but a nigga who'd crashed with the wings he'd been given, spent his years crawling with filth like the rest of us. Judgment was final, and Mookie would rot beneath earth.

His mother—the woman who'd gave him that stupid nickname hoping that she wouldn't have to spend life running around a Kenwood shack calling for two half-assed gimps barely alive to answer—she stood nearest the raised casket. Her tears flowed with sobs that drowned out Reverend Goode's preaching. A mother's pain was all the earthly send-off Mookie would get, least far as the fifty or so folk present heard. And a wasted pain it was. She was the one who didn't want Mookie to become the father. And other than dying, what would've saved him from that fate? True, Mookie seemed big-time in the end—golden, powerful Mookie. But living on Stony Island would've brought him down one way or the other, hobbled him eventually. If he'd survived the parking lot, his wounds should've left him with a limp and grunt like the ol man's. That king of Stony Island talk was just that, talk. So what was the reason for the mother's tears? Caught up in the moment, she must've been, for Mookie's end was a good thing, a saving thing. I knew.

Geri stood behind the woman, soft tears dropping down those chubby cheeks and swallowing her face. Enough tears she could make no effort at comforting the old woman, but not so many that she took anything from Mamma King's show. The sister rocked back and forth on the burial ground, swallowing and squinting as she looked above. Not at Mookie's box, but at the wet flakes dropping on his funeral.

Geri had to know better than wasting grief over her brother. They were blood, but it was Mookie's fault her life bloated up so fat and lazy. He hadn't stuffed garbage down her throat, just taken everything else away; he hadn't sold Leroy Cross that final junk, either, but a dead music man was his fault, no doubt. Left her with but a feast of waste and a bastard boy to love. She understood Mookie's burial as fate and justice then, so those weren't tears on her face. Just dingy snowflakes turning to raindrops as they touched her fat.

Mora stood toward the back of the crowd. Her face was dry, protected by the wide brim of a Easter hat. She held on to the older-looking negro man, gray and professional, at her side. And her head hadn't stopped shaking, not since she'd left Friday's wake. Mora, with her college schooling and Hyde Park manners, knew not to fake like Mookie being put in the ground was a loss worth pain. She'd took what she could from the hustler's life and moved on to a big-time negro—I saw the Jag they'd drove up in—a lawyer, doctor, professor, whatever. Profited off Mookie, then got herself a chump who was from the same place as she was, near the lake, and we all saw it. What point would there have been in showing more fake pain?

Near the grave, Isaiah stood with his mamma and grandmamma. He didn't cry either; wasn't good sense or respect for the preacher's words that kept him from showing hurt, not at all. He'd grown into too much the man for weak tears. Isaiah patted Mamma King on her black-covered shoulders, told her everything was all right. He was gonna take care of it, because he was the man of the family. Those were the words from his mouth, I knew, I heard. The boy turned and looked—stared, not peeked—at me when Mamma King was comforted. I heard, then I saw. His eyes begged to let go pain.

The metal rise howled through the cemetery, shook the ground. Isaiah turned to his uncle's grave—I'd found Johnny the Baptist under a hill of garbage, but buried Mookie King in a platinum box, under a solid stone tomb. *We shall overcome,* the trolls sang.

The casket was lowered past snow. Mamma King's comfort became screams as her daughter and grandson held her from collapsing.

Those weren't melted flakes on Geri's face, no, they were thick tears drying, not melting, into skin.

The crane backed away as the casket disappeared. Another machine lifted dirt the crane'd spent so long taking from earth, lifted and dumped the soil into its hole. Mamma King was quiet long enough for the reverend's last words to echo: "Who delivered us from death, and does deliver: in whom we trust that He will yet deliver us."

I listened as Mookie's family returned to Mister Shipp's limousines and the worshipers followed the parade back to Stony Island.

"I got two packages waiting for you, man. What're you doing? You was supposed to be here Thursday. It's Saturday, J.C. What's going on?"

I breathed into the pay phone and glanced down 47th Street. "Had a funeral to go to. Been busy as hell. You know that."

"A funeral? Whaddya mean, funeral? It don't take but a minute to bury a guy. What's that got to do with Thursday? You got my eighty K or what, goddamnit?"

"Get off me, Tony. I just got done seeing a brother I known my whole life put in the ground. Ain't an easy thing. Gimme a goddamn break."

"Who got put in the ground? Not that King fella? He ain't the one you're talking about, is he? Don't tell me you're over there mourning a guy who got what he had coming. It was you who buried him. You had him clipped, J.C., you done the work. What the fuck you crying for?"

"I ain't. I ain't shedding no tears. It was rough seeing it done, is all."

"Sorry, goddamnit." I heard the grin in his voice. "So when you gonna pick up these packages and pay me what you owe?"

"I don't know. Tuesday, I think. Yeah, Tuesday I'll be over there with your loot. You know Mookie was protected, that those who took him out are gonna have to pay for it themselves."

"Oh yeah?" Tony sighed. "What kinda protection did this fella have?"

"What you think? Protection from your people, whatever the hell y'all call yourselves now. Joe Defelice, that's the only protection that means anything around here."

"That's the word, huh? What else you gotta lemme know about, J.C.?"

"Plenty," I say. "The street says it was me who did Mookie—I was ordered to hit him by Tommy Ricci's gimp son. Now there's bullets coming for my ass, looking for payback." The Ricci boy was quiet. "Understand what I'm saying?"

"Better be careful, friend. Streets can be a dangerous place to be. Look out for yourself."

I patted my chest through the trench coat. "Ain't nothing to be concerned about here. I know this place, Forty-third and Forty-seventh at least. I'm safe. But if Mookie was protected like they say, Defelice's gonna come for your ass before anybody else's, gonna figure you should've known better. There'll be knocks at your door."

Tony laughed until there was nothing in his throat besides a wheeze. "My door? Why would my own people—ain't that what you just called um, *my people*—come here and do harm against me? Over what? Over some *melanzana*? A cocksucking spade? Don't fool yourself, brother."

"What the fuck is a 'mulinian'? You keep using that goddamn word. Told you not to talk that funny Italian shit to me long time ago. I don't—"

"A *melanzana* is an eggplant, friend, a plant who lives its life for no reason other than dying. You ain't figured that out?"

"Naw," I said, and leaned against the pay phone. I looked across the street and remembered walking through Snake Pit ashes with the Ricci boy years before. "I ain't."

"That's what *melanzana* means: dead, black plant. What makes you think my own'd touch me cause they think I had to do with squashing such an eggplant? That ain't how we work. You should understand by now, you're a smart guy. And I know none of these *melanzanas* is coming here to do harm to me. They don't got the balls for it. Do they, J.C.? And I got you to handle my business on that side of town, so I ain't gonna be on Forty-third Street no time soon. What else I got to worry about?"

I heard Janie in the conversation's background, the baptized Catholic laughing up high. "Nothing. Suppose you've got not a thing to worry about at all."

"Damn right," the Ricci boy said. I smelled the sweet cigar smoke circling his curls until it was swallowed by thick caramel lips. "You're the one who needs to be worried, my man. That home of yours is a bloody place."

28

I LET GO my mind as I chased our world, what was left of our world. Such a beautiful place it'd been once, 47th Street on north through Kenwood, back when I was a boy—like the beginning, God's Eden made just for us.

I drove on, driving and remembering Morris King junior as the only cat I'd ever looked up to in life. When he hit a baseball, it flew—true, it'd fall to the ground eventually, but for a good moment, it would fly. I couldn't hit like that, not mighty as Mookie, not like my man. He used to drive a red Thunderbird convertible that shined in the August sun. That was what we cruised up and down 47th Street in, that red convertible, shining as our part of the world sizzled. I loved that car.

And Mora, his woman, was the finest thing I ever laid eyes on. Smart, light, and pretty, she favored Lena Horne when we were young. Nobody else I knew had a female like her, definitely nobody from around our way. But even with Mora at his side, all the South Side honeys loved Mookie for his looks and his loot, and if not, then they loved him for all his pull on the strip. And it wasn't just the females—Black and white folks'd worshiped him for being a smooth cat. So of course I looked up to him. I'd been deserted in life and his shadow gave me a place to hide from the sun.

I never held much of anything one could call a real job for any time, so the only masters I'd known were Salvie Fuoco and Tommy Ricci. Evil men, demons, killers, what have you, they were all those things and worse. But we still spent our years driving their cars, dressing in their clothes, shooting their guns, praying to their cross, trying to be as close to what they were as possible. We knew we'd never truly become them, had to know we'd never be real gangsters. But since they wouldn't make us that, how much higher could they have let us climb, how much lower could they let us fall, in our skin?

In the end, Mookie became big-time running the Stony Island goings-on; and me, I made my way moving dope in a 43rd Street alley. It was a good trade we had, considering the money. While the world went through its recessions, depressions, peaks, and pits, its different presidents, our business turned its own smooth circle. There were no low points. Sin market didn't have bad days. Never.

Our souls? They were lost, had been for years. Maybe the prison shrinks were right; maybe if I'd come up with my father, if I'd had a father other than a mystery God, I would've known better than to sell myself. I'd made crazy cash in life, crazy paper money hustling the streets, all without a soul. Mookie, though, he had his old man and still pimped himself off. I chased our world as it ran into the dark outside the Cadillac windshield, watched it just about disappear.

Only as I pulled my Caddy to the curb at the beginning, 45th Street, did I catch it and see. The gimp on the living room couch was no more father to Mookie than the ghost who laid Mamma up was to me. The only real father he knew was a two-bit Sicilian street-tax collector who didn't respect us far as he could spit us. And blaming somebody for our wrong wasn't the point—Salvie did the best he knew to do with us. But if Salvie'd showed him the way, and I followed Mookie, kept on following until we just about disappeared in night, what more were we?

"Bastard!"

I stepped from the opened Caddy door and turned to the northwest, to the voice yelling for me, found two silver circles in the 45th Street night. Heard the hum of a running engine and waited for the voice to tell me its concern. "Who's there . . . what you want?"

I'd always been told—by Otis and Jaime Manuel, even by Salvie—that, after a man'd been shot, he didn't recollect the gun's actual firing, or the piercing of bullets. If he survived, the mind was supposed to wipe away the moment, too much pain to deal with. But I deserved no mercy. I'd see the orange flashes forever instead, bursting from the night in front and shaming those silver night-lights.

Blasts echoed against the 45th Street homes, like the noises Mookie's baseballs made long before. I dropped to the concrete, my arm burning, not hurtful so much, just hot. The door window had exploded, so maybe the pain was from flying glass pieces. Why did fire scream through me, then? I dropped my head against the door's leather upholstery, biting my lips to fight the tears. I was too much the man for tears, too strong for that.

I reached into the coat, grabbed hold of my chest and rubbed it, found no blood. I breathed and snatched the .45 from its holster, held it, felt it, pulled out the clip to make certain it was loaded. Couldn't go down like no scared slave. Those fools would fall with me.

Hadn't meant to, but with the tears choked in my eyes, I'd stopped making noise. I listened to air and the bullets, too, were gone. The fools walked my way, I heard that at least. I jumped to my knees, glass spilling from my clothes and clinking against the street; didn't matter if they saw, or if they heard, didn't matter if they fired again and put an end to me. Didn't matter, long as we went together.

I bent into the cracked space where there'd been a Caddy window and fired, let go the .45—into a black hole I sent rounds to drop them. There was a scream, high and girlish, then the stomp of boots running off on concrete. Like Sermon on 47th Street, the escape sounded. But I'd been in the game long enough to know better, so I fired until the scream was full of too much pain for its life to matter.

I stepped out from the door and blood ran down my left hand (my arm didn't even burn anymore, just hung) as I held the gun in my right. Counted the shots I'd fired up to five. Not too many that I had nothing more to put him in his grave, enough that he was laid out, waiting on me. I nodded as I walked. Those streets wouldn't fuck with J.C. Rose after that deed. Blasting a fool who'd come for me and leaving him to drown on 45th was enough to take back what all the welchers owed. Gimme my respect.

* * *

I looked in his eyes. Soft, clean eyes. Innocent, no matter the steel laying outside his fingers, those holes were. They didn't fix on me just then, but on the sky. So much like Mookie the boy had grown to look over the years. His nose was sharp like the uncle's, his skin brown and without mark, shining in the silver light. The only difference was in those innocent pupils jumping behind the boy's hurt.

Isaiah's blood left bullet-tears and made a pool before Grandma Rose's house. It was there my own wound dripped, blood in blood, lost in black. I kicked his shoulder and his eyes stopped on me.

I remembered Salvie putting a gun to my side before driving me to the Indiana Styx. Was that how I looked to Isaiah, like the end? "That was you shooting at me, boy? What's wrong with you?"

The noise he made was that of a baby shook from sleep. "I can't feel, J.C. My arms, I don't feel um. Can't stand."

"Don't try moving then. Help's coming. You'll be all right," I said. I searched the pit for what was nowhere near. What help was there for a punk who'd got what he had coming to him? Grandma Rose used to say it—"Live by evil, burn in its flames." And 47th Street Black, "What go round . . ."

Make sure the boy grows up right. Not like us.

Mookie knew our world. Why'd he go and tell me to fight the Word of the Lord as written in stone?

I waited for Isaiah's eyes to find me again. But the pupils darted between my face and the .45 without pausing. I shook my gun, felt both the weight of chrome and the clip not finished. When his eyes did slow, I lost myself in his stare. "Please. Please."

"Ain't got no more bullets," I lied, and threw the gat to the Caddy. Sounds of metal bouncing against gold filled the pit, and I bent over to drag Lazarus from his tomb. Couldn't stop until I'd reached the sidewalk grass. Then and there, I would've pointed the way, saved a boy from what he could not see. Carried the fool when living'd got too hard for him. Mookie'd told me to take care of his nephew, told me in a dream—figured if I did as he'd said, maybe I'd become the hero, J.C., for all time.

I felt pulling at my bloody wool, a weak pulling, barely there. I looked to the grass, saw begging fog fill Isaiah's eyes, taking the place of his years. I turned away before answering his tug, back to the night because I'd seen enough.

"Up there, boy. I found it."

He pulled harder, enough for the coat to press into my shoulder wound and hurt, but not for long. Strength left his little fingers, and the hand fell back to grass. I looked at him again, though I didn't want to. "What? God?" he wheezed.

"Not God, no God up there," I said, and jabbed at the black clouds with my good arm, pointing until his pupils rolled up much as they could. "Just heaven. In the black, I found it."

I listened to his whimpers, gave the world's salvation its last chance. When nothing came, I grabbed my knees and pulled them to me. His uncle's smile came to my mouth and we watched the night together. That joy on Mookie's face when they buried him: couldn't keep it from spreading my lips. I rested in the boy's mess and smiled because we were done dying.

About the Author

Bayo Ojikutu graduated from the University of Illinois–Champaign, and earned an M.A. in writing from DePaul University. *47th Street Black* is his first novel.